The Witch who Chases the Sun

Dawn Chen

CONTRARIAN PUBLISHING

Brooklyn, NY ✳ Est. 2024

Summary: Two witches, ex-lovers who survived the Second War, reunite and begin unraveling the mysteries of their village. Can the witches be each other's salvations or are they doomed to repeat the past that tore them apart?

Library of Congress Control Number: 2025942557
ISBN: 978-1-965422-09-0
ISBN (ebook): 978-1-965422-10-6

First Edition

Cover illustration and design by Kristi Zeyn
Book design by Jamie Ryu

To the ones who keep speaking out when the world is silent

Content Considerations

This novel contains content that may be disturbing to some readers. Content includes racism, racial harassment and bullying, microagressions, dismemberment, graphic depiction of war and colonization, graphic depiction of murder, PTSD, genocide, suicide, homophobia, executions, and religious bigotry.

Reader discretion is advised.

Contents

"Once upon a time, a witch fell in love with the sun.
Ever since then, she has been chasing her light."

—a prophecy scribbled down by The Oracle Anne
Barberry, at the age of six.

PART ONE

The Witch

1

Reunion

EVERYONE KNOWS ANNE is a fraud of an oracle. Every single scenario presented to her can be turned into a bloodbath filled with doom and gloom.

"Will I have children soon?"

"There is a future where you have children, but they will leave you at the age of maturity. Your husband will leave you, too, so maybe it's best if you don't."

"Will I pass the magician's assessment and become an official lineage bearer?"

"The last Inabrian magician lineage was recognised by royal decree over a century ago. The magician's assessment is a hoax by the Inabrian court to keep class division. You don't need an oracle to tell you the answer."

"Will my wife forgive me and join me and my daughter here soon?"

"I don't know. Why did your wife leave you in the first place?"

Her parlour is as off-putting as her personality. A large castle at the edge of the town that she inherited as a child when her father,

Mr. Perks, died in a coincidentally timed heart attack along with her mother the same year, in an accident. An orphaned child in a mansion, Anne's parlour is filled with silver cutlery collecting dust on black tablecloths. A suspicious jars filled with what appear to be dismembered body parts line the great hallways that lead to the place where she receives her guests.

The town murmurs about her sacrificing kittens to the Discord, who stood opposed to the Creator, in exchange for darker magic.

Not necessarily alchemy.

Ten years after the war between Inabri and Aixauh ended, the stigma that alchemy is a form of Discord's evil magic has largely lifted—thanks to the encouragement of Inabrian magicians and Aixauhan alchemists mingling over scholarly exchange as part of reparations following the war.

The reparation efforts were commendable in their intentions. But Chely Ying could not testify to their effectiveness. Sure, they allowed Aixauhan alchemists like herself to roam the lands of Inabri more freely, and the townsfolk in this oddly secluded area are surprisingly open-minded. After everything she's lost thanks to the war, Chely is not sure she believes ten years of peace is enough time to bridge centuries of root-deep differences between the Inabrians and Aixauhans.

However, that's beside the point. It is said the number of people who visit The Oracle's Castle only increases by the year. The Oracle's eccentricities fascinate tourists; they find this town on their own, motivated by a vaguely defined sense of hopefulness. Chely's own journey here is for a less instinctual reason, but after speaking to some of the tourists at The Inn, the way they describe The Oracle is almost as if she were a lamp that attracted them like moths.

Anne shows no preference for these tourists over the local towns-folk. Whoever comes to seek her advice is met with equal vulgarity and unpleasantry, to the point where Chely doubts any of those who visit The Oracle are interested in their actual fate, instead seeking only the atmosphere The Oracle's Castle and personality provide.

According to The Innkeeper, who's lived in the town for as long as he can remember with his only daughter, everyone goes to The Oracle's Castle at least once. Once was enough for The Innkeeper to call bullshit, but apparently not enough to be taken seriously by anyone he tries to warn as he polishes cups at the bar.

The Innkeeper's daughter, Naomi, might be the only born-and-bred girl in the area who hasn't visited Anne. It's almost a rite of passage for the town's teenagers to visit the dreaded oracle and come back with some ridiculous grumpy remarks, but Naomi is strictly forbidden from going by her father. Unlike most kids her age—and much unlike Chely in her own youth—Naomi actually obeys and respects her father's wishes.

The Oracle doesn't ask for any monetary compensation from those who visit her castle. This makes the motivation for her free service largely unclear. Chely's has a secret board of hypotheses, including maybe that Anne is doing all of it for shits and giggles. It hurts no one for some isolated, lunatic oracle to give unhelpful and sometimes mean responses to those who seek her fortune-telling. Every town needs a legend, a bit of fun that keeps the locals churning on with their otherwise boring lives.

The problem is that rumours around The Oracle have recently turned from benign to suspicious. It started off with one or two tourists who ran out on their tab at The Inn. The Innkeeper thought it was unfortunate but cut his losses. However, when he asked around the tavern, he learned that apparently those tourists did not come as a group; instead, they came as scattered arrivals who gathered together one day as companions to visit The Oracle's Castle.

No one saw them after that.

In fact, many people who came to visit The Oracle vanished after departing for the castle on the hill.

"I don't know, sounds too much like a coincidence for you to seek my help," Chely says to The Innkeeper on the first night she stays at The Inn. She's arrived during the same season for the past few years. The first Aixauhan alchemist most of the townsfolk have ever seen, yet her continued presence—alongside her charming, Chely hopes, personality—is a far more welcome sight around town than The Oracle by a fair margin. "You manage The Inn, sir. I think it's a huge stretch to say it's The Oracle who abducted those tourists. The tourists always come here for The Oracle Anne, no offence, but she's the main draw for your business to keep running, so of course they'd be visiting her at some point. It all sounds so…circumstantial."

The Innkeeper grumbles. "You say so now. That's because you've never stared into those cold grey eyes of hers," he says with a shiver. "Unlike you, alchemist, those kids who traveled here don't know shit about Inabrian magic. They have little knowledge of the war, how much the alchemists—sorry—and the magicians screwed us common folks up. They think it is a toy, that they can see some wonders and then go home at the end of the day unaffected."

No one can agree on the missing people's names. Chely spends a whole afternoon asking every drunkard and dullard at The Inn for information. The only helpful voice is Naomi, who is near the same age as the travelling kids. She tells Chely the names of the ones who went missing—all Inabrian, which is no surprise, as oracles aren't exactly fondly remembered by anyone that isn't Inabrian.

None of the missing kids are magicians or have magician lineage last names.

"But Anne herself doesn't have a magician lineage family name, either," Naomi says to Chely. "The folks around here aren't exactly kind. Some say she's a bastard of one of the lineages, and that's why she's bitter and mean. But I think she can be kind. I bumped into her a few times when she came to the market for groceries. She was nice to me. Father thinks I'm naïve."

"Maybe you are naïve," Chely muses. "Or maybe you are simply a product of peaceful times. Having faith in strangers cost my generation dearly in the war, and your father is older than me, so maybe he lived through the First War as well. It changes people, but that does not make you wrong. You are the first one who made me feel welcomed here, after all."

Naomi blushes. "Thank you, Chely," she says. "Truth to be told, I want to go visit The Oracle Anne myself. I was supposed to go with the kids who left without paying Father, but the tavern was busy all day, so I couldn't sneak away. I wonder if I should try to go again, if only to ask The Oracle face-to-face if she's had anything to do with the incidents."

"Hmm," Chely says. "I applaud you for your bravery. But maybe this is not the best time to do such a thing. Are there questions you wish to ask The Oracle about your future?"

Naomi's sapphire-blue eyes glisten for a moment. "Not my future, no."

What could the girl want from Anne? It isn't her business though. So instead of being nosy, Chely asks Naomi to go fetch her father so she can inform The Innkeeper of her plan.

The Oracle Anne has stayed in her castle with her crow from the age of seventeen to the age of twenty-seven, according to the older townsfolk. She never grew taller, but her blonde hair slowly dampened with the passing of years as if the dark clouds above the town had drenched her with age. She keeps a chalice of clear liquid in the middle of her house. The few guests who The Oracle gave serious answers to say that Anne would look into the chalice before speaking their future to them.

"You *sure* she's an oracle?" Chely asks The Innkeeper with a certain amount of amusement. Sure, there might be people missing, but this whole situation is still more comical to her than dire. "Only a few family lineages in all Inabri claim to have fortune-telling powers. And only *one* family among them claims to be oracles. The Oracle's power is different from that of a common seer. An oracle can only divine the larger picture—events that affect the globe, according to most records. And as far as I know, the only true oracle lineage nearly died out after the Second War. Surely you know that? I mean, if an Aixauhan like me knows the distinction, the good people of this town surely wouldn't expect any mundane predictions from an oracle, right?"

"We're not like you, Miss Ying." The Innkeeper sighs at the oblivious and good-natured alchemist from the east, whose unique, shifting red hair and dark eyes are both warm and kind. "The towns-folk love magic. It makes them feel fresh, closer to the Creator's magicians. We common people don't see it as something as technical as you do. She could be a fraud, a curse, a blind woman. As long as she calls herself The Oracle, the townsfolk will flock to her damned castle for the free show."

"Not going to lie," Chely says with a smile, "the way you speak of her, it's almost as if you have a personal vendetta. Could it be you're averse to magic? If you can house an Aixauhan alchemist without breaking a sweat, surely one of your own magicians, no matter how dubious the origin, isn't someone you fear."

The Innkeeper is a tall and well-built man in his late fifties. His hair has trims of grey tucked in with chestnut. For an Inabrian man, he maintains his hairline well. When Chely first came to this town a few years back, he was the one who offered her a place to stay without qualms.

"I was in the wars, Miss Ying." The Innkeeper's voice darkens. "Both of them. The magicians, the alchemists. I've seen things, while you were probably only a tiny baby in the first and Naomi's age in the second. After what I've seen… I don't believe the bullcrap they fed us about the alchemists being the Discord's minions. Evil. But magicians? They saw us, the common folk of Inabri, as nothing more than cannon fodder on the front lines. I don't believe that's the Creator's Will. Plus, I cannot imagine an Aixauhan alchemist like yourself is fond of them—you must have heard horror stories from your parents' generation, or your grandparents."

"Well, I can't argue with that," Chely concurs. "What do you wish me to do, then? I have to admit, I don't know that much about the magicians of Inabri. If it's my professional opinion you want, I won't be able to offer much expertise."

The Innkeeper lifts a brow, seemingly surprised by this admission. "But what about those fortune cookies you hand out every year when you come around town?"

"They're party favours." Chely flashes a mischievous grin. "The first flood of Inabrian and Aixauhan exchange came from food, and the restaurants always use these fortune cookies. They aren't a thing in Aixauh itself, mind you. Aixauhan alchemy values precision. Unlike the magicians who believe their powers to be based on feelings, the base of Aixauhan alchemy is math. Even the divination practised by alchemists is a form of practised calculation. It's not my field, regardless. The alchemy I practise isn't going to endear your townsfolk any more than the awful stereotypes perpetuated by the wars."

The Innkeeper goes silent, and for a moment Chely thinks he might crush her for that admission. However, what comes from Innkeeper's mouth is a stream of raucous laughter.

"I can't argue with that," The Innkeeper repeats Chely's line. His gruff tone takes on a lighter note, the face that so intimidates the troublemakers from the tavern turning into a kinder version with age-lines spread across it. It is a great transformation, as if finding a tiger purring like a house cat. "You do what you must do to survive, girl. I can't imagine surviving through the Second War being an Aix-auhan alchemist by yourself. All alone. By the Creator's name, you really were Naomi's age during that war, weren't you?"

Ah, so there's the real reason The Innkeeper is kind to her. He sees her as someone helpless, like his daughter. It is a gentle kind of love. For an Inabrian to see an alchemist as merely a girl who could be his daughter... Despite all The Innkeeper's overprotectiveness, Chely is warm as she faces him. If this is the future she and her friends fought for, if this was the reason Cole died, maybe it wasn't all a waste.

"I was Naomi's age," Chely admits. "But I wasn't alone. I had friends. Other kids to look out for. Sadly, they're all gone, one way or another. That's the thing about war—once it ends, relationships can't survive without being tainted by it."

"Isn't that the truth?" The Innkeeper asks. "My old army pals never speak to one another. I came back here for my inn, a family business. It keeps me grounded. But I've heard the worst fates for those who can't keep up with peacetime. Anyway, I don't care if you use little fortune cookies to tame the townsfolk's ignorance, Chely. Even if they're lies, no harm comes from them. They're like... sweet little promises. The Oracle, no, there's something deeply wrong with someone who professes themselves as seeing into the future and only gives others misery and doubt. Not to mention, she is probably a fraud. From what I have heard, none of the terrible things that came out of that wretched witch's mouth have ever come to fruition. It is just a show."

Witch. The term is rarely used by anyone in Inabri or Aixauh. It's a term designated to magical or alchemical practitioners whose crafts are malicious.

"If you believe The Oracle is responsible for the missing tourists, why don't you guys shut her down?" Chely tilts her head with genuine curiosity. The term "witch" is so scarcely thrown around, especially by an Inabrian toward their own magician, that it shows The Innkeeper's resentment toward Anne is probably not based on a hunch. "Take it to the authorities? From the way you describe her, she seems like the evil witch who hides in her scary tower, spreading misfortune with glee."

"I'm not proud to say this, but she *has* been good for business, bringing attention from the fancy media folks." The Innkeeper shrugs. "We can't afford to pass over the chance. It's terrible to say, but after the wars, the entirety of Inabri suffered catastrophically. We have to scramble together whatever means of income will keep this town running, no matter what. It's stupid, I know. Short-sighted."

"Right," Chely replies. "I understand that, I truly do. We do what we need to survive, to keep our loved ones safe. Speaking of loved ones, where is Naomi? I haven't seen her all day."

The Innkeeper rolls his eyes. "I don't know, girls that age," he says. "I am fortunate enough to have intercepted her attempt to go to the castle with those tourists. Teens. I know I can be hard on her, but it saved her from meeting the witch! Still, she's mad at me, I can tell. I know I can be overbearing, but I think she might be involved with some boy. It's not one of the tourists' kids, thank the Creator, since she's still sneaking out constantly. I wager it's the butcher's son. That's why she doesn't want to tell me."

"The butcher's son is like twice her age." Chely laughs. "Have some faith in the girl. I think Naomi can do much better."

Who knows, it might not be any son at all. It sounds like Naomi's more likely in love with The Oracle Anne herself.

"Right," The Innkeeper sighs. "You know, Chely, I hope she isn't stuck here with me, my Naomi. You probably think me harsh, but I wish I could raise her somewhere better than this place. I wish she went with her mother when—Too late though. This town isn't the best place for a girl like Naomi, no one her age to play with, not unless it's this season and the tourists' kids are around. I might be a brute, but I want the best for my daughter. And those kids who went missing? They are someone else's sons and daughters. I can't turn a blind eye to that—that's why I'm asking you, discreetly, to help me go sniff around the so-called oracle."

Chely sighs. Humanity glistens in The Innkeeper's eyes. The red-haired alchemist herself doesn't particularly harbour any familial ties of this kind with her own family, but she understands this is a sweet sentiment. The kind she can't say no to.

"I still don't think being a recluse is a good enough reason to suspect The Oracle of being behind anything," Chely says. "But I'll go to the castle and look around, if that calms your mind. In exchange for free lodgings for this year, that is. Is that okay with you?"

"Of course!" The Innkeeper beams. "Thank you so much, Chely. Thank you."

Chely puts her glass on the bar counter and waves goodbye to The Innkeeper. There is no need to tell him that visiting Anne's castle next was always the plan, even prior to The Innkeeper's request to look into the whole bizarre missing people incidents.

"I can see the business is going to bloom for you tonight, my friend," Chely bids goodbye to The Innkeeper. "Three brothers are coming in already. It's the time of the year when everyone starts to drink early."

"Gosh." The Innkeeper lets out a string of curses. "They better not get into a fight again and destroy my property. They still have the last brawl's tab to pay. May the Creator be with you, Chely. I think you might be exactly what this town needs to be free of that witch."

Chely nods without a reply. She doesn't say it out loud, but "may the Creator be with you" to an alchemist like her is nothing but a stab wound.

In the middle of the night, The Oracle holds the Chalice of Truth in her lap. She reads the words that tell her of the future. The war and calamity that lay in the future of the world before. Every single one of them sinks deep into her like teeth gnawing at rotten meat.

Chely wonders what Anne sees in the chalice these days since the war is over. There is always a future for The Oracle to behold, but without wars, can anything truly constitute a global scale event?

If the peace can last for longer than a few decades, does that mean The Oracle can finally sleep peacefully at night without Visions plaguing her mind?

Chely closes her eyes; the stench of sweat permeates the alleyway outside her window. Her wooden floor thumps beneath her feet at the rhythm of songs and screams. The Innkeeper didn't manage to tell the three brothers to bugger off, sadly.

It's the sound of celebration—maybe Naomi did find a boyfriend somewhere she wishes to spend the night with, away from her father and the tavern. It is the Solstice, after all.

In Chely's limited understanding of Inabrian traditions, the Solstice used to celebrate the Creator until it became more of a party season. It's the reason why Chely—and most other tourists—arrive in town.

Many years ago, Chely found the love of her life during the Solstice. It was the one stretch of time where the Inabrian magicians mingled with the common folk, it was where the red-haired alchemist found a lonely silhouette skulking at the corner of such festivities and struck up a conversation.

It turned out to be a conversation of a lifetime.

She smiles as she pulls out the letter Ark gave her. It was something the captain asked be delivered to The Oracle by hand on her death-bed. It took so long for Chely to find this town; it was buried in the middle of a wild patch of wilderness. That those missing tourist kids found this place solely based on their insistence on seeing The Oracle? That is a miracle all on its own.

A truly nameless town to hide in, Chely thinks. Anne Barberry has succeeded marvelously in secluding herself from the world.

At dawn, around six o'clock, when the noise has finally died down to snores and quiet mumbling, Chely Hawk steps out of her room at The Inn and heads toward the lone castle standing on the hill.

A black crow caws at her, no doubt alerted by Cheley's sudden intrusion on his human's heavily guarded premise.

"Are you The Oracle's new familiar?" Chely asks.

The black crow watches the red-haired alchemist with milky, filmed eyes. A wordless, judgmental creature. Amazing company for Anne, no doubt, since the emotion suits The Oracle perfectly.

"I mean no harm," Chely continues.

The crow's dark eyes stare into her soul. The guests who returned from the castle said that The Oracle called her familiar "Cole," which almost made Chely spill her drink onto her robes. It's a name that means nothing to most, but not to Chely.

Cole the Crow becomes silent as his smart little fluffy head con-siders the pros and cons of letting the red-haired alchemist into The Oracle's Castle before Chely bribes it with a glass full of catnip.

The familiar instantly perks his head up before his long beak transforms into a wet nose that sniffs the air repeatedly. Cole, now a black cat, nuzzles up to Chely's heels while meowing like the girl in red is his new best friend.

"There you go." Chely smiles as she strokes the space between the cat's ears. "Taking in a familiar, that's so unlike her. But I guess even The Oracle can't stand being truly alone. You really do remind me of your namesake. Maybe my visitation can bring Anne some joy?"

The familiar stares up at Chely with its milky eyes. It is uncanny how it seems to both welcome the alchemist and mock her.

Speaking of—the oracle of the castle stomps out in a grey dress with puffy sleeves. Her hair is dark to the point that it looks drenched in rain. However, Anne's forever expressionless face is now edged with the threat of an incoming storm.

"Why the fuck are you here, Cai-Li?" Anne demands without any of the presumed politeness and elegance expected of an oracle. Straight to the point, despite years of pretending she didn't know Chely was in town. The oracle remains one of the few Inabrians who manages to pronounce Chely's real name correctly. "Leave, *now!*"

"Hey, Annie." Chely beams. She holds out her arms as Anne charges into her embrace—only because it is too late to stop. "Dashing as ever! You look like you just dug up a grave. Did you see me coming?"

"Don't act smug." Anne bristles as she picks up her cat with a fury that makes the poor familiar squeak in dismay. "I told you never to come back. I should put a curse on you that makes you trip over your own feet for a week to prove how much I meant it."

"Hmm, we both know that's not your type of magic." Chely lets go of Anne and poor Cole, who almost got squashed by the hug like a pancake with fur. "Apparently, The Great Oracle has been saying mean words to those who seek her aid. Can't you just tell them that's not how oracles work and make them back off?"

"You've been handing fortune cookies to those folks in town to gain favours! You are using their gullibility to get your way too." Anne scowls at her, despite a small twitch at the corner of her mouth. "I've tried to tell them I can't see the solution to their pesky little problems because all I can see is the big picture. Yet they keep on coming."

"Maybe because their problems *are* their entire worlds, Annie," Chely says. "Ever thought of that?"

"No, they're not," Anne replies, as cold as stone. "If you came all the way for small talk, let me show you the way out."

"Wait," Chely says. "I'm not here for small talk. I'm here because someone from the town says that there are tourists missing, people who were last spotted heading toward your castle."

"Tourists?" Anne snickers. "There are tourists who come *here*? What in the Creator's name is here to see?"

"Well, *you*," Chely replies. She gestures vaguely toward Anne's whole attire. "You assumed the identity of this girl, a decade junior to your actual age, who the townsfolk remember to be the castle's original owner. Then you dress up in black, start offering divination sessions to the townsfolk—life advice filled with insults. I don't know, it sounds like what you Inabrians enjoy—a spectacle."

"Wow, okay, see who's talking," Anne responds with thorns. "*You*, Ying Cai-Li. The alchemist who turned dark. You think I know nothing of what has become of you since I left?"

Chely and Anne stare at each other for a few minutes. This is useless. It makes Chely's chest hurt. Just like how they parted: in bitter words.

Finally, Chely caves.

"Look, I'm not trying to look for trouble," she says. "I just... I missed you. No one has heard from you in ages. I'm not accusing you of anything. But you isolating yourself...it makes me worry, okay? We parted on bad terms; you left The Cottage without saying goodbye. I'm not trying to encroach on the life you've made here for yourself. I am checking up on you as an old friend. Are you okay?"

"I'm fine," Anne replies, stony, but her voice drained of hostility. "I have nothing to hide, not from you or anyone. I enjoy living alone, because people suck."

"The war gave you trust issues," Chely says. "I know."

"No shit," Anne says. "However, it's bad manners to turn an old friend away, I guess." The dark circles under Anne's eyes are deeper than Chely remembers. "I can make you a cup of tea before kicking you out."

"Aw, thanks." Chely jolts up in mock surprise, as if she didn't think Anne would offer, eventually. "You are such a big softie for someone the townsfolk say eats teenagers and likes to keep their body parts in jars."

"Is that what they are saying in the town?" Anne looks like she wants to go up to the highest tower in the stone castle she calls a home and leap off the tip without using a gravity-reverse spell. "Or is it your horrible, morbid sense of humour? Either way, I should have picked a better retirement location. Somewhere more remote."

"How do you get more remote than here?" Chely asks.

"I don't know," Anne says. "But you found this place, so it defeats the purpose."

They walk through the hallways with all curtains drawn shut to block out any semblance of daylight, an old habit of Anne's from ever since they were children. Anne says it's so she can sleep tight until the middle of the day without feeling anxious about waking up. It seems in the years they've been apart, the oracle's anxious nature has grown worse, seeing as windows are now barricaded by overflowing black velvet that blocks any light from seeping into the oracle's domain.

In this castle that seems to be cloaked in a permanent night, Anne Barberry's face is so gaunt, she appears to not have slept in a decade. Her unkempt blonde hair has become straw-like, her lips twirled downward.

They arrive at an equally dim-lit room. The only light source is the Chalice of Truth, which glows a soft, pearly white.

"May I?" Chely asks.

Anne waves her hand, giving the alchemist silent permission.

Chely snaps her fingers and the candles in the gas lamps around the room start to glow. Each of the lamps are misted and unclean, as if they belong in a tomb. The flame answers the alchemist's gentle call to burst out sparks of red and orange. They're giddy from finally being put to use. Chely can hear their laughter and thanks.

They start complaining to Chely all at once about how Anne neglects them. Chely offers them sympathetic smiles without taking sides. Fire is temperamental. Chi'You forbid she offers them her allegiance, and they end up starting a rebellion to burn down Anne's castle.

Anne, oblivious to the exchange the red-haired alchemist is having with her element, goes to the center of the room where the Chalice of Truth sits. The oracle chugs the liquid in the chalice as though it's water. It is definitely not water.

"Are you drinking?" Chely asks, concern lacing her voice.

"No, I tried quitting after I left you," Anne says. "So far, I've been successful at doing so. With you here, though? I see a future where I need brandy in my system to stay sane, Ying Cai-Li."

"Don't," Chely says. For the first time, the alchemist's voice dips closer to room temperature instead of its natural cheerful tone, like a burning stove. "If I'm truly such a headache-inducing component to you that it's causing you pain, then I'll go, as you ask."

Anne eyes Chely and then shakes her head. "It's fine," she says. "Not saying your unannounced visit isn't a nuisance. But if I drink again, it will be because of the Visions and memories that haunt me, not because of my annoying ex."

"Have you been overusing your magic?" Chely asks, ignoring the jab mixed in with the oracle's words.

Anne doesn't answer her, staring past Chely. The oracle goes to the stove, takes out some Earl Grey tea leaves from a tiny silver box sitting next to the chalice. She places the chalice on the stove where the log fire burns until the water is bubbling.

Then, Anne pulls out two cups from under the table. She probably only has multiple cups because there are constant visitors who ask for her divination, since it's apparent that if it were up to Anne, she'd prefer solitude with her familiar. Still, the fact she keeps more than one cup is a positive indication that the oracle—despite what her cruel words suggest—hasn't changed as much as Anne wishes.

After the tea is prepared, Anne pushes a cup toward Chely with just enough force that the cup clinks with the table and almost spills the tea.

"Thanks, Annie." Chely smiles back.

The Oracle returns a glare.

The Earl Grey is transparent, as clear as a cup of water. It is a small trick that might mesmerise any common folk who know nothing of magic, but Chely is used to it. She's watched Anne use that chalice for tea since they were teenagers.

The chalice drains the colour of any liquid poured into it. As clear as the freshest water. Some alchemists speculate it's because the Chalice of the Barberry Lineage drains spiritual power until whoever drinks from the chalice becomes soulless, like the colourless liquid within the chalice itself. Chely knows that's horseshit, since she very much has a soul and is alive after many afternoon tea sessions spent with Anne on their early dates.

Chely takes a sip, and her senses fill with the floral scent of an ordinary Earl Grey. Anne's magic manifests in weird ways. The tea tastes like it is made of water from the well next to their old cottage, with a special metallic flavour resonating in it. A magician's emotions leak into their everyday life, Chely recalls. How odd, for the

Inabrian magician's power, so tied to their emotions, to pour out like tea in an overflowing cup.

"Have you been practising that spell I told you to stop with?" Anne asks her expressionlessly, as if she were discussing the weather.

That ends the brief civility established between the oracle and the red-haired alchemist.

"Who is the girl you are pretending to be?" Chely asks in return. She smiles in a mirthless manner. "Is she dead? And where are the missing people who came to your castle?"

"How many times do I have to tell you? I have nothing to do with these missing people!" Anne's face floods with colour for the first time since Chely stepped into her home. "As for the girl I assumed the identity of, she's not dead. I met her while travelling. Her parents were planning to disappear off the face of Earth because they laundered money from the official Inabrian fund for the Reparation. She wanted to live with a family who loves her. She asked me for help, so I gave her a potion and told her to leave. The potion was to help her find a place where people will love her as she is. Somewhere no one knows her name. Last I heard, she is attending university in the northern Inabrian capital."

"Huh," Chely says. "That's a magnificent tale you came up with on the spot, Annie. When did you get so good at lying?"

"What do you want from me, Cai-Li?" Anne stands up and almost knocks over one of the jars that decorates her table. "You think I'm responsible for some missing kids? Kids who probably have someone who loves them waiting at home? I *know* how it feels to lose someone! We lost Cole. I lost him, and I didn't realise it at the time, but I lost you too. You drown yourself in sorrow."

"You can see into the *future*." The fire inside Chely tugs at the edge of her wooden bench. The candles that listened to the alchemist's command are getting sheepish, as they don't know who to side with:

the oracle who owns this castle or the alchemist that rekindled their flames? "You could have at least told me you saw him die. Even if we couldn't stop it from happening, it would have been better to know and prepare for the grief. Maybe we both could have made better decisions in the aftermath."

"That's what this is all about, is it?" Anne's face grows distant; a cold grin spreads across the oracle's facial muscles, which are strung taut. "I didn't tell you because I was afraid you'd want revenge against whoever killed him! Screw the circumstances that it was a mother-fucking war, screw the context—let's be honest here, you aren't the sort of person who cares about some random missing Inabrian kids. It's about your loss, your grief. That's why I saw his death in the first place! His death was the catalyst for events that changed the future of the world to come. Not something private to mourn for, but an excuse you tell yourself when you go down the path you're heading toward!"

Her words are met with silence. It's an old wound by now, Cole's death a scab that has healed after years of torment. Most of the time, Chely can think of it without feeling like her heart has been shred-ded into pieces. Ever since the day she held her brother's body as it slowly turned cold with crimson liquid scattered on the emerald grass, nothing has been the same.

"You are right, Annie," Chely whispers. "You're also a huge *hyp-ocrite*. You think I'm the only one making Cole's death all about myself? Letting it change me beyond recognition? Look around you. You have isolated yourself from the rest of the world in this tacky castle that scares everyone away. You masquerade around in your oracle persona so you can tell over-the-top stuff to people who are genuinely asking for help, and you feel satisfied by that? That's childish for someone who's pushing thirty. And if it makes you hap-py, sure, be a piece of shit for a living. Except this isn't who you are!

Can you honestly tell me you are satisfied? I think not. When did you last shower? What are those sleep potions you made that line the shelves? They seem very unprofessional, and they don't seem to work because you look like shit!"

Anne narrows her eyes at Chely. "I'm sorry my potion-making skills aren't up to alchemist-sanctioned standard," she scoffs. "But I don't need you to help me sleep. I don't need your company, or your unsolicited advice, and I don't need your half-baked accusations!"

Chely throws her hands up in the air. This whole argument is getting them nowhere; it sounds like every other fight they'd had in those last years. Familiar, but unpleasant.

"I'm sorry." Chely sighs. "I didn't come here to argue."

"No," Anne replies plainly. "I don't know what you are here for, Ying Cai-Li. We have nothing left to say to each other."

That is The Oracle speaking, the one that always values the truth, no matter how harsh it is.

"Okay," Chely changes tactics. "You are right. I'm not here for the missing kids. I'm here because I want to bring you home."

Anne freezes, clearly perturbed by the sincerity in a round of verbal sparring. "This is my home," The Oracle croaks out. "You are the intruder."

"You still should have told me that Cole was going to die," Chely says, not backing down.

"And you should have listened to me when I told you that you would *lose me* if you kept up with the black magic!" Anne snaps at the red-haired alchemist.

The chandelier above their head shudders. The candles scream bloody murder as the flames try to clammer, staying atop without raining fire down on the two women.

"Yeah, you're right." The smirk is gone from Chely's face. "I did lose you."

Anne's lips twitch.

Both of them aged. Both are old and exhausted. The girls who fell in love during the Solstice in their youth over tavern fire and joyful conversations are nothing more than a distant memory. A daydream long dead after it was dragged across the walk of life.

Chely with her alchemy in the colour of crimson and death, Anne with her Visions of the future and loneliness. They have strayed so far from where they started.

The only one who remained the same was Cole.

The chalice of water in the middle of Anne's table swirls like a tornado. The reflection changes in front of their eyes. It shows a sunny day in the woods, two girls and a boy laughing as they dash in and out of a cottage playing hide-and-seek. The light is blinding. Their laughter carries across the fields of flowers by the wind.

The kids shown in the chalice are undoubtedly Chely, Anne, and Cole.

Except the image portrayed in the chalice never took place, not in reality.

The three of them didn't meet under such happy circumstances. They never spent their childhoods so carefree.

They met as young adults, raised in the shadow of one war, only for another to crush into their generation, leaving half of them dead and the other half broken.

The fairytale versions of them in the chalice are simply that—a reflection of the oracle's unspoken desire.

"The Chalice of Truth, huh?" Chely stares into the cup.

"Oh, shut up," Anne murmurs. "Truth is subjective, so is the future. We choose to believe, so we become. That's the truth to me. The future I chose. I wish…it was the family I had from the very beginning."

They sit there together for a long time. Neither of them speak another word.

Chely knows, however, they're both thinking of the same thing for the first time in decades.

They watch as their younger selves live a peaceful life in a parallel universe.

The children grow into adolescents.

"We *are* a family. You, me, and Cole. Nothing can ever change that. Not where we come from, nor where we end up," Chely says. "That is the only truth that matters to me."

"Since you are going to live here for an indefinite time in my house—"

"Well, Annie," Chely points out cheerfully, "it's not really your *house*. It's more like your castle. Your very creepy castle you didn't really pay for. The Castle of Doom."

"Great, let's establish some ground rules for The Castle of Doom, Cai-Li," Anne says with a blank expression, unaffected by Chely's deliberate attempt at lightening the mood. The oracle was always a serious girl, but it appears she has grown into a truly grim adult.

Despite offering tea to Chely, the tension from a decade of unspoken emotions boils beneath the surface like hot lava. That cup of tea is the warmest thing she's felt in the castle so far, besides the dancing candles Chely lit so she wouldn't plummet to her death while ascending the stairs.

How does Anne see in this dark? It is an eternal question. The oracle navigates the hallway with the ease of someone who traces the palm of her own hand. It's like this place is engraved in the marrow of Anne's bones, its map carved into her veins.

"No dark magic," Anne says sternly. "Don't even try or I'll know."

Chely opens her mouth to say something.

"No, Cai-Li," Anne says.

"I didn't even say anything," Chely muses.

"You don't need to," Anne says. "I can hear the cogs in your brain."

"Can you really?"

Anne Barberry doesn't humour that with a proper response.

Chely smiles. "You know me. Even after seven years, we are still connected."

Anne scrunches her nose as if she is already regretting offering the castle as a sanctuary to the red-haired alchemist. If The Oracle was responsible for the missing children, this would be the moment she'd zap Chely out of existence out of sheer exasperation.

She doesn't though. Chely sees that as a point in favour of Anne's innocence, much to The Innkeeper's disappointment, probably.

The man isn't going to be happy to find out that Chely, in fact, knows the shady oracle, let alone the complicated history the two women share. Although Chely never intended to follow through with the promise she gave The Innkeeper, she does feel slightly apologetic that she never explained it wasn't Anne that he should be worried about.

"Okay, no dark magic." Chely raises her hands up in appeasement. "It is debatable though. What you Inabrians consider 'dark magic.'"

"I can't speak for all Aixauhan alchemists," Anne says as dead as she seems to be on the inside. "With the sample size of one Yamalan boy and one Aixauhan alchemist captain, I think both Cole and Captain Ark Li would say what you are doing is dark magic too."

"Okay, fine," Chely says. "No dark magic. It's like nothing's changed."

"You're wrong," Anne says, as if she can read Chely's thoughts. The blonde woman's voice is strained and reserved. "Everything has changed, Chely. We can't just pick up where we left off."

Chely nods. "I know," she says. "Doesn't mean we can't get to know each other again. Friends who haven't seen each other do that all the time. We can catch up on what we've been up to, or what new hobbies we've picked up in the last seven years. Don't you want to know what Maev is up to these days?"

"You're talking to Maev?" Anne's expression morphs slightly into that of surprise, the most emotion Chely has squeezed out of the oracle. "I thought she swore she'd stop talking to us if you kept up with the dark magic... Maybe you have changed since we last met."

"Okay, fine," Chely says in defeat. "Can we lay off the topic now that I've promised you?"

"I don't know," Anne replies. "Depends on how well you keep your promises."

Chely doesn't wish to admit Anne might have a point there. She's nearly abandoned the plan of searching for the missing kids after one nostalgic conversation with the oracle over some tea.

But she won't make the same mistake again.

As Chely steps into the guest room, her eyes widen. This space is almost like a different world from the rest of the castle. The curtain is a bright, sheer turquoise fabric, drawn to the side for the sun to stream in long golden rays. The bed is covered in milk-white sheets, with several pillows plopped on top of one another. There is a huge wardrobe made of wood that seems sturdy, carved with flowers. The floor is white marble, and the walls are painted a yellow in the shade of dandelion flowers.

Even the lamp is in the shape of a flower in blossom, with a crimson lampshade gilded with gold tips.

"Wow," Chely marvels at the sight. "This doesn't fit the aesthetic of the Barberrys. Did you decorate the room for me?"

"No, I saved the room for the kidnapped victims," Anne replies in a flat tone, which drains the amazement from the air quickly. The oracle leans against the doorframe as the red-haired alchemist turns her head in bafflement. "What? Too dark, too inconsiderate? Is the timing too poor? This isn't the Barberry Castle, Cai-Li."

"Er, no." Chely winces a bit at the implication of Anne's words. "I mean, of course it's not. Sorry, Anne. I didn't think before I spoke."

"What?" Anne waves a hand, her stoic face radiating the energy that she wants to move on from this topic. However, as she opens her mouth, that is proven to be the wrong assumption. "I do live in a creepy isolated castle that has way too many hidden compartments and wear too many black clothes. I might as well take in the other…interests of Brutus Barberry."

"That's not what I'm saying at all!" Chely lifts her head up. Her eyes feel like burning, how Anne says those words is like self-flagellation. It's more painful to the alchemist's ears than it appears to be to the oracle's. "I would never say that. I know you differ from them, more than anyone else. I just…remember you don't like black clothing."

Makes the dark circles under my eyes look more prominent. That was what Anne used to say. *I don't want to look more like a ghost beside you, Ying Cai-Li.*

"I still don't," Anne sighs. "This is my divination costume. It's the colour that makes people pack up and flee. Plus, it doesn't show stains of spilled drinks. Two birds, one stone."

Anne's familiar, again now a black crow perched on Anne's shoulder, gives a cry of protest.

"I think you offended Cole," Chely muses.

"Stay out of our business," Anne scoffs. But the alchemist hears the oracle lower her voice and mutter under her breath, "Sorry, Cole."

Chely sets down her suitcase on the rug, which is the same shade of red threaded with gold as the lamp.

"Are you going to stay there to watch me change?" Chely asks.

Anne's face contorts like someone has accidentally stabbed her toes. "Please enjoy your own fucking company," the oracle curses before storming off.

Seven years later, Anne Barberry is still as allergic to flirtation as she was when they were young. No one this easily flustered could be responsible for a dozen or so missing teens. They'd embarrass the great oracle to death with their shrewdness.

Ying Cai-Li takes off her brown boots, the ones she always wears as a traveler who often needs to trudge through woods and mountains to find alchemical components that can only be obtained under specific circumstances. The spirit core of a thousand-year-old tree, metal that can be mended into a hearth with enough spiritual energy to light up certain ingredients, or even a hungry ghost with no burial mound to claim.

She's relaxed in this room. It's downright luxurious compared to what Chely has grown used to on the road. Sometimes the alchemist almost forgets that, before anything else, Anne Barberry is a sheltered Inabrian girl with exuberant taste who grew up in a castle just like this one.

Anne is primarily known as an oracle, but with magic comes the convenience of making life agreeable. It means the Barberrys fashioned their ancestral castle with art and decorative magic that made it larger than life. The walls bore no cracks, the flames could be tweaked to perfectly accommodate the desired temperature of the castle's owner, the dining tables popped up delicacies like lobsters, and the wardrobes contained the latest Inabrian robes made in the softest material that it slid around the body like water.

Most of it is exaggeration, no doubt. But there is a grain of truth in it, which is that Anne is into architectural magic that makes rooms more surreal than they should be. When they lived together, Chely used to wake up in the morning to find The Cottage's wooden walls smelling of fresh-cut logs from the forest, and the muddy floor so pristine that she could walk barefoot on them. Plus, she added a bathtub to the washroom with extra space to boot, as if the oracle couldn't comprehend there were other ways of cleaning themselves.

It used to drive Cole mad, but it always made Chely smile. Secretly, Anne was a creature of comfort.

The renovation that Anne brought to The Cottage came one speck at a time over the course of several months that accumulated into seasons. Here in this castle, it is different, as if this entire room sprung into life as fast as the flick of a pen.

Anne's magic is growing, no doubt. It's incomprehensible, but not out of nowhere. The Inabrians and their boundless belief in what they deserve, the world answers to their magic in kind.

For Chely's magic, for lack of a better term—"alchemist" is simply the closest word the Inabrian language has for any Aixauhan imbued with beyond normal human properties—on the other hand, operates under a separate set of rules.

Aixauhan alchemist is an umbrella term for anything Aixauhan and magical. The Inabrian magicians are, as their title suggests, human magicians; but in Aixauh, everything has a soul. The trees, the flowers, a random rock; anything that has a spirit can become a human being through a magic-like means of gaining enough enlightenment. They were all lumped under the term "alchemists" in Inabri.

The official term for someone like Chely would be 炼丹师, more a "forger of fire-element magical orbs" than an "alchemist." The Ying Clan and most other alchemist clans who actively practised this type of magic are the closest to what the term "alchemists" suggests. Their craft mostly includes mixing ingredients through a process that creates magical components in shape of an orb—some of these orbs are medicine or poison. Others could soothe the ocean about to become a tsunami, grant people abnormal powers, or explode weapons of war.

The emperors of Aixauh sought an orb of immortality through the help of alchemy, but they often died of mercury poisoning, as it was the element symbolical of the unchanging soul between life and death in the Aixauh alchemical charts.

Just like Anne is an oracle with a knack for domestic decoration magic, Ying Cai-Li is an alchemist with a strong suit in a different magic as well.

That magic had driven Anne away.

Chely groans just thinking about it. "I really hope I don't fuck this up again," she says to the ceiling while falling back onto the comfy sheets. She can smell lavender in the fabric. Anne still loves mixing the same flavour of flower into her cleaning spells.

Chely closes her eyes and takes a breath filled with the damp yet calming scent of flowers and falls asleep after a long day.

There was a time when Chely brought all kinds of wildflowers to Anne. Freshly plucked from around The Cottage they lived in. Each day, a vase with a different blossom greeted her. Red peonies, blue bellflowers, purple lavender, wisteria, white lilies…

The other half of the flowers were for a less romantic purpose, which meant they went straight into Chely's cauldron to create the cleaning spell for all their laundry.

She remembers how Anne's face scrunched up when she found out where the leftover flowers went. Like a glass shattering on the ground, a perfect illusion breaking into pieces.

"Geez, who can believe it's been seven years?" Chely mumbles to the ceiling as she wakes up. She can still taste the smoke that once permeated the battlefield.

Magicians and alchemists clad in protection spells and armour had clashed into one another with all their strength. Debris of architecture crumbled into dust. Cities toppled overnight by the might of magic, the full scale of how the craftsmanship of magic turned into methods of destruction revealed to the common folk.

That was when the Inabrians invented the word "witch." Before the two wars, the magicians were thought of as untouchable divine lineages that were blessed by the Creator, while the alchemists were abominations who got their abilities through pagan sources. Until both sides committed mass slaughter of their civilians during the war, and the Inabrian public realised that when it rained acid or the ground cracked to swallow people whole, the source of the magic—Inabrian or Aixauhan—ceased to matter. They were all going to kill them excruciatingly.

The Innkeeper is not the only survivor of the wars to grow disillusioned by the concept of the magicians. Chely can relate.

The taste of salt and iron on her tongue as her mouth lay agape. Cole's body dropping like a puppet whose strings were cut. Sticky crimson liquid on her hands. The lone daisy blooming among the cracked earth of the battlefield was stained crimson too. Its head bent, petals drenched in red.

The soldier who killed Cole was not Inabrian, but rather an Aixauhan alchemist.

Before Chely can get too lost in her thoughts, Anne pushes the guestroom door open without warning.

"Hey, Annie." Chely beams, the nightmare forgotten. "Have you ever heard of a thing called knocking? What if you walk in on me changing half-naked?"

"My castle, my rules." Anne's face twitched. She hid it better this time. "Plus, it's not anything I haven't seen before."

Chely's smile widened. It seems like overnight the oracle decided if she can't make the alchemist stop antagonising her, then she may as well win the game.

The oracle's attire has changed. Anne is in a black robe with long open sleeves that hang loose like the sails of a ship. It's simplistic in design, nothing more than some laces on the hem. Compared to the intricate layers of her dress as The Oracle, Anne looks downright normal this morning, barring the unfortunate choice of colour.

"You look…cosy," Chely says. "Did you and your familiar agree you'd both only wear black or something?"

"Shut up, I'm wearing normal ass clothes," Anne says.

"I mean, sure," Chely says. "Normal clothing for a very rich hermit. Do you not keep up with the latest Inabrian court fashion, at least? You used to be so dedicated to it."

"That was before the war," Anne says. "We're not seventeen anymore."

"True." Chely shrugs. "I kind of noticed that among the population in town. There aren't a lot of teenagers. Other than the tourists. And Naomi."

"Naomi?" Anne asks, confused. "Who is that?"

"The Innkeeper's daughter," Chely says. "She said she's met you in town buying groceries from time to time and that you were nice to her?"

The oracle's face slackens. An indescribably dull expression settles over her features. Anne Barberry's grey eyes are dark and prowling like a thunderstorm diluted into a shade softer, like a dove's feathers.

Her face is inscrutable, like mist rising to block out the moon.

Anne replies in a hollow voice, "This town is no place for kids."

2

Born to Greatness

ANNE BARBERRY GREW up in a castle. It is less impressive than it sounds. Castles are so abundant in Inabri that even the smallest town with two streets and one tavern probably has one looming nearby in the background.

Inabrian history is marked with magician lineages fighting amongst one another. Before the Crown united the lineages into one whole, each lineage was gunning for greater control of their territory and land for themselves. The magicians might have been chosen by the Creator, but the Creator clearly was having a bad day and wanted to see people bash in one another's heads in creative ways en masse.

Terrible jokes aside, Anne's memories of The Barberry Castle are filled with childish wonder.

Stone walls with great views, watchtowers to climb where magicians used to decimate armies of men. Dungeons that were locked for very good reasons—and Anne learning to lock pick from the lineage of locksmiths. She always knew more than she was supposed to. With a knack for not caring about how morbid things could get, nothing could hurt a young Barberry oracle. Anne's world was once devoid of the concept of pain and suffering.

History was nothing but stories; the future was nothing but flashes of prismatic colour. The biggest problem on Anne's mind was how to deal with her parents when they got mad at her for breaking rules or etiquette.

She used to love sneaking into the sprawling town below the castle, especially during Solstice. The townsfolk recognised her on sight, with her signature white-blonde hair and metallic grey eyes. They knew Anne was the next oracle that would take up the mantle from her grandfather. They showered her with free food, lovely conversations, and odd trinkets they sold at their stands.

Sometimes, they'd ask Anne to tell them some small fortune. Whether their cheese would win the local competition, how many children they would have, what the weather would be like if they hung the laundry out to dry.

Anne would reply honestly: "I don't know unless I taste it." "You look too old to have any." "Even if it doesn't rain, it's still too damp for any clothes to dry."

They'd laugh, with their eternal kindness and patience extending to the foolish rudeness that only a Barberry child could afford to indulge in.

The Barberry Family Castle resided in the hills surrounded by greenery. It towered over the hustling and bustling town like a shadow. The Barberrys prided themselves on the gifts they got from the townsfolk but never debased themselves enough to mingle with them.

Anne always thought she'd grow up to be different. She found joy in the company of others; solitude was not for her. Her parents were not especially kind to each other, nor did she have many friends from the fellow magician lineages. The town was her home, she thought. They were her people.

She was The Oracle. The Creator blessed the Barberry Lineage with one of His greatest gifts—the Vision to peek into the future that was His grand design. Anne was not stupid, she knew she was The Oracle. Yet she hadn't realised that was *all* she was going to be to these people, in this town, in this castle. Anne Barberry was bound to the future of providing a solution to their infinite enquiries and problems.

Anne enjoyed the love and admiration that fixed role brought her, so she would have to bear the burden it became for the rest of her life. It was not long into her teenage years before her father told her that it was Anne's duty to serve the Barberry Lineage, which meant serving the Inabrian Army and the magicians in the war to come, for how else was she going to repay the years of doing what she wished without consequences?

Consequences, what a funny word. The Barberry family produced two kinds of people: the oracles and the rest. Her father, her aunts and uncles, her sisters. Everyone lived a consequence-free life, for they did not have to become the object of ridicule when they didn't deliver on the promise of the Barberry name.

Anne might have tasted joy as a child, but that joy was conditional. Like The Barberry Castle, it had yet to reveal its sinister roots to her eyes.

So, for years, Anne remained a spoiled brat, believing the town was her entire world and that her family deserved its place at the top. A beautiful, isolated story with no outside world to speak of.

Sometimes Anne wonders if her whole life was merely a dream. One she woke up from and only to find herself right back where she started.

Except this time, there is no more childish innocence to be lost. This time, the oracle is fully aware of the town's animosity and the discontent that runs beneath the surface, their desire to pull from her threads of the future. Anne Barberry is under no illusion that there is a power dynamic to her castle and their town.

She will take nothing from them, unlike her parents and grandparents. But they will get no hospitality from her. The Oracle owes nothing to the townsfolk who wish to pluck out her eyes to see into the future.

Anne's going to make them wish they could cut out her tongue. Then she can find some peace within her solace in the memories of the family she has found and lost.

She will never tell Ying Cai-Li that she dreams of the red-haired alchemist often.

When the oracle heard Cai-Li somehow found this town, Anne dreamed of the townsfolk with their permanent smiles and towering frames, the way she saw them as a child.

In that dream, Anne screamed for Cai-Li to run. She was too late; the town swallowed her love whole.

They didn't even spit out her bones.

The castle Anne lived in as a child is nothing like the castle she lives in now.

The curtains were always open to let in light. Chandeliers hung from the ceiling, sparkling like stars confined in crystal glass. Golden tapestries of the ancestors proudly stood in portraits encased in eternal youth.

All this, Anne's grandfather, Brutus Barberry, built on his own.

Anne's parents were social butterflies; they'd dance night after night at the gatherings of magicians. Expensive champagne swirled in tall glasses. They talked about Anne, boasted about how they were the parents of the destined oracle who would change the tides of the war to come.

It was hilarious. Neither Anne's mother nor father were in the First War themselves. Her father had been a pimply and prissy teenager, her mother an arrogant yet delicate flower. They didn't see into the future or the past; they lived fully in the present.

Anne sometimes thought about who she would've become if she had not been The Oracle. Did the Creator choose oracles to be born specifically to be the harbingers of war? There was no better explanation for why it was Brutus Barberry who got the gift of the Vision, who was the Barberry that carried the mantle in the First War, only for the power to pass not to his eldest son—Anne's oldest uncle—but to a granddaughter born into the family of the third son. Anne's father would have gotten no title or inheritance if Anne hadn't turned out to be the only Barberry child in her generation that was near adult-age during the Second War.

It was either the biggest coincidence in the world, or the Creator had a sick sense of humour. Thanks to the life Anne led, she unabashedly believed the latter to be true.

Despite the temporary truce, it was common knowledge after the First War that a second war among the Inabrian magicians loomed on the horizon. The First War took place on Aixauhan lands, with half of the Aixauhan alchemist clans wiped out. The Inabrian magicians lost sons and daughters, for sure, but that's what happens when you send armies to war.

No, the Second War was not one of survival for the Inabrian magicians—it was one of pride. Only when the Aixauhans brought the fire back onto Inabrian land did the Inabrian magicians regret poking the bear one time too hard.

The ten years of peacetime after the Second War left both sides weary, licking their wounds with equal amounts of damage. *Finally*,

Anne thought. The path to peace was forged when both parties became tired.

If they gathered enough strength to start killing one another again, Anne prayed that it was not within her or Cai-Li's lifetimes.

As a child, when everyone tells you that you are special, and you soak in those praises like a sponge. Anne used to go to gatherings of magicians, being introduced as the pride and joy of the Barberry family. Her head would tilt up in such self-importance, with the confidence of someone who deserved a punch in the face.

"The magical lineages who pass down the Creator's Magic by blood will also pass down the Creator's Will."

Little Anne had smiled as her parents patted her head, not yet realising the meaning of those words.

Years later, on her sixteenth birthday, which fell on the day of the Solstice, Grandfather Brutus would place within Anne's hand the Chalice of Truth—the heirloom passed down from oracle to oracle for as long as the Creator blessed them with the power of prophecy.

Anne took the chalice with her when she ran. It was a tool that helped the oracle stay sane. The prophecies spoken by The Oracle could be stored in the chalice for safekeeping, only to be remembered when Anne drank from it again.

She used the chalice as common glassware. Many afternoons for tea with Cole and Cai-Li in The Cottage, neither Aixauhan alchemists suffered any apparent side-effects from drinking from the sacred Chalice of Truth, even though the idea was they were supposed to burst into flames due to being born of impure dark magic.

Anne saw it as a giant middle finger to the entire Barberry legacy. But it wasn't enough. Nothing was enough to wash the conscience of a Barberry clean.

"Will you do anything and everything that is demanded of you for this family, Angelica Cassandra Barberry?"

"Yes, I will." Little Anne had puffed up her small chest and held her chubby cheeks high, leading all the adults in the room to chuckle in delight.

"We are so proud of you, honey," Mrs. Barberry had said. "You will be the greatest oracle, and you will define the future of the Barberry Lineage."

In her adolescence, Anne wasn't sure if she'd become the greatest oracle by the time she reached thirty, but she knew she was going to define the future of the Barberrys.

She was going to let the name die with her. Cheers to that, Grandpa.

But Brutus Barberry had once been once Anne's entire world. Despite their pride in her, Father and Mother had always been away. Anne had spent days popping her head out of the window at the gate covered with wisteria, waiting for her parents to show their faces, until her legs were sore. Grandpa Brutus would gently tell her it was time to go to sleep.

"Your parents are busy," Brutus had answered patiently whenever Anne had complained about how unfair it was. The soft creases on his forehead were marked by age. "Now, let's get back to your studies. Have you seen anything using the Vision beyond the magician who chases the sun?"

"No," Anne had replied, ashamed. "It's been years since I produced that prophecy, Grandpa. Do you think the Creator is mad at me? Am I ever going to see the future again?"

"Each Oracle grows at a different pace, my darling," Brutus had cooed to soothe his granddaughter's anxieties. "Your parents are eager, but they're also stupid. They see the glory of the Barberry name, but not the time spent to get there. Do you think I was born as well-versed as I am in the Vision now?"

The way Brutus had called Anne's parents stupid had made her chuckle, like any child easily impressed by those who sided with them. In those days, it had been like Anne and Brutus shared a secret. A secret that made them beyond the townsfolk, beyond the rest of the Barberrys, and beyond even Anne's parents.

"Yes," Anne had replied. Back then, she couldn't see a world where her grandfather was not a near-omniscient figure.

"Let me tell you a secret, my little duck," Brutus had said. "I came to my oracle power when I was twenty-five. My father was a lot like yours, prideful but useless. The Creator does not unfold the veil toward the future to anyone. He only does for those of us who stand at the precipice of time. An oracle is born to greatness. We do not see the futures of the common milk maid or farmer for a reason; we see the future because we are the ones who will *define* the future. I was there for the First War, and you will be there for the second."

"But the Vision I saw as a child had nothing to do with war," Anne had pouted. She had thought herself grown at eleven years of age. "It was about the stupid sun! I want to see a war, too!"

"You will, in time."

"What does a war look like in the Vision?"

Brutus's eyes had glistened with pure elation. "Glorious," he had whispered before kissing Anne on the forehead. "It is glorious."

Anne now wishes she could have vomited all over his perfectly tucked cravat. Alas, an oracle is sadly not awarded foresight into things that matter.

She doesn't yet know the meaning of her first Vision. It was like Brutus said: The Oracle could see those who would come to define history. He saw himself, once upon a time.

While Anne, she sees someone else.

3

The Innkeeper's Daughter

CHELY IS STARTING to get the hang of communicating with Anne. Namely, she doesn't.

Anne's idea of etiquette when inviting someone to stay at the castle is based on the same rules as hide-and-seek. Chely wakes up on her first morning. There are clean towels folded on the armchair. On the side is a note written in cursive: "Put your dirty clothes here at the end of the day." Without a signature, since it is pointless to think anyone other than The Oracle is haunting this castle.

Chely finds the guest room has en-suite facilities attached, mysteriously detaching itself from the wall like a tunnel leading to another dimension. The washroom is clean and bright, with notes dotting across the area, pointing out the different drawers. Every type of toiletry is accounted for. There is also an added drawer for al-chemical bath orbs, ones that smell floral and ones that are essential but flavourless. The kind Chely used to brew for Anne specifically—there is no apparent alternative source where Anne could get them here, isolated and alone.

"Are you stalking me, Annie?" Chely asks to the white ceiling, to no one's response.

After taking a shower with her own packed essentials, Chely takes a stroll through the castle. The guest room opens to the same hallway Chely and Anne walked across on the first day, except now the curtains are open.

"I'm going to search for where you hid the kidnapped victims," Chely says to the empty and dark hallways, again to no response.

Anne Barberry might have grown older and more disheveled, but she's also evolved in terms of waving away Chely's taunts. There was a time when the oracle would have argued with the alchemist about every single word of a sentence, back when there were no corpses in their metaphorical closets.

Chely gives up on talking to the dark on the second day; it becomes clear no one is listening when the alchemist's adventure of opening every closed door lining The Barberry Castle results in Chely slamming open Anne's own bedroom, where Anne is abed.

The oracle opens her eyes as the noise disturbs her sleep. However, the utter calmness in Anne's gaze is uncanny for someone who's been woken up in the middle of the afternoon.

"What the fuck, Cai-Li?" The oracle says calmly. "Get out of my face."

"Okay," Chely replies, speechless. "Why are you still sleeping? It's like 1:00 p.m."

"Do you see me asking about your life?" Anne asks.

"Er, no?"

"Good," The oracle says, expressionless as she remains in bed with her eyes already drifting closed again. "Stay out of mine."

"Okay," Chely says.

Anne means those words. Following that quiet and disturbing confrontation, Chely decides that if Anne is hiding the missing people in her Castle, it's probably not in one of the dozens of bedrooms.

The only forbidden area is the west wing. Except it isn't forbidden in the sense that Anne has shut it off with spells or wards using architectural magic—there is no material separation between the main body of the castle to that side of the castle. Chely is not sure it's even forbidden because *Anne* says so. Instead, it's the familiar, taking the form of a black crow, that vehemently blocks the alchemist no matter which direction she tries to approach the area from.

"I just want to cut through the area to reach the dining room, Cole," Chely tries to reason with the bird on the third day. "For breakfast?"

The black crow stares at Chely with his white filmy eyes, unblinking. When the red-haired alchemist tries to walk past him—as he's a fluffy ball of feathers perched on the wall while she is a human-sized creature—the crow starts cawing incessantly and pecks her with his pointy beak, sinking it right into Chely's skin.

Chely learns her lesson. She isn't going to win against a bird in an argument.

Anne sees the bruising left behind on Chely's skin from the battles waged between alchemist and familiar. The oracle's reaction is an impassioned glee that emanates from her statue-like face.

"What is in the west wing?" Chely asks Anne at breakfast. "What are you hiding?"

"Nothing," Anne replies. She bites into a fresh apple from the farmer's market that Chely got from her trip into town the other day. "It's Cole who is stopping you. Ask him."

"He's a bird," Chely replies, her nerves fraying at the edges as the black cat snores from where he's curled up on an empty chair along the long dining table that is too much for two people. "Sometimes other creatures. How am I supposed to understand him?"

"I don't know, Cai-Li." Anne doesn't look the alchemist in the eye. "Maybe if he struggled with you to keep you out, that means no."

"No…what?"

"I don't know," Anne replies. "That's between you and him."

A few days into the alchemist's stay, the oracle shamelessly threw a list of groceries at Chely and told her to go fetch the things. Chely stared at the list in utter bewilderment. Anne expected her to run errands just because she wished to stay. The underlying assumption that Chely would just take it seemed absurd.

Which was exactly why Chely went into town to get everything Anne asked for. The fresh apples sold at the stand with the man with the gigantic red beard, the honey from the girl with freckles on her nose, the freshly brewed wine from The Inn.

Chely's eyebrows had furrowed at that last item. There was no way The Innkeeper would agree to this.

"I don't think The Innkeeper likes you enough to supply you with alcohol," the alchemist had said. "Also, what about the no drinking rule?"

"The wine isn't for me," Anne had said. "It's for the guests who come by for divination."

"Since when is wine part of an oracle's divination ritual?" Chely had almost wished to laugh out loud at the clear trap set by Anne Barberry to mess with her. "I know how an oracle works, Annie. You see something or you don't."

"Since you're going to report my whereabouts to The Innkeeper anyway," Anne had said without blinking, "you might as well pick up some wine while you're there... if you're fine with selling out an old friend."

Chely hadn't been surprised Anne found out. The Oracle has more eyes than the alchemist can understand around the castle. It wouldn't be a stretch to say that she could see beyond the coming and goings in town.

"I'm not selling you out," Chely had replied stubbornly. "If you tell me where you stashed those missing kids, I can help you to better distract the townsfolk."

"I have nothing to do with those missing kids." Annehad eyed Chely with mild annoyance. "You are way too comfortable with being implicated in potential serial murders, Ying Cai-Li."

The moment that Chely got to the Inn, she understood how Anne got her alcohol supply.

Naomi was the one tending the bar, mopping it as clean as it could be in the late morning, when no one in town came to The Inn for drinks except for a few tourists staying there that were just waking up to grab a few pies that the kitchen offered around the clock.

"You are terrible at espionage, kid," Chely said. "So, this is how you got to know The Oracle. What did she offer you for the best wine in your father's cellar?"

Naomi's eyes were as round as the rims of the glasses she almost bumped onto the floor. Tears filled them instantly.

"Oh no," Naomi muttered. Her hair was in pigtails yesterday, making her look younger, barely more than a child. "How did you find out, Miss Ying? I thought we were discreet. Anne always comes in different disguises."

"It's okay, please don't cry." Chely felt like an asshole, which was possibly exactly what she was going to have to be to get some answers. "I meant it though. Is that where you disappeared to that other day? Your dad thinks you were off seeing some boy. Were you meeting with Anne instead?"

"What?" Naomi stammered, both at the first name basis the alchemist was on with The Oracle and because of the question. "No, not in *that* way! I'm exchanging favours with The Oracle because I went to see her the other day. I...I know Inabrian magicians have more power than their designated role, so I went to the castle to ask if Anne could get a message to my mother. She said yes, no strings attached. Only condition is I don't ask her how it is done. I feel horrible that my father says so many awful things about her, so I offered her wine… I mean, the wine in my father's cellar is always refilling. You know how it is. It's all I can give her. She says there's no need, but every time she brings me a message from my mum, I always hand her a jug or two."

"Oh, no worries. I know you guys aren't romantically involved," Chely said. "She's way older than she looks, and she isn't a creep. It's none of my business, anyway. I'm not going to tell your father about this. Not unless I want to spill my own beans regarding Anne."

"Oh." Naomi blinked in surprise. "What…? Do you know her, Miss Ying?"

"She's the sole reason I'm here," Chely replied nonchalantly. "I'm going to win her back or die trying."

Naomi chuckled. The Innkeeper's daughter clutched the bar, a little unsteady on her feet at this turn of events.

"Okay," she said. "Not going to lie. I am surprised. But it makes sense that you're here for Anne. What else would an Aixauhan alchemist be doing here? I mean, it makes no sense. Anne always seems lonely. I meant what I said last time—she really is nice."

Chely watched The Innkeeper's daughter thoughtfully. "You're right. I'm sorry, Anne didn't give me any message to deliver from your mother. Can you still give me that jug of wine?"

"Yeah, of course," Naomi said. The wispy girl felt more solid than she had since Chely met her. "… I'm leaving. Anne says my mother is waiting for me. I know Father is going to be furious. If I can bother you and The Oracle for one last favour. Take care of him, will you?"

Chely nodded. "Sure, kid."

Chely keeps an eye on the oracle for a few days. Anne never drinks; it mixed up badly with the alchemical orbs that Chely made her for sleep when they lived together. It messes up the oracle's sleep schedule, which messes with Anne's mental state further. the oracle's sanity is "hanging on like a single hair loose on the side of the cliff being dragged down by a tsunami of bullshit." Those were Anne's own words, not Chely's.

It's good to see Anne was being truthful when she told Chely she is in no habit of drinking. Chely fussed over Anne's intake of alchemically generated sleep medication for the years they lived together after the war. Anything triggered endless hours of pacing and insomnia in those early days. Light, noises, sometimes scents. That was why Chely agreed to make Anne the orbs to begin with, because the side-effects of the alchemy orbs that helped sleep—nausea, risk to kidney and lungs, addiction—proved to be less urgent than the immediate effects of chronic sleep deprivation—nightmares, anxiety flare-ups, flashbacks, suicidal ideation.

Now Anne is on her own. Chely is, in fact, worried the oracle has replaced the dependency she developed on the sleep medication orbs with something else more potent. Murdering innocent kids who come to her castle is a wild guess, which is unfair in retrospect. But the Anne that Chely witnessed during those breakdowns was someone else, like a container that carried around the war, cracked under heavy pressure.

However, counting out the first day where Anne had heavy eye-bags and a very grumpy attitude, the oracle is doing much better than Chely expected. The Anne who exists solely in Chely's memories is not a woman who can have someone barge into her room only to politely tell them to sod off and go straight back to bed.

Okay, maybe Anne's sleep schedule is a little screwed, but who cares about rising with the sun and going to bed with the moon after surviving a goddamned war where night and day melted into each other in one permanent frantic haze?

That is why, when noises come from under Chely's guestroom, the alchemist doesn't bother to investigate at first. She's getting used to the coexisting non-company that The Oracle prefers. It is less than what Chely desires, but it's what Anne feels comfortable with... that's enough. The alchemist is nearly convinced that nothing about the oracle has changed at all.

Except, that is, when Chely hears the voice of a guest who's entered the castle.

"Can you truly bring my mum to me, dear Oracle?"

"No," Anne's voice is the gentle water that runs across a valley. "What I can do is bring you to her."

Chely bolts up straight as an arrow.

The voice belongs to The Innkeeper's daughter.

Naomi.

4

A Spark in the Dark

THERE WAS AN annual gathering of Inabrian magician children just after the Solstice. A summer camp where younger children of the magician families would undergo a series of fun activities curated specifically to hone their lineage's magic. Older kids attended the summer camp as well; the ones who would take over their magician lineage's name one day were tasked with curating those activities and were instructed to bond with the younger kids of their fellow Inabrian magician lineages as mentors to guide them in the future to come.

In the beginning, these gatherings often ended in bloodshed; during the days when Inabrian magician lineages had no allegiance other than to their own families, each wishing to plot the demise of others. A gathering of their heirs was a sure path to destruction. Security increased following the Crown's establishment.

Nowadays, the gatherings are little more than an excuse for the parents of Inabrian magician parents to socialise child-free amongst themselves for a month or so.

In the decades following the end of the First War, there was also an increase of other nations' magic users who entered Inabri for scholarly exchange. Their children were often invited through courtesy to join the summer camp. One particular year, even some Aixauhan alchemist kids were asked to participate.

Thinking back, Anne doesn't believe for a second it was part of the Crown's attempt at Reparation. Instead, the Inabrian magician lineages knew this would have the opposite effect. After the First War, there came a huge change in the tides of power between the Inabrian magicians. Their hearts were shaken, as the First War proved not as fruitful and fulfilling as they thought. Bringing in the Aixauhan kids was almost like taking lambs to slaughter, a reminder to the youngest generation of the magician lineages' clans that there were the outsiders they should all focus on beyond their petty squabbles.

A common enemy, the age-old trick employed by any tyrant. Find a target for the people you lead to hate, so they can feel better about themselves in their misery.

Every summer beginning at the age of eight, all magician children spent their summer days growing up at the campsite. Anne was thirteen; technically, at that point, she should still have been in the children's cabin. But because two years prior, she had inherited the mantle of The Barberry Oracle, following Brutus Barberry's death, Anne was grouped with the older kids in the tents as creators and curators for the camp.

The camp was, in its function, trying to train the next generation of the Inabrian magician army. It was a clever trick. Anne's magician peers possessed their lineages' pride and an eagerness to prove themselves. So what if they did not notice the "activities" they set for the younger Inabrian kids were a tad outrageous? It was all in the name of some good old-fashioned fun.

So many of the ideas invented at the camp became the tactics driving behind the military minds of the Inabrian magician armies.

Acid rain clouds made by the water and weather magicians, electrocution fields by the lightning wielder lineage, the sink-cave that buried tens of thousands of people alive at once—collaborated by the magicians of earth and nature.

The same night Brutus Barberry died, eleven-year-old Anne had become the true Oracle. The Visions of the war to come accompanied her like bees to honey. Each of them grotesque, each of them bloody. The threads that connected the past, the present, and the future wove together in thirteen-year-old Anne's mind, even though there was not yet a clear map to knowing the extent of insidiousness of it all.

One thing was clear enough: Anne wanted no part in whatever was to come.

"Did you hear?" seventeen-year-old magician Lila Shaffield scooted close to her best friend, Nina. They shared Anne's tent, much to no one's delight. "There's this new girl at camp who's never came to the summer camp before. She's a tiny, quiet thing, an *Aixauhan alchemist*. She cannot speak properly. These parasites, coming to Inabri as if she and her people's magic aren't against the Creator! Savage magic of pagan gods. And she has no fucking clue she's here, far above her station among actual magicians of Inabri. She's such a moron, smiles all the time, even after we made it clear she's not welcome here."

"Yeah, I noticed! Her parents are apparently 'scholastic diplomats.' Since when are we exchanging magic with the Aixauhan alchemists? Their alchemy is tainted, inherently evil. Like, how dare they intrude into what is our inheritance? We're literally welcoming enemies into our fold just because the Crown wishes to play nice."

"Yes, did you see her in training today?" Nina said so loudly that Anne could hear her, even with her soundproof spell as thick as it could get. "She refused to turn that rock into a spider, muttering about how every inanimate thing has a soul inside of it and how tampering with the shape of a rock without its consent would be a violation. As if a bloody rock is a human being!"

Anne wanted to shut them up. Of course, she knew who they were speaking of—the girl with flaming red hair and midnight eyes. The girl from Aixauh had appeared in her Vision long before Anne had set eyes on her. But the person she had seen was the future version of this girl. Anne could not see her facial features, but she knew the smile the older girls spoke of.

In Anne's Vision, that woman with hair of shifting crimson had grinned as the dawn lit the sky aflame.

Anne did not speak up. The words of those older girls were annoying, but she did not care much for the plight of some weak Aixauhan girl with no self-respect, who *smiled* when surrounded by people who treated her like vermin. She knew the girl's name in passing: Ying Cai-Li, a name of a foreign land. A girl of pagan magic that existed outside of the gift offered by the Creator, who bestowed distinct magic craft solely upon the noble lineages of Inabrians.

The arrogance and fragility of a teenager torn, fully abandoning the indoctrination she underwent… Anne grimaces now at her younger self. Cai-Li would someday come to say how one views others is a mirror, that it shows no quality of those one looks down upon, but rather a projection of who one perceives oneself to be.

Anne wouldn't be sure know how true that was. The Inabrian magicians viewed themselves highly and saw the Aixauhan alchemists as nearly inhuman. It would be hard to see where the projection lay. However, with Anne herself, Cai-Li would hit the bull's eye.

Down the line, Anne would learn what Aixauhans practised was not magic, but something else. Not magic in the sense that it is spoken in the Inabrian tongue.

There was so much to learn from that thirteen-year-old brat who eventually opened her eyes.

The girl with flaming red hair and oak-brown eyes was also not the only one whose pagan magic went against the norm set by the Creator. There was a whole group of kids at the summer camp who huddled together like rabbits trying to watch one anothers' backs against a praying mantis.

There was a boy, Cole, who had translucent skin that one could see through like a piece of ice and hair as white as fresh milk. He and his people were of the Hima'aya mountain tribe of Yamala. They were often referred to as "the snow fairies" by the Inabrian common folk, half-joking and half-derogatory. They were Aixauhan by Inabrian's categorisation, but probably not by their own.

Anne's other Inabrian peers at the summer camp talked about how Cole and his kind had no mother or father, because they viewed the snow upon the mountain where they were born as their only parent. Which would be proven to be bullshit when Anne saw Cole's mother, whose black-and-white altar later resided in The Cottage, a woman who had the same white hair and blue eyes as Cole. The woman wore an Inabrian dress. There was something glassy in her eyes, something sorrowful at the tip of her smile.

"My bastard father abandoned us after my mum abandoned everything for him," Cole would explain. The early hostility in their friendship would not yet thaw by the wartime. "Is that what you are going to do to Cai-Li? She's something new, something unexpected. But when it comes down to it, you will go back to that ugly Castle and your cushy home. I won't let that happen. I won't let you discard my sworn sister like a wilted flower."

Anne would be indignant and angry at the time, and she would wonder who would care about *her* that much. After all, at the age when Cole and Cai-Li had forged their friendship, Anne's closest companions had been the Visions of the desolation to come.

Back then, Anne thought the idea of Cole and the other Yamalan kids having no parents made no sense. She believed it, because she had no other frame of reference. And for the Inabrian magician children whose magic was bestowed by the Creator, everything else daring to claim to be a form of magic was inherently primal. Except the alchemists; they were heathens and pagans, whose gods were the many disguises of Discord.

"That Yamalan boy can barely be counted as a magician! It's not like he practises magic, he just…is," Nina flippantly said. "Hell, he's hardly even *human*. The Yamalans are more like ice cubes that just happen to look humanoid. If I build a stone statue with a human face and enchant it, should it be considered alive? Why are these things here in a summer camp for actual *people?*"

Nina should have known better to say that in front of all the kids. The Inabrian magician lineages were supposedly good at lacing insults with nice words with politeness, reflecting their education. However, Anne guessed that sort of courtesy was extended only to those they considered human. Them not seeing the Yamalans and the alchemists as human beings was cruel. Even Anne's childish mind thought it was wrong. The severity of it eluded her grasp, as even if she wished to understand over the years, Anne's humanity was never in question.

It was a sunny afternoon, and the younger Inabrian magician kids were allowed free time in the courtyard to do whatever they wanted. The camp was located in a cleared-out field of ground of the Crown's land. Kids would sooner throw mud balls at one another than use their Creator-given magic. It was a sight that calmed Anne, the only time when she gained the sense that other Inabrian magician kids were children at all. They had a childhood like her own back in the town, when she had not yet known what it meant to be an oracle.

A precious and fleeting thing. Beautiful, nonetheless.

The teenage Inabrian magicians were tasked with watching the younger ones without letting things get out of hand. Inabrian common-folk servants did the most the unsavoury parts, but they weren't going to be helpful if the kids decided to start using magic to fight one another.

The older magician kids tossed off their robes, rolled their breeches above their knees or tied their dresses up into knots, so that they could dip their feet into the cool water of the river that ran through the open field. There was birdsong nearby, tiny flowers blooming before the season turned cold. Summer was nearly over, and so were the childhoods of these heirs coming to an end. They would have to learn to join the brutal politics of the Inabrian magician court. The friends they made there at camp would not last. Soon, the only ones they'd serve would be themselves and their lineages. Friends turned into enemies in the face of vested interests.

Love would become as precautious as a proposition of securing different lineages into a single line, combining the gifts of the Creator. Friendship would become a word that masked ill-intentions, and people tried to keep their allies close. Those closest to them were often the ones that possessed the most damning secrets.

Anne was not interested in breaking things that were once dear to her. She remained an observer. It seemed best to not love or befriend anyone when the promise of the future was that such joy would be used as a pawn against those you shared happy memories with.

The older Inabrian magician kids loved to murmur behind Anne's back that her family's prominence and her oracle status were the only reasons that brat hadn't yet been sent to a healer.

There was a part of Anne that knew she was a bit *wrong* by then. The way she felt social etiquette was a maze to navigate, harder to grasp than the flashes of the future in an oracle's Vision. She often found herself saying something that made a crowd fall into awkward silence, so Anne preferred to not speak at all. Some thought her arrogant, others thought her dim-witted. Truth was,

Anne's facial muscles were a bit stiff. She never knew what the right expression was for different occasions.

The magician lineage that specialised in manipulation of the mind had been called upon by Anne's father, and his diagnosis had been that Anne was perfectly fine.

After the Second War, as the lineages of the old would become despised by the common folk they ruled over, magic would soon divert its attention from warfare to medical, social, and other fields. There would eventually be a name invented for the mind Anne possessed. It's an achievement that lays far into the future of this tale, but it will be comforting to know that she is not alone, eventually.

Back to the memory. Anne thought little of the Inabrian kids' dismissal. She found their acquaintances tedious. She was content with her tea-brewing in The Chalice of Truth, something she'd started doing following the months when she'd discovered more about Brutus Barberry. She drank the liquid from the chalice in front of her parents, much to their horror. She made a habit of carrying the chalice and Earl Grey tea leaves ever since. The flavour of the tea brewed by the chalice was unique, something Anne found comforting, until the slightest deviation from such a taste would invoke a sense of dread within her.

Even with the distance Anne kept from her peers, she heard the commotion attracting the attention of the magician kids as they gathered. Laughter that was a pitch too high punctured Anne's eardrum.

"You knew what they were doing," Cole would say to Anne many years later. Or is it now? No, Cole's dead. This was the past. "You stood by and watched."

The grass under Cole's feet was covered in sparkling frost in mid-July. The boy looked so young. He was Anne's age, only a few months younger than her. None of that was knowledge privy to Anne at the time. All she saw was the nervous huff of frightened and eager Inabrian magician kids breathing out white fog as the temperature dropped.

"Did you care about us existing before you developed this obsession with Cai-Li?" Cole asked. His voice is not of a boy's. This is not the Cole from this part of her memories; it is the Cole who would bleed out on the battlefield. "If you hadn't fallen in love with her, would you have remained blind till the very end? Even after you found out the truth about your grandfather?"

Some of the older Inabrian magician heirs shook their heads in visible disapproval. Nina was known for her bullying tendencies—unbefitting as an heir of the magician lineages. It was perhaps why she felt the need to prove herself. Anne watched mutely and wondered if there was a future where she shared the same fate as Nina. If she were not The Oracle, what differentiated Anne from the other young magicians? If the power of The Oracle had passed down to Anne's baby sister instead of Anne, like Nina's lineage power had passed to her older sibling, would the same poison consume Anne until she became a husk of everything she hated?

No future. No past. No one fixed time in her head. Everything merged into one, pressing into her.

Cai-Li would say that regrets about the past surface for those who are discontent in the present. Anne would tell the red-haired alchemist she didn't know what she was talking about.

The Oracle has no past or future. Everything is there in her mind, happening at once. Threads trip over one another, forming one coherent picture briefly before crisscrossing into a tangled mess.

The younger magician kids watched with wide-eyed anticipation, the childish wonder of beholding a spectacle of cruelty, without being the subject of scorn. Would those kids who had snot dripping down their faces, who didn't fully comprehend what was happening, end up in combat? Would their hands be stained with blood, or would they be dead because they marched into a war believing in their parents' tales? A generation of magicians who learned hatred at camps like these, not knowing their true enemy was not the outsider, but their own families who would sacrifice them as soldiers in the name of the Crown for a pointless cause.

There would also be the Ninas and Lilas of that generation who would find their value through the war. Following the Reparation after the Second War, Anne would see the list of the Inabrian names of who awaited trials for crimes against humanity. There it would be—Lila's name written at the top of the list. Anne would stare at it for way too long. That night, she would take two orbs of the sleep medication Cai-Li made her to sleep.

All that remains of Anne's generation, those magician kids who thought they ruled the world…all that remains are monsters and corpses.

The boy named Cole shivered. His head lolled as he bit his lips. He stared at the ground as if he wished to melt into it. There were so many layers to this that it made Anne's heart ache, mostly remembering Cole like this, who was as foreboding as Anne came to know him to be during the war. He never should have looked small or afraid.

The Yamalan boy came to the camp about two months after Cai-Li had joined. That morning, he appeared with a brief explanation from the Magician Alliance that he was the ward of a minor magician lineage. His father wished for him to be better prepared to one day join the magician family name that Cole was supposed to assume.

Whoever Cole's father was, he hadn't bothered naming himself. A coward who Cole never wished to discuss. Anne spent the early part of her courtship with Cai-Li proving she differed from that man, that she'd never leave Cai-Li the same broken-hearted mess the way Cole's mum had on her deathbed.

"You will treat Cole with the same respect you reserve for any of your peers," the representative from the Magician Alliance told the magician kids at the camp. "He is one of you."

The greatest skill the Inabrian magicians taught their children was to lie. To themselves, to the common folk, to the people they stepped on and killed.

The older magician kids headed by Nina rounded up on Cole like a pack of wolves. The younger kids watched in awe.

Boring, a thirteen-year-old Anne thought. She didn't even bother putting down her chalice of tea.

Don't worry, Anne thinks to her younger self. *Every second you stand by, brat, is one you will spend repenting in the future.*

The life of an oracle is one of pretending to be blind. Anne once was amazing at dealing with the darkness that surrounded her in her Vision.

Death, destruction, desolation. When the worst of humanity became a lullaby that was played enough times, it became nothing but a daily routine. Anne had made friends with the darkness, aware her childhood with the townsfolk and Brutus Barberry had been nothing but fireflies: tiny lights that were snuffed out by the endless, choking night.

Until the sun came.

A strand of red hair caught Anne's vision as she was about to turn her attention away from this inconsequential situation. The oracle stood up toward the tent, wishing to get some sleep while everyone was busy being drawn to the debacle on the open fields.

There she was, a flicker of flame. Her vibrancy was out of place against the muted green and brown of the summer fields. A spark in the dark that ignited in Anne's grey irises.

The Aixauhan alchemist, with a name Anne could not yet pronounce, shuffled her way through the circle of Inabrian magicians like a blazing trail.

Cai-Li stood in front of Cole with a gentle smile on her face. It was something that would grow like a wildfire, eating away at Anne's heart for years to come. Not that the young alchemist would ever know. Anne hunkered in the dark while Cai-Li was light itself.

The red-haired girl took the boy's hand, his transparent tears dripping nearly imperceptibly against his ghostly cheeks.

Cai-Li's chin lifted high. Her brows were the arching wings of a bird about to take flight. A shadow of a smile spread across her face, as if she was unaware of the animosity that would soon devour her.

"You are a sad sight," the girl with hair the colours of flames and blood said. "Do you want to kill him? He is the son of one of you. What else you got other than way too many spit in your mouth?"

Cai-Li's words were practised shapes that belonged to someone who did not speak Inabrian as her native tongue. There was no shame on the alchemist girl's face as her words betrayed her in their inaccurate state.

The Inabrian magicians encircled Cole and Chely. They stared at her, some mimicking Cai-Li's Inabrian with a stutter. The crowd howled with laughter as if it was the greatest joke ever told.

Anne shivered. She wished she had stayed in the tent and slept in. The oracle was used to death in her Visions as well as nightmares, yet the thirteen-year-old was delicate around real conflict. A delicate blossom that thought seeing rain from afar was the same as being drowned.

"Oh no, look who's coming to the snow-boy's rescue," Lisa whistled. "He clearly can't speak up for himself, Aixauhan alchemist. What are you going to do? Fight your superiors?"

Cai-Li shook her head. The threat fell upon her like a branch into hearth-fire, incapable of disturbing its warmth. "My Ma and Ba are diplomats in Inabri. Scholars protected under law. You hurt me. Big trouble. You want your parents involved?"

There it is, Anne thinks. Across the gap of time, the older oracle sighs at the baby sun.

It was still summer; the days were long. The peacetime would soon end, something conjured up by children. A fairytale.

The Oracle misses the look on Cai-Li's face when the red-haired alchemist thought she could take on the world. The things Cai-Li believed in—first justice, then humanity, last merely the survival of their tiny family through the war.

Every one destroyed. What was left when one had to shed faith in the world like a snake shedding its skin?

The threat that Ying Cai-Li threw at the Inabrian kids was a double-edged sword. If this got out of hand, the Inabrian kids would get a slap on the wrist. What about the Ying family? Their scholar privilege might be revoked if their daughter was labelled a troublemaker?

Anne doesn't remember how that day ended. It is a piece of shattered glass. The Oracle cups it gently in her hands, if only to remember what it felt like for the first light to reach her after a long winter.

There are things in life one never forgets. The first time one stared death in the eye, the first time one tasted the fruits of love. From that day forward, every single one of Anne's first times had something to do with Ying Cai-Li.

The next day, Ying Cai-Li was taken away from the camp by the healing unit of the Magician Alliance, the alchemist girl's body half-fried by Lila's spell.

The young oracle learned on that day: there exist people like Ying Cai-Li, who stare down death, and all they do is smile gently and stand their ground.

5

Dark Magic

CHELY TAKES THE stairs down to the divination room. After a week of searching through the castle's halls, she is sure of the precise location and function of each room in this gloomy colossal castle.

The dining room that can host guests of an entire magician lineage, the guestrooms by the hundreds that no doubt were for even grander occasions. A ballroom that must have hosted the entire elite of Inabrian magicians, dancing and twirling long through the night. The library, with floor-to-ceiling bookshelves filled with tomes on every subject of magical research, even ones written in languages not of Inabri. Chely and Anne spent a wordless afternoon in that library. What Anne read was from the fiction section—a story about a man on a path of vengeance.

Chely knows the area below her guestroom is the divination room, the place that townsfolk and tourists clambered to for a chance to meet The Oracle. Chely went to have a look around.

The decorations in the divination room are a combination of the grimness of every other corner of the castle combined. There sits a round table with a pitch-black, hand-sewn tablecloth, adorned with white threads marking stars and constellations. Each major star The Oracle sees as important is marked by the shape of a skull.

On top of the round table, in the center, normally sits the Chalice of Truth, even though it was absent when Chely went snooping about in the room, due to Anne's improper use of the relic as her own personal mug. But the divination table was cluttered with other decorations:

Candleholders carved into the shape of crows with half-burnt candles, as if The Oracle had not bothered replacing them after the last session. An ugly and rusting vase with a bouquet of white roses that each blossomed with red rimming their edges, as if the petals had drunk in fresh blood. Skulls, real ones, with their caps removed, used as boxes for trinkets and crystals that Chely cannot name.

The divination room was especially cold, as if the air inside it was caught in deep autumn. The fireplace held no logs, only ashes. When Chely tried to call on her fire to ignite it so she could inspect the room closer, the fireplace did not obey the alchemist's request— no fire spirit lived there, scared away by the force that shadowed the room.

Now Anne's voice comes from that very cursed place, beckoning Naomi in with the promise of bringing Naomi to her mother. The silent change in the pitch from The Oracle's usual deadpan voice, something lurking within those words, makes Chely's skin crawl.

It is Anne, but it does not feel like Anne.

Chely darts to her belt with a string of small glass containers, each labelled and hosting a different sort of alchemical orb that achieves the effect of magician spells. One of them allows an alchemist to "see through layers of obstacles," which Chely usually uses to see what is on the other end of a forest to determine where to proceed on her travels. But she guesses it can also work to see what's happening through layers of stone, wood, and lime mortar.

Sure enough, as the alchemist presses the orb onto the floor, it's as if the white marble floor of the guestroom are clouds being pushed aside by an invisible flood of water. The orb is absorbed into the floor and effectively turns the material under Chely's feet into a layer of solid glass. She can clearly see from overhead.

Naomi, with her hair tied in pigtails, sits opposite Anne at the round table. Chely can only see the top of her head, so there is no discerning Naomi's expressions. However, from the way the girl's back hunches and her hands nervously clench into the fabric of her dress, Naomi is trying to conceal the fear and doubts in her head.

On the other side of the table is Anne. She wears the same gown Chely saw her in on the first day she arrived at the castle—the intricately crafted black gown with puff sleeves and more layers of silk cascading down her dress like waves. However, there is one odd addition to The Oracle's divination attire—a piece of black headwear with jewelry embedded into it. It goes around The Oracle's eyes and ears, rendering Anne's expression unreadable.

"Do I have to drink the wine?" Naomi's voice becomes clearer, thanks to the alchemical orb's effect.

Anne shakes her head. "It is for the guest," The Oracle says. There it is, the peculiar alien feeling edging into Anne's voice. It bellows as if spoken from somewhere far away, like the wind echoing in an empty cave instead of coming out of Anne's throat.

Naomi seems taken slightly aback by this. It's the same explanation that Anne had given Chely. What guest, though?

"By guest, do you mean my mum?"

The Oracle replies, "Yes, child. There is an ageless property in wine. The longer it is left to maturate—that is, the longer wine is left to stew after fermentation—the more valuable it becomes. Many things about Inabrian magic are tied to the symbolic property of the tools we use. Communication between long-lost loved ones becomes a sort of longing, growing more valuable because of the time spent in separation. Much like the price of wine."

"Okay," Naomi mutters. "That's very complicated. My mum liked wine, I think. I'm glad I don't have to drink it. Sometimes my father stays in the cellar and watch the wine barrel for hours."

"There is a reason why The Innkeeper's wine barrels kept refilling on their own," The Oracle says. "It is a physical manifestation of his longing for his wife. Your mother."

"It's like magic," Naomi says. "It's so weird, I never thought of my father as a magician."

This makes The Oracle laugh, a string of hollow noises that strike Chely's chest with woe. It is not Anne's laughter as the alchemist remembers it. Despite being hesitant and rare, Anne's laughs were concrete and infectious.

There is something deeply wrong with this scene that Chely can't put a finger on. It is like someone is wearing Anne's skin, speaking with Anne's voice, saying things within Anne's knowledge. Except it is not Anne. The thing that is speaking to Naomi is cold and inhuman.

"Your father is no magician," The Oracle replies. "The only magician here is Anne Barberry. The town, this castle, everything you and the souls here experience… All of it derives magic from her."

Naomi's voice trembles with the question that comes next. "Are you not Anne?"

"That is a question you need not concern yourself with," The Oracle replies. "You are here so I can bring you to your mother, and she is on the other side, waiting for you to come home. Your father has been selfish, and you have been cowardly. There is a reason people like him are drawn into this place, and there are reasons children like you are never here for long. He belongs here, not you. Those of your age often possess an equal amount of immense guilt and responsibility. You carry the weight and sins of your father, when what you need to realise is that they do not define you."

"My father can be tough," Naomi says. The same words she recited to Chely. "He can be better. I know there is good in him. Can you let him come with me to meet Mum?"

"No." The Oracle crushes the pigtailed girl's dream with one word. "You cannot love someone back from ruination. It is The Innkeeper's job to find a way out on his own. It's time for you to let go and think of your own happiness."

Naomi's heaving breaths are the only noises coming from the divination room as The Oracle falls silent.

"Okay," Naomi says, voice tight like there are tears in her eyes. "You're right, Anne. I want to go with my mum."

The Oracle nods. She grabs the jug of wine that Chely brought from The Inn earlier that day and pours the dark velvet liquid into The Chalice of Truth. In the darkness, the density and colour of the wine is undifferentiable from that of blood.

However, as soon as the liquid touches the chalice, the half-lit candles spring to life. Chely blinks in surprise; she does not feel the call of the flames as an alchemist…which means the candles are not burning with fire. The dancing figures twirling around the candles are pearl white, lacking smoke or warmth. They are fragments of a human soul.

The white flames dancing on the candles chant, "*Naomi,*" their voices ethereal with the unity and synchronicity of a choir.

Meanwhile, the blood-like wine begins to drain from the bottom of the chalice. An invisible mouth opens up and takes it in huge gulps. A satisfied sigh echoes alongside the gentle sound of Naomi's name.

"Mama?" Naomi asks, her voice filled with fragile hope. The girl raises her head to each candle, as if unsure which she should greet with joy. "Are you here?"

"*Yes, darling. I'm here.*"

The white dancing figures over the candles swirl into the air before settling on the floor, creating a spiral as they find their purchase to become one. A woman's face forms, down to the aged lines around her eyes, the threads of her hair, the tip of her smile.

The chalice is completely empty of wine as the candle lights fuse to become Naomi's mother.

Naomi runs into the arms of the figure of light. The light is contagious; the girl's face congeals with her mother's light. The tears that brew in her eyes do not fall, as her mother's embrace cancels out the pain and longing in the girl's heart. Whatever tether that has kept Naomi here in the town with her father is gone.

"*Thank you, Anne,*" the voice of Naomi's mother says before the light begins to fade from the room, ready to leave nothing but darkness behind. "*Can you give me my husband as well? He watched you grow up, ever since you were a child. That has to count for something.*"

"I am not Anne Barberry," The Oracle replies without compassion. "You have been gone a very long time, Cecile. The bad blood between The Innkeeper and Anne is personal. There is no way out for him. Even if the town is clear of all its residents, he alone will remain trapped."

Naomi's mother sighs. There is a weariness to her otherwise weightless and free form. However, she relents.

"*Thank you, Anne,*" Naomi repeats.

The light snuffs out like snow melting into nothingness. The divination room is plunged into darkness. The Oracle sits alone. Chely is stunned beyond the ability to move, her brain scrambling to make sense of what she's just witnessed.

The lone figure left in the divination room does not give the alchemist any chance to recuperate. Anne, whose eyes are still covered by the headpiece, snaps her gaze to the ceiling.

"I know you are there, Blood Hawk," The Oracle muses, her voice metallic and sharp. "Is this answer satisfying enough?"

Chely, whose worst quality has been described as not knowing when to back down, replies.

"No. Not even close."

The next morning, Chely finds Anne in the dining room at breakfast. The oracle's hair is in a messy state, like she tossed and turned for the whole night.

The food on the table is the usual sort of Inabrian cuisine. Several plates of cheese, ham, lettuce, fresh fruits—slices of apples, green and purple grapes, a pomegranate cut open with the seeds spilling out—butter, jam. The smell of Earl Grey wafts from The Chalice of Truth.

Anne is holding a bread-cutting knife; the serrated edges almost send Chely fleeing from the room. The oracle's eyes are bloodshot, and her gaze upon the loaf of bread is downright murderous. Coupled with the emotionless look on The Oracle's stone-like face, it is an ominous sight after yesterday.

"Are you going to come in or are you going to lurk at the door?"

The oracle's voice nearly makes Chely jump out of her skin. It's been ages since anyone has got a rise out of the red-haired alchemist like that.

Anne must know that, as the gaze she turns on Chely is clearly one of amusement. She finishes cutting her bread and starts picking various choices from the table to make a sandwich.

"Er..." Chely's words are like stones stuck in her lungs. "Did you sleep well last night?"

Nothing in Anne's posture suggests anything out of the ordinary happened. The otherworldly pressure that exuded from The Oracle last night, like a noose that tightened around Chely's neck, is gone. Replacing it is Anne's usual disheveled look that comes along with being an out-of-touch hermit living alone in an isolated castle. Unbrushed hair, simple black nightdress—the threads fraying at the edge of its hem—black bags under her heavy eyelids.

"Not really," Anne says, picking up her sandwich. "Nightmares. Also, I have an annoying red-haired ex roaming the halls who has no sense of boundaries."

Chely chuckles. "Ha, yeah. That would be me."

The black crow sits on Anne's left shoulder and watches Chely with his milky-filmed eyes. He caws at the oracle, which makes Anne's gaze fixate on the alchemist.

"Is it true, Cole?" Anne asks.

The familiar cocks his feathery little head to the side, which is not hard to infer the meaning of.

"Cole says you were spying on me last night," the oracle says. Her grey eyes are the same shade as the bread knife that was just in her hand.

"Yes, I was," Chely confirms, since there is no point dancing around it. Doesn't she remember? "Although I don't know what right you have to judge, seeing as you clearly sent your familiar to spy on me too."

The black crow directs a more aggressive caw at the alchemist.

"Cole is his own being," Anne replies. "We choose to live together. Doesn't mean I control his actions. He distrusts you, Cai-Li. It seems, for a very good reason."

"Okay, fine." Chely throws her hands in the air. Let caution go fuck itself. If the oracle wants to shut her up by sending the glowing beam of light after the alchemist to be dragged into wherever Naomi went, she would have done so by now. "I watched your...meeting with Naomi. The divination room, it's right downstairs from my guestroom, yeah? I saw you summon Naomi's mother—or what appeared to be her mother, at least—and Naomi disappear into thin air."

The lines around The Oracle's eyes crease. Anne does not seem to be caught red-handed. Instead, she is giving the alchemist a perplexed look.

"Who are you talking about, Cai-Li?" Anne asks. "Who the hell is Naomi?"

The audacity strikes Chely so hard, her mouth opens and closes like that of a goldfish, until the gasps of air form words at last.

"Are you kidding me?" Chely replies. She sees the same jug hanging on the side of the table that she took from Naomi, the one containing wine that is no longer there. "The Innkeeper's daughter! Your sole wine supplier? Her father hates your guts, but you helped her contact her mum somehow? And then last night you fed her to a heatless, dancing white blob? Are you seriously playing dumb?"

Anne puts her sandwich down on the table. The oracle's face is completely closed off, her eyes that were slightly ajar and playful are now wakeful and alert.

"I don't know what you are talking about, Cai-Li." Anne Barberry marches across the dining room to stare Chely directly in the eye. "There has never been a Naomi in this town. We both know The Innkeeper. He had a wife, yes—she took their daughter away after the war. I last saw The Innkeeper's wife pregnant, but I didn't even know it was a girl until you brought it up."

Chely's black eyes are inches away from Anne's. The oracle's eyes are a whole thunderstorm. The lighter grey of a dove's feather crashes into the grey of metal. Bright and sharp, without a blemish or concealment.

Chely has stared into those same eyes countless times. Before, it was followed by the warmth of the oracle's lips. Now, the only thing lying between them are ashes from the past.

"You are not lying," Chely says. She knows Anne Barberry's eyes like she knows the palm of her own hand. The Oracle truly has no idea what she's talking about. "Hmm, you don't remember. Interesting."

"What don't I remember?" Anne challenges. It is her whose face blazes with heat and accusation. "Answer my question, Ying Cai-Li! What are you doing here at my castle? The constant banging open of doors, the way you pester me with questions as if you want to rekindle something that is long dead. You say you are here for me, but then you go overturning my whole castle so what…? You think you will find the skeletons of those missing tourist kids you babbled about?"

"How come you remember the tourist kids, but not Naomi?" Chely asks. "It's like The Innkeeper's daughter has zapped out of existence. But you haven't denied the tourist kids and their names. Why is that?"

Anne shakes her head wildly. "That's not the point," she says. "If you are here investigating me, just say so."

"I mean, kind of," Chely replies curtly. "Fun story, The Innkeeper. He's the one who asked me to look into the missing kids. But now, with Naomi gone, I guess he will look up and down for her. You might have forgotten what happened, but it doesn't mean he or the townsfolk will as well."

"So, that's it," Anne replies. There is levity to her voice that almost sounds like disappointment. It is way too close to the growls of a wounded animal. "You are here because you believe I am responsible for the missing youngsters? Not just suspicious, you have been convinced it is the truth from the moment you walked into my home?"

The hurt that leaks into Anne's voice makes Chely laugh. "Oh, come on, Annie," she says. "Don't play coy. This castle you live in, don't you think it's a bit off how convenient it is? A girl who is also called Anne, who looks nearly identical to you, asks you for help to replace her so you can 'save' her from her abusive family? Not to mention The Innkeeper, yes, we both know him. But do you remember from where? The wine that automatically fills itself in the cellar, a castle sitting on the hill overlooking a town in the middle of nowhere, the knowledge you possess of the town and the townsfolk despite never showing your face there. It's all too insular, don't you think? It's all too *surreal.*"

The black crow caws, his voice tearing through Chely's words as the familiar descends onto the alchemist and pulled on Chely's hair. It cuts the alchemist's rant short.

Anne, whose eyes now are as round as alchemical orbs, stares at the grey walls as if she is surrounded by a colourless layer that cloaked her five senses. She does not appear surprised, nor does she seem to be listening.

When the oracle opens her mouth, it is clear that Chely's hypothesis is true. The words the red-haired alchemist threw in Anne's direction slide off her like water without the oracle noticing.

"If you truly suspect me of foul play," Anne Barberry says. "You can go sleep in that damn inn in town with the creaky bed and all the drunk brutes puking outside your room every night. After everything you have done, I don't know what makes you think you have the right to come into my house and accuse me of *dark magic,* Ying Cai-Li."

It feels like someone pounded on her chest, the smile dissipating from Chely's face. "You think this is about *dark magic?*" Chely swallows down a mouthful of bile before continuing. "I'm not here because of some grudge, Annie. I am trying to help. There are kids missing. Yes, I want to find out why. I know there is a good reason that will explain the weird things that are happening around this town and in your castle. I don't think you're intentionally doing anything, but denial isn't going to spare anyone."

"No," Anne answers swiftly. "You think I'm capable of kill innocent kids, Ying Cai-Li? After everything we went through in the war? After all the good we did together? You should know I will not do anything to kids like Maev, like *us*. If you don't, then we truly have nothing more to say."

"Oh, really?" Chely stands up instinctually. "That's rich, given it is what you accused me of doing after the war. You said you didn't know me anymore, because of the *dark magic* I was practising. You didn't think about what was going on from my perspective at all—you were going to leave either way, weren't you? Because you think you are better than me, an Inabrian Creator-chosen magician. You are awfully good at choosing when you wish to become blind, Annie. At least I did what I did with my eyes wide open, while you scramble away from your own actions like a goddamn coward."

"Oh, I'm a coward?" Anne laughs. There it is, the full-chested bellowing that was missing from The Oracle's laugh in the divination room last night. "It's better to be a coward than a *liar*. The years after the war ended, the radio kept on talking about the Inabrian magicians who paid their way out of going to the Court of Reparation. Every single name that came onto the radio ended up a corpse the next day. You, gone from our cottage, from our *bed*. You came home every day with infinite excuses. I never asked, because I wished it to last. We lost everything in the war. I told myself I couldn't lose you too."

Anne's voice grows hoarse and cracked, drenching the room in deadly silence.

"Annie, I'm sorry." Chely looks up at Anne, her chest fills with ice, but she refuses to let her gaze move away from her ex's anger. "I cannot say I regret any of it. At the time—it just felt like the only way. After everything those magicians did, I couldn't let them get away with it. I thought by not telling you, I was sparing you the grief and conflict. I thought it was kind to not have to force you to choose *again*, between your country and me."

Anne shakes her head. The oracle is trembling despite the heat in the room becoming unbearable. The fireplace cracks with red, orange, and blue amber. Nothing like the magic in the divination room that is devoid of warmth.

"I already made my choice," Anne says. "When I chose to join you and Cole in war. When I chose to fall in love with you. I do not regret a second of it, Ying Cai-Li, do you hear me? I never need you to make me feel better. We were supposed to be in this together!"

"I know," Chely replies. "That's why I'm here. We can be together, Annie. But you have got to let me in. You can't live in this castle, denying what is happening around you. *Because* of you. I can help you. Let me help you."

"You should go." Anne's voice is flat and final. "Go get a room at The Inn. Leave, Ying Cai-Li. Go back to your life. There is nothing left here for you."

6

Human Nature

"ALMOST ALL PEOPLE are inherently evil." This was the most common thing Grandpa Brutus said to Anne as she grew up. "Not every single one of them, some of the willing ones can be taught to see another way. However, most of them cannot. Especially magic users who aren't chosen by the Creator. We Inabrian magicians, our magic is imbued with our humanity. While they? They take it without asking. That is evil, do you see? Assume the absolute worst of people, so you don't give them the chance to destroy us when the time comes."

It was the most fundamental part of every Inabrian magician family's preparation process for the heir to hate the use of magic beyond the Inabrian lineages. In their opinion, their hatred made them better weapons for the wars to come.

Brutus Barberry had served in the First War, so the bogeymen, of course, took the shape of the Aixauhan alchemists. But there were other magic users all around the world. In Anne's limited lifetime, she'd met Soul-Gazers, who could cross between the realm of the living and the dead; she'd met the Yamalans, who were both human and nature; and she'd met Ying Cai-Li, who was an alchemist but also part of the sun herself.

In her oracle state, Anne would see more than that. She would gaze into the vast land of the past and future. Inabri is nothing but a handful of islands, and the magicians divide their magic in ways confined to the lineages like barnacles trying to stop a ship from sailing. She would see the vast grassland where people danced with magic in every gesture, see the rainforest that rose where people communicated through one another with echo-like songs, see the civilisation buried in the deep ocean, where humans much like themselves lived in an underwater empire after their city had drowned.

When she was eleven, however, Anne believed Brutus's words.

Maybe a piece of those speeches Brutus gave planted a thorn in Anne's heart, even after denouncing her family, after loving Cai-Li and Cole, after the war where she tried to do as much good as possible.

That thorn remained, somehow. Anne has learned to ignore it mostly, but there is no doubt it is still there.

Is Ying Cai-Li right? Did she live a whole life only to come back to the beginning, like she was walking in a circle?

Did she become exactly the kind of oracle Brutus Barberry was?

On the night of the murder, Brutus had been tending to a barberry bush outside their house. It had several long tentacle-like branches sticking out of its head. It looked like a hedgehog, if hedgehogs were green and had leaves.

It was the most beautiful thing, Anne had thought. She had liked to close her eyes at night and imagine its funny-looking shape. It had calmed her down, especially when the Visions got too bad.

The things she saw could be horrible. There had been an unprecedented degree of blood and gore in them lately. Although Brutus had promised Anne it was all a natural way of the Barberry oracles, it hadn't stopped Anne from crying as she watched the blood paint a beautiful white hillside as red as the sky when the sun goes down.

"What have you seen?" Brutus would come into her room and pick up Anne, who was still screaming and kicking at thin air. "Don't be scared. Tell me everything."

"So…so many people died," Anne would say. She couldn't comprehend how many people there were. The way bees littered a hive at the height of its activity, there would be so many bodies strung across the ground that their blood would feed the soil over countless months, even years. There would be people who emerged from those grounds, scarlet and wide-eyed as they were whisked home but without one or several of their limbs. "It's scary, Grandpa. I don't want it. Make it go away!"

Brutus would squeeze Anne's hand as if it were a squishy toy, his face wrinkled with gentle kindness and endless patience. "It's okay, my little duck," he would whisper into her ears. "Do you want me to stay with you for the rest of the night?"

Anne would. She always did, ever since she started seeing those things, those gnarly things that made her wish she did not need to sleep.

"Very well. Do you want me to sing our nursery rhyme to you?"

"Hmm-uhm," Anne would say, already feeling better.

"Okay," Brutus would nudge tiny Anne's nose.

"Bloody barberry bush sitting on the hill,
marking a lonely castle still.
The sun shines and the caw whines,
Where did the bloody barberries go?
There it rolled across the green grass field,
Down the chimney into somebody's well,
Up the deck onto somebody's sail.

Bloody barberry bush knows it all,

it could go wherever the Creator wills."

That was normally where Anne would drift to sleep. The nursery rhyme was one Brutus had written specifically for Anne. It was his Vision of her, Grandpa had proudly proclaimed. The most Barberry in their lineage to ever come. Anne had asked exactly what the rhymes meant. Brutus hadn't known, but he had promised it would be great.

He had believed in Anne. Brutus Barberry had utter, unyielding faith in his granddaughter to become the next oracle who would change the world in the Barberry name.

It is the downside of having the Vision, Anne think. Very much like how she had seen Cai-Li as the rising sun in her childhood Vision, only for her to be majorly disappointed in Cai-Li when her girlfriend was so changed by the war—like everyone was changed. Anne is sure now that she was Brutus's Vision of the future, for oracles can only see those who define the future on a global scale.

Anne thought the world of Cai-Li.

Brutus, however, had seen Anne as the end of the world.

You see, children rarely think about the lyrics they hum along with, even though Anne had always been a sensitive child and imagined the barberry bush with paint instead of blood. Deep down, she still always knew it was weirdly fucked up.

What kind of sick bastard would tell a kid about a bunch of plants covered in blood?

Years later, a teenage Anne complained loudly about it to Cai-Li during their first dates at the pub. Half-drunk on wine while the tailor's son, whose inn was tentatively open for business, watched warily as The Barberry Oracle loudly screamed about her family's bloody history.

Cai-Li was never abhorred by Anne's words recounting the many disturbing deeds. The red-haired alchemist would stifle down a laugh, as she found it to be hilarious.

"Nooooone of this is funny, Ying Cai-Li," Anne slurred with her weak constitution against alcohol. She'd had only three glasses of ale. "I'm telling you what he did to your people. What the hell is wrong with you?"

"Oh, don't get me wrong," Cai-Li said. "The things the Inabrian magicians have done to Aixauhan alchemist clans? They are horrendous, Annie. But I also grew up hearing about them. It's not something that's possible to escape, not when everyone from our parents' generation all have missing relatives. Not to mention entire clans whose family names were wiped out."

"Then how can you be…smiling?"

"Because I am here, sitting with Brutus Barberry's granddaughter," Cai-Li said. "And she is learning. Maybe there is hope for Inabri after all. Maybe, if you are the example of what Inabrian magicians can be, not all hope is lost."

"The bar is so low, it is literally in the underworld with Discord," Anne blabbered. "It's not your job, Ying Cai-Li, to see hope in those who want to murder you."

"I know. It's *your job*, Barberry," Cai-Li said. "My duty is to my people, and your duty is to yours. However, in an ideal world where we both survive, what's coming? Then our job might be trying our best to make the same goal possible for the world. A better and kinder place, where the war doesn't come every other generation, where no one is crushed by the wheel like ants. Don't you want that?"

Anne desperately wanted that. And they succeeded. Even if their effort was indeed equivalent to a bunch of ants scrambling to stop the war but crushed to smithereens by it. However, that they fought against the tide at all, that felt good.

"We are together," Cai-Li would say after the war. "As long as we see the humanity in each other, then no matter how many of us emerge to the other side, we have won."

That version of Ying Cai-Li exists now only in Anne's memories. Memories like old family portraits, with oil paint cracked and peeling off.

Still, Anne sometimes watches the memories on her own. She relives the days where Cai-Li taught her to see a different side of humanity. Brutus had believed human nature was evil, and he had proven to be a great example of that. Cai-Li believed human nature was good. Except the red-haired alchemist eventually changed her mind on that, as well.

A young Cai-Li always found humour in the darkest of rhymes. If someone recited their completely screwed up childhood memories to their date when they had only been going out for like two weeks, Anne would have bolted out of there and never looked back. That is why, Anne supposes, she has never had a long-term relationship outside of Ying Cai-Li.

Anne always imagined she fell in love with Cai-Li's inherent goodness. But maybe it was the opposite—maybe they were both messed up on the inside, and that was what drew them to each other.

Not their goodness, but their mutual capacity for wretchedness.

What happened was, on the night Brutus died, Anne didn't fall asleep after she was told that particular nursery rhyme. She was twelve, long past the time girls should be comforted by nursery rhymes.

She lived in a castle where no child in her social circle needed anything from their parents, other than her two-year-old sister. Her Oracle Visions were becoming more and more visceral. Everything had come up like they were always meant to be, so why would she question the morality of the world?

The previous night, however, Anne Barberry had a dream, odd even by the Barberry family standards. She had seen the summer camp of Inabrian magicians, something that had not yet happened. She had seen an Aixauhan girl's hair shimmer under the sun in crimson and a Yamalan boy with his head bowed in silent defeat.

Like all dreams, it had been sweet and gentle. That had not lasted.

After the dreams ended, she'd had another Vision.

A wailing, like that of an animal. It had pierced Anne's ears like a piece of chalk striking across a blackboard.

It had come from a man's throat. The man had a huge hole in his chest. Chunks of flesh and meat detached from the rest of his torso, falling to the ground like rotten fruits from a tree.

"Annie," the man had muttered. His voice had been hoarse and distorted as blood clouted his vocal cords and blossomed up his lips. "This…is not your fault."

Anne had seen herself fall to the ground. The hands that had reached out in her Vision were huge. There, her arms had not been the gangling awkwardness of her preteen body, but elongated and elegant like that of an adult. She had seen her arms trembling as Anne had clumsily fumbled to cover the gaping hole that nearly tore the man in two.

It had been the result of some form of magic, young Anne's mind thought objectively. An animalistic cry had spurred out from her elder self's throat, but the oracle girl had not yet met this man in real life. Her sorrow and grief had been distant, like watching a wildfire from kilometers away.

"It…is…not…your…fault."

Those words had been so light as the man died. Last words meant to comfort someone else.

The man had stopped breathing. His body had crumbled to the

ground. His soul, it must have had wings, for Anne had heard a fluttering of noise like that of a bird taking flight into the Heavens, into the Creator's Realm.

For some reason, the young Anne Barberry had been sure this was a man who deserved to go to the Creator's Realm. But he wouldn't, because Cole of the Yamalan would refuse the Inabrian Creator, whose name was the reason his life was cut short.

There, on Cole's torn-open chest, a barberry bush had grown. Its berries had been as red as a rose and as hot as liquid iron. The parasitic plant had overtaken the boy's heart with glee. Colours had drained from Cole's face until he rotted into the ground.

A gurgling sound had come from the dead man's corpse.

What had come out sounded eerily like a crow's caw.

"I can't," Anne sobbed into Brutus's shoulder. "I don't want to see these things anymore."

Brutus patted her head without a word. The weeping child was inconsolable, so her grandfather let Anne cry until she got tired and bored.

"Shh…" her grandpa whispered. "Don't be silly. It's a gift, my little duck. You'll get used to it one day."

"How?" Anne asked, wide-eyed and a little more than horrified. "How can I unsee that?"

Brutus considered that for a moment. Anne did not know if he thought about helping or not, maybe about wiping her memories out. That was what Brutus did—something Anne discovered after digging through the Barberry library, Grandpa Brutus's personal archive. Memory-altering spells. So many of them. Primarily those applied to children without damaging their brain.

How much had Anne forgotten before Brutus died? How much of her childhood was true? The town filled with friendly faces—was there truly not one of them who threw a stone at her? Anne will never know the answer. She does not grieve for herself as much as one might expect her to.

She wishes to leave everything Barberry behind. So what if she had no childhood? For a while, all that mattered was that she had a future. A future which Cai-Li promised her was possible.

The moron that Anne was. No one wants to know what happens in the future, not when their future is a tragedy without reprieve. Hope is for those who have everything to lose.

All those people who have come to her castle throughout the years, they were not looking for truth. The answers they sought were always a remedy or recompensation for their past.

Trivial. Childish. Unimportant.

The people who asked for children with their partner wanted a guarantee of their partner's loyalty. The people who asked for The Oracle to predict their future as becoming the head of a new Inabrian magician lineage were, in fact, asking for a favour from the heir of the Barberry name. The people who wanted to know what their future occupations were did not know to cherish what they had at the present.

They always end up moping around town. Anne cannot judge, because she was one of them.

But the kids? What they ask of her is different. They ask her about the future, not because they want reassurance or help, but because they believe they can change the course of their fate.

There was a time when Anne saw that same spark in the dark, the hope for a better future. That fire which dances in their eyes is the belief that human nature is one of goodness. One worth fighting for, one worth dying for.

Like the fire lit within Anne by a certain Aixauhan alchemist, the oracle does not wish to be the one to snuff that candle of hope out.

"What did you see?" Brutus Barberry asked Anne. "Maybe if you talked about it, then we can sort it out."

"People dying," Anne repeated. She didn't understand why it wasn't getting through to her usually understanding grandpa. "So many people are dying. No, not just dying. They were murdered. They were murdered by *magic*."

"People always die, my darling duck. No matter by magic or natural causes," Brutus hummed to her, as if he was stating something obvious instead of something incomprehensible. "You can't prevent it. Everything great requires the deaths of those who do not deserve to live in the Creator's grace."

"How…" Anne started, rightfully horrified. "How can you say that? There was a boy. A Yamalan boy, I think? He was talking to me as if I was his friend!"

"Hmmm. Nonsense, my little duck. People are horrible, Anne. But you learned from our lessons, right? The Yamalans are not humans. They are deceptive creatures. They are merely pretending to be humans."

Anne blinked. "That is what you always say," she screeched. "But if human nature is so abhorrent, why would anyone want to become one? You're contradicting yourself, Grandpa."

"Ah, here we go again." Brutus sighed. The gentle creasing from his aged face darkened. "You are so adamant about the truth, so stubborn that you know not when to compromise. It will be the death of you."

That was when the doorbell rang.

7

Barberries

AFTER KINDLY REMOVING herself from Anne's castle, imagine the ghastly surprise that waits Chely as she walks into a field of barberry bushes on the hilltop of The Barberry Castle.

That is to say, the *new* Barberry Castle. The one Anne Barberry is living in. The one Anne is apparently the legal owner of. Where kids disappeared into, like Naomi.

Chely did some digging before she came here.

There was indeed a girl who went by the name of Anne Perks. She did not live in a castle though. She was an Inabrian commoner, whose family lived in a barn near the territory belonging to the Barberrys. Anne Perks was named after Anne Barberry, the last oracle of the magician lineage that occupied that piece of land, which was apparently a common tradition among Inabrians.

In the Barberry household, the older generation had a lot of boys called Brutus. After Anne and her sister Patricia were born, a lot of girls were named after them. There are so many Annes, in fact, that there is a saying that if someone threw a rock in any town or village on Barberry land, they'd be able to hit an Anne.

Anne Perks was one such unfortunate naming coincidence. The girl did have a father whose work during the war promoted him to quite a high station in the Inabrian system of power. He and his wife did flee after the war, leaving little Anne Perks behind to tend to the farm.

Anne Perks, however, died of a lung disease around the same time Anne Barberry left Chely at The Cottage and never came back.

A decade later, they are still trying to stick all the broken pieces back together.

When Chely heard The Innkeeper talking about the missing children, the fate of the Anne Perks, whose identity Anne Barberry had assumed, came to mind. Cai-Li has the vague suspicion that Anne Perks is the first of the many, as the alchemist remembers the girl not just by name. Both The Oracle and Cai-Li were at Anne Perks's deathbed when the girl requested the last oracle of the Barberry clan to come to her barn.

Usually, Anne Barberry was not the kind to indulge in the endless letters that overflowed the mailbox at The Cottage. She often threw them into the nearest fire available, which always ended up as a nasty surprise for Chely when the flames cried to the alchemist about being fed garbage.

Anne Perks's letter was delivered right when Chely forbade Anne Barberry from burning the letters. The red-haired alchemist told the oracle that maybe they ought to go visit the girl before her death, if only to can grant her a peaceful rest.

"A peaceful rest?" The Oracle Anne snickered. "This child is dying, Cai-Li. How is an oracle going to help her? Her death isn't going to impact the world. Or should I make up some tale that she will miraculously be healed?"

"I don't know," Cai-Li said. "Possibly? But the girl clearly is an orphan, and with all the kids we saw during the war who were orphaned, I feel like we can maybe help this one too."

"I'm not lying to a girl and saying that she's going to get better when it's death awaiting her at the end," Anne replied. "That's fucked up, Ying Cai-Li. We helped those orphans during the war so they could live. There is no point tending to a girl who is for sure going to die. Giving hope to those who have none is cruelty, not mercy."

In the end, Cai-Li won, for they did end up going to see Anne Perks. The girl was tended to by the people in her village, which sat on the outskirts of the land that belonged to the Barberrys. It was far away from the battlefields and the fanatic-like worship of most of the towns closer to The Barberry Castle.

Anne Perks saw Anne Barberry, her namesake. The little girl's eyes brightened like embers that were about to go out. She held out a hand to The Oracle.

"I want to be just like you, Oracle," Anne Perks said.

Cai-Li had not seen fear so naked on Anne Barberry's face in years.

The Oracle asked, trembling, "Why would you want that, child?"

"Because you are a kind person," Anne Perks said. "I heard what you did in the war. You aren't like your family or mine. You didn't help the Inabrians do awful things to other people. You ran away. You helped people! You are free. I wish to be free like you. Do you think there will be freedom where I'm going, Oracle?"

Anne Barberry did not respond for a while, but when she opened her mouth, she gave her namesake a signature answer.

"I don't know what death is like, sadly. I'm still alive. I know a girl your age though. Her name is Maev. She can walk into the land of the dead, and I'll give you her address so you can send a letter."

That was the Anne Barberry that Chely was in love with. That she's still in love with. Pragmatic, yes. Cold? Sometimes. But never a liar, always sincere. That is the oracle that Chely came all the way here for. Someone who had absolutely no chance of being involved in the disappearance of kids by inviting them into The Barberry Castle.

Yet, all Chely can see within her view are miles upon miles of barberry bushes, with the kind of barberries that aren't even supposed to be growing on this side of the fucking globe.

This castle is not just a copy of the old Barberry Lineage Castle. It *is* the same Barberry Castle. The Oracle brought it to this place, somehow, alongside her grief and her regrets.

Anne Barberry brought The Castle with her.

The town is covered in snow. The wind blows Chely's cloak into the air like a ship's open sail, and the fur trimming agitates the alchemist's neck like her frying nerves.

It's as if overnight, the season changed without Chely knowing. The previously bustling farmer's market has gone quiet. Most of the shops—the butcher, the florist, the place where they sold small plates of desserts—are closed as well.

The lights on each side of the town's street are dim. Chely lets her power extend to the candles and lamps of each household. Their stoves are lit; their fires are kindling. So, the town hasn't become a ghost town. It's only that the townsfolk moved indoors to keep themselves warm.

A part of her wonders if this is The Oracle's doing, a warning to the red-haired alchemist to turn back. That part of Chely is responsible for her risking everything to reunite with Anne, wishing for some kind of happy ending.

Another part of Chely thinks bleakly to herself: maybe the time has passed. There are things that cannot be put back together once broken. Maybe whatever was lost when Anne left The Cottage that day was one of them. The thing that broke between them—it could be called trust, it could be called hope. Whatever it is, love cannot exist without it, like fire finding no purchase or confinement. The kind of love that will engulf anything flammable in its path. The kind that needs to be extinguished.

"What are you doing out on a day like this?"

A familiar voice cuts through the roaring winter wind. Chely whirls around to see The Innkeeper. He is wearing an animal-skin coat bundled up to his neck, his face reddened by the cold like a radish.

"I've just returned from The Oracle's Castle," Chely answers numbly. Usually, she'd be able to come up with something better on the spot. But today is not one of those days, so the truth slips out. "I'm sorry, Innkeeper. I couldn't find the kids, and Naomi—"

The Innkeeper's eyes blink slowly. "Naomi?" His voice dips into the coldness of the surrounding snow. "Is that one of the tourist kids that went missing? You found something about them?"

"I, uh—" Chely blanches. An awful feeling settles on her heart, a heaviness tinged with sorrow. "She's your…never mind."

It seems The Innkeeper's memories are gone. There's no point in pursuing something lost.

"That name is a kind of nostalgic," The Innkeeper says. His eyes flutter closed as in deep thought. "It was on the list of baby names me and my wife came up with before I went off to war. She was pregnant. I knew only by the letters that were sent to the front lines. If it was a boy, we would call him Friedrich. If it was a girl, the child would be Naomi."

"Yeah, sorry to dredge up the past." Chely sighs. "I better find lodging elsewhere."

"Nonsense, child." The Innkeeper comes close to the red-haired alchemist. He is nearly twice Chely's height, and his broad shoulders firmly block the wind that cuts into Chely like a thousand knives. "You always stay at The Inn when you are here in town. Come on."

The Inn is warm and quiet. The hearth fire that usually roars like the patrons of the downstairs tavern has now relinquished to the soft, warm orange of twilight at sundown.

"Here's your drink." The Innkeeper places a mug of something in front of Chely.

It is a wine-like liquid. That colour and the strong scent instantly tell Chely it's alcohol. After what she's seen, this feels like a bad joke.

"I'm not sure I'm in the mood for wine," Chely says. "Sorry."

"No need to apologise," The Innkeeper says. "You don't need to drink it. I mainly busted it out because…it's Feuerzangenbowle."

"It's what?" Chely will chew her tongue raw trying to pronounce that, so she doesn't try. If there's thing Ying Cai-Li understands too well, it is how bad it feels for something or someone's name to be butchered by a foreign tongue. "Is this even an Inabrian drink?"

"No, one of the tourist boys who went missing is from a country up north, across the narrow canal that separates Inabri from the rest of the continent. They share our religion, but not our language. The boy says this is a favourite festive drink of theirs for winter. The name means 'fire tongs punch.'"

"Huh," Chely says. "Sounds more like a torture method instead of a drink."

"Your mind can get quite dark, Aixauhan alchemist," The Innkeeper chuckles.

He doesn't leave the dark liquid in front of Chely. Instead, The Innkeeper goes through the bar, finds a box of sugar cubes, snatches one out and places it in Chely's hand.

"What am I supposed to do with this?" Chely looks at the sugar cube in confusion.

"Light it on fire, alchemist," The Innkeeper says. "Then drop it into the drink."

Chely does as she is told, persuading the fire element to ignite the sugar cube. Once the cube has started to brown, Chely pops it into the mug.

Fire erupts from the dark liquid. Yellow flames followed by orange sparks, then a deep cerulean blue. The sugar cube quickly disintegrates into the drink, yet the flames keep burning on the surface of the blood-like liquid.

"Impressive, huh?" The Innkeeper asks. He stares at the liquid, mesmerised.

"Sure," Chely says politely, not wanting to ruin The Innkeeper's mood by suggesting that this is nothing to the grandiose capabilities of the fire element, things she sees daily.

"I know it's not much for an alchemist." The Innkeeper detects the white lie. "But it's one of the first things my wife showed me when we got together. This…fire drink. We shared it every winter before I went off to war and came back to an empty home. I thought I'd get to share it with our daughter someday. But life doesn't exactly go according to plan, does it?"

Come to think of it, neither Friedrich nor Naomi are Inabrian names. Perhaps they originated from the same place as The Innkeeper's wife, a country up north on this continent.

"Hm. Is that where your wife went? Back to her home country."

"Honestly, I didn't go looking," The Innkeeper says. "It's clear she didn't want me to follow. The last letter I found was on the day I came back from the war. It said that she delivered alone, with no surgeon or medical magicians beside her, since everyone had gone off to war. Our baby was a girl. I don't know if her name is Naomi, or if my wife changed it to something else. My wife…she said she'd heard enough of what our Inabrian magicians were doing on the front line. That she knew what my family abided by working for the Barberry family as tailors, while knowing what Brutus Barberry was responsible for in the First War. She called me wicked and that she was not going to raise a child with a man like that."

Chely lets out a desperate laugh. Not that she hasn't speculated that was the reason that The Innkeeper's wife left him. The Innkeeper might not remember, but Chely had met him before this town. In his younger years, he'd been an apprentice to his father—the Barberry family's personal tailor.

"She's right," Chely bites out mercilessly. She sees her eyes reflected in the fire dancing on dark maroon liquid. "If you know what Brutus Barberry did to my people and you joined them in the Second War regardless, then you *are* wicked."

The Innkeeper sighs. "I know," he says morosely. "I just…I never knew an Aixauhan alchemist personally before. When I was a young man, I bought into the ideas the Inabrian magicians preached, that the magic practised outside the Creator's appointed lineages was evil. But now things are different. I am not that man anymore. No, not just me. Inabri is no longer the same as it was decades ago. The wars opened our eyes. We know now the Inabrian magicians don't care about the common folks—"

"So, that's what it took?" The rage scorches inside her like a sunbird. It is Ying Cai-Li's core, even if the alchemist hides it well behind smiles and jokes. She is made of anger, decades old and ever growing. "It takes you suffering as well for you to care what your country did to those beyond your borders. Our humanity, a talking point, a moral enlightenment. You never valued our humanity for simply existing. The fickleness of Inabrian goodness—if that's why you invited me into your home, Innkeeper, save it. I'm not here to absolve your guilty conscience. I have my own demons, and I'm no Inabrian saint you wish to confess your sins to. If your Creator is real, then I hope He fucking damns you for eternity."

Chely knocks the mug onto the ground. The liquid splashes across The Inn's floor in a splatter pattern ominously close to a slashed throat. Except this is not murder, there is no need for it. Every strand of The Innkeeper's suffering, he brought unto himself.

An idea has been brewing in the back of Chely's mind about the peculiarities of this town, of its purpose. That idea is taking form and shape, as it emerges into full view of colour and meaning.

"I know we did was wrong," The Innkeeper stands up and speaks. "But what would you have done, alchemist? When your whole life, you've been taught to hate someone, when your whole country is marching onto the same battlefield, what would you have done?"

"I don't know," Chely replies coldly as she grabs her coat and heads for the door. "But I know someone who made the right choice. She made the right choice, over and over again. The hard choice. They had to force-feed her memory loss spells in an attempt to stop her. She *still* made the right choice. And what did the world give back to her? Nothing. Doing the right thing destroyed her, yet she did so anyway."

When Chely leaves and slams the door shut, she now understands her position here in Anne's town.

No matter what is going on with the oracle, the alchemist would rather spend her days before Anne kills her in that creepy castle. Whatever Anne Barberry has become, she is still the girl who once made the right choice at the worst time.

Chely will choose to believe in that, no matter the cost.

Of course, Chely Ying camps within the range of the barberry bushes. It's the logical conclusion, because despite knowing from the colour of the barberry fruits that they are exactly the kind that can poison people, there is no way Anne Barberry of all people would want to use them to murder someone.

At least, that's what the alchemist tells herself as she collects a sample of the barberries.

Barberries as a fruit are a constant Chely has seen in her travels across the globe. The evergreen shrub can withstand any kind of temperature in all kinds of different geographical locations. The Aixauhan pirate captain they sailed with during the Second War said she came from a clan in a province that primarily used barberries as a medicinal ingredient. Anne was apparently so unnerved by this fact that she ended up throwing up over the deck. When Chely asked Anne if she was okay, the oracle's face was the pale shade of the moon. Anne insisted she was seasick, that was all. It took a lot of time before Chely figured out the real reason why she was so impacted by the revelation.

It is also very hypocritical of Chely to think that, since she wouldn't be opposed to Anne murdering people who deserved to die with poisonous plants. Like Brutus Barberry, for example.

It wasn't like Chely didn't have the blood of one or two—or a *dozen*—lives on her hands.

The barberry bushes are symbolic to The Oracle. The thorns prick Chely's fingers when she tries to cut some fruits from its branches. Yet the plant is stubbornly unchanging, no matter what climate it encounters. It changes colour from continent to continent; its flavour and usage changes as well.

But the eternal presence of it, no matter where Chely went on her journey, was soothing. During those years without Anne Barberry, everywhere Ying Cai-Li went, there were always barberry bushes that sprung up from the wilderness. Far from villages and towns and cities, but always a sight to behold.

On some continents, their fruit and leaves grow in the wild in the shade of wildfire, a mesmerising sight that inspires awe within those who behold it. Others, however, are a mute blue and purple like the colour of a person's face on their sickbed, puking their guts out.

A huge contrast. Temperamental. A kind of plant that's filled with personality.

The barberry fruits that Chely harvested induced hallucinations, cooled fevers, served as a counter-poison due to being toxic themselves. The undiscovered properties were exponential. She always took a sample of the local barberries, no matter where she went.

During the first years after the war had ended, it was some kind of inside joke between them. Chely would come home, her travelling cloak dirty and frayed, while Anne fussed over how long she'd been gone. *Again.* Chely would place a small vessel of the barberry sample in Anne's hand.

"Forgive me," Chely would say. "I thought of you no matter where I went."

For a while, it worked. Anne's face would turn red, and she'd be so flustered by Chely's shamelessness that the oracle's pent-up rage would bubble into feeble protests that bore no real heat.

It would distract the oracle enough that, for years, the blood-stains on Chely's travelling cloak would go unnoticed. Chely's travelling cloak was a shade darker than wine, so it was hard to tell.

Long ago, Anne had sewn a pattern of the sun onto that travelling cloak, golden threads against a maroon background, while humming an ancient Inabrian lullaby with disturbing lyrics. It had suited Chely.

It was on the last night of one particular trip when Anne set to mending travelling cloak that she discovered the soot mixed with blood—dark clouds that covered the rays of the pattern of yellow sunshine.

That was the reason they fought, which ended in Anne storming off into the night.

She never came back to The Cottage.

After Chely cuts a tiny string of barberry sample into her vials, it occurs to her she has no alchemical equipment with which to test the vegetation. The alchemist left most of her equipment in her overnight travelling suitcase, which she didn't take with her after her short-fused explosive fight with The Oracle that landed her outside.

It is such a childish mistake that it feels out of character. Chely tells herself she and Anne went through a war together, and the townsfolk aren't the friendliest bunch in existence. Their isolation and hatred for Anne might even stoke some of them to take extreme measures to ensure the witch in the castle be *dealt* with.

That is exactly the reason the alchemist is risking the possibility of hypothermia to sleep outside right after heavy snow. Not that the snow stays long before thawing into nothing. Weird weather around these parts, but nothing about this place hasn't screamed suspicious so far during Chely's visits.

Anne must have a good reason, the alchemist reassures herself as she asks the logs she piled up to burst into flame.

Chely wants to imagine she is a safe place Anne can vent these murderous feelings to. Once upon a time, at least. It's not like the oracle has been making friends since they last saw each other. She knows there is something going on; it doesn't scare her as much as piss her off.

Honestly, if Anne is murdering people and watering her plants with the blood of the innocent or something, why would she be judging Chely about dark magic? That makes no sense.

Chely certainly isn't going to judge Anne, that's for sure.

A part of her wonders what Cole would say if he were alive to see what his friends had become. He'd probably push both the alchemist and the oracle off a cliff.

Chely is happy to settle on that conclusion as the fire cackles to life. Chely Ying tries to chuckle with it, as she has been trying to light the fire with coal and bare hands for the last hour.

The fire logs are unnecessary, technically speaking. Chely can just light a fire with the element that runs through her blood. Fire is to her core as blood is to any other person. It doesn't take a second thought to make it happen, unlike when Chely is trying to use any other element for alchemy purposes. Water, earth, metal, wood. Those require the alchemist to take from the wild for a concoction, but fire? That comes to the tips of Chely's fingers.

The red-haired alchemist sometimes envies the magic users in Aixauh's system of alchemy, who are primarily gifted with the element of metal. How much easier it could be to achieve the alchemical prowess that other alchemists struggle for a lifetime to achieve! Like mercury, the metallic element that millennia of Aixauhan emperors across the dynasties poisoned themselves with on their path of wanting to achieve immortality.

The fire laughs at the night-time sky. Chely closes her eyes as she calls on the spirit of fire, Chi'You, the name of the sun god. In the forest, it is eerie, like a single ghost wanders through a silent graveyard, searching their bones charred white.

The fields outside The Barberry Castle are dark and suffocating, like a cloth that covers the sun's eyes. That's not what Chi'You murmurs to Chely though. The fire god is lonely; he once had nine brothers to gossip with, but now he is alone in the sky.

Contrary to popular belief, Chi'You loves the night. Once upon a time, his brothers took turns lighting up the sky. This gave the young Chi'You a lot of time to explore the world in human disguises. He loved the world at night so much that his heart ached at the sorrows that visited humanity at night. The humans with evil thoughts who tainted their hearts would maim and kill in the cover of darkness. The crops stopped growing and the temperature dropped until no one came out to play anymore.

Chi'You wished to change that. He desperately sought to ease humanity's suffering. This convinced him that he was going to be the solution to humanity's problem, never a good sign in Chely's opinion. He led his other nine brothers up into the sky, to light the way for humanity in an everlasting day.

It proved to be disastrous, as Earth was not made for there to be ten suns in the sky. Humans stopped going to bed. They exhausted their strength, yet the heat killed the crops, regardless. Famine and hunger swept the lands of Aixauh. Until one day, a divine archer shot nine of the ten suns down, so that night could come again.

Chi'You wept at the deaths of his brothers. He went off to complain to his mother, the Mother Goddess of the Heavenly Court that ruled beside the Jade Emperor. The heroic archer Hou'Yi accepted the unjust punishment the Heavens dealt him and became mortal.

Moral of the story: the Sun is a real spoiled dickhead. That's what Chely tells the flames every time they spark to life.

No matter how much Hou'Yi paid for Chi'You's mistakes, the Sun still complained about it to every alchemist with the fire element as their spiritual core since time immemorial. Most alchemists listened out of politeness, or sheer duty, or the simple fact it was the Sun talking to them and they didn't want to risk his wrath. Chely, however, was sick of Chi'You's bullshit.

Chi'You is a horrible conversational partner. His words come in bursts of glitter that can eat your face if you aren't careful, and he is as unintelligible to a fire alchemist's ear as any crackling fire pit is to an ordinary human. The only reason Chely is forced to listen to him at all is because her alchemist clan is one with a particular connection to the Sun. It made the Ying Clan's hair red as flames, which put Chely in an awkward situation during the Second War, as neither Inabrian magicians nor Aixauhan alchemists could tell from a distance which country she was from. This, combined with Cole's mixed-heritage and Anne's Inabrian magician features, made for the perfect distraction for them to sneak in and out of the lines of conflict, but proved to be extra annoying during Chely's travels in post-war time during the Reparation.

Chi'You's flame flicks to life under Chely's command. Once the Sun's big mouth opens a slice, Chely can already hear the same over-regurgitated verse coming out of its mouth.

"I really wish you would learn to shut up," Chely mutters back unhappily. Today of all days. She rarely likes to argue with the actual fucking sun that gives her power and life, but it has been a very long day so far, and the alchemist is about to light herself up even without Chi'You's usual theatrics. "Maybe if you learned to shut up, your brothers wouldn't have been murdered. I don't know, maybe that would've saved you a lot of guilt. You always talk about how much you hate Hou'Yi, but I know you. You just feel guilty, because if you had the self-awareness to know you aren't the saviour of the universe, maybe not everyone you loved would have been shot down like flies."

The fire accumulating on the logs hisses at her before snuffing itself out in an instant. The spirit of Chi'You is offended, and like the petulant child he is, he's decided the best recourse is to run off and sulk, leaving nothing behind but a few breaths of ashy snickers in their wake.

"…Am I interrupting some ancient self-help Aixauhan ritual?"

The Oracle's voice saunters through the dark night, seconds after Chely's world was plunged into darkness.

"Cai-Li, we need to talk." Anne Barberry's voice continues, and it is more searing than the sun god. "I think you might be right."

Chely is used to campfire, leather strapped hiking boots, and a thick fur cloak. For the most part, she's slept in tents and lodged at rented cabins or barns where she was hired to vanquish whatever magical disturbances were in the area, using alchemy to protect people from all sorts of things that threatened their lives, travelling from village to village, city to city, town to town. Like a phantom that defends the mundane from other phantoms.

After the war, Anne and Chely moved back to The Cottage, mostly. It was not the same without Cole. Anne nested up in the home the Yamalan boy had left behind and dedicated her life to scholarly pursuits like sending letters to other magician lineages who didn't consider the last oracle of the Barberry Lineage a traitor, gathering petitions with diplomats and officials for reforms and curating consultations for witnesses of the First and Second Wars to come to The Cottage for interviews, which the oracle would jot down with dedication.

The scrolls of papers Anne gathered in those years as the oracle practised her hermit lifestyle proved to be fruitful. The stacks of interviews soon turned so thick they had to be bound into piles until Chely asked why the hell Anne wouldn't consider publishing them into books—an idea which the oracle took seriously and ran with in a way Chely didn't expect.

Soon there were people visiting The Cottage asking for Anne every day, and the guests became more and more high-profile. Court officials, historians and scholars, governors, and even rulers.

Chely watched as Anne made a life for herself following the war. The oracle was onto something big. Somehow, by studying the past, Anne was getting further into the future than she ever had with her

Visions. Anne Barberry was going to make a name for herself in history. Chely knew that as a fact.

Of course, with the amount of attention Anne was getting for her historical research, the tension grew in The Cottage. Soon, Chely found the oracle withdrawing from her.

Anne burned away midnight oil to verify every source she was going to include in the new historical records documenting the First and Second Inabri-Aixauhan wars. She'd fall asleep at first sunrise, which was when Chely usually headed out for another day of her journeys abroad.

Chely left sleep medication orbs in the top drawer for Anne to find. Anne left freshly done laundry and notes in the same place. They shared a bed and a home, but words exchanged became less and less of a priority. It was as if they had grown bored with each other as peace finally dawned on them, when the first years of their life together were filled with secrecy, turbulent emotions, and uncertainty.

Chely found death threats and burned them to ashes with her fire. She didn't want Anne to find them, and also didn't bring them to the oracle's attention. The alchemist left her growing unrest as something unsaid, a crouching beast waiting to devour those she held most dear.

Maybe Anne had found the bloodstains on Chely's travel cloak, the yellowed papers containing disturbing images and words warranting concern, the evidence of dark magic abound next to the very cottage they made their home, long before she confronted Chely that fateful night.

The oracle simply hadn't wished to tell Chely because she wanted to keep hold of the illusion that they were both happy. Chely accused Anne of being ignorant to the things she did not wish to see, but the alchemist had ample practice in the art herself.

However, Anne was marching forward into the future by finding her way backward. While Chely? She was growing more and more nostalgic for the days where it had been the three of them at The Cottage, instead of the tenth official who wished to consult Anne about her most recent writing on the Inabri-Aixauhan conflict tracing a century back.

Chely found herself wishing she'd stayed in that war. It had been a bloody and confusing time, but The Cottage was quiet, Cole was there, Anne was not so far away. The flowers bloomed, the birds sang, and they spoke their thoughts aloud.

Ying Cai-Li knew who she was back then, who and what she had to protect. She no longer does. As the war ended, so too did the fight that had defined the alchemist her entire life.

During those years, Anne's head overflowed with thoughts of her own past. Chely traveled to Aixauh, the hometown she never knew. Her grandfather and grandmother were the heads of one of the Ying Clans, the greatest alchemists to ever exist. They'd taken in practitioners for hundreds of years. Their line of alchemic studies was a mountain they had laid brick by brick, and their understanding with the spirit core was the result of cutting down another mountain day by day.

The Ying Clan was rumoured to be descendants of the Qin Emperor himself, the first emperor who united the land of Aixauh. And every single one of them shared the same red hair as Chely. No one treated such a fact as odd. They saw it as a signature, something worthy of respect. No one asked Chely to prove her allegiance. Even the ordinary people who lived in the city her clan occupied were kind to her solely due to Chely's family.

It gave the alchemist a glimpse of a different life. A window where Chely saw a past and future where Anne Barberry alone lived.

A space of peace and tranquility where she didn't have to fight every day to prove her existence. A lifetime of being a spoiled brat instead of stepping outside her comfort zone.

Anne would never leave, Chely thought. She'd wondered for years, as she never knew how Anne could throw such a life away for a war and a lifetime of trauma. Why would The Oracle abandon her title because she had a conscience? Or because she hadn't wanted innocent people to die in the war?

If they were to switch places, Chely would trade the Inabrians and their lives in a blink of her eyes. She'd never think of them twice, let alone fall in love with an Inabrian magician, if only she'd grown up as part of the prestigious Ying Clan.

Anne was surely an idiot, no doubt.

The last name Ying was more a conscious choice on the part of Chely's ancestors. The Qin emperor sought immortality using alchemy, which had led to mercury poisoning—a very popular hobby and form of death for Aixauhan emperors. It takes a particular sort of arrogance to have the audacity to crown oneself the Emperor of Beginning, but one is above even him because the Ying Clan is famous for producing the best alchemists in all the contemporary Aixauhan lands.

That was why Chely's mum and dad had said they took their daughter away from the Ying Clan in Aixauh, to give her a better life than what the strict rule of the clan, who forced them into becoming a mad alchemist types who chased nothing but immortality, could provide. So, their solution was to plunge themselves into Inabri, a country that was historically founded on the eradication of any magic on the lands that were outside the Inabrian magician lineages.

Chely has a lot to credit her parents for, but being a liar is a skill she's honed herself. Because that is a shit explanation that even a toddler can call bullshit on.

When the war broke out, Chely's parents left Inabri as swiftly as they came. It was easy for them, since Chely cut contact with them first due to their objection to her association with Cole, who the Aixauhan alchemists apparently found to be beneath them.

Chely was drinking tea in The Cottage she shared with Anne and Cole at the time she got the message about her parents abandoning their daughter. She and Anne had been dating for about two years at that point, which was pretty much an eternity in the eyes of two sixteen-year-olds.

In one's youth, the good parts of life seem like they will last forever. The Cottage was evergreen; the stones were gathering moss, and the test Chely ran on the well testified the level of lead inside was becoming undrinkable for most humans. Cole, who The Cottage belonged to, started filtering the water by pouring it through his hand instead of going to the market. Anne almost spit it right back into Cole's face one morning as the Yamalan excitedly told them about the new system of water source they had going on.

"Sorry," Anne repeated, her face was bright green like leaves of a spring tree. "What do you mean the water is poisoned, but it's okay because you made it safe?"

"Ew." Cole's light blue eyes bulged in disgust. "Well, that was fresh water. It's such a waste. Since it has your saliva inside, no one can drink it. The well's going to take a few weeks to regather that bucket of water you just ruined, unless we get a sudden monsoon season."

"I'm sorry, am I the only one listening to this?" Anne sat back, clearly having lost her appetite. "Didn't Cai-Li say the well is lead-poisoned?"

"Yeah." Chely took a sip of her tea. "It's probably safe though. The lead level is always insane, but it's never affected Cole, and after running through him, it doesn't seem to have poisoned me so far. You'll probably be fine too."

"Do you ever hear the words that come out of your mouth, Ying Cai-Li?" Anne muttered. "They're so wrong, I don't even know where to begin."

"It's fine," Chely reassured her girlfriend. "Cole knows what he's doing."

"Yes, Cai-Li made it sound super weird." Cole rolled his eyes. "I wouldn't poison my best friend's girlfriend, even if they're Inabrian scum."

"Wow, okay," Anne said. "I'm going to die. Check my corpse if you ever loved me, Cai-Li. You'll know who killed me."

"Cole's fine," Cai-Li said. "His thoughts of stabbing you have gone since we started dating over a year ago."

"I'm sorry. Did you say he had thoughts of *stabbing* me?" Anne spluttered. "I think I'm going to be sick."

"Why are you such a pain in the ass?" Cole rolled his eyes. "Your people literally planned to murder everyone like me and Chely not even a century ago. I suppose you're different because you fell in love with one of us?"

"*Technically*," Anne replied with a deadly glare, "there is a historical precedent of the Aixauhan alchemist clans persecuting the spirits of the wild like the Yamalans too. The Ying Clan was one of them. It's not always just us Inabrians against you, you know?"

"She's right," Chely said.

Anne and Cole spoke in unison: "Shut up if you're not going to help, Ying Cai-Li."

"Okay, okay…"

"What is your problem, Barberry?" Cole snorted. "I don't care about other Aixauhan alchemists. I only know Chely, and she's fine with The Cottage when it's just me, my mum, and her living here by ourselves. Everything's been a problem since *you* moved in. Why is nothing good enough for you?"

"Probably because you constantly have a stick up your ass about how I'm sleeping with Cai-Li," Anne responded in a deadpan tone.

"Ew, keep that to yourself!"

Chely's best friend and girlfriend never got along in those early days. Cole resented Anne for being a Barberry, while Anne was willfully ignorant, which honestly irritated Chely as much as it irritated Cole.

Yet it was nostalgic, the silliness of those banters. They fought like kids, wild and unruly, blossoming like the vibrant spring flowers surrounding The Cottage, without knowing peace was a fleeting season of illusion. The war soon swiped in and realigned their priorities toward the same one true enemy.

Back then, not all liquid brewed by Anne's hand could turn as transparent and clear as if it were distilled from the highest snowy mountains. That was Cole's ability alone. Anne was still very new to not living in a castle, which didn't help. Chely and Cole often exchanged glances that made Anne gawk. They thought they were discreet, but Anne knew the nonverbal communication the two shared. The oracle was never jealous but did feel left out.

"What?" Anne glared back at them like she wanted to cook them for breakfast instead of the eggs.

"Annie," Chely said tentatively. Her voice was a mix of childish idleness and softness. "You only know how to make a three-course meal."

"Yeah," Cole resonated with his mouth in a flat line, looking like he'd swallowed his own mouth. "By that, she means every meal you make is so tiny and unnecessary. You can't be full even after like ten Anne-meals a day. There's a war coming. Do you want to starve us to death before someone burns down The Cottage?"

Chely forced her laugh into a choked noise. Anne's eyes seemed to get closer and closer despite not moving a single inch.

"Cole," Chely whispered quietly to the boy, who was basically her sworn brother, "I think she's angry."

"Oh, how could you tell?" Anne snapped in the background. Her voice was the same emotionless desert, except it was getting closer to a screech.

"Chely," Cole continued regardless, "I think you should have better taste in girlfriends. Anyone would do, really, other than this pampered oracle princess who would be dead without us."

"Cai-Li doesn't want me dead," Anne's tone was deadly sincere. "She needs someone to keep her bed warm."

Chely almost had to peel them off each other before Anne and Cole inevitably blew a hole in the wall with the spells they were beginning to utter. At the time, Chely thought despairingly how impossible it would be for them all to survive an oncoming war together, if the two closest people to her were ready to kill each other over petty disagreements on the daily.

That was when Chely got the message from her parents.

And a single note, written in Aixauhan. 长命百岁. *"Wish you live to a hundred."*

Chely eyed that piece of paper intensely enough that she could have scorched a hole through it; Chi'You never answered Chely's call without making it into a huge mess. On that day, the flame burned without a single sound. It was the Sun himself who noticed the callousness of that sentence.

Chely's parents were hundreds of years old, born alchemists in a clan that harboured the secrets of Aixauhan dynasties. They were mortal only in the flimsiest of senses, their longevity ensured by their connection to the sun god. That they left that note behind for their teenage daughter, wishing she might live to see a mere one hundred years…

It was downright petty, or it would be if Chely was at the age where she wished her parents would accept her—the trait of entitled children raised in a prestigious alchemist clan. Chely never dared ask Anne outright, but the red-haired alchemist thought about how much more similar she was to the oracle than she was to Cole.

In another lifetime, I could be everything you are, the red-haired alchemist almost said to Anne on numerous mornings as they woke up next to each other. *All the privileges in the world, with none of the consequences. In that world, Oracle, I surely would not have fallen in love with you.*

In the present, Chely stares into Anne's eyes.

"I'm right about what?" asks the red-haired alchemist.

There it is, the capacity for cruelty. Ying Cai-Li has never been more aware of how she could be her parents' child. There is something dark inside her that is not present in Anne—the burning desire to be proven right, the earth-shattering ego of the sun born of good will, but ended in destruction.

The night has climbed further and further, its shadow elongated like a dragon, the tail unable to be perceived by human vision. The darkness swallows up the world into its belly.

"You're right about the things that happened at this castle, Cai-Li." Anne's eyes are the same silverish grey. However, in the dark, they're like reflections of the moon in the water—observant and bright. "And I...I want to say that I could never be involved in such things. Missing children? That's so much like the bloody past of the Barberrys you know I don't want to be a part of. But it would be a lie to say that my memories are entirely reliable. There were so many memory spells done on me that maybe there is some rotten legacy left in me too. Whether I wish to admit it or not."

"There is nothing rotten inside you, Anne Barberry," Chely says.

"Oh." Anne's left eyebrow curls up. "Is that why you took a sample of the barberry fruit? Let me guess, you're going to check it for blood."

Chely stares at the barberry bushes, wondering if she will have to eat some soon to get out of this embarrassment.

"You left your alchemistry set at my castle," Anne continues, as if not noticing the piercing note her words landed on. "Right next to the cooking pots in the kitchen. Not going to lie, kind of gross. You have to come back to get it."

The red-haired alchemist freezes in surprise, but a smile floats onto her face. "Huh. You're still a snob about food."

"Not wanting to be poisoned is not the same as being a snob," Anne replies dryly. "I've told you so many times. I almost poured some kind of liquid metal into my frying pan instead of oil—you need to label your shit if we're going to live under the same roof again."

Chely smirks. "So, you learned how to cook?"

"Nothing beyond eggs."

"Boiled or fried?"

"Kind of both? I mean, eggs are easy and can't go wrong—"

"Hmmm," Chely hums.

There is an understanding that floods the oracle's face.

"You're making fun of me." Anne facepalms. "The Creator above, I can't believe I fell for that."

"The Creator can't blame you," Cai-Li says. "It's been a while since you've been out to meet people, hasn't it?"

"I made up my mind to be vulnerable with you." Anne's face turns a shade colder. "And you are fucking with me. That's so typical."

"I really wish we were doing that," Chely said cheerfully.

"You know what?" Anne throws her hands up into the air. "This is a mistake. Go test the barberries somewhere else. You can come and find me if it's got a missing kid's traces on it, so I can decide if I should kill myself."

Coldness runs down Chely's spine, the same as the day she received that last note from her parents. "No, I'd prefer you alive."

"Okay." Anne turns her eyes away. "We're going to find out what happened to those kids. I don't know what's going on here, Ying Cai-Li. I don't know who Naomi is. But if you say there is a possibility their disappearance is connected to me, then I do not want to take chances. You're full of shit, but you are not one to hurt kids."

"Hmmm." Chely shrugs. "Yeah, definitely not kids."

"Okay," the oracle says. "That's good enough for me. Let's go back before my toes freeze off."

8

First Encounter with Death

WHAT HAPPENED AT The Barberry Castle that night is a secret Anne will take to her grave.

Not the part about the murder. That was obvious to anyone who found the mangled body of Brutus Barberry in the yards, bits and pieces tangled with the barberry vines, very much looking like ten dozen screaming hedgehogs bumped into him at the same time.

It was gruesome, unexpected. She would never admit to anyone that Brutus Barberry was one of the people whose deaths haunted her dreams. Because it was unfair, for everyone else who died in the Second War was innocent in one way or another. While Brutus? He had it coming.

Sometimes Anne wonders if she tells herself something enough times, then with thing become true as well? Because a life without dreaming of the night of Brutus Barberry's murder is easier, as if Anne hadn't had a normal reaction to her grandpa getting murdered, then she'd have one less thing for those she allied with to hate and criticise her about.

The truth remains. She dreams about Brutus's death as much as she dreams about Cole's. There is something fundamentally wrong with that fact. Something unfair, that no matter how much Anne wishes to scrub her heart raw and clean, it is to no avail.

Anne should have seen it coming, given she is The Oracle and all. But you can't expect a kid who does not yet understand the concept of war to predict the consequences of war. No matter how powerful that child becomes at predicting the future.

The night of the murder was the first time Anne Barberry encountered those consequences.

The doorbell rang.

"Are Father and Mother arriving home?" Anne asked Brutus. She was feeling sleepy. She kept on forcing her eyelids to open when they drooped like melted candle wax.

"No." Brutus's eyes narrowed, suddenly were strange and unfocused. "Go back to bed, my duckling. Don't come out, no matter what you hear."

"What?" Anne sensed the urgency in her grandfather's words. "What is going on? Grandpa? No one is supposed to come at this hour." Not with all the magical wards placed around Barberry Castle, not when the barberry bushes that dotted around the hill like the stars dotting the sky acted as a barrier that dissuaded anyone from trespassing.

"An old grudge," Brutus replied, calm and collected. "I can handle it. Anne, no matter what happens, remember the lessons I taught you. There will be a war."

"Why are you saying these things?" Anne was confused as the alarm started to glow red in her head. "What do you mean by war?"

"War, my girl," Brutus smiled at her in a way that was kind and gentle, "is something you will shine in. Remember my lessons, be the oracle that will lead the Barberry Lineage into glory."

At this time, Anne did not know the definition of glory in war. The bloodshed that cost one to survive was already hard to carry; the glory that Brutus dreamed of was built on a mountain of corpses.

Back then, those words brought tears to a younger Anne's eyes. She could hear the strange implication of goodbye etched away in Brutus's words. Children are sensitive creatures who know to read between the lines. Each of them are oracles in their own right, predicting what might happen from between the lines of the adults in their lives who assure them everything will be all right when that was never the case.

The front door banged open. A gust of wind swept across the castle, sharp as a knife, with a tinge of salt and storm clouds. Anne would one day be closer acquainted with the fundamental elements that lay within Aixauhan alchemists' cores: metal, wood, water, fire, earth. The murderer of Brutus Barberry had a core of water, the element of most Aixauhan alchemist healer clans, Cai-Li said.

The feeling Anne got that night was indeed a sense of being drowned. A white mist rose in the hallways and rooms. Anne tasted salt on her tongue, as if the water came not from wells, but from the seaside.

The chandeliers jingled like windchimes, the kind that Cai-Li would one day put up on The Cottage windows to test for ghosts. Another Aixauhan tradition that ominously told the identity of the assailant.

A vengeful ghost, Anne thought. A ghost that came to haunt Brutus from his past while Anne got caught in the crossfire.

There was shouting. Things were smashed on the ground. Windows splintered into a thousand shards, and the curtains whipped so high the fabric tore into shreds.

The alchemist might have possessed the element of water, but it was boiling hot. The kind that if one put their hands in, their meat would be cooked in an instant.

A stranger's voice echoed through the castle. It bounced across the old walls, coming from all sides. There was her grandfather's reply, which was uttered in a more muted yet conspicuous tone.

Brutus Barberry was trying to tame a hurricane. A hurricane that had built up for years, originating from across the ocean, on the land where the First War took place.

Anne couldn't stop trembling as she hid. Yet there was a sense of curiosity and wonder, too pampered at that age to know there were situations one should avoid in order to not get hurt.

She carefully slipped out of her bed and followed the trail of voices down the winding staircase. Almost tripping over herself several times, sweet and stupid little Anne was worried about her darling grandfather. She was a small child yet brave enough to think she could be of help.

When she finally got into the proximity of the front door, survival instincts sparked in Anne Barberry for the first time.

She didn't rush in as her grandfather's saviour as she'd originally planned.

All she did was peek through the curtains and watch.

There was a woman with pitch black hair. She is faceless in Anne's memories, has been devoid of features for years. What Anne does remember are the emotions that imbued in the woman's every word. Fury and agony. Concepts that Anne understood from a distance, concepts that Anne would only learn after she experienced them herself.

"I have finally found you," the woman said, as if a whole war were stuffed into her chest, so what came out was nothing but muffled breaths. "You have no idea how long I have waited for this."

"You have found the wrong person," Brutus said to her. He raised his hands in a placating gesture, but his brows lifted in a way that suggested to Anne that, like always, her grandpa had complete control over the situation.

No, who was Anne kidding? Brutus Barberry appeared to have control of the situation because he was used to it. It was a fact he took for granted. A life devoid of consequence and accountability. The life of an Inabrian magician of the great Barberry Lineage.

"Oh, that's rich." The woman's laughter was sharp and deliberate. "You people are funny sometimes. You come into my country, slaughter my family, and then go back to your castles and your riches, thinking you can walk away from the war and what you have done. Funny, I guess it has something to do with the fact you think we'd never fight back? That someone like me would forget the face of the monster who strung my family up like dead pigs?"

"No, of course not. I know your grievances—but I was merely a messenger," Brutus replied quickly. He didn't sound meek, only confused. "You should be looking for the Inabrian magicians who were battle-trained. Their magic was what killed most of your people. I was merely a spokesperson, a figurehead. Nobody wants a war. I only joined like everybody else."

Anne's eyebrows scrunched up. A tiny part of her screamed about how that was not what Brutus had told her. But her mind was so fearful of the black-haired woman, who looked like the shadowy denizens of Discord that were told in Inabrian bedtime stories, that the healthy question was squashed.

"Funny how you all say that. A figurehead, a foot soldier, just doing their jobs. You Inabrian magicians truly are unimaginative. For a bunch of murderers whose brains come up with the most colourful torture methods, you guys sure are bad at begging for mercy."

"What do you mean?" Brutus's voice lost some of its heat. "Ollie, Logan, Henry—"

"Yes, yes." The woman nodded as if she were drinking in the sight of the despair descending over Brutus Barberry. Her voice rose to a singsong pitch, giddy with bloodthirsty delight.

"They all are dead. I picked them off one by one. Not easy, mind you. Trying to find you was like trying to find a needle from an ocean. You are the last on my list to kill. There is a very good reason for that. I longed for the fear you show on your face now, knowing all your old lackeys were dropping like flies. I've done my research, Brutus Barberry. You were no mere soldier. The Great Oracle himself. With your Vision, you hand-selected the alchemist clans that would have become the worst obstacles for the great Inabri in the war."

A needle from an ocean. She wanted to say a needle in a haystack, Anne corrected instinctively. It was an odd phrasing, as if translated from a different language of a faraway land.

The woman loomed closer to where Brutus stood. Anne let out a little squeak from where she was hiding. This was her last chance to do something.

"What was that noise?" The woman swirled around, and her eyes pinned onto where Anne was. The girl's courage evaporated; her hands flung to cover her mouth. She tried hard not to cry out. "Who is there?"

Anne imagined herself as a ghost. A ghost who did something wrong in life and was about to be dragged into the Underworld by Discord. Not that such a thing was possible, according to Brutus, for Inabrian magicians were chosen by the Creator. They would rest in the Creator's kingdom up in the clouds.

Sometimes, Anne wonders how delusional Brutus Barberry was, how delusional the entirety of Inabri was, that for centuries they took such a statement as fact.

"There is no one there." The panic that flooded Brutus's voice was that of the grandfather Anne adored. An old man who doted on his granddaughter with his whole heart. "Why don't we talk about this outside?"

Anne watched the scene unfold. She now can recolour her memories with the woman's features, like adding paint to a dried-up portrait.

The woman's eyes were dark onyx stones. She had the darker complexion of the Aixauhan southern coastal cities. Her muscular build indicated years of military training. She was average height yet possessed an imposing aura, the kind that made her allies rely on her and her enemies tremble in fear.

Anne could only accurately describe it after having seen what the ocean looked like. It's a long story, involving three stowaways with a bunch of stray orphans they picked up along the way. But before vomiting her guts out in a vessel stuck in the middle of nowhere with black waves knocking against the only ground within miles upon miles, Anne would have said Cole's eyes were the colour of the sea—the sea on the beachside, clear and turquoise, where one can see all the seaweed and shells washed ashore.

The true ocean, which Anne would later found out, was unending, merciless, and devoured anyone who deluded themselves into thinking they could bargain with it.

Anne can't remember the rest of the night, because as soon as the woman with the ocean-black eyes turned back onto her grandfather, Anne *ran*. Her Vision that once brought her so much pride leaked away from her eyes along with the tears. She could barely think clearly.

She tripped twenty times over the stairs. Later, Anne would discover a scar on her lower lip that must have been from scraping against something sharp on that night. It is now a little white line only visible when her jaw hangs open, like when she witnessed Chely's red hair appearing in the chalice—where all her oracle abilities lie nowadays—a few summers ago.

It is a wonder, perhaps, that the woman who broke into Barberry Castle never caught up with Anne. She was a tiny girl caged in a large castle far away from the nearest town, like an insect trapped in amber, nowhere to run and nowhere to hide.

She was twelve, and the world had just exploded in front of her.

Anne curled up in her bed. For the rest of the night, she would close her eyes and try to wash away what she saw. She told herself over and over again that her grandpa would be all right. There was no way he would be harmed. All Anne had to do was wait, and wait, and wait.

The twelve-year-old oracle drifted into sleep somewhere down the line and woke up to the morning rays.

The castle was silent and drenched with shadows. Anne stumbled out of her bed, drowsy and heavy-eyed. She walked through the halls past the Barberry ancestors' portraits, past the divination room, past the library. All the way back to the front door.

She stepped out the ornate doors. Whoever intruded into Barberry Castle hadn't bothered to close it. Anne heard the hinges being blown back; the creaking noise felt like it was mincing her bones.

She found Brutus's dead body lying there in the bushes. For two days, Anne did not sleep or eat. They were a haze as she sat next to Brutus Barberry's corpse, trying to make sense of her overturned world. Then her parents came home to find the horror that had been bestowed upon their family.

As her mother cried out in shock and embraced Anne in her arms, her father's composed face fell to cinders.

Anne's face, however, was as calm and emotionless as the winter frost.

"I saw what is buried under this hill," The Oracle said. "Is that why he died? If so, then he deserved it."

Her mother's cries intensified, while her father's fist struck Anne's face. The impact was nothing, merely a moment of blindness.

Violence was nothing, not even when it came from her own family members. Everything started to reassemble for the young oracle.

Violence was nothing. The truth she discovered as her childhood shattered—that was the secret that Anne could not bear.

The barberries that were on the Barberry hilltop used to be dark blue, the shade of night hard to decipher from the colour of ink. After that night, they all turned red. Red like the crimson shade of the setting sun, red like the blood that ran through their veins.

Anne's sister still calls her sometimes to talk about how they could return the barberries at home back to the colour they used to be.

Only people who haven't seen the sight of war can talk about washing off the blood with some bleach and a few magic spells.

9

The Reveal

CHELY IS IN the kitchen. The morning sun is gentle yet judgmental after a sleepless night. Still, she pulls all the curtains open, because why the hell anyone would keep the curtains drawn in this kind of pleasant weather is a mystery.

She hums a little tune of an old Aixauhan song under her breath as she works with the test tubes and measuring cups, spoons made of copper and silver needles that can detect the mercury level by turning black if something indeed showed its venomous properties.

There is smoke everywhere. Another reason she opened the windows. Not that the small windows of a medieval castle are helping much with clearing out the air. How Anne lives in a hellhole like this is beyond Chely's understanding.

It is a relaxed and chill morning, especially considering Chely almost become homeless last night. She really is enjoying it until Anne stumbles up to the kitchen door, sweating and swearing like an old sailor instead of a proper oracle.

"When I say we'll figure this out together," the oracle screams at Chely from across the large kitchen space, "I didn't mean at five in the morning! I also didn't mean for you to be doing the alchemical examination in the kitchen where I store my food!"

The familiar named after their deceased friend, Cole, curls himself into a ball of fluff as he takes the shape of a black cat. He doesn't seem too antagonistic toward Chely this morning, which is a nice change of pace. Chely would have almost thought she personally wronged the familiar somehow with how much he constantly pierced Chely with those milky, filmed eyes.

"I don't have all the ingredients needed for the test." Chely waves a hand at Anne. "Your kitchen, however, should be renamed an encyclopedia of storage where every possible magical vegetation can be found somewhere. I never knew you to be a collector, Annie. Some of these ingredients I only even know exist through travelling! Oh, and good morning."

"No, I didn't collect them." Anne's eyes turn dark. "They were… always there."

A rather ominous remark, Chely thinks. She brushes it off easier now that she's getting used to this new version of her ex.

"Slept all right?"

"No," Anne says. "I *wish* I was still fucking unconscious, but the possibility of being a serial killer kind of ruined my ability to sleep."

"Look, Annie." Chely wears a face mask to prevent the alchemy pot that is heated to a metal-melting degree from burning her face off. She concentrates on the texture and smell of the solution brewing in the pot before she carefully drops the sample of barberry fruit in. "No one is saying you're a murderer. Honestly, there is something weird going on here, but from what I witnessed that night. Your… Oracle form? Seemed to be doing what Naomi wished for. It was probably a transportation spell or a summoning spell. Wine is often used for communicating with spirits of another realm in Inabrian tradition, right?"

"It is," Anne replies, unconvinced. "But if this Naomi—you say she's The Innkeeper's grown daughter?—really was here in the castle, why is she the only one that I wiped from my memory? I remember the missing tourist kids, how they looked and how they sounded. I even know one of them is from the countries north of Inabri. He said they have snow mountains there for sport, and he gave me a very potent drink that can be set on fire."

"Wait, what?" Chely is hearing this for the first time. "You mean the tourist kids *did* come to the castle? I thought you said you had never met them."

"No, I said I have nothing to do with their disappearances because they never came to the castle," Anne says. "I met them at The Inn—don't look so surprised, Cai-Li, I'm not as much of a hermit as you imagined. I love The Innkeeper's pies, so I go there occasionally in different disguises. Those kids were nice and reminded me of the orphans we traveled with during the war. We talked; they were horrified when I revealed I was the witch they had come all this way for. I scolded them for objectifying me. Said they were treating me like a tourist attraction, and I told them I can't see the future in the sense they imagined. They were polite, kind of chastised since they found out I'm an actual human being. I thought they had just left town until you told me otherwise."

"Er, yeah," Chely says. "That's not what The Innkeeper says. He says the kids were making trips to your castle."

"I don't know if you should trust The Innkeeper," Anne snickers. There is something personal vendetta going on here that Chely isn't grasping. "He might act nice, but he's a downright creep."

"Okay." Chely remembers the conversation she had with The Innkeeper before storming out of The Inn. "Maybe he isn't the most reliable source. I wouldn't have believed it if it were his words alone though. Naomi, the girl you didn't just wipe from your memory, but seemingly also The Innkeeper's—she was supposed to meet up with the tourist group of kids and go to your castle the night they disappeared, but it was Solstice, and The Inn was too busy, so she didn't manage to join them."

"The Innkeeper doesn't remember, either?" Anne's brows furrow. "That's…I don't know what to say. I thought maybe it was possible for me not to have remembered something that proved to be detrimental to my own mental stability. But you're saying that not only were my memories wiped, but The Innkeeper's too?"

The suspicion creeping back into Anne's voice makes Chely look up from her experiment.

"Not again." The red-haired alchemist rolls her eyes. "I know Naomi existed, all right? I saw what I saw."

"You *think* you saw what you saw," Anne's voice turns cold. "You came and accused me of having missing memories. How do I know you have nothing to do with the kids' disappearance? I don't think you'd hurt kids, but dark magic and necromancy come with side-effects to the one who dabbles in them. They corrode the practitioner's sanity. If Naomi only existed for you and no one else in this town, isn't what you say about me true about yourself too?"

"I know you think that since you've been gone I've spiraled into some kind of abyss where I do nothing but dark magic all day for fun," Chely says, "but do you really think that's what's happening here? That I'd come all this way to the middle of nowhere, exactly where you live, so I could kidnap kids and make them into stew or something? Oh, also knocking on your door asking for reconciliation, but then making up the story of a girl who doesn't exist to make things more complicated. It's reaching, Annie."

"Fine, I guess you make a good point," the oracle says. "Why practise dark magic in my face when you always tried to hide it from me when we were together? That's a very valid question indeed. I guess that clears your possible participation in whatever the fuck is happening, at least."

Anne might be fully sincere, but the way she phrases the sentences is all kinds of unpleasant. *Typical*, Chely thinks.

"You don't need to stand here and watch," Chely says. "The result won't come until the fruit is entirely decomposed by the solution, and analysing the spiritual fragments of the plant that are aligned with an enlightened version of the spiritual core that belonged solely to the human body is going to take a while."

Anne stares at Chely as if the alchemist has grown two heads. It was the same look the oracle used to give her whenever the latter went on a rant about the intricacy of the alchemical process.

"The way you talk about alchemy makes me wonder if I even speak a human language," Anne says. "It's almost like you're describing a recipe for making soup."

"That's exactly how I feel when you go on one of your oracle tangents," Chely replies. "You make it sound like you are tripping on some hallucinogenic herbs."

"I mean, yeah." Anne shrugs as she walks toward the adjacent dining room. "What's for breakfast?"

Chicken broth sits on the table nearby. Chely learned how to make it during the war. The flavour of chicken doesn't need much seasoning, and the fat that makes the soup so tasty comes from nothing but the meat itself. It's a dish served to pregnant women to nurture their babies, with Aixauhan alchemist healers mixing herbs while brewing them in pots that have alchemical properties that preserve qi—the name for spirit and life force in Aixauhan—to nurture in a swift and painless birth.

At least those were the words taught to Chely by an Aixauhan alchemist from a healer clan. Like everything in Aixauh, it was second-handed knowledge. Chely has never explained those words to another person, as it felt wrong when coming out of her mouth. She doesn't know how to make the kind of chicken broth that has healing properties, but the taste is nice.

Cole and Anne both loved the dish. Chely herself couldn't eat it, as she'd watched the pinkish skin turn white and wrinkled, until every bit of sinew peeled off the bone. It reminded her too much of the war, which was why she'd stopped eating meat altogether. The texture and taste brought the sight of corpses into Chely's mind. Their bodies in piles, maggots and flies opening holes in the flesh…

"Tastes amazing," Anne's voice comes from the dining room. The oracle drags Chely out from her momentary lapse in time. "What are these fungi floating in the soup? They made it taste so much better. I haven't seen them in any encyclopaedias before."

"Oh." Chely masters her smile and lightens her voice. It's like a spell in itself to cover up the damage in her mind. "It's 香菇, they're native to the forest ranges next to the ocean. There's no translation. It's kind of just like 'sweet-scented mushrooms.' I don't think there is anything similar on this continent. Inabrian mushrooms are flavourless, no offence. The ones I used were dried up. They were nurtured by natural rainwater and grew on dead logs in the forest. The people of the coastal towns harvest them as a tradition. Last time I visited her, Captain Ark refused to let me go unless I packed some with me."

"Oh." Anne's voice turns wooden. "Is that what the captain spends her retirement days after the war doing? Sending people dried, dead plants for fun?"

"Well, she *is* a healer." Chely shrugs. It's kind of a miracle Anne didn't instantly fly the bowl across the room after hearing Ark Li's name. "She's naturally knowledgeable about this kind of stuff."

"Well, guess you really can't judge a book by its cover," is all that comes from the dining room. "Have you eaten?"

"Nope, I'm fine," Chely responds, surprised at how calm Anne appears to be with the information.

Chely watches the white smoke enveloping the room in a haze. The grandfather clock in the kitchen ticks by with a steady rhythm, like heels knocking on a wooden floor. No noise other than the sound of soup slurping comes from the dining room. Not long after, Anne waves her hand around to clear a path for herself into the kitchen to ask for more, and Chely gestures to the pot on the stove next to the alchemical blood-test cauldron.

Anne looks at the stove and then turns around to Chely. "Are you actually trying to poison me?"

"No," Chely replies. "I don't know why, but this is the only available fireplace in the entire kitchen. It's almost like whoever built this kitchen has never seen the interior of one. Or know how much it takes to feed a castle full of people."

Anne narrows her eyes at the fireplace. Her face churns in confusion, as if seeing a clog jamming its course of work.

"Fair point," the oracle finally says.

The smell of the chicken broth floats across the kitchen and out the door, which Chely left open to disperse the smoke of the alchemy concoction. The black cat seems to have found the two women boring and left for a walk. Now, a squawking sound comes rumbling into the kitchen, its indignant voice accusatory, as if complaining someone forgot to invite him to the party.

The familiar is in its black crow's form as its beak emerges from the smoke. His eyes carry from Chely to Anne. Something feels strange to Chely as his gaze levels onto the alchemist.

"I was about to tell you," Anne says, her voice casual, "you're just going to have it all to yourself if you know."

The black crow caws at The Oracle. Vengefully, he turns in a flash of wind to the shape of a cat. His face digs right into the pot of chicken broth. Slithers of chicken meat stick to his fur as he lifts his smug face in triumph.

"Typical," Anne mutters as she stands up. "Bastard."

The familiar doesn't respond as he savours the broth. Chely thinks that must mean the pot is ruined for the oracle, but Anne grabs the pot from the stove to refill her bowl.

"Hm," Chely says. "This is interesting."

"What is interesting?" Anne asks as she finishes another bowl of chicken broth in the kitchen. Her eyebrows perk up.

"Nothing," Chely replies. The grandfather clock strikes twelve o'clock on the wall. "The alchemical test is done."

Anne coughs loudly. She chokes on her last few gulps.

"You really need to slow down," Chely says. "Instead of acting like you haven't eaten anything in the last ten years."

"Bugger off," the oracle says. "What's the result?"

"The barberry outside has boiled down to its essence. Now I can see all the properties it possesses. Like, for example, what kind of barberry is it? How long has it existed by the spiritual duration of their spirit's existence, was someone murdered and dumped on top of it, and is the colour natural or soaked with blood?"

"The only relevant part of that sentence is the last third of it," Anne notes. "I forgot how excited I get about this type of magic."

Chely sticks out her tongue. "From your tone, I can tell you mean something derogatory," the alchemist says enthusiastically. "However, I need to remind you every kind of magic is a double-edged sword. The cleaning spell that gets stains out of the peskiest fabric can also make a person bleed from every orifice until they die of blood loss."

"I really hope you don't say that because you tried it yourself," Anne replies in a monotone voice.

"Haha, no. Think it in your own words, Oracle. The past informs the present. The future is merely a map traced by dots from today into tomorrow. The past and future reflect each other, all that."

"Do I actually sound like that?" Anne asks. "If so, no wonder I have such a poor reputation amongst the townsfolk."

"You have poor customer reviews from the townsfolk because you are mean to them, Annie. And no one knows the opinion of the tourists and their feedback on your divination sessions because they all went missing."

"Unless you're suggesting I murder kids because they didn't like the result of my divination sessions with them, you're not making any sense." Anne waves her hand at Chely's work of art. "Do you at least have something to show for whatever that was?"

"Oh, yeah." Chely pours what remains in the little ornate cup into the chalice after taking out all the variants that make the liquid barberries irrelevant to the matter at hand. "Go ahead, drink it."

"What?" Anne asks. The black crow crowds into them as well, with his head tilted to the side.

"Drink it," Chely smiles and repeats. "Then you'll know everything you want an answer to."

"All right," Anne says dryly. "You scooped that out of the alchemy pot. It's...I don't know, possibly mixed with human blood samples and poisoned barberries. Is this some kind of test?"

"Oh no." Chely shakes her head. "I think I know what's happening here. The pattern shown through the alchemy process is what tells me a story, not the resulting product. Don't worry, the barberry bushes outside your castle aren't tainted by blood."

"How do you know?" Anne's lips tremble as if the oracle is having difficulty comprehending those words. "They're red."

"Yeah, the barberries outside your house are a subspecies of *Berberis vulgaris.* They're native to the Inabrian geographical location of this hill," Chely says cheerfully. "I was wrong. This isn't the same castle as the one you grew up in. Sorry, my mistake. Their fruits are red, not cursed or soaked in blood or anything."

"That means…" Anne's voice turns soft, her eyes glimmering under the light. The perpetual greyness within her eyes, like storm clouds, almost turn a shade of blue. "That means there are no dead children buried under them."

"No." Chely's smile widens. "Nothing sinister or weird. They're just…barberry bushes. I mean, they're still poisonous and bitter. Barberry fruits have magical properties, and they're linked to your emotions. So, there is a lesson in there for you, I think. You are grumpy and scary."

"This isn't a joke, Ying Cai-Li."

"I'm not treating it as one, Annie," Chely says with finality in her voice. "Those kids aren't under the bushes. I can promise you that."

What the red-haired alchemist doesn't say is that as the barberry fruit sample dissolved into the fire, the flames churned in a dance that also told Chely the story of the kids who came into the castle. In hindsight, it's obvious what has been happening all along.

It is nothing outside of what Chely should have expected. It brings a smile to the alchemist's face as the barberry sample tells her the fate of those children who entered Anne's castle over the last seven years. She knows their voices, Naomi's among them, each of them clear and sure. No screams. No uncertainty. No loss.

Those children are at peace. How odd is that? They are not to be peaceful, given their young age and the facts that remain. Yet that's the impression they leave upon The Barberry Castle—this one that Anne, the supposed terrifying Oracle, lives in—they came with weariness in their hearts, and left with serenity. Into the arms of those who loved them.

"Wait, that doesn't make sense." Anne runs a hand through her tangled hair. She is no longer looking at Chely. Her gaze is focused somewhere past Chely's shoulders, out the open window where atop the hill the barberry bushes bloomed. "The barberry bushes I had around our castle as a child… It's not exactly here, but it's nearby. Its—its fruits are blue and black. It was only after Brutus died that they turned that unnatural shade of red. They were red, I thought, because they were soaked in blood. Like the creepy lullaby he always sang to me as a child."

Chely sighs. There is no side-stepping the difficult part. The relief that the red-haired alchemist feels must be the opposite of what is happening to The Barberry Oracle now that Anne clearly remembers the truth of this place.

"Brutus Barberry was a man who deserves what he got," Chely says. She holds out the same concoction the sample left behind, a gesture of good will for the oracle. A thank-you gift from the kids who visited Anne over the years. They beckon The Oracle to open her eyes. They wish for the lonely woman to notice she is not so alone.

"It is not him alone that's buried underneath the bushes that surrounded your castle, is it, Annie? You thought of the crimson fruits of the naturally occurring barberries of your own yard as something unnatural—because the ones that were planted around the Old Barberry Castle where you grew up as a child, they were…*Berberis julianae*. With their fruits black and blue."

Anne shakes as if something is unravelling from within her. "Yes—No? I don't…" Her emotionless face rocks as if an earthquake has happened underneath. "I don't understand."

"You see, I saw blue and black barberries for the first time when I went to visit Captain Ark five years ago." Chely turns away from Anne's pale eyes. She is rarely fazed by things like this, but it is Anne, goddammit.

This is why I don't always like the truth, Annie. It is painful, and it is cruel. Don't you wish to live in a fantasy with me? Why do I have to break it for you?

"*Berberis julianae* is native to the southern coast of Aixauh. It's otherwise known as the Wintergreen Barberry. Some of their leaves turn red approaching winter, but never their fruit. It's the kind of barberry commonly found in the province that Ark came from. She asks me to take her to see the barberries in the same woods where she knows the best herbs to brew chicken broth grow."

Anne, to her credit, doesn't scream "impossible" or storm out of the kitchen. She doesn't even seem that surprised, which is almost worse. The oracle looks like she was expecting this to some degree, like when Chely used to tell her the next day's weather would suck, or that Cole had *accidentally* picked up another child orphaned by the war into their travelling stack. The Oracle's Vision probably doesn't involve any of those things, but they are foreseeable enough that it doesn't prompt a reaction out of Anne.

"I know," The Oracle says as if in a trance. Her hands stop shaking as a calmness settles across her skin. It's as if someone struggling against a riptide has given in to the water as the last bubble escapes their mouth. "*Berberis julianae* recognises the blood of the Li Clan—the healers who use them as ingredients. They are red as a warning for if anyone of Li blood spills onto the land."

Chely watches quietly as Anne Barberry fades away. There she is, The Oracle who saw past Chely's detection spell the day Naomi went into the white light. The Eyeless Oracle. The Oracle who is Anne but also is not.

"Anne never told you," The Oracle says calmly, her voice as cold as a full moon on a winter night. "It is the same reason she never told you she foresaw Cole's death. Do you hate her, Ying Cai-Li?"

"No, of course not," the red-haired alchemist says. "Not even Captain Ark hates you as much as you hate yourself."

"I'm not Anne," The Oracle insists.

"Sure," Chely chuckles. She rolls the orb of the concoction of the congealed alchemy test into on her palm. "You might not have told me what your family has done, but I'm not blind to history, Annie. Brutus Barberry massacred Aixauhan alchemists in the thousands, all by himself. It is said he brought back tons of plants from where he murdered innocents and planted them around The Barberry Castle like trophies. It is also rumoured he took human specimens with him. Hid their bones under the plants that eventually became red after drinking in the blood from them."

"No tale spoken by the Aixauhans is worse than the truth." The Oracle's face is flat. "I think your parents must not have told you the worst parts. They wanted to save you the heartache, the horrendous fact that plagued your new lover. Tell me, how could you love Anne Barberry after learning the truth?"

Chely laughs at the question, which makes a tiny indent between The Oracle's smooth brows, the only blemished part of this being. It must be whatever lives inside of Anne. The part that is passed down through the Barberry Lineage, the unfeeling power that sees the past and future while remaining impartial.

The thing that Anne wishes herself to become but never managed to.

"You mean my parents who knew the fates befallen their fellow alchemists, but did nothing other than dump their teenage daughter to face a coming war? The Ying Clan, which was in line with the Inabrians in their belief that Cole is subhuman because he is a spirit of the wild?" Chely narrows her eyes in a flash of anger that tastes like blood. "We are more alike than you'd like to admit, Annie. I'm no sun, no matter how many times you told me that during the war. I cannot see how that's true. Being an oracle is a matter of perspective, isn't it? Anne is great with perspective, unlike you, Eyeless Oracle. The truth that matters to me is that Anne never once wavers in her conviction to see humanity in every living thing. I want her back."

"You are treading on ground that has not been walked before," The Oracle snickers. The indent between her eyebrows grows a concave, almost like a crack on top of a perfect porcelain cup. "You are the reason that Anne Barberry is here. The townsfolk who are stuck here—they are souls who don't deserve to move on. She—I have been trying to help the children who made it here by mistake to reach the other side. While you, Blood Hawk, are attempting to disrupt the natural balance of things!"

"Yes." Chely's face opens wildly to the possibility. She chases after it like an obsession, half-livid and feverish. It is the sole drive that has kept her going in the darkest of times. The war rages on, and she is not stepping down. "I am going to win, Eyeless Oracle. Stand aside and watch."

The liquid that boils in Anne's eye sockets slips out like melted metal, liquid silver as they trickle down The Oracle's pale face like tear stains. Chely tries not to let her heart hitch as she holds onto the orb and prepares for what is to come.

"You have lost your mind." The Oracle lunges at the red-haired alchemist. "You are even worse than the woman who murdered Brutus Barberry in front of a child!"

Chely easily dodges to the side with a twist of her shoulders. Anne's slim and slight form speaks of sleep deprivation and malnutrition. The oracle hasn't taken care of herself. The alchemist, on the other hand, has been busy since the war ended.

"The captain is dead, Annie," Chely replies with sadness. "Let Ark Li and Brutus Barberry go. Their feud is of a war from before we were even born. We need to start thinking of the future instead of the past."

The Oracle collides with the utensils that hang alongside the wall. The black crow squawks in alarm as he sweeps down to defend The Oracle as she fumbles with her eyes gone.

Chely has no idea why the black crow hasn't fallen into silence like the rest of Anne's creations with her knocked out. She pops open a container on her belt, an alchemical orb that freezes the motions of creatures temporarily, and aims at the familiar.

The black crow halts as if he is trapped by the air itself. He lets out a caw, desperate and angry. It sends chills down Chely's spine. It reminds her of the birds that flew above corpses in the war.

Like Anne, it is as if the familiar's eyes turn a different shade as he stares into Chely with emotions about to flood out.

"I'm sorry," the red-haired alchemist says. Whether it is to Anne or the familiar, Chely doesn't know.

Chely then bends down and pries open the crumbled oracle's mouth, and she pops the orb made of barberry onto her tongue. Anne's body scrunches up as memories hit the person inside.

Ying Cai-Li stands in the kitchen. Her form is silent and alone. She loosens the hold on the crow, whose first movement is to get to the oracle's side and peck at Anne's hair helplessly with his beak.

She watches the havoc she brings to Anne's house and wonders if the oracle knew this would happen from the moment Chely had walked through the front door.

The crow's voice grows desperate as the oracle remains on the ground.

"She's going to wake up, don't worry," says the red-haired alchemist. "Captain Ark's last gift will not be in vain. Besides, I still have a letter to deliver to Annie on her behalf."

10

On a Solo Sail

THAT'S HOW THE trip down memory lane starts. Because Ying Cai-Li stuffed an alchemical candy orb down Anne's throat.

It is bitter and sour, much like Cai-Li said it would be. It tastes like tears and ocean water, salty and un-nurturing.

Fucking asshole, Anne thinks to herself dimly. She should have let Cai-Li freeze to death in the wintery cold outside her castle.

Memories flutter across her mind like broken pieces of glass. Each piece is like a mirror, reflecting her face in different stages of her life. Each piece a knife, cutting her apart as Anne screams without sound.

Death by a thousand cuts would hurt less. The Aixauhan torture method saved for the worst of criminals. It would be fitting, as the Barberrys should be executed by the ghosts they left behind.

Ying Cai-Li stands in front of The Oracle, the smiling face that has tricked Anne once again. How many times is Anne going to fall for Cai-Li? How many times until Anne learns the lesson that the girl she loved is never coming back?

Her red hair flutters like the feathers of a crimson bird of prey, the dancing flame of the sun. The grin cuts across her face like a wound instead of a smile, never reaching her pitch-black eyes.

Anne's hero, gone. What is left behind is a mere husk, wearing a mask.

"Why are you doing this?" Anne wants to ask. She finally crawls her way to the present. Her past, an avalanche; her future, a tsunami. The Oracle who studied history knows the future and past, while Anne…she is merely an ant squashed under the boot of time.

"You think shutting out the memories is saving you, Annie." Cai-Li turns around and her appearance is of her younger self. The sun of her youth, joyful and brave. The spark in the dark, the rising hope of Anne's abyss of a life. Yet her face has a merciless quality to it. "It is not. It's killing you. Don't you see? The children you thought you killed, you saved them instead. But you suppressed that into your subconscious. Why? It's easier for you to believe yourself a monster like Brutus Barberry than for you to come to terms with the truth."

"The truth?" Anne's eyes swirl back to Cai-Li. "What is the truth?"

The red-haired alchemist softens. There are constellations beginning to dot Cai-Li's eyes.

"That you can't change the future, nor the past. Captain Ark Li's family, Cole's death, Cai-Li's descent. You are merely a witness, Annie. There is nothing you could have done to make things better or worse."

When the captain of the ship turned the cargo hold they were hiding in upside-down, Anne should have been worried about what would happen to them.

Cole was seeping into the floor, seasick from way too much salt in the air and way too low of an altitude. He was from the mountains and not made for sea-voyage. The orphans all huddled together like a bunch of lost lemmings, ready to jump ship if one of them thought it would be an easier death than whatever awaited them on board.

Chely was the only one who could still maintain a straight face and form half a sentence. The red-haired alchemist was the shield that stood in front of the group. A natural-born leader, Cai-Li led them through the acid rain and sinking earth. She snuck them onto this ship with the hope of it heading west of the conflict zone. But there had been something wrong with the information about which ship they were supposed to get on. This one they landed on had engaged in battles with both the Inabrian magicians and Aixauhan alchemists, and it had no intention of sailing away from the cannon fire and red-rinsed ocean at all.

The red-haired alchemist squeezed Anne's hand so tight the oracle felt like her bones would break.

Anne could be of no help to her girlfriend. The sea dislocated all her organs into a jumbled mess, and Anne feared if she opened her mouth, all that would come out was bile. The oracle couldn't feel her lungs through the burning sensation left by to the starvation and seasickness.

Anne tried to use spells against seasickness for herself and the kids. She didn't dare to try it on Cole, because who knew how it would react to the boy's unique constitution? Chely had politely declined the offer with a reassuring smile, but Anne knew she was seeing how Anne was about to faint and didn't think Anne could utter the vowels of the magic required correctly out of her trembling mouth. She was correct, so Anne didn't push. Gods knew there were two opposing magical armies out there trying to kill and torture them. Death by Anne's poor healing skills would be a pathetic way to end after their lame attempt at heroism.

Yet, this *was* the end. They had tried their best. They did what they had set out to do, to save as many kids as they could along the way while surviving this brutal war. Anne had seen everything with her very human sight that her childhood self had seen as an oracle. The ground covered with corpses as far as the eye could reach, the screams that used to sound like nails scraping against a chalkboard that were now just part of the daily routine.

They made it out alive to the docks. Half-alive. They lost several kids along the way, not to mention the parents of said kids. Ten cities and countless villages down the map, or whatever charred remains that were left behind after the armies had marched through where people used to inhabit. Magic or modern weaponry, everything that people could kill one another with had been tested and used, again and again.

"There will be such an influx of ghosts into the Afterlife," Chely whispered to Anne and Cole, in a desperate attempt to keep them awake. She was trying to be discreet, so the children didn't hear them.

"Shut up," Cole and Anne answered unanimously, not caring whether they were a little loud or not. The kids they traveled with had seen enough. A little mention of *the mountain of dead bodies* was not going to change that.

They would soon join them, Anne thought. The crew, with their swords and hooks and whatever the fuck that piece of wet wood was, are all aiming their weapons at them. They were millions of miles from land. There was no escape.

Such magic existed that could be used for teleportation, but they couldn't be monitored or performed with one person alone, so no matter how good at this shit Chely could be, she wouldn't be able to save them all, because Anne knew she'd be no help at all, and Cole was *dying anyway* because of the salt. Even if they weren't discovered, he wouldn't survive the fever that had grabbed onto him like a barnacle for long enough to reach land. Not without the right medication, which Chely could not make without access to a bowl-adjacent object in which to boil ingredients.

Even if she had the ingredients, the red-haired alchemist had admitted to herself that the Ying Clan were no healers. Chely had said it was more likely she might accidentally turn their friend into the living dead if she tried her hands on him.

"Stay back," Chely said sternly and clearly to the murderous pirate crew, who were closing in on them like a bunch of sea lions. She was made of a fire that even the high sea couldn't quench. When Anne told her girlfriend she was the only reason they hadn't fallen apart, Chely laughed.

Ying Cai-Li always said that she was fire. The one who held them together was Cole. After saving each other multiple times in the line of fire, the initial animosity between the oracle and the Yamalan boy became old news. They stared into Death's eyes too many times together for them to not become friends.

Why was Cole the one holding them together? Cai-Li's answer would be that Cole's spiritual core was metal. A malleable kind of metal that was almost a liquid. He adapted and changed form, but his essence stayed the same.

"That's what we need for the world after the war," Cai-Li would say. "Not water, but the kind of metal Cole is made of. By the end, he might be the only recognisable one among us all."

But what they needed now was fire. That was Chely.

"You cannot kill us without your captain present. It is against the Pirate Code among the free seafarers in Aixauhan waters."

"Seriously, girl?" One of the crewmen with a hatchet laughed at the same time as Anne muttered. Chely side-eyed Anne with an exasperated look. "You think we became the most feared crew on these waters by obeying the Code?"

"Well," Cole said to Chely while hiccupping out blood. His blood was the colour of grass. It was supposed to be transparent, just like the rest of him. That was not a good sign. "Not going to lie, Cai-Li. He's got a point."

Chely chuckled affectionately and morosely. Her face softened like a goldfish. With cheeks bulging outward because of a reverse-effect of dehydration and the colour of her hair, Ying Cai-Li was looking increasingly like a koi fish. The fish was supposed to be the Aixauhan symbol of royalty and good fortune. That was funny, Anne thought. Or, it would have been if they weren't about to fucking die.

"Shut up and lie down, Cole," the red-haired alchemist chided softly to her very sick, sworn brother. "Please don't question my authority in front of the people who are about to kill us."

"Please pay more attention to the fact that they are *about to kill us,* then," Anne bit back with the strength of a turtle being boiled alive without its shell on white-hot sand, dry and hoarse.

"Are you guys always so talkative before being killed?" A fourth voice joined their desperate attempt at humour before dying, sounding curious yet amused.

It was not one of the kids, who were still scared shitless and would be traumatized for the rest of their lives. Anne saw her own life flash before her eyes, knowing she was not going anywhere good after death. Being The Oracle, being the heir to the Barberry house, bearing the cursed legacy of what she knew—she would not meet the Creator and His peace. But the kids, they deserved something better. She'd heard of an afterlife from other nations, Aixauhans' belief in reincarnation cycles, or just the wide realms of a mirror world where no pain or sorrow could reach them. Children, especially dead children, after being destroyed by this war, deserved something better.

"Oh, gosh," the voice that intercepted sounded nearly aghast. "I thought we were like a bunch of army deserters or something. What we got is a bunch of kids instead?"

"Yes," Cai-Li desperately argued. "We've got kids here. They're orphans, their parents died in the war. You can kill me, but leave Anne and Cole alone. I heard the pirate ships always need free hands, and the kids can be of help. Some of them are magicians, like Maev.

She can walk into the afterlife and back. Just…the kids need familiar faces to be able to stay calm. Take me and let my friends live."

"Hmm," the voice hummed, nearly amused. "What are you talking about, child? I'm saying that *all* of you are kids. How old are you and the other oldest two? Sixteen, seventeen, eighteen? That's the age of adults in my book. If you're not enlisted, then we have no reason to kill you."

The voice belonged to a woman with a straw hat. Anne wanted to scream about what kind of asshole would wear a straw hat in the middle of the fucking ocean, but she had lost the nerve to do so. The woman wore an oversized coat that had been bleached out of colour by the sea salt, her features were that of an Aixauhan—straight black hair tied together by a piece of leather, black eyes shining like stars blinking across the velvety night sky—except those familiar features on Chely were arranged differently enough to make up a nightmare instead of a dream. The woman had no accent, but her attire indicated she was presenting herself more distinctly as an Aixauhan than Chely ever had.

"You must be the captain," Chely swiftly, without showing hesitation. "Nice to meet you."

The captain eyed them from under the hat that covered half of her face. "Smart observation," she said coolly while judging the stowaways.

Anne didn't know that they were much to look at. Yes, they looked half-dead. Could they please move the hell on?

"Are you deserters?"

"An Inabrian girl, a half-Inabrian and half-Yamalan boy, and an Aixauhan girl? Deserters? Together?" Anne laughed hysterically. She really didn't care if she was about to lose it, or about the careful tap Chely placed on her shoulder. "Come on, anyone with a pair of working eyeballs can see that we are not deserters."

"Really?" The captain's gaze rose to Anne, her onyx eyes swiftly checking the oracle up and down. "I have trouble telling Inabrians apart from one another. But you seem familiar. Are you famous, Inabrian child? I feel like I have seen you somewhere."

"Annie, goddammit," Cole muttered weakly, his voice as coarse as sandpaper. "The captain is so clearly Aixauhan. Do you need to draw attention to yourself? Are you stupid? It's clear you are the first they'll kill."

"Fuck off, Cole," Anne said back. "If they're willing to kill an Inabrian civilian who they confessed they see as a child, then they are no better than the Inabrian magicians who stoked the rightful grudge most Aixauhans have against Inabri. Isn't that right?"

Chely took a step forward and pushed Anne behind her. Cole was too sick to stand for Chely to shield.

"Enough," the red-haired alchemist said calmly to them, as if she were a shepherd and they had simply wandered off the right path. Chely turned back to the pirate captain. "My girlfriend does make a good point though. We are not soldiers. We are just trying to get the kids somewhere safe on land."

"Girlfriend, huh?" The pirate captain whistled. A fascination seemed to rise in her as she concentrated on Anne and Chely's intertwined fingers. "Young lovers. A girl from Inabri and a girl from Aixauh. How in the gods' name did that happen? Now that's worth keeping you alive, if only for you to tell me and my crew that tale."

"There's no story," Cai-Li replied. "We are going to survive this war and grow old together. That's all you need to know, Captain."

The captain eyed Chely up and down. She nodded once as if impressed by the bold claim. "You have some guts, girl. To be so firmly in your belief that you will survive the war when you're on death's door," she said, her voice casual. "It's as if you've seen the future."

"That's ridiculous." The lie rolled off the red-haired alchemist's tongue as natural as breathing. "There are few people who can see into the future, no matter which nation's practitioners of the craft you are talking about. We Aixauhans have no recorded talent in our millennia-old history. And the Inabrians…the Barberry Lineage announced their heir died of a mysterious illness right before the war started, didn't they? That was supposed to be the last oracle they produced."

"Well, that's true. But if you have a girl who can walk into and out of death with you"—The captain gestured at Maev, who tried to hide behind Anne and Cai-Li—"there might be other…unexpected talents among you. You appear fearless and bright, and you are an Aixauhan with red hair. It's not far-fetched to guess you probably have a blood connection to the Ying Clan. I cannot imagine why they would abandon one of their oh-so-bright children. Although, I guess if you're being lovey-dovey with an Inabrian girl, I can understand why they left you to fend for yourself."

That somehow made Anne's skin crawl. She was fine with the pirate captain insulting her; the Creator knew the amount of distrust and confusion that spread through the people when Cai-Li offered them help while she was accompanied by Anne Barberry. But this captain… there was something unsettling about her, like she knew where the vital parts of a human soul were and had learned how to twist the knife where it hurt for the living.

"My parents left because they were heartless jerks." Cai-Li's reply was determined and unwavering. "I choose my family now. You are an Aixauhan yourself, Captain? Then you'd know the Ying Clan is also known for their ambivalence to the common folk of Aixauh and their callousness to the Yamalans. I don't think they are your friends, even if we share the same nationality. My parents might have left me, but I have no doubt you know more than I do about how the Ying Clan left the rest of the alchemists and Aixauh to the Inabrian wolves in the last war."

A shadow danced across the pirate captain's face, but it was replaced by a satisfied smirk.

"You are quite right," the captain said. "Being a descendant of the Ying Clan would not endear you to any Aixauhan at all. But what you just said—that's something I can see potential in. You have a backbone, Ying Clan girl."

The pirate captain's words were verging on friendly. Her voice was somehow a rasp yet an unfathomably deep abyss, like a sea monster with salt sunk into its sharpened teeth but whose stomach had no end to it. Anne heard an underlying bloodlust under the compliment; the captain gave her the feeling of being lured into the belly of a shark without knowing why it was keeping them alive.

Chely's hand tightened around Anne's. Anne detected her discomfort despite not knowing how she could look sicker after weeks at sea. The red-haired alchemist flashed a reassuring smile that did little to soothe the weird gnawing in Anne's stomach. She tried to keep the warmth that traveled from Chely's palm to hers alive, but it was quickly dissolved by the chill and damp air of the ship's hull.

The children whimpered. Maev, who had dark brown skin and amber eyes, pulled at Anne's soaked skirt and whispered to the oracle, "This captain woman has cracks in her aura."

The girl, one who was only ten at the time, had the rare power of a Soul-Gazer. Along with the ability to travel between the realm of the living and the dead, Maev could also see the aura of a living person's soul.

"They're the kind of cracks that formed around the Inabrian soldiers who killed Mama and Papa. The kind that belong to those who enjoy sending at least one soul across the gates of death. I don't think we should stay on this ship."

That's just great, Anne thought. The oracle's dehydration was catching up to her mind so that she was halfway delirious. Of course, the pirate captain was some kind of murderer who enjoyed killing people. They were pirates, after all, renegades who ruled the sea, plundering the villages on the coast of their own people.

Realistically speaking, Anne was pretty sure they wouldn't be staying on the ship for much longer either way, since the crew looked ready to throw them overboard to be chewed on by whatever lurked in the ocean. But she couldn't say that to a girl whose mother had stepped on a landmine two weeks into the war, whose father had tried to keep it together for his little girl but wasted away until he couldn't outrun the soldiers one night as they were fleeing the acidic rain that ate away at everything it touched.

Acid rain. Had it been invented by the Inabrian magicians or an Aixauhan alchemists? Which side had killed Maev's father? Did it even matter? Anne couldn't discern the answer. When she was Maev's age, Anne had been taught the monsters were the Aixauhan alchemists. When she'd fallen in love with Cai-Li and gotten to know Cole, the monsters had become the Inabrian magicians. However, since the war started, the line between the two had blurred until it didn't matter anymore.

There are three kinds of people in a war—the people who are murderers, the people who are family, and the people who are in the afterlife.

No one ever talks about it, but surviving through a war is most akin to being drunk. In the beginning, you taste the bitterness and want to spit the disgusting liquid out. However, the people around you tell you to indulge in it—*just one more drop. Don't protest.* If you fight against it, then they'll hold your head down and force the alcohol down your throat as you're kicking and screaming until you become as drunk as everyone around you.

After the war would end, Anne would experience a withdrawal period from war. She would review so many letters and historical documents, talk to Inabrian magicians and common folk soldiers, talk to Aixauhan alchemists and their soldiers, talk to the civilians caught in the middle, talk to those who'd lost their family, as well as those who'd taken family away from others. Victims, war criminals, bystanders, survivors.

Clarity like water would sooth the drunkenness away bit by bit. It would be a long and grueling process, to wake up from a war. The mentality of us versus them, that would be the part Anne got good at recovering from. The hangover would linger in nightmares and sleep deprivation, in headaches and occasional memory loss. But Anne would know it was part of the process—she was healing.

Being drunk might have been comfortable. War made people who were caught in it dependent on it, almost like an addiction. Cole perished because he didn't get the chance to leave the war; Cai-Li—she lived, all right. But Anne sees the alchemist in her Castle, whose red hair is both fire and blood, and she realises that Cai-Li might never have purged the toxin of war from her veins.

"We won't let anything happen to you." Anne patted Maev on the head. Her conscience screamed alongside her sanity, because that was obviously a lie. "I promise you."

Do I really have the right to blame Cai-Li when I lied to myself, too, in order to survive the war? People shouldn't make promises they know they can't keep.

"Can you see it?" Maev asked, curiosity somehow overtaking the fear. Children were relentlessly resilient. "Did your Vision tell you we'll safely survive this?"

The spark of hope that glittered across the girl's eyes was like a galaxy safe from the bleakness of the abyss surrounding it. Anne turned her head away uncomfortably. She really couldn't answer that.

"Some of us," The Oracle replied.

She *foresaw* the war. She foresaw chaos and carnage. What she didn't foresee was whether the children would grow up or not. The

Oracle could only see things on a large scale, which basically rendered her Magic useless for those who needed it the most.

"We are counting on you having a backbone too, Captain." Chely's composed voice resonated through the cabin, like bells on towers. "I have seen enough of the Aixauhan navy in this war to know the way you run your crew is the same as they do their soldiers. You are a defector, aren't you? Maybe not from the war, but you are a *pirate.* You owe allegiance to no one other than your own conscience."

Little flames jumped in Chely Ying's eyes, flickers of them licking the edge of her hair. The ship's hull was dim. The red-haired alchemist glowed like a human torch.

The captain stared at Chely for a prolonged amount of time. Her eyebrows scrunched together. After an excruciating staring contest, where Anne could feel Chely's hand growing warmer and sweatier as it went on, the captain finally let go and shook her head.

"You are right, girl," The captain laughed. "You are indeed a Ying Clan alchemist. If I kill you and your friends, who knows whether you'd burn down my ship or not? You and your sunbird blood. After all, my ship is my and my crew's home. And it's very flammable. You are a pirate's natural enemy."

"Thank you." Chely smiled good-naturedly. "That idea did cross my mind, yes."

"Typical," Cole said weakly from the ground. He had a small smile on his face now that they had avoided mortal danger. "That's my sworn sister, ladies and gentlemen. A suicidal maniac who never tells her friends about her plans. Annie, you really should think about breaking up with this idiot after the war is over." He coughed very hard after finishing that sentence.

"Are you okay?" Anne ran toward him and knelt on the ground beside him. "You're speaking nonsense, Cole."

She put out a hand for him to grab. The boy coyly gave her a fist bump instead.

"No shit," Cole wheezed out. "We're pirates!"

"You are not," the captain commented dryly in the background. "We're dropping you at the nearest port that hasn't been sacked by the armies."

"Can you get him a medic?" Chely asked concernedly, but she kept her cool. "I know this is a pirate ship, but…"

"She can heal him," Anne cut off Chely's words and turned her gaze upon the captain.

"What?" The captain wasn't confused so much as she was surprised.

"Chely's not the only one who shows signs of being an alchemist." Anne waved her hand quickly. She was too sick to dig deep into the thought, but this much was clear—she was not willfully ignorant enough to gamble with Cole's life. "Every Aixauhan ship has a healer. They're from minor alchemist clans. Alchemy is not traditionally used for healing. So, the healer clans are not as well-known as the old names like the Yings among your people. There's no one in your crew who appears to have alchemical power. That means…you are not just the captain of the ship, but also an alchemist. A healer alchemist."

"Huh." The captain watched Anne as if she wanted to plunge a sword into her skull. Her words teetered close to danger. "For an Inabrian girl, you sure are knowledgeable about Aixauhan alchemists and our history. I wonder…did the Ying girl give you these detailed introspections or perhaps—"

"I told her." Chely stepped up instantly. "I am a big fan of history."

Cai-Li had told Anne nothing of the sort. The red-haired alchemist was more likely to burn history documents as kindling than read them for fun. Chely was so eager to bury her past, as if trying to bury the memories of her parents.

The pirate captain didn't question further. Anne doesn't know if it was mercy or true ignorance. Ark Li would be a mystery till the very end.

"Maybe what you have is true love, then," the captain mused. "There were many Inabrians in my time who lived amongst the town where my clan resided. They sometimes fell in love with Aixauhans; sometimes they even bore children. Much like the Yamalan boy, he's mixed, right? But I'm guessing it didn't end well. That's how almost all Inabrian-Aixauhan love stories end. In another lifetime, it could be a fairytale. But in the world now, it is nothing but a fantasy. I don't know what your history is, but from the sizable samples I have, Ying alchemist, your girlfriend knows more than most of those Inabrians who spent decades in my town, spreading the words of their Creator, coming to my parents' place when they contracted disease— as is common for people who go to a place not meant for them—only to stand on the Inabri army's side when our clan was slaughtered."

"I'm sorry," Anne said instinctively. She didn't even know the extent to which she should be sorry, at least not then, when the captain hadn't yet announced her family name.

"No, Annie. You aren't responsible for whatever happened. You were not even conceived when the last war happened!" Chely snarled. There was rage that spiked through the patient facade. "Captain, I've heard of the healer clans. I know that, unlike the older alchemical families, you see the Yamalans as celestial and divine. So, can I assume you will help keep my sworn brother here alive?"

"I do have the blood of a healer clan," the captain said. "But like you, Ying girl, I very much have nothing to do with my parents other than my family name. I chose a life at sea first as a soldier, then as a pirate. I've taken more lives than I've ever saved. The knowledge I do possess, I learned in my youth. I can't make any promises, but yes, you are right, I will try my best for one of the Yamalans. They are the purest of souls; they earned their life through gaining enlightenment. Unlike us, who are born of flesh and bone. Their souls are pure, devoid of sin."

Sin? Anne thought faintly. That was a weird thing to hear an alchemist say. The Aixauhan alchemists did have their gods, but never had Anne Barberry hear Cai-Li speak of the concept of *sin* as if there was divine morality in Aixauhan gods.

However, that was the limitation of Anne's perspective. She was a Barberry at her core; how much did she truly know of the Aixauhans, no matter how much research she did? Unless she transcended her birth and became an immortal observer, Anne Barberry would forever be an Inabrian magician first.

"Er, I wouldn't say I'm devoid of sin or anything," Cole said weakly. "I'm not a snob. The whole concept of pure souls sounds way too much like Inabrian magician mumbo-jumbo. Reminds me of Anne before she grew a brain."

"Wow," Anne muttered sarcastically. "Thanks a lot, Cole."

"You're welcome," Cole grunted as he rolled onto his back. "Now, Captain Weirdo. Please help if I'm, like, holy or something. Last time I felt this bad was when I ate Anne's cooking."

"You better heal fast, Cole," Anne said, "so I don't feel bad when I drop-kick you off the fucking deck."

"Okay," the captain said as she watched the interaction. She pulled the straw hat off and let her face be seen in full. "Oran and Logan, get the Yamalan boy to the medicine cabin. Prepare some fresh water; I'll cool it down. The Yamalans do better when the temperature is closer to that of their homeland, with its high altitudes. What is your element, boy?"

"Er, metal?" Cole replied.

"Okay, that's the broad category." The captain waved her hand impatiently. "What kind of metal?"

Cole's eyes went to Chely, as if lost. "Just metal?" he said, confused. "That's what everyone has for their element, right? Metal, wood, water, fire, or earth?"

"No, that's the way Aixauhan alchemists categorise the elements in broad strokes," the captain said. "I can see you don't know much about yourself, Yamalan boy. I can help you learn as you heal. For now, tell me, what is your other name? The one your Yamalan parents gave you in their language."

Cole paused for a moment before he said, "Shui-Yin. My mum called me Shui-Yin."

"That's in Northern Aixauhan." The captain's brows furrowed as if in disapproval. "What has happened since I last saw your people? The Yamalans have their own language."

"My mum traveled with Cai-Li's parents," Cole replied. "So, I guess maybe that's why?"

Chely's face scrunched up in embarrassment. "Unfortunately, yes," she confirmed.

"Okay." The captain shook her head. "The Ying Clan, what the hell. I guess that's what happens when one believes themselves to be a descendant of emperors and gods. That's sacrilege, to ask a Yamalan spirit to take on an Aixauhan name. No wonder you call him by a meaningless Inabrian syllable, Ying girl."

"I know, right?" Chely answered flatly. "I hate it too."

"I'm happy you think I'm really cool," Cole said. "But can you, like, help me first instead of being offended by my name on my behalf? I'm still dying."

"Right," the captain said. She ordered two of the crew members to come forward and lift Cole up with surprising gentleness and practice. "Yi-Tian, get some dried hyacinth orchid; some of his wounds look infected. Omizu, too, just in case he starts coughing out blood. Also, crack open a few seawater measurement scales for the element the boy needs, from my alchemy kit, from the kitchen cabin, anything we have on the ship that has the boy's element in them."

Anne had no idea what was going on. "What are they talking about, Cai-Li?" she asked Chely eagerly.

"Shui-Yin," Chely replied. "The Yamalans' elements aren't like ours. Well, mine. We alchemists, we're flesh and bone, we have blood like you. It's different for the Yamalans. They have blood, yes, but it's not the same. Their elements are quite literal, and therefore more specific."

That didn't answer Anne's question. She still felt like her head was in the clouds.

"Don't question it too much, girl," the captain said. "What Yamalan elements are to them is what the future is for you. It's not possible to articulate to those who do not know."

Anne nodded. There was something glaringly wrong with that sentence that stared Anne Barberry in the face for years. Only now does the oracle hear it clearly.

A cold creeps down her spine. A glimpse of white bones sticking out of the ground…

She must have noticed though. Not intentionally, yet the suspicion would be a thorn that lodged in her heart. Anne would never trust the captain, not even after the woman saved them from oblivion. The way the captain bit into the words, "the future," it was as if she wished to shatter them with her canine teeth.

Chely, however, was almost glowing with fascination.

"You are really a healer, aren't you?" Chely said. "I'm sorry for my rudeness. It's just…I thought the healer clans had mostly gone, because…"

"You are right; I'm the last of my clan," the captain replied. "My name is Ark Li. You can call me Captain Ark."

11

Drunk

CHELY CARRIES ANNE back to her room. The Oracle's slackened form fills the red-haired alchemist with guilt.

Anne's familiar, the black crow that had desperately tried to ward Chely off, has gone somewhere to sulk. Chely initially anticipated further animosity from Anne's companion, but the familiar seems to realise there is nothing more to be done. Either the familiar thinks he can no longer save Anne from Chely's clutches, or he knows Chely's intentions are not malicious.

It's most likely the former, but a small part of Chely wishes it were the latter.

The Inabrians see black crows as a harbinger of death, same as the black cat, a symbol of misfortune. But the Aixauhans have no such beliefs; crows and cats are creatures of great intelligence and are among the spirits of the wild who gain enlightenment—bird and cat spirits are among the most common.

All of this is second-hand knowledge, passed down by Chely's parents and Captain Ark Li—broken pieces of the red-haired alchemist's heritage that run in her veins yet are as distant as the sun god to his human descendants.

"So, does it really come as that much of a surprise?" Chely mutters as she lays Anne on the soft sheets of her bed. The alchemist runs her fingers through the oracle's stream of hair. Soft as silk. Luminescent like liquid gold. "That I inherited the second-hand callousness from my parents, and the second-hand rage from the captain?"

The worst example of an Aixauhan alchemist.

Captain Ark Li is the one who taught Chely about the different herbs and plants of Aixauh, which significantly expanded her horizons when it came to alchemy.

The intricacy of ingredients listed in the Aixauhan language that was often lost in translation was one thing The captain helped Chely with the most. Chely studied alchemy in her mother tongue, with the ingredients written by millennia of Aixauhan alchemists for their students who resided in Aixauh. No one had particularly curated an encyclopaedia for Aixauhan alchemists who had to make do with substitution of such ingredients in the Inabrian geographical ecosphere.

For example, parsley and coriander. Both of them were translated into the same word in Aixauhan writing: 香菜, meaning the "leaves with a sweet scent." So, imagine twelve-year-old Chely's surprise when she put parsley into her mixing instead of coriander and realised that it called upon ghosts instead of coming out as an edible soup. Or the time when she asked for "daisy tea" and was laughed at by the entire magician summer camp when what Chely meant was chrysanthemum tea—both flowers were of the same shortened name of 菊花 (Ju-hua) in Aixauhan. There were endless mix-ups like this, and those were only the herbs you could eat or drink. Chely can't even count the accidents she's had while making alchemy-related things.

Ark Li was the first alchemist Chely met who was an expert on the subject. Being from a healer clan of alchemists, the well-traveled captain was the closest to a master of substituting different ingredients found on foreign land by incorporating them into traditional Aixauhan alchemical formulas that Chely could get. Chely knew it from the moment Captain Ark saved Cole by cracking open all the measuring meters and thermometers from the ship. The captain knew what Cole needed simply by asking his name. Something that, despite their lifelong friendship, Chely somehow didn't think about.

Ark Li was the kind of alchemist that Ying Cai-Li strived to become. Everything Chely wished she was but was not thanks to her parents. The captain was the reflection in the mirror that Chely wished to see of herself, a version of Ying Cai-Li who grew up among the hills and lakes of her ancestors, knowing the name of every blade of grass, the shape of every leaf, the traces of the gods and animal spirits dancing in the air. All of it had come to Chely as textbook names and descriptions under her alchemist parents' explanations and guidance, but it had never been lively as if she'd borne the sight and taste of Aixauh with her own five senses.

Unlike Chely, who had been disregarded by her parents, Captain Ark Li carried the legacy of her clan as a healer. The sole surviving member of a renowned alchemist clan.

There was a purpose to the captain's alchemist identity. There was a history.

The red-haired alchemist did not know back then that history and purpose born from war were nothing to envy.

Two years after the war ended, Anne told Chely the story of Brutus Barberry, from his role in the First War until his gruesome end. They were having a quiet night in The Cottage. It was the middle of summer; flower fields were in full blossom, and only the sound of birds chirped in the distance.

They were having dinner together, and Chely can't remember what they were eating. However, she does remember that Anne was in a good mood—she'd gotten her first contract from a publisher asking her to join Reparation historians in compiling the first volumes of written accounts of the First and Second Inabrian-Aixauhan Wars. The endless nights of showing dedication to the past by tireless correspondence and interviews were paying off, and The Oracle's name was becoming known in both Inabri and Aixauh as one of a peacemaker.

In celebration of Anne's new career trajectory, Chely insisted they open a bottle of wine. It made Anne crinkle her nose, but the oracle was sleeping better than the year before. The need for sleep-inducing alchemical orbs had become infrequent, so the responsible Anne Barberry relented to Chely's stubborn insistence of the alcohol.

Anne drank from the Chalice of Truth. One full cup in, the oracle was already slurring her words. Chely drank the rest straight from the bottle, which the alchemist emptied in less than three gulps, making Anne laugh giddily.

"How—how do you manage to drink like a sailor?"

"Well, we were kind of sailors for a while in the war." Chely watched Anne's red cheeks. There was a dreamy smile on the oracle's face, as if a spell had made the marble stone into malleable white yeast. The red-haired alchemist drank in the sight of her love being drenched in joy more so than the taste of fine wine. "You didn't join us, but the captain invited me and Cole to many drinking sessions. She beat us every single time, given I have the Ying Clan's element of fire and Cole with his Yamalan element of metal. Captain Ark might have seemed like a rock, but seeing her drunk...? It truly was the biggest reminder that she is flesh and bone."

The smile blossoming on Anne's face withered away. Solemnity overtook the reddened cheeks of the drunk oracle.

"She *is* just a human being, isn't she?" Anne asked, her pitch low and voice small. "Flesh and blood."

"I mean, yeah," Chely said. "I know she scares you or whatever, but to be honest, the captain's not that much older than us. And when you see her trying to cope with a hangover, or when she tended to Cole's wound? There was a softness in her, like she was once someone's older sister."

Chely expected the oracle to scoff or snicker at the mention of the captain's name. The three of them had never met up following the war, despite being the few familiar remaining faces from that time. A cloud settled over Anne's face whenever the captain was brought up; despite fighting side by side till the very end, something still blocked Anne's ability to perceive the captain as more than the steely exterior Ark put on.

This time, however, with the sun setting outside The Cottage, making the sky the pinkish hue of a flower bud, a soft breeze carried a few strands of Anne's hair into the air, and a single tear rolled down the oracle's face.

"She *was* someone's older sister," Anne said. "There is something I need to tell you, Cai-Li."

The wine loosened the oracle's tongue. It was on that beautiful and peaceful day that Anne told Chely how she had witnessed the murder of her grandfather Brutus.

And that the oracle had known for a long time that the captain had been the murderer that night.

The Oracle found out the truth herself not long after they made the captain's acquaintance. Then, Anne shrugged it off and moved on with the war, telling no one. Not Chely. Not Cole.

When Anne finally told Chely about the past that entangled the Barberrys and the Lis, she said it in a calm tone, as if recounting someone else's story.

The oracle spoke about Ark Li as if what she had done to Anne's grandfather was just another puzzle piece that fit into the bigger picture. A picture that Anne increasingly grasped at as if she weren't part of it.

Watching Anne as the twilight flooded into The Cottage, Chely, for the first time, had the thought that she might not be able to catch up with Anne.

"Why didn't you tell me any of this?" Chely slammed the bottle onto the table, almost shattering the glass. "If I had known you saw the captain murder someone in front of you, I would have got us out of there as soon as I could!"

Anne was surprised at this. "Why would you do that?"

"Because she *murdered* your grandfather in front of you!" Chely spat out. "You are traumatised by it! And *don't* say that's not the case. I've heard you scream for your grandpa in your nightmares enough times to know it still affects you. Gosh, Annie! Why didn't you tell me?"

"Because…" Anne's face was perplexed. Her voice, however, was as calm as the surface of a still pond. "Ark Li had a reason. Brutus Barberry was responsible for the death of her entire clan. Not to mention the more horrifying things he did to…well, you know. It made sense for her to want revenge for her people. You can surely relate as her fellow Aixauhan alchemist—you've seen the Inabrian magician lineage's ideologies, you've experienced their prejudice and hate."

"Sure, she had a reason to be angry," Chely said. "But that doesn't negate the fact you have the right to be angry too! She knew there was a child in the castle, as you said yourself. Killing someone's grandpa in front of a child? That's fucked up!"

"You don't have to keep calling Brutus my grandfather in order to humanise him." Anne sighed. "I know you hate the Inabrian magicians, Cai-Li. He's a monster and deserved his end."

"For fuck's sake, I'm not trying to *humanise* him!" Chely yelled. A primal urge made her huff out sparks of fire. "I'm angry *for* you, Annie! I'm angry for my girlfriend, who saw someone she loved killed in front of her! Just because he deserved to die doesn't mean you don't have the right to grieve, Annie. You know that, right?"

From Anne's silence, Chely got the distinct feeling the oracle did not agree at all.

The red-haired alchemist lets Anne rest in her room for a full day and night. The orb of remembrance is not easily digested. It will be some time before it takes effect. The memories won't rush back to Anne in one go.

Most likely, the oracle will wake up with a massive hangover, thinking most of the memories rushing back to her are just a dream. Chely might still have a few days—when Anne is sobering up, groggy and confused—before she truly loses Annie for good.

"Anne?" The red-haired alchemist knocks on Anne's bedroom door. "Are you awake?"

"Do you think I would forget what happened, Ying Cai-Li?"

Chely's heart seizes. The door opens from the inside. Anne Barberry emerges from behind. Her eyes are misty and unseeing, like The Oracle yesterday.

"You are…" Chely whispers under her breath. Those grey eyes do not have the metallic clarity of a silver dagger. This is not Anne.

"Annie, I know this looks bad, but I can explain."

The oracle's stonelike face breaks apart into a giant grin.

"What is there to explain?" Anne's breath catches inches away from Chely; there is the floral scent of Earl Grey within it. However, there is also something sweet and pungent in that breath, like ethanol. "We talked about Ark. I told you the truth about what happened to Brutus Barberry, and then I passed out after drinking."

Chely pauses for a moment.

Sure, the orb of remembrance can make the subject feel like they're hungover from a drunken night. But it shouldn't do the opposite of what it is intended for—namely, help Anne remember the truth of this place rather than stirring her deeper into memory alteration.

The red-haired alchemist rummages through her memory of the previous day, trying to surmise what could have gone wrong to prompt this to happen.

"Oh, crap." Chely's brain snaps in half as she thinks of the properties of ethanol—

A clear and colourless liquid.

Chely thinks back to the alchemical process yesterday as she mixed the ingredients for the orb of remembrance. A heavy white smoke blurred her vision. She remembers putting in a crucial ingredient: a clear and colourless liquid.

Only, it was not supposed to be ethanol.

Chely's hand quickly settles on her belt, which she takes with her everywhere, which holds alchemical vials containing the most important ingredients. She checks the labels of each vial, and there it is—the critical mistake she made.

The vial containing ethanol is empty, while the one next to it, containing the correct ingredient that was supposed to make up the orb of remembrance, is full.

"Shit," Chely curses again.

"What—what is that?" Anne slurs. She stumbles close to Chely's chest as the oracle screws her eyes to focus on the label on the full vial. "M…"

"Nothing," Chely announces loudly. She swipes the end of her shirt to cover the vials on her belt. "It's nothing you need to concern yourself with, Annie."

Anne's eyes, however, are filled with a hardness that wasn't there before.

"I know what it is, Cai-Li." the oracle's voice is soft like a breeze that chides the petals of a bluebell to lower its head. "You're not letting it go, are you? I know what you are doing, but it's not what Cole would have wanted. You've gotta stop. I cannot lose you too."

Chely's eyes widen. It is as if someone's suddenly poured acid onto her face. The red-haired alchemist is dragged back to the days after the war just ended. At that time, Anne was still trying to make their relationship work. Chely suspected the oracle knew what the red-haired alchemist was doing behind her back, yet Anne never said a word until she left.

These words are not from the Anne Barberry of today, but from the Anne Barberry of ten years ago. The same Anne who told Chely of the truth of Ark Li in a desperate attempt to dissuade her lover from walking down the same, wrong path.

"I'm sorry, Annie," Chely replies to the drunk Anne. She wishes they were back at The Cottage, instead of here at this castle. "There is no going back now, I'm afraid."

The Oracle, however, does not reply. "I love you, Ying Cai-Li." She falls forward into Chely's arms with a string of giggles before passing out again.

"You are very drunk, Annie," Chely replies. "Let's get you to bed."

Chely stays in Anne's room for the rest of the day. It takes a while before the ethanol wears off, and every time the oracle wakes up and asks for water, Chely gives Anne some with the correct ingredient for orb of remembrance mixed in.

As a seasoned alchemist, Chely should have known better. This will have to suffice though. The orb of remembrance is partly for helping Anne to regain her memory and partly for helping the oracle to get out of this place. It isn't too late, the red-haired alchemist hopes.

When The Oracle is awake, however, she has an awful lot to say about Captain Ark Li.

"Captain Ark Li was a real asshole," Anne shouts to the ceiling. "Honestly, screwwwww her. I knooooow she had a good reason to, like, want to kill Brutus Barberry dead. But, like, really? Couldn't she have picked a better time? The superb strategist captain, my ass. The woman didn't even knoooow how to plot a goddamn fucking murder without having a child in the way. Idiot."

"Right," Chely says. She helps Anne to lie back down before the oracle can hit her head on the headboard. "I, er, I suppose the captain wasn't thinking straight, exactly. People don't tend to be logical when committing murder out of revenge, Annie. That's kind of the point."

"How do you know what it feels like to want revenge?" Anne asks. "You are literally okay with dating me, an Inabrian magician, part of one of the lineages that are responsible for the slaughtering of Aixauhan alchemists."

Chely sighs. "I do feel vengeful on behalf of the Aixauhan alchemists, my love." There is no point in hiding it any longer, not when Anne won't remember this conversation. It is nearly done. "Not going to lie, I understand why Ark did what she did. I don't… I never felt that sort of allegiance to the Aixauhan alchemists. It's because I lost things I truly valued that I understand the kind of rage that could turn a healer of the Li Clan into a cold-blooded murderer."

"Don't say things like that, silly." Anne's eyes turn tearful. "You are the one destined…destined to survive the war and accomplish something unprecedented with youuur life. Ying Cai-Li, promise me you won't waste your life on someone unworthy."

"Annie…" Chely's heart hitches. She wipes away Anne's tears. "It's like you always say: we should not make promises we can't keep."

"Boooooooooo," Anne lets out a long, dismayed sound. "Such a killjoy. Chely, what have you become?"

"I don't know, Annie." Chely tries not to let the emotions that are eating away at her stomach show on her face. "I don't know."

Chely remembers the only time she met Anne as a child. The oracle looked bored, and her eyes were the colour of storm clouds under the tree's shade. Hollowness and burden made the girl look more tired than her age under the bright sun of summer.

The red-haired alchemist once thought she was the one who could put colour back into Anne's face, with flirtatious words and pecks on the cheek.

Chely wanted to be the one who lifted that burden from Anne's shoulder. Again. Again and again.

When Anne finally starts snoring, Chely confesses to the dark.

"I lied, Annie. I know what I've become."

A monster.

Anne drops onto the bed and falls asleep like a rock.

She acts like Chely is a safe harbour, as if there isn't a rift between them that Anne made sure to let Chely know will never be bridged. A mistake that Chely cannot unmake, nor does the alchemist offer to.

"I think I could use some of the alcohol Anne left behind," Chely mutters to herself before carefully closing the door behind her and walking down the hallway as silently as she can.

That is when she hears the knock at the door.

It doesn't make sense for Chely to be able to hear what goes on at the front door this deep into the castle. But if she's learned anything, it is that the Barberry Castle has more layers than it first appears. It is a winding trap of endless corridors and zig-zagging patterns. No wonder it was such huge news when Ark Li successfully broke into a castle with so much defence magic piling up around it that it's like a thick mist.

It is probably one of the townspeople or tourists who are here for The Oracle's Vision, Chely thinks.

As it takes her a bit of time to find the door, the knocking continued in a rhythmic yet increasingly impatient beat.

"Coming!" Chely says loudly as she gets to the door. "I'm sorry, The Oracle is not really in the headspace to provide her services—"

The person blasts the castle door open. Bits of debris catch in Chely's hair. The red-haired alchemist is knocked away by the blow upon impact.

"Where is Annie, Blood Hawk?" Maev Yahaya asks with an enraged look on her face. The black crow, who was missing for the whole day, is perched upon her shoulder. His white eyes settle on Chely with a look of disdain that mirrors Maev's. "I cannot let you do this to her!"

The girl holds nothing back at all. Maev has grown tall in the ten years since the war. Chely coughs her lungs out as she pulls herself back up. The world is a kaleidoscope, spinning out of control.

"It's too late, Maev," the red-haired alchemist croaks. The grin that breaks out on Ying Cai-Li's face is a wicked and remorseful thing. Chely smears a hand across her face, and it comes out bloody. "I see you found Anne's familiar. Did he lead the way for you? Or was it the missing kids who Anne helped send off into the afterlife?"

12

The Children of War

MAEV YAHAYA IS not dead. She is a Soul-Gazer who simply can peek into the paths souls take along their journey toward the afterlife.

It was a useful tool during the war. It kept Maev alive as a child to avoid the parts of the battlefield where tens upon thousands of freshly deceased wailed on the road. However, it hadn't kept her parents alive.

The afterlife is many-branched. It diverges into large chunks before deviating again into smaller strings until it becomes the grand shape of an eternal tree whose roots run deep and branches reach high.

There are as many afterlives as there are different kinds of magic. Maev's power is one that neither Inabrian magicians nor Aixauhan alchemists could decipher. Her family were merchants, travelling across the globe like nomads. Unfortunately caught in the middle of a war zone.

She almost followed her parents' ghosts right into the afterlife. Everything was on fire. The acid rain melted away the skin and flesh of those around her. She watched their souls wiggle out from their bodies, each squirming and writhing in agony as they became smokeless white flames, each taken away to somewhere Maev couldn't follow. Including her parents.

Maev was ready to try to follow her father, whose skeleton lay next to her but whose soul beckoned her to come with him, when Ying Cai-Li found her.

"Annie! Cole! There is someone left alive! A child, I think."

The red-haired alchemist was a warm silhouette. Grey ashes flew across the sky, mingled with white bones and ghosts, black charcoaled souls. Maev's eyes were almost scorched by the intensity of the older girl's hair. The crimson hue was not close to dark maroon, the colour of blood, but the shifting colours of bright fire blossoming on logs as her family camped outdoors on their travelling.

Maev thinks back on how she must have looked—a dark-skinned girl on the brink of death, standing next to her father's corpse. A liability to anyone who would take her in. Neither Inabrian nor Aixauhan, she'd starve in the carnage. No one would bother to save a child in war, not when that child was not theirs.

"I'm going with my dad," Maev muttered in the language of her people. She then switched to Inabrian, to the dancing flame in front of her. "I won't stay here. Don't worry."

The dancing flame stopped moving. The red-haired alchemist came close to Maev's blurred view. She gently reached out with the palm of her hand, which Maev stared at with confusion and numbness.

"Is that your dad next to you?" Ying Cai-Li asked. The red-haired alchemist pointed at the skeleton next to her.

Distantly, Maev thought she heard a gasping sound. A woman with yellow hair like dandelion flowers covered her mouth with her hands. A young man whose eyes were sapphire blue and hair was milk-white made a choked noise.

Maev would come to know them as Anne and Cole. They were not a woman and a man, but a girl and a boy. Not until Maev had lived past Cole's age, and kept living till she reached Anne's age, would she finally understand that despite how big they had looked from her childish vantage point, the three were the age of barely grown adults.

A bunch of smaller hands clutched their torn clothes. Children huddled behind the two more distant figures like a pack of hungry cubs. They blurred together, each one eyeing Maev with curiosity, each one followed by white ghosts of their parents like Maev's own father. They wished to take their children away to a safer afterlife where there was no pain and sorrow yet wished their children could survive the war intact.

"Not the fleshless corpse," Maev scrunched up her nose and said to the dancing flame. She pointed to her dad, who stood featureless beside Ying Cai-Li, a white, colourless flame next to the alchemist's scarlet hue. "He is right next to you. He's holding out his hand. Leave me here, and I'll join him soon."

The calmness in her voice made the flame-haired alchemist hitch. A string of emotions flashed across Ying Cai-Li's face. Shock, confusion, pity, but in the end, resolution.

Maev would not have imagined that one day those expressions could be wiped clean from the alchemist's face. The vibrant dancing fire of Ying Cai-Li who could not hide herself, like a stove failing to conceal its warmth. Those emotions would one day burn to ashes and leave nothing but a smiling husk behind.

"You can see the dead?" Ying Cai-Li's voice asked in awe. "That's… gosh, that's some terrible gift you've been blessed with, being a child born from war."

Maev shook her head. "It's not a terrible gift," she replied. "Death is not painful; it is like going home. There is no home here, can't you see? Everything is burning to the ground. Leave me, I'll be another mouth to feed."

Despite telling the red-haired alchemist off three times, Ying Cai-Li did not turn her gaze away from Maev once. She stood there with a conviction that belonged only to the gods, determined to save the child in front of her, no matter the odds.

"Your dad will always be waiting," Cai-Li said. "He will be on the other side. You will join him one day, so why the hurry?"

The red-haired alchemist held out a hand to the tiny Soul-Gazer.

Side by side, Cai-Li's crimson flame silhouette and the spirit of Maev's father both offered a hand. Both smiling, each asking Maev to join them.

"Maev, come with me," her father beckoned. "Let's go to your mother. She's waiting for us."

Maev saw the world waiting for her on the other side. The enchanted night where fire logs burned, where she'd once again lay her head on her mother's lap as she fell asleep while the caravan rumbled across bumpy roads, where her father gently ran his hands through her hair and called her his Little Soul-Gazer.

Any other child might be tempted by the view.

Maev saw the afterlife with one eye, and life with another.

She reached out her tiny palm and put her hand in Ying Cai-Li's.

Maev chose life. Every single time.

The red-haired alchemist smiled. Not a hollow smile that did not reach her eyes, but a smile that warmed Maev's heart.

The child of war was reborn in the alchemist's arms. Maev would grow up in a more peaceful world thanks to those who saved her.

Every line of magic and every worldview leads to one form of the afterlife.

The afterlife is the destination, but the souls linger sometimes in places called the In-Between. There can be many causes for this delay. Some are like Maev's parents, who stayed at an In-Between until Maev presumed to be at her peaceful end, so the family can reunite and get on a caravan to continue their travels. Ying Cai-Li was right; the peaceful afterlife is always there waiting. There is no rush to meet up with those lost.

So, before Maev died, she wasn't going to sneak around these In-Between places. She wanted to give her parents time, and she wanted the reunion to mean something. There are rules to the living and the dead that a Soul-Gazer learned to respect, especially a Soul-Gazer who was also a child of war.

Death is trivial and mundane; the afterlife is vast and eternal. Life is the most fascinating and precious state to be in, not death.

Maev did travel through the afterlife though. During the war, she had asked the ghosts of the In-Between and the afterlife to point the group away from conflict zones that resulted in mountains of corpses. After the war, Maev's gift gave those who'd lost their loved ones comfort, as she became the messenger for the living to the dead and vice versa.

There were so many words she carried from one side to the other. Maev made it her living. However, there was only one rule. A rule she built upon the foundation of the philosophy that had formed when the red-haired alchemist saved Maev's life.

"No matter what you wish to communicate to your loved one, you have to do it with the intention of letting go. I will not be the facilitator of your joining your dead loved ones, nor will I deliver the eagerness from the dead for the living to quench the thirst of the eventual reunion. I am here to help you move on so you can live your life in full."

It worked for the most part. Maev felt good about herself. She might have been born during wartime, but the child of war grew up to become an adult of peacetime. Most of the children from the group that Cole, Anne, and Cai-Li had picked up managed to blend into the era of peace quite well.

When Maev visited her friends, she found their ghostly parents no longer hovered around them. That put a smile on Maev's face.

It was thanks to their three heroes that so many ghosts were at peace. And that so many children lived to see tomorrow.

"What happened?"

When Maev barged into The Cottage, she didn't waste time on courtesy. The place was like a second home to her, to all the orphans who were saved by The Cottage's occupants during the war. A place they'd always be welcomed in without questions asked.

"She can't be…I saw her yesterday! She came by to say that she was going to visit someone for an interview. How can she be dead?"

Chely's hair had grown from the short length she'd kept it as a teenager. The dancing flame that bloomed from the sides of her ear combusted into a cloud of scarlet and shriveled into maroon as it poured down the sides of her head. It was like seeing a volcano chopped in half by a gigantic axe for the lava to bleed out and cool into red earth. The rotting corpse of a fire god whose blood was wetting the earth after being shot down from the sky.

"I'm really sorry," Chely said to Maev with a patient look on her face and a sad smile. The red-haired alchemist ritualistically tried to comfort Maev, as it was instinct baked into her. "Anne and I had a fight. It was my fault. Anne stormed out. I waited for her from dusk till dawn, but she never returned. I went through her stuff and found her calendar. She planned to meet up with Patricia—her sister. I didn't know where they were supposed to meet, so I went asking around in the town. The Innkeeper—he was the tailor's son.

I met him through Anne—he says that the Barberry family left, except for Patricia. She still lived at the Castle."

"What—" Maev heaved. She drew the natural conclusion from the words of the alchemist. It didn't make any sense. "Isn't…isn't Anne's sister younger than I am? Wasn't she a kid when the Second War ended? How does she have anything to do with Anne being…?"

"Yeah." Chely's face was calm as she said, "I found Anne's body there. Patricia is the one responsible. The wards around The Barberry Castle lift for no one other than those of the Barberry Lineage, and the ones invited into it by the blood of the lineage. After Brutus Barberry's murder, they took a lot more precautions to shield themselves. But I guess they didn't take into account the fact that the castle never disowned Anne. So, I went in without much problem."

Maev didn't know what else to say. Her lips trembled as Cai-Li recounted the events in a calm tone.

"Do you think they can save her?" Maev asked as tears ran down her face. "They must be able to save her, right? I mean, Patricia was her family. How bad can it be? How can anyone that young be so filled with hate for their own sister?"

"Anne's gone, Maevy." Cai-Li shook her head. A dream-like smile floated onto her face, like the white belly of a dead fish floating on the river. "They took her to the medical unit. But Patricia knew what she was doing. They couldn't do much for Anne. They were trying to tell me to have hope, but we've seen bodies that are beyond help. Anne's body was beyond help. She's gone."

Maev fell onto the ground. There was something detached about Anne Barberry that almost made Maev think it was an impossible truth. No matter how kind Anne had been to her, there had always been a distant air surrounding The Oracle. A wall built up between the blonde-haired Inabrian and the rest of the kids.

The Soul-Gazer had once thought it was because The Oracle was an Inabrian magician. The Inabrians all had a similar air about them that seemed to distance them from the rest. But Maev had been a child, and she had not understood that sometimes people hold others at arm's length because they wish to protect them.

During many nights, as the older teens tried to distract the orphan kids from the smell of mass graves, they had told stories. Anne had told Maev of the prophecy she'd had as a child, the one with the sun rising after the war. That had been the only time the orphans crowded to The Oracle instead of the red-haired alchemist who blistered with hope or the Yamalan boy who made them laugh.

Anne had been serious, her face forever fastened into the same expression. She had been solemn, which made her scary. But when Anne told stories, The Oracle had sucked the kids in as if her voice were enchanted. How Anne described things, with the grim face and sincerity, had made the words that came out of her mouth contain gravity.

Anne had told Maev and the other kids of the old Inabrian magicians and how, before their Crown had united them, they used to fight one another in bloody battles. It had been a time of mages and knights and monsters who cannot be found. In that tale, the surrounding war had seemed to be an afterthought, background noise, a mere interlude of a greater world churning out grand narratives that the kids were a part of. In Anne's story, life and death had seemed to blur together.

Maev never liked ghosts before. She had thought of them as nothing more than remnants of their colourful living selves. Yet, in Anne's words, Maev had seen the value of ghosts—they had become characters of flesh and blood, become humans who, at their cores, were both evil and misunderstood. One would think stories like that would be too much for kids during a war.

Anne had never shied away from it. The Oracle had seemed to understand what it was like to be a child who saw death. It had not been cruelty that drove Anne to tell those stories, but a sense of trust. When she had told the kids of the past, Maev had known it was trust. A trust that Anne had shared with them, knowing the true values of those stories were being heard and brought into the future with them.

Because in Anne's story, the heroes had always won in the end. Maev would later find out that the histories The Oracle recited to the kids had not been entirely historically accurate. After all, history is cruel. Anne was nothing but precise in the stories she told others, judging by the twenty references she would use to verify just one account of events after the Second War's end. The Oracle, who would become a historian, had known the power of stories, and she had known the story that Maev and the other kids needed to carry on.

That had been the gentleness of The Oracle. Anne had never been a fire that emitted warmth, but she had been a steady stone that laid the foundation of Maev's belief to embrace the future.

"Do you think she foresaw this?" Maev asked Chely, her voice small.

"No," Chely said. "That's not how oracles work, Maev. You know that."

"Yeah, true," Maev whispered. The sorrow hung like a stone, heavy on her chest. Her lungs were on fire. Because of how quiet Chely was, Maev felt like she had no right to cry without the alchemist doing so first. "It's just, it's so unfair! She did everything she could, and this is what the world gives back to her."

Chely's hand found the Soul-Gazer's back. "Good intentions never helped anyone," the red alchemist said calmly. "Have I ever told you the story of the sunbird Chi'You and his brothers? He wanted to save humanity, only to burn it to the ground."

Maev gurgled at the mention of that. Yes, of course she remembered. Chely was many things, but a good storyteller was not one of them. The red-haired alchemist had an odd fixation with old myths of Aixauhan gods. Unlike Anne, however, Chely's stories often left Maev feeling cold on the inside.

"Yes," Maev replied. "Anne told you to stop. She said that kind of depressing story helped no one. Plus, it had the logic of gods instead of the logic of people. Stories are supposed to serve people. Especially stories of the dead. They are supposed to mean something."

Chely hummed and stood up. "Let me make you some food."

The red-haired alchemist cooked for them as if Maev were still a child who needed comforting instead of answers.

They ate in silence. Maev stayed the night. The Soul-Gazer went into Anne Barberry's bedroom. What she found was a library where every available surface overflowed with some kind of historical record, book, or interview. Pen and paper littered the sheets where Anne slept, ink stains left unwashed as if the owner had vanished in a hurry and could come back at any moment.

She's never going to come back, Maev thought.

"Do you want me to go find Anne in the afterlife?" Maev asked Chely.

"No, love." The red-haired alchemist twirled the maroon hair spilling down from her head. The same dreamy smile on Chely's face felt unnerving instead of forceful. "I doubt Anne would want to see me, even if you could find her."

"Why?" Maev asked.

Chely did not give Maev a straight answer. "We had a fight," she said. "Anne found out something that I didn't want her to know. She confronted me about it before she left The Cottage. I knew she was trying to get back in contact with her family again, and I couldn't understand why. Now I know. What I did pushed her away. It pushed her so far that she felt the need to go looking for a connection elsewhere. That led to her death."

"It's not your fault," Maev insisted.

"Oh, I know." Chely shook her head. The red-haired alchemist's voice was unbothered. "The ones at fault are the ones who killed Annie. No one else. Patricia and The Innkeeper. One committed the murder, the other helped."

"Wait, The Innkeeper helped Patricia kill Anne…?" Maev's head felt fuzzy. "Why would he tell you where to find Patricia then?"

The light that came into The Cottage held a pinkish hue of twilight. It was the soft colour of fresh blossoms in spring, but also the colour of intestines and guts spilling out of a human body.

There it was, the dancing flame that lit up the grey and white sky on the day of the war when Maev reached out to touch Ying Cai-Li's hand, the hand that guided the Soul-Gazer to choose a difficult, colourful life instead of a peaceful, pale death.

Chely's eyes were awash with waves of red. The black pearls of the red-haired alchemist's eyes were set ablaze by the setting sun.

"Well, I tortured The Innkeeper until he told me where Anne was." Chely smiled. "She trusted him. Can you believe it? He was part of her childhood in that town. Annie hated the Barberry name, yet she held onto the hope there was something worth saving in that damn place. It took some effort. He was a soldier in the Second War, you see. His wife left him to join the war. He kept his loyalty to the Barberry house after all that was said and done. As for Patricia, well… I can tell you an eye for an eye does make the whole world blind. But it doesn't matter, does it? Anne's dead, so she can't see anything, anyway. No amount of Patricia's blood can bring her back, unless…"

A sudden realisation hit Maev like a shooting star. Yes, it was so obvious. All the rumours about necromancy and the Aixauhan alchemist who was driven mad by the war.

"You don't need me to deliver a message to Anne," Maev inhaled a sharp breath. "You are planning to do so yourself! I didn't believe them, I couldn't—but it is true, isn't it? You were…you *are* going to try to tear through the fabric between life and death. "

"To wake her up." Chely shrugged with the same blood-soaked eyes. "I can already manifest in the In-Between Town for a little while. It is quite a neat place, you know. The scenery and logic governing that town is almost like what Anne dreamed. It's funny, I found The Innkeeper there. He has a daughter, you know? The girl looked much older than her actual age. I wonder why…"

Maev stared at Chely, wide-eyed. "That's…" She shook her head repeatedly, not knowing if she should be horrified or comforted. "That's beyond messed up, Ying Cai-Li. I can see souls as they are. They are pure aura and have no physical limitations. You can't reverse a soul's wish to remain. Anne, she's at an In-Between place? That probably means she's waiting for you. Please don't rush. You can't pull a soul back against her wishes."

"Well," Chely said, as if none of this was news to her, "Anne is stubborn, but I can convince her."

"You can *convince her*?" Maev stood up quickly and pushed the cup filled with tea away from her. "That's not how life and death work, Chely. It's not up to you or her. Life and death are a line, primordial forces of nature. You can't simply *change a dying soul's mind* and expect her to come back. Anne would tell you this is fucking insane!"

"People keep saying that." Chely sighed calmly, the smile dropping from her face like a pebble against a calming lake. "You know what else is insane, Maev? The fact that the Inabrian magicians kept pulling this shit and getting away with it. The Barberrys… I haven't told you about the atrocities they've committed against the Aixau-han alchemists. Captain Ark killed Brutus, and Anne tried to kill what remained of that legacy. However, it didn't fucking work. Now she's dead, slain by the same poison she so desperately righted her whole life. She spent the years after the war trying to give the next generation hope. For what? For people like Patricia Barberry? The kind of privileged and bigoted little shits who've never known the shape of war other than the warped, glorified version from their Inabrian magician parents' tongues? I've had enough of it. There is no primordial force of nature, Maev. No Creator or Discord. I can be a god like Chi'You, I don't care if I have to burn the world to the ground if that's what I have to do to get her back."

"What are you saying?" Maev asked, horrified by the implications of those words. "You want to become a god?"

"I don't care about being a god," Chely spat, her face twisted in anger and elation. Her face warped like melting wax. "My parents wanted to be gods. The Ying Clan lauded themselves for being closer to Chi'You. No, that's stupid. It makes one blind to one's own humanity. I do not want to be a god, Maev. What I want is to demand things back from Death after it's done nothing but take from me."

13

The Necromancer

THERE IS A legend in Aixauh. Once, there was a spirit born of stone and nature in the shape of a monkey, who petitioned the Heavenly Court for a position among them. They attained immortality three times. Once, by beating the entire Underworld Household so that the Yan King of the Underworld could strike their name off the List of the Dead. Another by drinking the fruit wine at the Celebration of the Mother Goddess of the West. The only way the Heavenly Court thought they could execute the Monkey King was by letting the most powerful alchemist boil them and dissolve their immortalities in a cauldron for seven days and seven nights—but instead, when they opened the lid, the alchemy had given the Monkey King one last layer of immortality. That was the last.

For a very long time after the war ended, Chely thought things would get better.

Cole was gone. So were a lot of the children they'd sworn to protect. Chely didn't want to talk to her parents, not that her parents ever came searching.

However, they were still alive. Anne was there with her, despite nights when she woke up screaming from nightmares that plagued her sleep or nights where there was no sleep at all, Chely was always there for Anne to hold her girlfriend until the terrors left them alone for a little while.

Those days were bleak, but they were bleak in a way that was hopeful. Like waiting for dawn, knowing the darkness was almost coming to an end. The war had been the crimson sunset that took away colours from the world, and the end of that must mean the sun would shine again very soon.

They had to march through the night through bushes with sharpened thorns for a while, but Chely and Anne would be all right. They had each other. Chely had to hold on to that thought.

Then Anne was gone, taken away in the same Barberry Castle the oracle had left behind. Anne had given everything to break away from her family's cursed bloody legacy. She was good, and she was kind, and that ended up killing her.

In a cruel twist of fate, the Vision could not warn Anne of her own demise, because The Oracle's own death was on too small a scale for it to matter. The death of a single person after the war? It was nothing more than a fly dropping dead after a storm in fate's eyes.

It might have been just a drop in an infinite ocean, but it was Chely's whole world.

Now that Anne was gone, there was nothing to hold the alchemist back any longer.

Death is nothing, Chely thought. *Death is nothing but a hand that takes away everything.*

It was time to demand something back from the thing that had taken everything from her.

"What do you think you can do to me, Maev?" Chely asks.

Her hair is no longer in the same disheveled state it was in when Maev last saw her, right after Anne's death. "Your power is not useful in combat, while I had a lot of practice during and after the war. I'm not going to fight you, my friend. I saved your life as a child, and I do not wish to hurt you."

Maev's eyes are one black and one white, the Eyes of Yin-Yang—that's the name the Aixauhan alchemists granted to Soul-Gazers. There are people with Maev's power everywhere, but there are so few, it's like winning a game of chance.

The black crow caws from where he perches on Maev's shoulder, as if declaring he is not buying Chely's words.

"I know I can't win a fight against you, Cai-Li," Maev replies, her eyes filled with determination. "But I thought about what you said. You said you are going to convince Anne's soul to come back, and that's exactly why I am here, Chely. I will convince you to abort this foolish plan."

Chely sighs. "No offence, Maevy," the red-haired alchemist says, "but I think you know the deeds of my doing now. I have been practising necromancy. You know I am the rumoured Blood Hawk. I know you see me as your hero, which is why I think you should find a better role model."

Maev's lips thin to a line. "I won't be the one to convince you," the Soul-Gazer says. "Do you want to know how I got here? I followed the spirits of the kids that Anne sent to the afterlife beyond the In-Between. They come here filled with guilt. But Annie, she helps them move on. They want the best for Anne. That's why they guided me here. So I can stop you."

That is when a burst of white light blinds Chely. The smokeless white flame is just like Naomi—the girl who drank the wine and disappeared with her mother.

Just as she anticipated, the first voice that comes from the white light is indeed Naomi's.

"Hi, Chely," Naomi greets Chely politely. The lines surrounding her are the petite and shy girl taken as The Innkeeper's daughter, yet she is nothing but a blazing white blob without colouration. "I didn't know my father was responsible for Anne's death. If I'd known… I'm so very sorry. You and Anne must be close. I admire your courage in being civil to my father despite the part he played in the tragedy that happened to Anne."

Chely's face can't help but soften. "What did I say to you, Naomi?" the red-haired alchemist replies. "I will keep your secret from your father. He doesn't deserve my forgiveness or mercy. But you deserve better than this town, and if loving Anne taught me anything, it's that no one is responsible for their family's mistakes."

"Yes, thank you," Naomi says, her white flame voice younger than she appeared in the town. Which Chely thinks makes sense. There is no way Naomi could have reached the age of a teenager if The Innkeeper's wife left The Innkeeper for joining the war. The sad truth crept into Chely's mind—yes, Naomi died much younger than she appeared. A girl who was at most in her preteens. A loving daughter whose mother died, maybe from the same cause as Naomi's death. A kind daughter who remained in the prison with the father who never once showed up for her in her lifetime, just to keep him company.

"Are you here to tell me I should let Anne go into the afterlife?" Chely asks, not unkindly. "I can see the appeal to you, Naomi. You are an innocent soul, unlike the denizens of the town who deserved to be trapped here by Anne's judgement. Your soul has gone to a better place, and Anne deserves the peace you have now. I do not object to that fact."

"The Oracle helped me to move on," Naomi says. Her pigtails made sense. She was the age to wear pigtails without it being odd when she died. "Don't you want her to be at peace too? I can see how much you love her, Chely. And you are a kind person. I know that. You want the best for Anne, don't you?"

"Yes, I do indeed want the best for Anne," Chely says. "But I don't believe what is best for Anne is to leave the In-Between and go to the afterlife. I can give her a chance at a life. Isn't that what you would want, too, if you were given a chance to grow up? Experiencing the sunshine on your face as you wake up every morning. That's what I want to give Anne. Tell me, Naomi, if you had a chance at a life, would you really think the afterlife is the best way to go?"

The white flame that was Naomi's soul stills. Her silhouette hunches, as if unable to offer a clear answer.

However, another voice came from another white flame figure. "That's bullshit, Naomi." It is the voice of a boy who is going through puberty. "We talked to The Oracle. She reassured us that our guilt that led us here is not our fault, but the fault of those who imposed such guilt onto us. And I can tell The Oracle carries that guilt as well. She is trapping herself here because of it. We owe The Oracle for the gift she gave us. We owe it to help guide her on to the afterlife to be at peace."

The boy who speaks has an accent that belongs to the nation that live in the snowy mountain ranges north of the Inabrian island. He has a tall build, his shoulders wide, and if judging by his height alone, people might assume he is a grown-up. But Chely remembers The Innkeeper's tale of a tourist boy who taught him to make Feuerzangenbowle. A boy who disappeared with the rest of his group after they visited The Oracle's Castle.

"Ah, I see." Chely pinches her cheek with genuine amusement. "So, the so-called divination with The Oracle has nothing to do with divining the future at all. It is simply a cover-up for the true purpose of the visits. The Oracle is the gatekeeper of this In-Between place. The townsfolk, who are chided by Anne with mean words, are sent back to the town, trapped because The Oracle deemed them guilty enough to not deserve to leave. While the so-called 'missing tourists' kids'… You are the ones Anne guides to the afterlife beyond the In-Between, to reach your true Afterlife—be it heaven, some kind of fantasy land, or the Cycle of Reincarnation."

"Yes." The white flames of the northern boy and Naomi are joined by a dozen more. No, a hundred more. Each of them is a white flame, tall yet narrow. But when all of them stand shoulder to shoulder, they make up a wall that blocks the hallway. "We want to help Anne, like Anne helped us."

"Hmmm," Chely hums as she observes the determination of the youth. They are cute. It warms the red-haired necromancer's heart. Sadly, despite their best intentions, none of them know Anne Barberry. They only met The Oracle, not Annie.

"You guys are so adamant about the fact that Anne wants to leave this place, including you, Maev," Chely says. She strolls up to the dark-skinned Soul-Gazer with dual-coloured eyes. Maev doesn't back down. What a brave woman she has grown up to be. Pride wells in Chely's heart, despite the inappropriate timing. "However, there is one thing you haven't thought through—Anne Barberry might be the queen of the In-Between, but she's trapped here too. Because she believes she deserves the punishment. As much as she deems the townsfolk to be trapped in this In-Between space, Anne Barberry is also judged by The Oracle as deserving to be here. That's why her memories are wiped like the townsfolk's. She might be the one powering the In-Between, but she is both a warden and a willing prisoner."

"What are you talking about?" Maev shakes her head. "Anne did everything right in her life. You are putting words in Anne's mouth, Chely."

"No, I'm not," Chely replies cooly. "Let me ask you, Maev. How are you better than me, if you and your group of afterlife kids drag Anne to the afterlife because you believe she deserves better than the In-Between, without her having all of her memories restored to know the truth of this place and make an informed decision on her own?"

Maev's mouth opens and closes. The white flames fall silent. Chely knows that she's won this round.

These kids are just kids. They care about Anne. Naïve. Oh, how Chely envies their naivety. They wish to honour Anne's choice, thinking that if Anne regains her memories, then that automatically means Anne will be at peace because she *did all the right things*.

That's not how guilt works. Guilt is a poison. When Anne Barberry regains her memories, Chely knows the guilt will return to Annie like a tsunami. Because despite doing nothing wrong in one's life, one can still be crushed by guilt for a million different reasons.

"How about this?" Chely raises her hand and points to the door. "Maev, you can check in with Anne anytime you like. But only after her memories come back to her fully can we know what Anne truly wants, whether it is what you wish for her—to pass on peacefully into the afterlife—or if she wants my way—to return to the realm of the living through my necromancy."

The ghosts fall silent, and so does Maev. The only dissent comes in the form of the black crow, who croaks out in protest of the plan.

"You seem to be particularly hostile to me, Cole." Chely smiles at the familiar. "I know you can communicate with Anne somehow. I apologise for freezing you in the air when I fed Anne the orb of remembrance. But for Annie's sake, please pretend to be normal around her before the orb takes full effect. You don't want to risk messing up Anne's head before she regains all her memories, do you?"

The black crow's milky eyes bore into Chely's with such vehement hatred that if glares could kill, Chely would drop dead then and there.

Still, Chely knows she's won. Because everyone in this room is an honest person who values Anne Barberry's autonomy and choice. Each of them respects Anne enough to wish for the choice to be Anne's once she recovers.

"Fine, Ying Cai-Li." Maev's lips tremble as she backs away out of the door. Her form becomes translucent as the Soul-Gazer fades from the In-Between back to the land of the living. "I will come back. The crow can travel through the In-Between and the living realm. He will tell me when Anne is back to herself again, so no more tricks, Chely. You no longer have my trust."

Chely smiles. Once upon a time, hearing those words from the girl she saved from the rubble of an acid-drenched battlefield would have made the red-haired alchemist's conscience twitch in pain. But that hero is gone; what remains of Ying Cai-Li has learned there is no reward for doing things the right way.

So, the ghosts disperse back into the afterlife, leaving behind Ying Cai-Li, the necromancer who successfully manipulated Maev and the other kids into leaving.

Anne is right. Chely has become an exceptional liar in the years they have been apart.

"I'm going to bed," Chely tells the crow, who throws a stink-eye at her. "You better check on Anne. I don't know what she's going to wake up to, or at what stage her memories are coming back. But I suppose you'll want to be by her side when she gets better."

14

Remembrance

ANNE WAKES UP with a very nasty hangover.

What have you done? her mind screams at her.

Anne groans at the ceiling. This whole year feels like a huge mistake.

Sometimes, in the past decade, Anne has thought she lost her mind and her grip on reality. Like for example, when Anne impersonated a girl with the same name as her living in a creepy ass castle in the middle of nowhere so said Perks girl could leave this creepy-ass town in the middle of nowhere, because that poor girl's family were a bunch of creeps. And Anne couldn't do much about it other than take the Perks girl's place so that girl could go live a new life under a new name, even though The Oracle did not know where.

At least, that's the story Anne's mind tells itself. Yet with Ying Cai-Li barging back into her life, throwing around wild yet sensible accusations, the oracle has increasingly felt the view in front of her shatter like a fallen chandelier.

Anne tries to remember the Perks girl and her parents. Their faces are all clouded by a white mist. Featureless. She thinks of their voices. No, there is not a single sound that comes to mind. The memories replaying in Anne's head are spoken with her own voice, as if she were acting out a story all by herself.

How much of it made sense? None, none of it made any damn sense. Why would a girl who had the same name as Anne conveniently live in a creepy castle that was almost identical to The Barberry Castle, which Anne spent her life outrunning? How did Anne even get here to begin with? Those were questions that fleetingly perched in the oracle's mind, but that she never had time to delve into too deep.

Making sense is an overrated sentiment. Anne is alone, she is safe; she is content to be with her familiar and the occasional tourists coming to her for divination sessions. Those tourists are always kids, lost and confused, but with wild curiosity and hope in their eyes.

Anne likes kids. It was the kids they saved that kept Anne sane during and after the war. Cole's death was gut-wrenching. Chely's growing distance and changing personality filled Anne with anxieties, the Barberry name and the survivor's guilt. Everything was pointless, but the idea that they saved some kids… That was enough to sustain Anne into believing it was all worth it.

Children, they bounce back. Anne wants a better tomorrow for them, not just survival for herself. She doesn't want the kids who lived through the Second War becoming as ignorant as Anne herself was growing up, being told horrifying lies by the likes of Brutus Barberry instead of the truth.

There will be no Third War. Anne will make sure of it for the rest of her life. The Oracle set aside her Vision, which told her prophecies that did no good other than stoke uncertainty in the human mind, and dedicated her life to the study of history. Only by observing the past and learning the truth from it could the children not repeat the mistakes of their forbearers.

However, a cold pit that opens up in Anne's stomach. A vortex that threatens to swallow her whole with its bleakness.

An overwhelming sensation that somehow Anne has failed sinks into her stomach.

Anne was so, so certain that it was what she would dedicate the rest of her life to doing. Then how did she end up here? In this castle isolated from the world? It was not her intention to do so, nor is this the kind of person she wishes to be.

War muddled everything. It drove Anne to learn that sometimes it's better not to question what one is given. She has a sense of peace here. So long as she doesn't poke around too hard with logic, Anne can keep living with this oblivious sense of peace.

She has spent her whole life so far being drowned in other people's sorrow and pain. Being an oracle itself is like a one-way ticket to insanity. Anne Barberry paid for her family's debt by being The Oracle and saving those kids during the war. Her power activated again and again, each time muddying the lines between space and time, until reality was nothing but a crescendo of nonsensical sequences of scenes that Anne could no longer care if they were real or not.

Cole's bleeding body in her arms? Yes, that had happened at the end of the war, but it was also happening as Anne sat with the interviewees who came to her recounting similar events. So many of them were Cole's age, some of them soldiers, some of them civilians. The initial disgust Anne felt for the soldiers quickly dissipated as one boy who was Cole's age broke down in the middle of describing how he'd watched every one of his friends die.

They were all kids. They had no choice. The winner of a war is a nation. As for the soldiers, none of them enjoy the victory. At least compared to them. Cole, Anne, and Chely went into the war with their eyes wide open. None of them bought into patriotism, so their respective country's betrayal of their soldiers was something they were spared from.

The death of her friend. The sobs of her interviewees. The begging for mercy from Brutus Barberry.

The war never ended. The war is happening right there in Anne's mind.

It is happening when Anne brews tea with the chalice; it is happening as she jogs down the sobbing confessions of the witnesses who lost everything in the Second War.

The mountains of corpses, children—Maev especially—crying at the sight of their dead parents. Rain enchanted by Inabrian magicians that ate away at people's skin, unearthing white bones beneath. Screaming Aixauhan alchemists who died in their homes, killed by a man wearing the younger face of Brutus Barberry. Aixauhan alchemists poisoning the refugee camp's water source so people's bodies became contorted into a bloated mess of flesh and bone. Magicians who screamed *"please spare our kids"* as they tried to convey the importance of the lineages. Common Inabrian and Aixauhan people, caught in a war between blood feuds of the magically gifted of their nations, with the tiniest defence and the worst number of casualties.

They died in Anne's head, a choir of harmonious sounds she learned to go about her daily routine with.

None of it makes sense, but nothing truly did for a very long time. Anne Barberry knows she lost her mind somewhere along the way, but even that hardly registered.

Chely's face has aged over the years. The fresh baby face of an Aixauhan girl who was fearless at summer camp, the vibrant light in Ying Cai-Li's smile was as it was lit up in the pub during their first dates. Then blood, blood a shade darker, splattered across Chely's face, blood that caked her ruby-like hair into brown knots.

Chely, what did you do? What have you become?

The girl Anne fell in love with, the girl that became Anne's hope and salvation, the girl that was all that was good and right in the world. Anne's own tiny lighthouse, her own beacon of hope.

Gone. Gone. Gone.

Yet not gone at the same time, as Anne hears the alchemist's footsteps around the castle. Chely is there with her, physically there in The Barberry Castle with Anne.

However, Anne vaguely remembers a time when things made sense. Having sense is an overrated concept, but dear Creator, does Anne wish she survived the war with her sense intact. Maybe if Anne was a little more lucid, she could have stopped it from happening. Except she doesn't even know what she is thinking of stopping from happening. It has already happened. It is too late. It is always too late.

Being an oracle is not an identity. The Sight is a parasite that eats away at one's own individual existence, instead of a concrete magical power that one can hold in one's hand like the carefully balanced scales of the alchemists. The Inabrian magicians see magic as water, and the water flowing in Anne's veins is a hallucinogen pumped into her in the form of blood since the time of her conception.

Poisoned at birth, a bloody legacy that Anne never agreed to take.

15

A Letter to the Next Generation

DEAR ANNE,

I want to give you the answer I never gave you while I was alive.

Yes, I was the person who broke into Barberry Castle that night and killed Brutus Barberry, your grandfather. It was a premeditated murder. I had been tracking Brutus Barberry for years. All I knew at the start was his face. I did not know he was the famous Oracle of your country. I did not know he came from a long line of magicians who were known to predict the future.

All I knew was his face, because it was the face of the man who led the troops that decimated my city in the First War. That face that gave the order through the command chain line to slaughter every single person in my clan. Anyone with an Aixauhan face and an alchemist family name, no matter if they were soldiers or civilians.

Bodies piled up into mountains on the streets. Our streets burned and crumbled into dust. The screaming and fleeing crowd stumbled over one another. People who weren't slaughtered were trampled to death. Everyone I knew was gone in the blink of an eye.

You might not know, Anne Barberry—although I'm sure Cai-Li knows, and maybe she told you—of a time when Aixauh was a rising nation growing at an exponential speed thanks to our alchemists. They channelled the gods of our world, for the first time in five millennia, had alchemists and shamans and Daoists reaching to the gods like they did in the time right after the Creation of the Universe.

Thanks to our alchemists, our economy was growing. We advanced at a rate that surprised the Inabrians. Our agriculture-based land turned into one that could rival your country in less than a decade.

My parents' generation, they were the ones that lifted Aixauh up into becoming a global power. We were formerly a small alchemist clan. The Li Clan was unlike the Ying Clan; we had no distinct ancestry tracing back to emperors and alchemists of old. My parents were the ones to make the Li Clan a name that was respected among Aixauhans. They didn't know that doing so was also painting a target on our backs in the eyes of the Inabrians.

We thought alchemy was what would finally put Aixauh at the same level as Inabri, with your noble lineages of magicians that claimed divine favouritism for your position at the center of the global stage. We thought we were earning your respect; instead, what we got was your jealousy and ire. We wished for equality, but Inabri could only settle for a world where it stood atop everyone else.

We should have known; your country was never one that allowed others to prosper alongside it. If you were Chosen by your Creator, then it was against Inabrian doctrine that the Aixauhan "pagans" could ever reach anything close to the might of your blessed magicians.

It took decades for the tension to build. When the First War broke out, no one should have been surprised. Yet, we *were* surprised, at your savagery and at your inhumanity.

My parents were healers. They dedicated their lives to saving people. When the First War started, they were told to evacuate, as the country could not risk losing them, since we knew how valuable our alchemists were. After the First War ended, people like my parents were needed by the country to rebuild. But my parents did not choose to flee like cowards. They said that alchemy exists for the Aixauhan people, and they were not abandoning them to ensure the safety of our own clan.

My parents were offered a way out, and they threw it away because they believed in doing what was right. It was the stupidest thing they could have ever done for me and my baby sister, and it was a mistake I swore that I would never replicate.

The Inabrians came. They knocked down our door with trained soldiers. Magicians with elemental magic were turned into weapons of war. It was unthinkable to my parents in their naivety. Despite all their accomplishments in alchemy, never once did they think of using it to defend themselves. It veers too close to the selfish pursuit of dark magic, they would have said. The Li Clan did not wish to be another alchemist branch that was obsessed over immortality, who crossed lines for selfish gains rather than benefitting the masses.

Such silly ideals proved to be fatal. A troop led by your grandfather himself stormed my house. He pinpointed the Li Clan as targets because in his Visions, Brutus Barberry saw us as a future threat to his precious Inabrian descendants.

He was there to witness the execution of my parents. Hanged in the square. Not just my parents—my cousins, my aunts, even my grandpa who could not leave his bed were marched out by heavily armed magicians under Brutus's command. Their bodies were left up there for a week for everyone to see.

"*Let them know.*" Those were the words that came out of his mouth. Brutus Barberry. "*Let them know that the Creator would not allow these heathens and their blasphemous witchcraft to thrive.*"

We alchemists had our own gods, but none of us were bold enough to claim that we spoke for the Heavenly Court. You Inabrians clearly did not share that sentiment. The Barberry Lineage, your whole legacy, was built to be a speaker for your Creator.

As my parents wept and begged for me and my little sister to be spared, Brutus Barberry grinned and said: "*That is an amazing idea. Maybe your kids would make good specimens, so that we'd know how to treat blasphemous mutations among your children. They'd be spared and contribute to making a better world where your kind is eradicated like the vermin you are.*"

He then held out a chalice, one that contained a clear liquid. "*The Elixir of Truth,*" he called it. What it turned out to be was an exceptionally cruel execution method for alchemists, as it melted an alchemist's body from the inside out.

For us, everything has a spirit; when we die, our spirits go back into the Cycle of Reincarnation. We might become insects, a blade of grass, or a piece of rock. Yet, we might be able to gain form after enough years of cultivation. That is why not all alchemists or magical beings in our world are human from birth — like your friend, Cole, who was born from the wise water of the Himalayan mountains. His ancestors were mountain streams that learned to gain a human form over millennia of cultivation. They gained sentience and reached enlightenment. They became humans in their own right; they *earned* their humanity. Unlike us alchemists and you magicians, who take our humanity for granted, the Yamalans are miracles that prove no one gets to decide who has the right to exist. Not our gods, not your Creator, NO ONE.

But your Chalice of Truth, it destroys that life force from existence. The ability for humans to cultivate into alchemists or spirits who reach enlightenment is eradicated.

Brutus Barberry did not just order the execution of my parents. Your grandfather extinguished their souls. There will be no Reincarnation for my parents. They saved countless lives across their short mortal years, and their reward was to be eradicated by your zealous grandfather.

They were gone. No afterlife, no journey beyond Death. *Do you understand what that means?*

I watched as the clear liquid was forced down my parents' throats. I watched them writhe. I watched them scream. I watched their pink innards turn inside out.

Your grandfather kept his promise; he spared me and my sister as specimens. But before he could take us away, the Aixauhan navy that was originally supposed to escort my family to safety came back. Too little too late for the rest of the Li Clan, but just enough time to save me. The last living member of the Li Clan to survive your grandfather's cleansing.

They saved me, but not my sister.

I joined the navy, since there was nothing left for me anywhere else. But in my heart, a flicker of hope still burned. My sister was taken by the Inabrians, and she was alive the last I saw her. I dedicated my life to finding her, as I hoped against all odds she had survived somehow.

You told me that day you stormed into my captain's cabin that The Barberry Oracle could only foresee the future of the bigger picture. I told you to get out. But I believed you, because Brutus Barberry's prediction was right—the Li Clan would be the end of the Barberry Lineage.

Your grandfather made the mistake of letting me live, which meant there was still one last Li alchemist who could take revenge against the Barberrys

And I succeeded in ending the Barberrys, didn't I? Your grandfather is dead, you were there on my ship, the last Oracle, a traitor to the Inabrians because you fell in love with an alchemist. I might not have liked you, but believe me when I say I loved Cai-Li. She was the final nail in the coffin that the Barberry ended with my help. Just as your grandfather feared it would all those years ago.

You see, the prophecy Brutus predicted was not of the Li Clan being the end of Inabrians, but the end of the Barberry name.

His selfish desire to keep his family line alive made him wipe out mine.

The First War ended before I reached adulthood. I stayed in the navy for the rest of my teenage years. I worked my way up the ranks. I became the captain of the ship that saved my life, as the old captain took me as his successor.

When I took my position as captain, I led a mutiny that branded me and my crew pirates. Because I was going to save my sister, and I was not going to serve a country that left its citizens to die. My parents stayed behind, and I am their daughter. I would sail for the people—for those who needed help during the war—and would not become a coward who only followed orders, adding more fuel to the pyre of war.

I survived both of the Wars. Both the one that took my parents, and the one where I met you and Cai-Li. Aixauh is safe.

There are no more Barberry oracles or Li alchemists left alive on Earth as you are reading this letter. I know that for sure.

That leads us to the final question—the question that you asked me that day.

"Why?"

Why did I kill Brutus Barberry, but not you?

It's simple, really.

You were a child, and you didn't deserve to die.

I found my sister, you know?

I found her bones in the barberry bushes that surrounded your family's castle. The same day I found you, the little girl who hid behind the curtains as I avenged my parents. Your grandfather, Brutus

Barberry, who said he would make good specimens out of us, kept his promise.

How do I know the bones were hers? Well, because the Barberry bushes turned red as my alchemy contacted the ground.

Barberries were a common ingredient of alchemists from my province. My parents used them as remedies for aches. Throughout the ages, the barberries that grew on our lands came to recognise the blood of Aixauhan alchemists. They recognise us as family. Their fruits were imbued with our spirit; they gained a sense of a familial bond with us.

When a Li alchemist's blood spilled onto the barberries that grew on our lands, they would turn red. And on that night, my alchemy woke the barberry bushes surrounding your family's castle like lighting a thousand red lanterns. Crimson hues dotted the hills as if blood was soaking into the grounds on which your family's castle stood.

I found my sister's bones, amongst hundreds of others, using a blood-match elixir I brewed myself.

All those bones, with sizes belonging to children and young teens, all of them were buried under those barberry bushes. The species of barberries native to Inabrian land were blue and black. But those that grew around the Barberry Castle? They were blood red. Because they grew feeding on the bodies of alchemist children like my sister's. Alchemist children's blood watered your groves. They nurtured your childhood home.

I collected enough of the bones to piece half of my sister together. A lifetime of hope of seeing her whole again, and it was nothing but a fruitless endeavour.

But the truth was, I didn't do it out of hope. I didn't do it for her. I knew my sister was gone, but I had to keep going. I had to make Brutus Barberry pay for his crimes. I had to have my revenge, or otherwise why was I spared when everyone I know was gone? I was not the Li Clan's hope—I was merely their vengeance set loose on the world.

When I saw you and Cai-Li on my ship, it was like watching something so abhorrent yet wonderful.

An Aixauhan alchemist and an Inabrian magician. In love.

The way you held Cai-Li's hand, as if she was all that mattered in the world. The way you cared for Cole, that Yamalan boy, it scorched my eyes.

I knew who you were the second I saw you. You have Brutus Barberry's blond hair, like strands of golden thread. You have his grey eyes, the same soft sheen that could see into the future.

When I killed Brutus, it did not feel like anything. You could not have possibly seen it, but my sister's bones were lying in my pockets as I tortured the man who murdered her to death. But there you were, the last Barberry standing on the hull of my ship, the ship of the last member of the Li Clan.

And I knew that this was what Brutus Barberry was afraid of all those years ago—not that some alchemist family might wipe out the Barberry oracles by force, but that one of his descendants would be a true Seer. An oracle that saw through the bullcrap that was fed to them, and who knew right from wrong.

You are the embodiment of his greatest fear. You are the true legacy Brutus Barberry wished to avoid. Someone who has The Oracle's Vision but will make a new future alongside Aixauhan alchemists.

And, gods forbid, you and Cai-Li ignited my hope.

By helping you, I would kill Brutus again and again and again. If I helped you, I would ensure the cycle of violence that trapped us all in these generational wars could end with me alone.

You and Cai-Li, you were the future of the world that I wished to see. One where love and hope were not childish daydreams, but the truth that all others might aspire to be.

That is the true reason I never answered your question that day when you posed it to me.

Why?

Because I didn't want my story to crush your hope. My story was one written in tragedy. I wish for yours to be different. And for it to be different, you have to focus on the future, not the past that plagues you.

You and Cai-Li. And Cole of the Yamalan.

You three made me believe that maybe there is something beyond dead children's bones that lie after the war.

I am going to die soon, Anne Barberry. I deserve it.

You do not.

Please live on, Oracle of the Barberry House.

You and Cai-Li are the horizon I see as I close my eyes. The dawn of a new possibility between our countries.

Hope.

Do not lose sight of it.

Sincerely yours,
Ark Li

PART TWO

The Sun

16

Five Years Ago

CHELY YING WAS an alchemist. She was supposed to be prepared for this kind of situation.

On her deathbed, Captain Ark Li looked nothing like her ferocious and charismatic self Chely had always known. The captain's face was caving in, skin clinging tightly onto its skeleton. A powerful figure, once a powerful sword, melted back into hot metal in a blacksmith's workspace to await its final disposal.

Her leg, lost during the Second War, had healed to a smooth stump. It was the only human part remaining on the captain's body that didn't look completely liquified, like ice under the summer sun.

A tinge of vinegar and fish left in the blaring heat for months on end permeated the room. It was like witnessing the decomposition of a corpse, despite the fact that the person in question hadn't yet met their end.

"Quite a horrible sight, isn't it?"

The gaping hole opened in almost the shape of a smashed cake. For a moment, Chely didn't realise she was being spoken to.

"Don't be so surprised, Blood Hawk," Ark Li choked out. "This is the result of lifelong alchemy that went against the natural order of things. You'll be here one day, too, if you keep up with what you're doing now."

"You don't deserve this, Ark," Chely said, her voice calm and her smile firm. But the muscles on her face felt strained and brittle. "Everyone does horrible things in times of war. You were just unlucky that your lifespan was smack-filled with them."

"Maybe," Ark said. She tried to sit up with the help of her right arm, which wobbled like jelly and failed to hold her weight. "I am not worried about myself. Wherever I go in the afterlife or the Reincarnation Cycle, that's someone else's decision. What are you going from here on out? That's what I want to know."

Chely shrugged. "So, you've heard." She sighed, knowing what would probably come next. "How did you find out?"

One of Captain Ark's eyes was already missing; only a bloody socket remained. The other was a dark abyss, with light slowly leaking as the sands in the hourglass of her life ticked away.

"News of what The Blood Hawk has been doing is scattered across the land, Cai-Li." Ark pronounced Chely's Aixauhan name clearer than anyone else in her life. "Each corpse of those who were responsible for the worst crimes of the Second War were found with a piece missing. An eye, a finger, a slice of skin. I collected the newspapers before my body started decaying as well. You have almost assembled enough anatomical parts to form a full human body."

Chely nodded. There was no point in denying it. Not to the person who had dragged her and the others through the worst stretches of war.

"You speak it as someone who attempted to do the same thing," Chely said. "Didn't you?"

"Yes. My parents, at first. But their spirits were destroyed. Then, my sister, but like all alchemists in Aixauhan history, I failed." Ark waved her hand dismissively. "I am about to die and join her, so the failure doesn't hurt that much anymore. Still, for years I craved a solution to bring her back, to successfully brew the Elixir of Immortality. But there is no hope of success. You know that, right? You're doomed to fail, and the ramifications will lead you to the mess I am in now."

"Then I guess I'll embrace my fate. I am no different from any alchemist that came before me," Chely said. "The emperor who, a thousand years ago, made Aixauh what it is today. Ying Zheng, the Founding Emperor of Qin. He kept trying to become immortal, even till the end of his days."

"Yes, he died of mercury poisoning." Ark laughed, almost nostalgic. "Ma and Ba used to tell me that all the time. Every alchemist parent tells their child as soon as they can understand human speech. *To never be like the Emperor of Qin. Who seeks to prolong life beyond its natural ending?* Even as they experimented with the same hope of one day attaining the secret remedy behind their child's back. Were your parents not like that?"

"No, not really." Chely shrugged. "The Ying Clan is…peculiar. My parents' greatest wish was to be like the Emperor of Qin. So is the doctrine of the Ying Clan. To rebuild the prosperous age of the Qin dynasty."

"Oh." Ark's voice stopped, clearly not having anticipated that answer. "Well, so all the rumours are true, the Ying Clan is filled with narcissistic assholes with god complexes. You and Anne have more in common than I thought."

"Anne was not a narcissistic asshole with a god complex," Chely replied.

"I am not saying that. I'm saying both of you are running away from the legacy of something awful. And that's probably why you were drawn to each other," Ark Li mused, wise as she was in her prime. "I am not your mother, but after everything we have been through together, I feel obligated to fill that role and ask you to reconsider. Turn back; it is not what Cole of the Yamalan would have wanted. It is certainly not what Anne Barberry would want for herself."

"I know," Chely said firmly. "I am doing it for selfish reasons, Captain. But I will do it, nonetheless."

Ark sighed. "Okay, I guess if I cannot stop you, I might as well help you. Wait until I take my last breath…then you can take what you have come to collect."

"You don't have to," Chely said.

She knew how she must have looked, a vulture instead of a hawk, circling the dying body of a woman who was the closest thing she had to a mother, ready to pluck at the remains as soon as the captain left this mortal coil.

"Well, if you are set to complete the ritual to bring Anne back, then you can have my remaining eye," Ark said. "I am giving you my consent. Freely given. That was the last requirement of the ritual, right? An eye from a person on their deathbed who volunteers it."

"I think that's why you failed the ritual," Chely said, her smile turning genuine. "Because after everything, you never had it in you to ask someone you love to die for your selfish goals."

"No, you silly, sweet child." Ark rolled her remaining eye. "It's because everyone I ever loved was already dead."

Captain Ark died soon after Chely departed from the healing unit of the Magician Alliance, taking the remaining eye from the captain's

eye socket with her, and the letter containing the life story of Ark Li and her history with the Barberry family.

In her last moments, as the captain stared into the darkness, she thought that death might not be so different from how she'd always existed. An endless darkness, with nothing more to see than the void in her head.

Then she woke up again.

In her blurry view, Ark Li saw the sky a magnificent cerulean blue. Clouds rolled in waves, sea-foam crushed onto sandy beaches. The breeze carried the salty tang of the ocean. Her dark hair was taken up with a ribbon.

There was no smell of gunpowder. No screams of agony. No taste of death on the tip of her tongue.

She stood at the helm of a ship with her heart as light as a feather. Her limbs no longer felt like they were made of lead or acid. The pain and hatred were nothing but a distant dream that someone had whispered to her a long time ago.

There, her parents were waving at her with smiles on their faces. Her little sister held up a wooden sword, a gap in her teeth instead of white bone shards.

"欢迎回家."

Welcome home.

"How is this possible?" she asked her parents. "I thought you were gone for good."

"傻孩子, 你真的以为他们的魔法能战胜公正的阎王爷吗?"

"Our silly girl," her parents chided, as if Ark were still a child that had knocked over a precious vase. "You really think their magic can conquer the justice and mercy of the righteous Judge of the Underworld?"

Ark smiled. It was truly silly of her to think the Inabrians had gotten it right somehow, that with the Elixir of Truth, they could extinguish the souls of Aixauhan alchemists who'd lived their lives good and true.

Somewhere during all the war and bloodshed, she'd stopped believing the tales of her people.

Ark no longer remembered why it had taken her so long as she stepped forward and joined her family on the journey beyond.

A place with no sorrow or pain. No war or vengeance.

The captain did not notice a crow flying across the white sails of her new ship. A black ink spot on the white and blue canvas, soundlessly witnessing the reunion before leaving without a sound.

17

The Truth of Anne Barberry

Chely Hawk said this as the world shattered into a million different colours.

The summer camp where white blossoms grew across green fields. The grey metallic ship on a black sea. The brown cabin washed in morning dew, drenched in the flavour of fresh wood and the stone well with its perpetual reek of moisture.

A red silhouette dancing like a tiny flame. Giggling playfully, full of delight.

The sound of a magician whose magic twisted Anne's body as she crumpled to the ground. The magician who tortured her had the blonde hair of the Barberry family. No, the magician was of the Barberry family, Anne's own sister, once innocent and sweet like a dandelion. Now her face twisted with rage as the snarling word "traitor" spilled out of her mouth.

Black fabric adorned the castle like a veil in mourning. The body was blown to bits with screams of agony. Charred soil split from the explosions. The ringing in her head…

A scarlet crescendo the colour of blood, laughing louder as it grew taller and taller.

A body lay on the ground. The call for a ceasefire. The funeral. The white of wedding gowns. The barberry bushes that surrounded the castle. The teal ivy which crawled across the Barberry estate. The steps she took into the old nightmare. The rays of sunlight streaming from the window.

Her sister. Her sister, who she hadn't seen in so many years.

"*Traitor.*"

Everything turned crimson. It engulfed everything in Anne's sight. It was warm and sticky. The texture reminded her of the fresh dough she'd baked that morning before leaving the cabin.

"*You are not my family.*" The last words that came out of Anne's mouth were a grim realisation. As reality swam around the dying oracle, blood streamed from her body where her bones were twisting and tearing open flesh, her limbs bending to impossible angles.

Somehow, Anne was not dead. She reached out with a trembling finger toward her sister, her murderer, and said: "You cannot keep me here. I have someone waiting for me back home."

The crimson spread like branches and roots, creating cracks in the room that was blacked out by heavy curtains and black ornaments.

"You mean your dirty Aixauhan lover?" her sister, the true successor of the Barberry name, spat in Anne's face. "You left us for her? I will go after her next."

"Oh, I'm not worried about her safety," Anne choked out. "You have no idea what Ying Cai-Li is capable of. Don't go after her for your own good, little sister."

The last Barberry did not believe her. That was fine with Anne. Her sister had become what their grandfather once was. It was sad, because Anne had seen in her Vision a different possibility. She and her sister, hand in hand, lifting the Barberry name out of its bloody roots.

You can't save everyone, Chely's words came back to her.

You were right, this was a terrible mistake, Anne thought. *Wait for me, Chely. I am coming home.*

As The Oracle fell to the ground, her entire life flashed before her eyes.

Anne Barberry was a girl hiding behind a curtain as her grandfather was brutally murdered. The sweat dampened her forehead as she felt a scream die in her throat.

Anne Barberry was the bystander who first met the transparent boy and the eternally smiling girl as they were bullied while she did nothing. She felt a tingling in her heart as if a bee had stung her, unable to say what was wrong but feeling uneasy.

Anne Barberry was the teenager who kissed Chely Hawk in the streets as the surrounding people stared in disgust at the Aix-auhan alchemist and the Inabrian oracle. The warmth of Chely's lips was like a torch that blazed out all the murmurs lurking in the shadows.

Anne Barberry was a refugee of war, starved and terrified as magician fire and alchemical acid rain took away her senses. Bodies piled up into mountains; blood flowed into rivers. Mass graves filled with maggots and the stench of death. Vacant eyes. Human flesh. Life rendered meaningless by the droves in which people died.

Anne Barberry was the oracle who sailed on a ship, who foresaw the attacks that would befall them. The captain of the ship was a murderer, but it hardly mattered when *everyone* was a murderer. Captain Ark and Anne had a shared goal: both of them wanted to keep their loved ones alive.

So many versions of Anne Barberry flooded into the oracle's mind all at once that none of those versions felt real anymore. She was the shadow cast on the wall, a forgotten afterthought. She was the witness to Anne Barberry's past and future, yet none of them felt like herself.

I am going home.

As all the colours blended together into a rainbow, it brought forth the most magnificent dream she had ever seen. The colour of a summer day where everything was tinted with the heightened concentration of light.

Anne Barberry stood atop a hill. The sun shone, and the weather was warm. Everything thrived with an eagerness that was impossible for life on the earth. Wildflowers of every shade, bluebells, and lily-of-the-valley hanging down their heads, sunflowers and dandelions washed in blazing yellow, wisteria dripping from vines atop trees, and green grass growing lush like emerald.

The field rolled on endlessly under her feet, a limitless ocean wave that rose and fell as far as the eye could see. She could hear birds taking flight, hear streams of the river laughing. She could smell the air as crisp as the first bite of an apple.

Anne Barberry stood there on the hill from dusk to dawn. Unmoving. Her legs did not grow numb, and her mind did not falter.

She knew this hilltop. It was the same place where Barberry Castle had loomed for centuries and probably would for centuries to come.

The flowers replaced the barberry bushes. There was no sea of crimson with white bones buried underneath. The fresh blossoms were of every colour one could imagine, except for red.

No one interrupted her. She was alone.

The utter vacancy of it all was what she had always thought Heaven would look like.

Anne Barberry stood there as the clouds were washed into a pinkish hue by the sunset. The entire world took on a dreamy daze, as if beckoning her to lie on the grass, promising a soft bed of eternal rest.

She could spend the rest of her existence there, engulfed by the aroma of flowers. She thought it would smell like lavender, taste like honey, with the consistency of a nice cup of warm tea with milk and sugar next to a stove.

She'd slowly break apart into a hundred, a thousand, a million tiny pieces. Her veins would bleed the same colour as pinkish twilight, her skin would become the clouds, her tears would wash away the bad weather. And her nightmares—her nightmares would become the fields of flowers with no thorns.

I'm going home.

She closed her eyes and surrendered.

"No. Hang on. No."

Her eyes snapped open. The voice came from the sky, like a nova exploding into a meteor shower.

The clouds parted as if fleeing from the heat of the orb that had crashed through the stratosphere. The flowers and grass turned away, afraid of being blinded by the light.

There it was.

A blazing crimson sun.

Its tentacles reached out like the thrashing limbs of a creature desperately reaching shore before it drowned. The colour shifted from white to yellow to red as the fire swung across the silent yet peaceful fields like a giant awoken from ancient slumber. It roared with the voice of a thousand lion prides and burned with the intensity of a dying star crying for its dying universe.

The air around the sun rippled as it set everything on fire, blurred with uncertainty of existence against the determination of the golden and crimson orb.

This cannot be the end.

The sun screamed in agony and glory.

I am going home to you, she said to the weeping sun.

It was no more than a complaint or resignation. It was a murmur, reassuring the sun that it would keep on shining until the end of time.

I still have something left to tell you, Chely.

Anne Barberry scorned Chely Ying's supposed lies, called the love of her life a liar, when Anne herself had kept the biggest secret of them all.

I should have told Cole when I had the chance.

The man she had seen dying in her Visions from the nightmare on the day Brutus Barberry was killed. The man who had been shot in front of Anne, whose last words in The Oracle's Vision were a crow's caw.

I knew he was going to die. I knew it would break your heart. I'm sorry. I should have told you. If you had been more prepared, maybe you wouldn't have done what you did.

Anne Barberry's first prophecy of an individual's death as The Oracle was that of Cole of the Yamalan.

In the Vision, the man was always shot right in front of Anne.

That blast of magic from the hands of an Aixauhan soldier was meant for her, the Inabrian magician, not for him.

Cole stepped in front of Anne, an invisible shield the soldier could not see.

His last words, like a crow's caw as he choked on his own blood:

"They cannot have you, Annie. You are one of us."

Anne Barberry was killed by her own sister using the same spell that felled their grandfather Brutus Barberry, the same spell that tore all those children's bones from their bodies. The last victim in a line of buried sins littered over The Barberry Castle.

The murder of the last oracle happened three years after the war. Anne thought the war was over. Chely did not. They had an argument, which had made Anne storm out of The Cottage in the heat of the moment.

Anne had gotten the invitation to go home on the same day as first wave of rebuilding began. The letter welcoming her back promised reconciliation and the mending of broken family relations.

Chely had told her it was not a good idea.

"That hasn't been your home for over a decade, Annie. You might have hope for the future, but they do not. The war ended the prestige of the Inabrian lineages; the common folk of Inabri saw how those in power failed to protect them. They have nothing left to lose. If you go visit The Barberry Castle now, whoever is there to welcome you is someone that will be plotting your death!"

Anne thought of the barberry bushes. Of the endless halls covered in velvet. Of the small town that was always huffing. She wondered if it was still untainted by the legacy of the Barberry family, going on about its mundane daily routine except for when the residents wished to seek their fortunes from her grandfather.

"Don't worry, Chely," Anne replied sternly, with a trace of coldness. "The war made monsters out of all of us. You are the best example, yet I come home to you every day. Why should this be different?"

As the warm blood leaked out of Anne's body, spreading into tendrils of crimson, the barberry fruit she had watched blossom on the chest of Cole's corpse in that Vision, the fruit that had haunted her whole life, came back to her.

The colour of death is the same colour as your hair in the wind, my love.

Chely, Cai-Li (彩黎). The magnificent sunset.

You were right.

I promised I'd come home to you.
I don't think I will be able to. Not this time.
I'm sorry.
I love you, my sun.
I wish our parting words had not been so unkind.

Later, the people who found Anne Barberry's remains would say she had crawled all the way from inside the castle to the side of the hill.

Anne would bleed out across the barberry bushes. Her blood would stain the stems and roots red.

All the newspapers would have a public "In Memoriam" post dedicated in her name. They would paint her as the tragic hero of the notorious Barberry Lineage, an oracle who sought justice and redemption for her family's war crimes.

They would say her name would forever be remembered as a martyr, that she was truly "a hero born into a world where the odds were set against her."

Anne would read those newspapers, even though she would later forget.

She would tear them to shreds.

She was no hero.

She would just want to go home.

Her whole life had been spent on escaping the nightmare of this castle, yet there she was.

Her body fed into the same veins of hate and war and meaningless deaths, thanks to her grandfather's hatred passing down to her generation.

It was all meaningless. The Oracle felt a scream tear through her chest as she stared into the endless bushes in the night. *My whole life was wasted on this hilltop with nothing to spare.*

She'd been naïve enough to think she could ever escape Barberry Castle. Even after two wars and countless deaths, she still wanted to believe her grandfather was wrong, that the castle belonged to her now as she was The Oracle.

That her sister, who was ten years Anne's junior, was not poisoned by the toxins of war.

That her family would somehow embrace her after everything that had happened; through the hatred and despair, Anne dared to think the Barberrys could be more than their ancestor's sins, more than Brutus Barberry, more than what destroyed innocent families like Captain Ark Li's.

Anne was wrong.

In the end, The Oracle could not have predicted that her death at another Barberry's hand would be the last straw that pushed Ying Cai-Li into the deep end.

There were no flowers. The grass was dry and brown. The air was damp.

In the middle of a winter night, there was no light or warmth. The sun had gone down hours ago.

She blinked.

In the distance, a cabin sat with a windmill on top.

She blinked.

There were flowers everywhere. Now, the middle of the summer.

She blinked.

A crow crashed to the ground, turned into water, then into a boy. Cole.

The boy scratched his head. *Can't say I'm too happy to see you so soon, Annie.*

I'm sorry. She fell to the ground. *I'm so sorry.* She begged him for forgiveness.

Cole was taken aback. *Gosh, Anne, what is this for?*

I foresaw your death in that war, The Oracle confessed. *I should have warned you. I should have told you to run as fast as you could.*

And leave Chely behind with you alone? Cole shook his head. *As if that was ever going to happen, Barberry.*

She picked up her head and took the outstretched hand Cole offered her.

It's okay, Anne.

Cole's voice turned into a familiar crow's caw.

Welcome home.

18

The Blood Hawk

THE BLOOD HAWK'S day started off at 6:00 a.m., when the sun had just come out from the horizon.

She first spread some seeds on the open windowsill, overlooking the woods. The birds never came instantly. They'd only come when Chely was not there anymore. Like thieves sneaking to take what was meant for them in the first place, terrified at the possibility of encountering the crimson-haired alchemist. The birds knew, even though they always ate what she put out. They could still taste the salty metallic aftermath of bloodstained hands.

Birds were magical, Cole always used to say. Everyone's soul was shaped like a bird.

No one referred to Ying Cai-Li by her true name anymore.

They called her The Blood Hawk, a bird of prey that dabbled in the darkest of magic and left a trail of bodies in her wake.

"Anne, you have the aura of a black swan."

"What? Why?" Anne lifted her brows. This was maybe the third time she and Cole had talked on friendly terms, back when Chely and Anne had first started dating. "Does that have some special meaning among Aixauhan alchemists?"

"No," Chely said. "I only found out this was a thing with the Yamalan Clan after I met Cole when we were kids at summer camp."

"Yes," Cole proudly nodded. "You were a snob, Anne Barberry."

Anne's face flushed, and Chely was confused.

"We met Anne at the summer camp?" Chely turned her face to look at Anne. She tried hard to picture her new girlfriend as a child.

She imagined a girl with golden locks streaming down her face, as if woven by a golden thread spun from the sun itself. The child in her mind was blurry, but with cherubic cheeks and pigeon-grey eyes. The same as the religious paintings of the Inabrian Creator drawn on ceilings of ancient architecture. Mixed by a perfect alchemic combo. Lacking in childish clumsiness and holding her stature in practised grace.

It was a pretty picture, but it was only a picture. Like illusions conjured by artists who used magic to make paintings move at galleries to enhance the experience.

"No, we didn't," the real Anne's gruff tone snapped Chely out of her trance. "We didn't meet until last summer at the pub. After Chely and I started going out."

"Yes, we did," Cole corrected. His voice was suspicious and hostile. "You watched me get bullied by those older magician kids. They didn't think I deserved to be there. They didn't think I was a person; they called me a 'thing.' Chely stood up for me, and she ended up in the hospital. You did nothing but stand amongst the other Inabrians and watch the show."

"You mean the healing unit of the Magician Alliance," Anne said expressionlessly. "It's not a normal hospital."

Cole's jaw dropped; he gasped as if he couldn't believe what was coming out of Anne's mouth.

"*See?*" He turned to Chely, who was regretting her choice to introduce her new girlfriend to her best friend. "She's just like the rest of them! What do you even see in her?!"

"Honestly," Anne replied in the tone of a dry rock, "I don't know either."

Cole's family, the Yamalan Clan, was known to have cottages spread around the globe. They were nomads, travelling across the land with no barriers or bounds. They could be anyone and anything, as their shapeshifting powers meant no one could stop them from doing so.

For the first years after the war, Chely had a daily routine of sitting in front of The Cottage, staring into the distance.

Every single shapeless orb that moved evoked a human being. As they got closer, she poked up her head like a hare. The scene played out in front of her eyes as the shapes elongated and grew closer, the Yamalan Clans' transparent natural state of being reflecting the sunlight like waves in the ocean, sparkling as if made of blinking stars.

However, once they got close enough, it became clear that it was a deer or a raccoon or a bear. All kinds of creatures passed by this corner of the woods.

No one from the Yamalan Clan had come in the past ten years. No one in Cole's family had ever claimed his body. It was as if they were avoiding this cottage in particular, the one that had invited outsiders inside—an Inabrian oracle and a rogue necromancer alchemist.

The year after Cole was killed, Chely preserved his body with mercury, cinnabar, sulphur, and gold.

The ingredients the Emperor of the Qin used to prolong his life and attempt to pursue immortality. He who had united Aixauh thousands of years ago into one empire and centralised all the different regional branches of alchemy into one coherent system that the alchemists still followed to this very day.

"Didn't the Emperor of Qin die of mercury poisoning?" Anne watched as Chely worked, quietly at first.

"Yes," Chely replied. Her eyes were sore from trying not to get the poisonous alchemical composition on herself, as well as from being unable to look away from Cole's dead body for days. "His corpse remained unmarked by age. Even when archaeologists unearthed him from the ancient tomb."

"That's ironic." Anne let out a dry chuckle that sounded more like a cough. "Sometimes what kills us is what preserves us beyond death."

When he was alive, Cole had been a never-ending water current. Always laughing and changing. Adaptable without complaint. Able to sustain any temperature. His heart was as clear and transparent as his form.

War had not managed to mould and change him. Death, however, had.

In death, his spirit had started to defuse. Cole's humanoid form shifted and faded back into nature day by day. What fell away first had been his hair, those wavering strands of dancing light condensing into black charred grassroot after a wildfire.

Then it had been his eyes. They had been a mixture of glacier blue and daisy white in life, but they'd slowly cooled into the colour of umber.

Lastly, it had been his skin. It had turned ash grey, as if he were turning into the remains of a failed alchemical experiment.

"Let him go," Anne said. "You cannot bring him back; it's not what he would have wanted."

He had been a living, breathing stream of magic. The Yamalan's natural cycle of mortality would see their remains dissolved into the land wherever their bodies found themselves.

If they were buried in the woods, they would become soil that hosted nutrients that helped the tree take stronger roots next spring. If their body was left in the river or thrown into the ocean, they'd dissolve into water like raindrops and become part of the whole. If they were fed to animals, they'd become whatever that creature's diet required.

"We learned to take our forms thanks to this world we were born into. They gave us the knowledge to cultivate ourselves into sentient beings," Cole explained with a content smile on his face. "When we die, it is a debt we pay back to the world in gratitude. To become whatever it needs us to be."

Cole's body, however, did not go back to the world.

"This is fucked up, Cai-Li." Anne's voice cracked after shouting at each other for what felt like centuries. "Cole deserves to be laid to rest! Not kept as some kind of zombie monument by dark magic because you refuse to let him go!"

"I don't want to do this anymore than you do," Chely argued. "But they need Cole's body as evidence so they can condemn the soldier who killed him. They need to be able to identify the time of death! We can't let Cole's murderer get away with this by saying he was just another casualty of war—the war was over by then. That man murdered Cole in cold blood."

"The trial for that soldier is scheduled *three years* from now, minimum!" Anne rubbed her temples, her hands trembling. She was having increasing migraines; The Oracle was now burdened by both Visions of the future and the nightmares of the past.

"They were not supposed to use alchemy against the civilians. I know what you are going through. But the ceasefire orders did not reach where we were in time. He blasted the deadly blow at *me*, Chely. That Aixauhan soldier saw my face, the face of the enemy. Cole dove in front of me. If you are so hell-bent on blaming someone for his death, blame *me*."

"It doesn't matter." Chely remembered the heavy waters of grief that had submerged her ever since she had first seen the solid body of Cole of the Yamalan lying on the ground. So still, as if he were a statue made of diamonds. Magic still coursed through him, not yet realising he was gone.

There were no wounds from the blow that killed him. Cole's eyes were still open. He looked stunned and confused, as if he'd accidentally tripped and fallen down. As if all he needed to stand again was for Chely to reach out a hand and he'd roll back up, laughing at how clumsy he was for face-planting against the ground.

Three years after the war, the trials were no longer broadcast. Other than those prosecuted and the ones roped into doing it. Everyone had largely moved on by then.

The soldier who had killed Cole was an alchemist, as well, specialising in architectural work. The kind of people Aixauh desperately needed to rebuild from the devastation of the war.

The case was dismissed.

Anne laid Cole on the ground next to the creek not far from The Cottage, under a tree that was barren after being struck by lightning.

The next spring, after Cole's body was buried underneath it, new branches sprouted from the previously dead trunk. White and pink flowers bloomed alongside green leaves. In autumn, Anne picked fresh apples hanging from the tree's branches. So plentiful were the fruits that they fell to the ground.

"Look at that," Anne said as she put the most radiant red apple into Chely's hand. "It's Cole. He's still with us. And he said these ones resemble the colour as your hair and your cheeks. Delicious enough to take a bite."

"Stop. Your attempt at flirtation is so embarrassing. Stick to wordplay with your prophecies, Oracle," Chely replied.

She took a bite of the apple. It was as fresh as the air outside.

The war was over.

It was a new beginning.

After about three hours of wasting her time thinking someone might stop by The Cottage between 7:00 a.m. and 10:00 a.m., Chely turned off the kettle on the stove that always had Earl Grey tea inside.

Fewer and fewer people had come to visit over the years. Maev was the only one after half a decade that Chely still expected to show up despite their time being spent mostly in silence.

Ark used to visit a lot too. However, after the wound she'd suffered from the war caught up to her, requiring her to remain an inpatient at the healing unit of the Magician Alliance full-time, there was no one else to prepare tea for.

As for the reputation of The Blood Hawk, the assassin whose hands were drenched in blood and who took body parts from war criminals who escaped justice, it became more and more known. Some people were disgusted by her. Some feared her. Some admired her and even cheered the name on in secret.

Nonetheless, they all distanced from Ying Cai-Li.

No one outright accused her of being a murderer and necromancer; it was the last kindness they could offer to a grieving and lonely woman who'd never moved on from the war.

The stove had been built specifically for alchemists who required a never-ending fire, one on which the temperature could be unaltered for weeks depending on the elixir that was brewing, but Chely rarely used it for that purpose these days.

She mostly gave lectures at different universities, being the one they called every time they needed someone to be a flesh and bone example for the students to learn from to specialise in "Alchemical Application in War."

Chely would teach these young alchemists, who were the same ages as Maev, Kong-Ming, and the other orphans they had picked up during the war had been. They'd lived through it—she could see it in their eyes. They had all seen ruined buildings, heard the explosions, lost family and friends, been driven out of their homes into an unknown future in which one did not live but merely survived.

She taught them the application of alchemy in war. The way to determine where the corpses had been before death by the dirt on their suits, the production of deadly elixirs that could melt someone's flesh or make their muscles age for decades.

Chely had learned half of them during the war, and she'd invented the other half to live through it.

Now, she was preparing a new generation of kids for another war in the future.

"Why do you keep brewing Earl Grey?" Maev had asked Chely the last time she had come to visit. "You don't like it. Ark doesn't like it. It's not the kind of tea from Aixauh. I don't mind it, but you know I only drink water since any kind of caffeine could impede my sense of direction when I walk into the afterlife and back."

"Anne likes it," Chely replied. "She says that Earl Grey tea drunk from the Chalice of Truth gave the most accurate and clear image of prophecies for an oracle."

Maev's eyes were unreadable as she turned her head away.

"The Chalice was used by Brutus Barberry in the First War as an execution tool for alchemists," Maev murmured. "Anne didn't know that, so I understand why she didn't throw it away. I hear the ghosts talking. Ark's parents were killed by that chalice. The captain doesn't have the heart to tell you. It's kind of messed up that you're using it like a teakettle."

"The history of it doesn't matter," Chely replied. "This chalice is like Anne; I don't care what it was used for by some old dead Inabrian man, my girlfriend used it for tea and divination, and that'll be all it is to me."

Maev was speechless for a few seconds. "Anne cared about history," she said at last. "Anne knew that history is what brought us here. She saw the bigger picture. She was an oracle, and she knew the past and the future are intrinsically connected. Anne would tell you to throw that chalice away."

"Anne can tell me to fuck off herself once she's back," Chely replied, her voice growing into a dark rumble. "Until then, I'll do whatever I want."

The child who was no longer a child had learned by that point it was meaningless to argue with The Blood Hawk.

Chely knew what Maev wanted to say.

Anne Barberry was not coming back.

They got married three years after the war ended, days after Cole was buried.

"We are literally dancing on his grave," Anne commented expressionlessly.

It had a specific kind of effect when The Oracle made her grim observations while wearing a white wedding dress that cascaded around her like the folded wings of a swan. A bouquet of red roses and pink lilies in her hand were the only colouration.

"If he were here, he'd be happy for us," Chely replied with a smile on her face. For the first time in a while, it didn't feel like a lie.

Chely wore a black suit with gold and red threads sewn onto the hem, the neck, and the sleeves. Anne had chosen it from the store in the town that lay at the foot of the hill where Barberry Castle stood.

The tailor there was talkative; he said he'd always wanted to open a pub and an inn with a restaurant because he loved to make pies. Anne's face had twisted more than Chely had ever seen as the oracle hand-signed at Chely to quit it when the tailor had offered them some pie while he went to grab the suit.

Chely had almost choked on it. She'd coughed as the crust, which was as hard as stone, lodged in her throat.

Anne had groaned before bursting into laughter.

If she could have stopped the scene at that moment, Chely would have willingly eaten the tailor's rock pies for breakfast the rest of her life.

"We can choose something else. This suit was pre-ordered by my family when they agreed on an arranged marriage when I was, like, six." Anne furrowed her brows at Chely as she tried on the suit. It was magnificent, but hung loose on Chely, seeing as it'd been meant for the Barberry Oracle's future *husband*.

"You mean your cousin who was a general in the war and was sentenced to life imprisonment for crimes against humanity?" Chely asked.

"Yes." Anne sighed. "So, maybe this isn't the best idea."

"Why not?" Chely smirked. She lifted her chin at her reflection in the mirror. "Surely I look better than a potential incestuous groom."

"Don't get me wrong," Anne replied, so serious that it was hard to tell if she was being sincere or sarcastic for anyone who didn't know her well. "You look great in black and in suits. I just don't think we should risk it. Magic barriers and wars have already been placed on the wedding so no one will crash it due to the attention we're attracting."

"That's the point," Chely replied. She twirled in a purposefully flamboyant manner and mimicked a posh accent she'd picked up from Anne. "We will set an example, my lady oracle. For everyone to see the notorious Barberry heir marry an Aixauhan alchemist while said alchemist wears the suit that was meant for her intended. It's a message to the world—the war is over, and the world is ours."

"The war is over, and the world is ours." Anne chewed on those words. "I like that."

"Thank you." Chely bowed as if she had just made a speech to a live audience. "Thank you."

"Shut up." Anne rolled her eyes and turned away. "I'll go tell the tailor to modify the suit to fit your build. Let's just hope my family doesn't hunt us down on our honeymoon once they find out."

Chely's smile stayed on her face until Anne left the room.

Then it fell, as fleeting as a ghost.

Speaking of ghosts...

"You must be the tailor's deceased wife," Chely said to the ash-grey spectator in a torn uniform and missing an arm and a leg. "You've been following us around from the village edge. Do you have something you want to tell your husband? I can pass it on for you."

The ghost of the tailor's wife stared back at Chely dully, her jaw opened and closed in a twisted manner. Saliva dripped out along with blood from the wound on her head.

"Okay." Chely nodded. The mumbled noise from the ghost's crushed windpipe did not form words that made sense. But three years into practising necromancy, Ying Cai-Li could already understand ghosts without knowing exactly what they said. "I'll tell him everything you told me."

Pearl-like specks formed on the ghost's dead and decaying cheeks. The ghost closed her eyes and evaporated like rain on the side of the road.

"Were you talking to someone?" Anne barged through the door, an uncharacteristically panicked, wild look on her face. The tailor followed behind her, discombobulated. He was holding the coat and leaning back, as he must not be used to the graceful Barberry Oracle acting so unlike he remembered.

Chely did not know what Anne was like as a child. The Anne she'd fallen in love with was graceful but always had the attitude of someone who stood on the edge of a cliff.

It was unfathomable to imagine that Anne Barberry must have been happy and careless, once upon a time.

The power of The Oracle manifested when one was a preteen. That meant there once had been an Anne who didn't awake in the middle of the night screaming and crying. A young girl who did not know how many ways a man could die, who was capable of being surprised by the cruel deeds humans were capable of.

It probably wouldn't have lasted, since the war would have taken all their childhood innocence soon enough.

A part of Chely idly hoped, against all reason, to go back to the summer when they were all children. The summer both Cole and Anne remembered but Chely had somehow forgotten.

They'd have more years together spent in innocence, when they knew not what war was other than from stories told by the previous generations.

"No one at all," Chely replied with a smile. Lying to Anne had been hard at first, but Chely found it got easier every time. "Not a single living soul other than us."

"I have your suit." The tailor frowned as he cut in. "Er, is everything all right? Ms. Barberry and…Ms. Barberry?"

"Her last name's Ying," Anne replied dryly.

"The Aixauhan character for winning (赢), certainly appropriate here," Chely added with a smile. "Thanks a lot; the suit fits great.

Your pie tasted great too. Becoming an innkeeper is definitely a wonderful idea. I'm sure your lodging would be magnificent."

"The tailor who did the wedding gown for you and Anne died a few weeks ago," Maev said. "I saw him in the In-Between the other day. He's an innkeeper there. His pies look good. I'd have taken a bite if dead people's food wouldn't trap me there forever."

"I wouldn't recommend it if you want to keep your teeth," Chely replied honestly. "He's one of those people who are gifted at things they did not like to do and terrible at the things they *did* want to do."

"Just like you," Maev said poignantly.

"I don't know what you mean," Chely said.

"You know exactly what I mean," Maev replied. "How many more souls will I have to find in the In-Between who tell the tale of being slaughtered by The Blood Hawk?"

"If they hate being killed so much, maybe they'd have thought twice before inflicting the same thing on thousands upon thousands of other people."

"She *knows*, Chely!" Maev's mounting frustration was a terrifying force, the helpless little girl in the war who Chely carried from her mother's dying embrace had grown up to become a better person in a better world. "She might not be conscious of it with the selectiveness of her awareness, but The Oracle who sees the past and future is the queen of the In-Between. She's the magic center of it all. Anne knows everything you are doing in her name."

Chely shrugged. "Let me guess," she said with a faint smile. "She hates my guts."

"Yes," Maev fumed. "She's living in the equivalent of her old family's castle, never coming down to mingle with any of the souls in the town who are passing through. You're not helping her. You are hurting her."

"She doesn't need to," Chely said. "They're all dead, and she is still alive. When I'm done, she'll have plenty of time to socialise with the living. When I'm done, she'll outlive them."

"If everyone's a bird, then what kind of bird am I?"

"If I'm a black swan, then you're probably a hummingbird," Anne suggested. "Since the shapes of our souls are based on the first impressions Cole had of us. Then I am evil, and you're sweet as hell."

"I don't know," Cole said, deep in thought. "You guys just got together. You don't know her as well as I do, Barberry. There's a lot more to Ying Cai-Li than you could ever imagine."

"Is this where you want to insert a speech about how Chely is too good for me, Cole?" Anne bit back.

Chely chuckled. It was a sunny day as she lay back against the tree. The birds were singing, and the sun was out. Warmth seeped into the air like a honeycomb.

"Actually, Cole thinks I'm a horrifying bird of prey," Chely said.

"Hey, don't tell her that!" Cole protested. "Plus, if you didn't like the idea, why make it into your unofficial last name?"

"Hawk?" Realisation dawned on Anne's face. "Is that where Chely Hawk came from?"

"Yeah." Chely smiled. "My last name is Ying. It is the character for winning (贏), and the last name of the Founding Emperor of Aixauh, who first sought immortality through alchemy. It is also the pronunciation of the character for hawks and eagles (鷹)."

Cole gave a long-suffering sigh. "If I had known how many times you were going to explain it like it was the name of some worldwide-known figure, I'd never have told you that."

"The hawk with the red hair." Anne smiled like the first rays of sunlight hitting the ground in the morning. "The Blood Hawk. That is as theatrical as a black swan."

"I think they'd look cool together." Chely couldn't help but smile back.

"Get a room," Cole groaned.

When the news of the war's end reached them, Chely thought life would truly begin. That was before Cole had died. Blasted in the head in the lingering panic and confusion of the battlefield.

Followed not long after by Anne. Swallowed by the same hatred and resentment in the ominous Barberry Castle she'd tried to outrun.

Even Captain Ark, who'd lived through both of the wars, finally succumbed to death from a wound sustained in the end.

That was all the reward and compensation playing heroes had gotten them.

There was no beginning.

They said the war was over, because lying to themselves was the only way society could move on. Turning a blind eye to the generations engulfed by the gaping mouth of a monster, forever stuck in the inferno cycle of hatred and violence and loss.

The war raged on.

Standing in the middle of the woods in her serene cabin, Chely was alone.

The Blood Hawk wailed a deafening cry.

The only ones who heard it were the creatures of the forest, who dared not come near the cottage on the hill.

19

The Crow

"DID YOU KILL my sister?"

When Anne Barberry opens her eyes again, the misty dullness is gone. The queen of the In-Between, finally aware of her crown.

On the surface, nothing appears to have changed. The Castle is still draped in black fabric that blocks out any sunlight, a looming dark hole determined to keep the outside world too intimidated to ever venture in.

The breakfast Chely is cooking sizzles on the stove. The smell of crispy bacon and scrambled eggs dances around the room.

"Before I answer that question"—Chely grabs the kettle that is boiling water on its own with a heating spell—"do you want some tea?"

"Do I want some *tea*?" Anne whispers, unbelieving. A decade's worth of suppressed emotions electrify her all at once.

And Chely just stands there, as if all Anne forgot was to turn off the light charm on her way out last night when she was passed out drunk.

"No, Chely." Anne's head pounds. "I want to know why you threw your life away in pursuit of the fucking dead!" For some indescribable reason, she is still hungover from last night.

The edges of Chely's lips are still quirked up, smiling sweet and tempting like a red-spotted poisonous mushroom.

"I will tell you everything you want to know," The Blood Hawk says, unaffected by Anne, who is about to explode in a blazing glory. "I have questions for you too. We've been fooling around long enough. It's time to get down to business."

"You mean the business of using dismembered body parts of people you've murdered in a dark magic ritual to resurrect me?"

"Yes," Chely says. "See, we're on the same page."

"No," Anne replies, shaking her head as her eardrums rang like a bell tower. "No. Not this again. This absolute nonchalance of yours despite the actual gravity of the situation…"

Chely chuckles softly. "I've missed this," she said. "I've missed you."

Silence descends on them like frost despite the stove fire.

"Oh no," Chely yelps, which jerks Anne into reality.

Anne's eyes bulge as an unnamable emotion catches in her throat. "What?!"

"The bacon is burnt!"

Chely pulls the pan away from the stove and shows Anne the shrivelled-up pieces of meat that are now a pathetic, dry brown. Anne stared at the burnt bacon for a few seconds before huffing out a breath. The currents swirling in her mind threatening to drag her down can wait.

The Oracle lifts up a hand. The air buzzes around them like a hornet's nest let loose. The charred bacon and blackened scrambled eggs lift into the air limply on their own, line up, and fling themselves into the open stove fire.

"Are there any eggs left?" Anne asks.

Mutely, Chely nods and passes the carton she got fresh from the market down in town that morning.

An earthquake-like tremor shakes the hanging pots and kitchen utensils. They sing in unison, clinking against the stone wall like a choir following Anne's direction as the orchestrator. Herbs hanging from the ceiling—parsley, basil and chives—are plucked away from the ribbons holding them suspended. They swim from the roof like fish to lie obediently down on the cutting board.

Vials and jars click against one another like windchimes as Anne locates olive oil, sea salt, and black pepper. A tiny silver spoon with a handle sculpted in the shape of a swan carefully scoops the needed ingredients into one of the measuring cups Chely brought with her.

"I feel like I am obligated to let you know, Annie," Chely interjects, sounding slightly sheepish, "that cup you're using is the one I usually use for necromancy."

Anne pauses before immediately dumping the entire measuring cup into the fire.

Chely makes a wheezing sound but then sees the grim look on Anne's face and stifles the sound into a cough. "Um…" The formidable Blood Hawk scratches her head like a child caught not washing her hands properly. "Are you making an omelette?"

In response, Anne gives the tiniest wave and one of the kitchen knives comes to life, jumping a little with excitement at finally being put to use. It shivers in excitement and is about to start a musical number about how rusty it was getting because the mistress of the castle never calls on them for any sort of actual cooking—before a deadly look from Anne shuts it up.

"I'll take that as a yes," Chely relents wisely.

"Don't look so stunned," the oracle replies without meeting the alchemist's eyes. "Contrary to what you and Cole believe, I am actually capable of cooking."

"Right." Chely laughs, her face puffing up like sourdough drenched in yeast. "Only took you about ten years."

Anne tells herself it is the newly awakened awareness that she is the creator and the center of the magic that makes this place exist—that is why her heart races in exhilaration and her pulse skips at the simple look of bewilderment and wonder on Chely's face.

The sense of steadiness filling her senses again has nothing to do with The Blood Hawk. The necromancer. The murderer Anne's wife has become.

It's the feeling of finding water in a desert after a week of dehydration. It's the feeling of being stuck in a cold and damp cave as a line of rope is thrown down.

It's probably the alcohol from last night, Anne thinks. She must still be drunk.

She should be screaming and crying and throwing up.

It makes no sense that she didn't fall apart at the revelation she's been dead for seven years. Or the memory of what this place truly is, illuminated in front of her eyes like a thousand candles that she alone can control.

This version of Barberry Castle. The town down the hill. The non-existent girl whose family Anne Barberry supposedly "took over." The townspeople who hate her, and from whom she hides, who also seek her aid. All the sorrows and tribulations and lived experiences of the last decade are nothing but smoke and mirrors. A land where everyone's memories have been wiped away—all trapped by the dying magic of an evil witch who lay in perpetual slumber.

They may not remember why as they go along their daily routine. The Innkeeper whose inn hosted Chely before she found her way to the castle. Those children and "tourists" who disappeared, who Chely said were the subjects of gossip in town, the rumours about how they all went missing after a divination session with The Oracle.

For a decade, the townsfolk feared and hated the witch in black who lived in her castle on the hill, but they never marched with pitchforks and torches to burn it down.

Why?

Anne used to think it was fear of her power, or some unspoken understanding that if the townsfolk planned on doing anything, The Oracle would surely foresee their futile attempt.

Now she knows the answer.

"Only took me about ten years," Anne repeats Chely's words as the passage of time dawns on her. The reality of what she's done. The shame rises like a phoenix from the ashes. She doesn't have the moral high ground to chastise Chely. Not when, in her own way, Anne has been trapping the dead she thought deserving here with her.

The tears that brew in a cauldron behind her eyes finally overflow, like a patch of healthy soil slowly eroded by rainwater as the trees died and their roots held no longer. The persona of Anne Barberry is unravelling, like peeling back the skin of an orange, exposing the sour and juicy fruit inside. Or more like flaying the skin off a person, leaving behind only the meaty remains for crows to peck on.

"All this time," Anne's voice broke like a dam. "I thought you were the one I was angry at. But no, it was myself. I am the monster that turned you into this. If we had never met, none of these terrible things would have happened."

"Annie." Chely's voice grows soft and vulnerable, as if, in taking off the mask she wore, now everything is out in the open. Unbothered by the confrontation of her own horrific actions, the red-haired alchemist is disturbed to see the oracle's face scrunched up in pain.

"Of course you have a right to be angry at me. I—I violated your corpse. I knew you'd find peace, and still, I selfishly wanted you back. You were able to forgive your family and go home to your sister even after everything that happened—you wouldn't have wanted to be pulled back by necromancy. I made my own choices. But you, you are trapped here because of the consequences that should befall your sister and grandfather, not because you wanted to be."

Anne crossed over to the other side. She finally chased up to the sun on that hilltop with The Cottage surrounded by wildflowers at dawn.

Cole was there. Anne found Cole there.

Still, it was not Chely's necromancy that brought Anne Barberry to this place. It was not recompense for what the other Barberrys had done.

Cai-Li might have made the mistake of being overly fixated on the past, but that did not mean Anne was the role model of someone who had stepped into the future.

"No," Anne replies. "Chely. You were right."

"Right about what?" Chely furrows her brows in confusion.

Anne's lips quiver. "Come along, I think it's better I show you in person."

After breakfast, Anne and Chely head to the divination room.

The heavy black velvet curtains are drawn to the sides, away from the windows. The chandeliers with their muted yellow dancing across the halls are gone, replaced by the blinding clarity of daylight streaming in.

That's when Chely finally notices the portraits hanging across every inch of every wall in Barberry Castle.

When the curtains were down, the faces on the portraits were submerged in darkness. Every single one is a similarly shaped phantom, faceless figures who are part of the furniture that contribute to the intentionally creepy atmosphere Anne prefers. The sunlight now illuminates the portraits, bringing their faces front and center.

Their alabaster skin painted with oil that is devoid of bumps or flaws. Each with their head tilted and looking proudly at the painter with their pigeon-grey eyes and sandy blond hair.

The men are all wearing uniforms, the same uniform that—even a decade later—makes Chely's brows twitch. The design has changed throughout the generations of the men in these portraits; the only constant is their puffed-up chests and squared shoulders.

Blood on the uniform. Uniformed men with weapons in hand. Same proud look as they decapitate one of the orphans they brought along with them. Uniformed soldiers on opposite sides send cannonballs into their ship. Uniformed soldiers round up alchemists, so many soldiers that they all blend together into the same shade, like a grassy terrain.

Until red blossoms among them.

Red, the colour of the alchemists who died at their hands. Chely watches as they huddle together in the hiding place and watch the execution carry on.

In a sea of green uniforms, Chely knows from the moment the red blossoms like spider lilies—the flower that blooms on the shores of the Yellow Fountain that leads to the afterlife in Aixauhan tradition—before the screaming and pleading starts.

Chely shakes her head and counts her breaths. She uses the technique that has slowly become a habit in the past decade, passed to her by Captain Ark, who's dealt with the way war warps one's mind much longer than she has.

"Imagine you're on a solo sail," Ark said. "The ocean is deep and turbulent, but it is beneath you. Your feet are safely on deck."

In the beginning, it was hard. Like dealing with thunderstorms and a kraken ready to drag her down. These days, it is more like a drizzle of rain.

However, Chely hears Anne's breath quicken as they pass by the portraits. The Oracle's fists are clenched, leaving half-moons of white nail marks on her palms. Anne's eyes are focused straight ahead, as if the portraits are alive and moving, their eyes following her, monsters ready to climb out to chase her down the hall.

The women and children are always wearing long silk dresses, with their cheeks a cherry pink. The girls all have long hair, slightly curled, like willow branches but gilded with gold.

"*You know, Barberry. Outside of Inabri, we see you people as ghosts.*" Cole's voice chases past Chely's mind like a breeze. It is so close, so vivid. "*Right, Chely?*"

"They surely do all look like ghosts," Chely murmurs as if beckoned by the spirit of her best friend.

Anne turns her head, on her face a fractured, mirthless smile. "That's what Cole used to say," the oracle recounts softly. "When you and I had just started dating. Before he got used to it, he'd always tell me it was because we have skin so pale it only belonged to ghosts and dead bodies after all the warmth and blood of life had leaked out."

"*Caw.*" The crow, Anne's familiar, flies in from the now-open windows with a disgruntled noise.

"I think your familiar is trying to say his namesake didn't mean it like that," Chely says.

"My familiar?" Anne asks, as if the crow isn't perched right on her shoulder. "Oh, you mean Cole? Right..."

The crow's eyes are not those of normal birds; they are a milky, foam white. Almost...transparent. Chely did not notice how its eyes shine like pearls as if they were made of mist, not until the sun is allowed in with the curtains gone.

"Did you not name your familiar after him?" Chely drinks in Anne's serious obliviousness like milk with honey.

"Well," Anne says. "I think it would be better for him to explain himself."

The black crow lets out one final, defiant caw before it melts into water and recreates itself into his human form.

The boy Chely kept in the same shape as the day he died for years. The brother they buried under the tree. The one who has remained forever young and unchanged by time, whose eyes are as clear as the fresh river stream and white snow, unblemished and untainted by neither war nor death.

"Hi, Chely," Cole of the Yamalan greets her. "It's been a long time."

"They all hate us here, Cai-Li," Cole cried that night when he snuck into Chely's tent. "Why did Mama send us here to this place where all the other kids hate us?"

"I think A'yi (Auntie) just wanted us to make some Inabrian friends," Chely replied. "I'm sure not all of them are like that. We just haven't met the good ones yet."

They were children, sent to this summer camp for Inabrian magical children by their parents so that, theoretically, they could blend in better. *Assimilate.*

"I don't want to be their friend," Cole grumbled. "None of them stood up for me. Only you did."

"Well," Chely said, "they're probably just afraid. None of them have really seen people like us before. They'll get used to it soon enough."

"I doubt it," Cole replied. "There was a war. Mum said that's where she met Dad. She tried to make it sound like it wasn't that big of a deal. But how could it not be, if she is so sad all the time?"

Chely's parents had shown they were not bothered by any war, not even one that had led to the deaths of tens of thousands of their fellow alchemists. They had set their sights on a higher plane. They were descendants of the Qin emperor, not some nameless alchemist clan with no claim to fame. That was what they said.

They lived longer than the average human being, alchemist or not.

Chely's mother was a distant descendant of one of the Golden Crows (金乌). As it was said, there were ten Golden Crows born in the sky of Aixauh, all of them made of feathers of crimson and yellow flames. They were so bright that there was eternal daylight on the land of Aixauh. At the same time, humans suffered endless famines because their scorching heat left no crops to grow.

The famous archer Hou'Yi shot nine of the Golden Crows down to stop their eternal flames from causing endless famines for the humans. He was then punished to become a mortal alongside his wife, Chang'E, who could not stand the short and meaningless life of a human and became the Moon Goddess of Night, leaving her husband behind.

"There is a lesson for you." Chely's mother told her the tale from the day she could understand tongues. "I could have been a goddess, and you could have lived for centuries. We are children of the Sun, yet now we are mere candle flames that will last for the blink of an eye."

"Is that why you married Father?" Chely had asked, naïve yet perceptive. "Because he is the closest you can get to a chance at immortality like your godly ancestors?"

"Aren't you a clever one?" Her mother had chuckled. "Of course, silly. Why else would you marry someone?"

Chely's father had been an apprentice of the Ying Clan who had taken on the clan's last name. An alchemist branch that traced its way back thousands of years to the Founder of Aixauh, Ying Zheng, the First Emperor of Qin. The emperor who drank mercury and died of poisoning, believing his alchemists had concocted a successful elixir that would grant him immortality. To rule the Empire of Aixauh until the end of time.

The Qin Empire had turned into dust within the next generation due to Ying Zheng's sons and their infighting over the throne, but the Qin's system of law and governance marked the beginning of Aixauh for millennia to come.

So, too, did the Founding Emperor's ambition of seeking immortality become the pursuit of all alchemists of Aixauh.

The passion alchemists had for immortality died out over the next few millennia. Mostly because alchemists found more pressing matters to focus on, more interesting things to explore. Or just another mortal crisis to endure.

After all, there were enough problems to keep one human occupied in one finite lifetime.

Unlike the Yamalans, who had exceedingly long threads of life built into them as they were born from the energy between the celestial and Earth, human alchemists lived a mere handful of decades before perishing.

The Ying family was different. They kept their traditions alive.

Chely Hawk's descent into what amounted to necromancy did not come from nowhere, as one of the reasons that magicians who went to Aixauh started the war was the belief that all alchemists were like the Ying Clan, who pursued immortality against the Creator's design, bypassing the allowed limitation of magic.

Chely didn't really believe in a singular Creator, for in her eyes her parents were basically gods.

Her parents had both been in their hundreds when they had Chely. Another mortal child, who was an alchemist by blood but nothing like them. They held no anger toward the ghosts from across the ocean who had slaughtered their people, as they'd seen enough bloodshed and death in their time.

They'd watched their children come and go, and, like two ancient trees, they'd grown bored with seeing the same green grass every year. They were not immortal, for even gods die in Aixauh. Everyone returns to the Reincarnation Cycle eventually.

Chely grew from a chubby infant to a stumbling child to a young woman, all without seeing a single strand of hair on her father's head turn grey, nor counting a single wrinkle added onto her mother's face. It wasn't even a surprise when they left when the war started; for them, it was nothing more than seeing a temporary vacation spot caught on fire.

They moved on.

Cole was supposed to be the same. His section of the Yamalan Clan was the crystallisation of the natural glaciers upon the peak of the mountain. Their children were born as rarely as their elderly died. If Cole had stayed on the Yamalan mountains among his people, he would have lived like Chely's parents. Had it not been for his mother, who was exiled for marrying a foreign magician, Cole of the Yamalan would not have known what the word "death" meant.

Cole's mother had loved Cole, but she had still doomed him to an early grave.

"Auntie is a kind woman," Chely once said to Cole, when she had not yet fallen in love, and was the war was not yet anywhere near their youth. "But it was a mistake for her to leave that mountain. You could have lived for centuries; now you'll only live a fraction of that."

"You don't know what you're talking about," Cole defended his mum, naturally, as any child would. "Mum said it's better to live a short life filled with love, rather than existing for centuries without feeling the passage of time."

"That can't be right," Chely argued. "If you live longer, you'd be able to find another love. Living a long life should make it easier to find love, not the other way around."

"I don't know," Cole said. "I have never fallen in love before."

"I think you will find out one day," Chely replied, feeling sorry for herself. "You'll at least still live past a century. I think I'll die of old age before I ever know what love is all about."

Not many years later, Cole's mother grew sick.

The Yamalan Clan was never supposed to leave the mountain range for long. She faded away bit by bit.

First went her hair, strands of it dislodging from her head like maple leaves falling in autumn. "I'm as bald as an egg," Auntie joked. "Cole, do you think your father will still recognise me when he notices my head is twice the size as before?"

Then her blood started to run dry. Yamalan blood was not red, so the only sign of the loss was that her body slowly shriveled like a piece of fruit in the sun. Then, her skin started peeling off her body. Afterward, she lost sinew and flesh.

When they buried her, all that was left was her bone.

Chely had learned a lot about the anatomy of a body by watching her best friend's mum die a drawn-out death.

They put the remains into the ocean, for that was what Cole wanted. He wished for his mother to find her way back to the land from which they came. Chely hoped that would truly be the case. She didn't comment on how unrealistic it was for bone dust to drift all the way to the nearest shore in Aixauh.

Nevertheless, that was not the point of a funeral. The dead did not care what you did with their remains.

The dead did not care about much at all.

For if they did, Cole's mother would never have left her son with that empty and broken look on his face.

"Mum was uttering his name until the very end, Cai-Li," Cole told Chely during his mother's funeral. The ocean breeze tasted of salt and tears.

"She must have loved him," Chely said, carefully, so as to not provoke her brother who was so deep in grief.

"Yes, she loved him." Cole laughed. He did not look at Chely, choosing instead to focus on the seagulls flying by. "A man who didn't even let his son carry on his family name. He convinced her to abandon her clan for him. He promised she'd be loved in his homeland. Look at her now, nothing but dust and bone. You were right. Life is too short for love to be worth the risk."

Chely didn't know what to say to that, so she remained silent.

Eventually, Chely offered the only way she knew how. "Do you want revenge on your father? Shall we go after him and have him pay for what he did to your mother?"

Cole's anguish and anger were the height of the Yamalan mountains, unreachable in their altitude and secluded in windstorms enough to strand any hiker who dared to venture up.

However, as deadly and unending as his grief was, it was still burning cold. An isolated solitude. It destroyed nothing but Cole himself, contained within the flesh and bone of a single person.

That was why he needed Chely to voice those words.

For so many years, Cole and Chely were each other's driftwood.

Two identically confused, magical kids from Aixauh, who'd wandered a little far from home and found themselves thrown into the fiery pit of the Underworld where there were ghosts everywhere who wanted to eat them alive. Cole was the glacier that cooled Chely's fire so she didn't leave a bloody trail behind her in a world that was hell-bent on breaking them down.

But at that moment, he needed her to provide the warmth of wrath. Even if that wrath came from the suns that had once caused famine and drought. Even if it left behind no survivors.

"Yes," Cole replied. "If there is ever going to be a war, I want to fight in it. For my mother. For all the kids like us."

"You're dating *who*?!"

They were in the middle of a tavern, and Cole was fully ready to flip the table and crush every single customer within a ten-mile radius.

Chely smiled at all the eyebrows raised their way.

"Sorry, carry on," she urged them as she got up. "My brother here is just a little drunk."

Cole protested. "I literally cannot get drunk—"

"Shut up and walk," Chely warned him through gritted teeth. "You just destroyed the number one date spot in this town where Annie and I can meet up without anyone giving a shit."

"Er, do you care if I give a shit?" Cole snapped. At least he had the decency to lower his voice now that they had ended up in the streets at midnight.

"Yes," Chely admitted. "That's why I'm telling you this."

"A little too late! Since you are already calling her 'Annie' as if she's your pony or something instead of the current oracle to the most famous war criminals—"

"I knew her a long time before I asked her out, Cole. She didn't even know who I was. She didn't care that I'm Aixauhan or an alchemist—"

"My father didn't care that Mum was Yamalan, either," Cole bit back. "It's a passive declaration of apathy, not *love*. Especially not when the person telling you that is The Barberry Oracle, the heir to Brutus Barberry, who headed the biggest Aixauhan alchemist massacre in history. The one who told his men to slaughter as many alchemist children as they could find since he predicted they would lose that last war!"

A cloaked figure wearing all black suddenly appeared from the tavern door, clearly following them out.

Chely facepalmed. This was not how she wanted this to go down at all.

Cole watched in utter bewilderment as the individual who joined them unwelcomed pulled back her hood, revealing a pale face framed by golden locks, like a gilded lily drawn on canvas in oil paintings.

"I think it will be a good argument for having me on your side," Anne Barberry said coolly, uncaring about the dropping temperature her appearance had added to the conversation, "when I tell you I know for sure there is another war coming."

"I'm sorry, Ms. Barberry!" The tailor clasped his hands as he knelt on the ground and pleaded. "I had nothing to do with your death. I'm so, so sorry. Please, just let me go! Please!"

The figure looming in front of him was clothed in black velvet. The gown dragging behind her merged into shadow. Her face was obscured by a veil as dark as storm clouds, hiding any traces of emotion from the view of the man begging for his soul.

Golden locks cascaded down her shoulder, as ghastly close to white electricity against the overwhelming darkness, bearing an unnatural shine. They were blindingly bright yet had all the warmth zapped away from the colour. Like newly born yellow ducklings plucked of all their feathers, or sunflowers that had bleached off their warm yellow petals, leaving behind an empty and harrowing husk.

"Falsehoods and lies."

Graceful yet damning. The deceased oracle, clothed in unending sorrow, replied with no vulgarity or vengeance or displeasure.

Her voice was a bottomless well, dry of water.

Her gaze was a world that was permanently stuck in winter, where night went on for eternity. A place where no seeds could sprout, no animals could roam, no flowers could bloom, and no life could inhabit. All because of the emptiness in the sky where the sun should be.

"You were the one who delivered the invitation from Anne Barberry's younger sister." She laid the accusation before the man on the ground, who was scrambling like an insect about to drown. "The one who led The Oracle back to that castle where she was killed."

"Yes, I did deliver the invitation! But I didn't know she was going to kill you!" The tailor howled in desperation. The liquid from the Chalice of Truth prevented him from saying an outright lie, but he was still not speaking the truth. "Please, you can't trap me here forever! My wife… She is waiting in the afterlife for me. Have mercy!"

"No lies hold for long after drinking from the Chalice of Truth." She watched him, almost pityingly. "Not even the white lies we tell ourselves."

"All right, all right!" the man howled as he caved. "I knew your family saw you as a traitor. I knew they still stuck firm to the beliefs they held through the two wars. I knew there was a chance it was a trap, but I did not care."

"I had just gotten married." A rush of blinding rage overcame her. It was a flash of pain and crimson. The last thing she ever felt, the thorny vines of barberry bushes pricking her skin. "Chely loved the suit you made her. Cole had only just been buried. The war was finally over. We had only just begun."

Ugly sobs broke out from the tailor's voice. He clasped his hands together.

"I'm so, so sorry." The man reached out to grab the hem of her dress. In her astonishment, his hand actually touched the soft fabric, where previously there had only been shadows. "I was just a tailor. Your family was my whole business. My entire livelihood! I could not refuse a request from your sister. Not after I lost my wife in the war to the Aixauhans. She was a magician—she served the country until the very end. I could not betray her memory."

"Because the war reaped your wife and your future"—The Oracle knelt down as she lifted her black veil—"you decided to pass the misery along. Another ripple in the pond leading to another monster being born. Another cycle of hatred, grief, and loss. Another dead body added to the never-ending graveyard called war."

The tailor finally saw under her veil. For that, he screamed and screamed until he lost his mind. Two empty, mangled holes sat where eyes should have been, hollowed out as black soot and puss leaking out as white maggots laid eggs in the center.

She was not Anne Barberry. Anne Barberry was the girl who lived in a cottage in the middle of the woods. The girl who deliberately forgot all that had happened, who lived in an eternal daydream of sitting with her red-haired lover underneath the evergreen tree that grew out of the soul seed of her dear brother.

She was not The Oracle either. The Oracle of Barberry Castle, who rejected her family's legacy by plucking her own eyes out so she could forget the cursed Sight that saw into the future. The future she used a lifetime to outrun, the future she returned to in death.

Anne Barberry had heard the tailor's story from Chely the night of their wedding. Anne Barberry had given him sympathy as she learned of his deceased wife. Anne Barberry had forgiven the tailor and understood his plight.

The Oracle did none of those things. The Oracle stared at the man with nothing but emptiness and rage. A pathetic creature who had taken her life from her yet still had the audacity to ask her for mercy. He would remain in this pit of misery with her forever.

"You will have your dream, but only half of it," she said somberly as she delivered the final verdict. "You will become The Innkeeper of the town below the hills. You will make excellent pies and cook. You will have plenty of customers. You will remain here, idly happy. You will never leave or remember you once had a wife. Forever. Until this place ends with me."

The tailor disappeared, fading away bit by bit like stardust. The Oracle room cleared until it was ready to welcome another new arrival.

The tailor had died, but The Innkeeper was born.

So was every other soul that set foot in the In-Between.

They had all come to seek The Oracle to determine their futures.

None of them had moved on. All of them had died.

The only answer The Oracle ever gave was that they would remain here, in the town next to the hill, alongside her castle standing in its solitude.

For good people did not come to this place at all.

Those souls who wandered onto the terrain of The Oracle in black were attracted to her like echoes through the mountains. They shared the same desire for isolation. The same sins and the same empty future.

"It's done," she murmured. Her empty eye sockets saw nothing in particular.

"Do you always have to be so dramatic?" A voice came from the open doors. "He's knocked out cold. You're talking to yourself."

A boy with furrowed brows, who appeared out of thin air, who had the voice of a crow, spoke to her.

She could not see Cole of the Yamalan. Not when she was The Eyeless Oracle and the queen of the In-Between. Anne Barberry could, but only as a familiar. Guilt clouded Annes eyes, for she still could not face the ghost of one of her best friends knowing she had predicted his death without warning him first.

It was getting harder to tell who she was herself, day by day, as she slowly blurred the line of where Anne ended and The Oracle began.

"You should leave, Cole," The Oracle said. "You do not belong in this place. At least one of us has to be at peace."

"I could never be at peace." Cole leaned on the door and kept it open for her. "Not while you are here, and Chely is chopping off people's body parts for some necromantic ritual."

"Then you are dooming yourself forever." The Oracle's features softened as she told the boy of the mountains. "You were right to warn Chely not to trust me that day outside of the tavern. I kept the truth from you. I saw you in my Visions, yet I still let you die for me."

"You flatter yourself, Annie." Cole shook his head. "I chose my own fate by shielding you from death. You can keep blaming yourself forever, but I would do it again if given another chance."

"You chose wrong," she replied cruelly. "You could have had another century if you hadn't stepped in the path of death before me, Cole of the Yamalan. See where it has gotten us? I'm dead only three years after the war anyhow. You sacrificed yourself for a temporary delay."

"That's where you and Chely are both wrong," Cole said. "Those three years were the best time of your and Chely's lives. You lived your happy ending in that short time. It's more than what I had in a lifetime, more than what Captain Ark got in hers. Knowing I gave the two of you three years of true happiness? That is enough for me."

"How can you be so sure of your choice?"

"I am not sure," Cole said as his colourless eyes watched Anne. "That's why I'm still here, Annie. I want to see how your and Chely's story will end. And I hope against all odds that it is another happy ending."

20

The Sun

"I WISH I could say it's nice we're all back together," Cole says. "But sincerely, you guys, *what the fuck?*"

Anne and Chely exchange sheepish glances.

The boy of the Yamalan has his glacier-white eyes fixed on them, making The Oracle and The Blood Hawk, arguably two of the most powerful magic users in this realm, both look down at the ground like children being scolded by their elders.

So, it's wise to say this reunion is going very well.

Ten minutes ago, when Cole first transformed from his soul shape of a crow back to his human form, Anne thought this was going to go very differently. Chely, whose eyes were filled with joyful tears, was about to bear-hug Cole, who looked as youthful and light as he did in life, untouched by age…

"Shui-Yin (水银)," Chely let out a trembling gasp. The necromancer's mask completely shattered. She sounded simultaneously about to burst out laughing or start crying, a tsunami at the same time. "How is this possible?"

The Blood Hawk's black eyes, which were empty pits of an abyss, had suddenly become dark soil newly being given life by drizzling rain. It was like witnessing a seed sprout between hard stones. Anne couldn't help but feel a small smile tug at her face, alongside a bitter sense of guilt.

Not The Blood Hawk. Not the necromancer. Not the murderer.

This was Chely Ying, the short red-haired girl who'd once bought a drink at the tavern for the sad-looking blonde girl who was pathetically drinking alone in the corner while reading a book.

"You must be The Barberry Oracle."

Anne lifted her head from her book. The redhead had popped out of nowhere. She almost had a heart attack as she noticed the features of the girl's face.

Eyes as dark as night, willowy frame, and a plum nose. Despite having flame-red hair, this girl's facial features and her accent were both unmistakably Aixauhan.

"Mind if I join you?" the unwelcome intruder asked as she waved to the tavern maid to tend to their table.

Anne sat frozen in her seat. "I was just leaving," she squeezed out, her voice sounding like a bad musician's piano skills. "You can have the table."

The red-haired Aixauhan girl smirked, cutting through Anne's awkward attempt at a polite escape like a knife. "Ah, I doubt anyone will come and bother you for being the oracle of the famous Barberry Lineage," the girl said. "Otherwise, you'd have been trampled to death by now. You know that."

Anne did not respond but nodded, as she didn't want to provoke this girl, who seemed to have no qualms about breaking the unspoken rules of this tavern.

"I know," she said to the girl. "I come here for that very purpose. Now, what would an Aixauhan alchemist be doing here?"

The red-haired girl chuckled, as if Anne's voice was one of friendly warmth instead of careful distance. "What gave away the fact that I'm an alchemist?"

"The ingredients on your belt," Anne replied. "They're from the Aixauhan market in the back alley. Your red hair is almost impossible for Aixauhans, but I've heard of the Ying Clan. Your ties to the fire god and the Sun in your mythos made your clan famous even among the Inabrians."

"Or I could have just visited a parlour," the girl replied casually. "Red hair suits me well, don't you think?"

Anne didn't have the best social skills, but even she thought maybe this girl was daft beyond measure for not recognising she was unwanted company.

"I'm sorry, but if you want to gut me for the war crimes my family has committed against your people," Anne said, exhausted, "you'll probably have to wait till I walk out into the streets and find a dark corner to do the deed. You'd get caught here in the open."

The girl gawked at Anne, as if she'd said something impossible and unimaginably bleak, instead of something perfectly plausible. A silent moment passed before the girl let out another laugh. Her voice sounded like the crackling of a hearth fire—lively and warm, but not enough to burn.

"I guess you are right," the alchemist girl responded. "But just the fact you recognise your family's atrocities in the war is enough of an indication that we can be friends."

"*Friends?*" Anne blurted out. She didn't know if she should call this girl stupid or brave or just completely lacking in any social consciousness of what she was saying. "Are you drunk?"

"No, I think you are." The girl pointed a finger at Anne's cheeks. They were flushed red under the dim light of the tavern. "You have been drinking and reading all night. Without ordering any food."

"I could just be very good at drinking." Anne blushed, not knowing if the heat in her chest and cheeks was because of the cider or anger or—for some Creator-forsaken reason—because the girl's hair was reminding her randomly of a prophecy she'd made as a child. The one about the sun.

"Sure," the girl mused. "Try to stand up without falling over."

"Why should I listen to you?" Anne bit back. "I don't even know you."

"My name is Chely Ying," the girl with red hair—Chely—said. "And I know you, Anne Barberry. Now, I think we should order something to eat before you pass out."

"Cai-Li," Cole replies. He uses Chely's Aixauhan name as a response to Chely using his. "You've grown old."

This response clearly catches Chely off-guard. The alchemist regains her senses quickly, as she always does.

"I'm in my thirties, Cole," The Blood Hawk says innocently. "I look normal for my age. You and Anne, however, both look like you're barely twenty. Maev's age. That's weirder, I'd say."

"Well, we're dead," Anne replies. "We stop aging when we die, so we *are* technically still around twenty."

"Cole is dead," Chely retorts. "And his body became a tree, while his spirit... became a crow? *You* aren't technically dead. You've been around in the In-Between for the last seven years. That means you are in your thirties too. The only reason you appear not to have aged at all is because you're vain, Annie."

"I am not," Anne says drily. "I am the least vain person on the Creator's green Earth."

"Yeah," Cole replies, sarcasm dripping from his voice. "I mean, look around. What kind of person with this kind of interior decor could be vain in any possible way?"

He gestures to the crystal chandeliers, the black velvet curtains, the white marble statues lining the hallway, and the wool carpet on the floor. Lastly, at Anne, who is currently still in the black lace dress that she went to bed in.

The dress is wrinkled, but it still has intricate patterns sewn across almost every surface with black and purple threads. The puff sleeves have white pearls as buttons, forged for centuries in oysters.

"I've seen your wardrobe for the past decade, Annie," Cole comments as if he's been locked in a dungeon and tortured for that duration of time. "This is your least extravagant outfit. They're practically your pajamas. And your closet is literally extended with an enhancement spell that makes the inside infinitely large. Last time I checked, it was the size of a ballroom."

"Wow," Chely says.

"Cole's been back for three minutes, and you're already ganging up on me." Anne turns to Cole. "Typical."

"No, no, no." Cole shakes his finger and advances on her. The humour leaks from his face quickly enough. "You don't get to complain, *Annie*. If Chely hadn't acted as a catalyst that forced you into remembering the past, I'd still be stuck as a bloody crow whenever you aren't The Oracle who is erasing everyone's memory in this town and keeping them trapped in some weird form of self-flagellation for not telling me you saw me die!"

Anne's face blanches. She's as pale as the marble statues. She lowers her head and turns her eyes away.

"Cole," Chely interjects, surprising Anne. Her tone is steely. "Anne didn't do it consciously. She had crossed over into death. She didn't choose to lose her memory. I was the one who brought her back, which led to the creation of the In-Between. She only did what she did to cope with what my necromancy had put on her and you. She didn't know—"

Why is Chely defending her? Anne feels like the floor has tilted and gravity is disappearing. Did the alchemist not hear what Cole said?

I kept the fact that I knew he was going to die from you. I was the one who let him go into the war to die. I was the one who killed him.

"Oh, don't even get me started." Cole's voice grows deeper. In contrast to his boyish looks, his voice is raspy and deep, like a crow's caw instead of the voice of a young man. "The Great Blood Hawk, Ying Cai-Li (贏彩黎). Who told you to go against nature and *my wishes* by keeping my dead body like some fucked up war souvenir for almost three years? Did you even consider why I was also dragged into the In-Between, Cai-Li? Despite the fact that I am *fully dead,* and Annie had always left the door open for me?"

Chely's face falls. Anne has never witnessed Chely look so ashen. It makes her heart twitch.

Unnatural. It is like watching the sun burn itself out. *Unnatural.*

It was her sixteenth birthday. The age for a daughter of nobility to debut into the official social circle of their class. For any other daughter of noble magician lineages, it would simply be like they were fresh fruit picked from the tree, put on the market to be sold for the most suitable marriage.

Creator knew how much Anne envied those girls who got to have such a simple fate with a set role and minimum responsibility.

To come from a magical lineage meant that one would surely marry someone who was also from such a lineage. There were only so many magicians among the nobility. As their magic was passed down noble lines—each family was known for one specialty. For the last names of magicians, they guarded their children as a form of preserving their currency and consolidating their power.

For unlike the barbarians heretics and the savage Aixauhan alchemists and other abnormal humanoid creatures who masqueraded as Creator-chosen magicians, the noble houses of magicians were said to be made differently by the Creator, who had given them gifts so they could keep this world pure from the unruly wild things that dared to exist outside of the confines of those the Creator had chosen.

It had been years since summer camp. Anne had long since learned why those kids had picked on the Yamalan boy and the girl with hair of flames. Why Brutus, her grandfather, had wished to eradicate the alchemists and the Yamalans.

And because she was not just any daughter of the nobility, but The Oracle of the Barberry Family, Anne's debutante ball was not much of a ball, but more a bunch of drunken magicians who shook her hands while spitting into her face with the same rhetoric for hours on end.

"My lovely little swan, you will save us all." Anne's mother kissed her forehead.

"The land of Aixauh is one Discord has complete control over," Anne's father, head of the Magical Alliance, puffed up his chest while he gave the speech to a room of eager magicians.

"Unlike us, who are the chosen protectors of the Creator's world, that land beyond the ocean is a place where evil runs rampant. There is no order to who is given the power. Instead, the blasphemous alchemists claim that these wicked and unnatural crafts of theirs were invented by themselves.

"Yes, the human alchemists have been corrupted into believing they learned miracles only the Creator could dole out. That is not even the worst part. More abhorrent, there are those among them who are born of Discord. Demons who have the intelligence of mankind, but with powers and lifespans the Creator did not intend for any one species other than humanity to have!"

"It's *unnatural!*" someone jeered.

Another quickly chimed in. "We must go to *war* against them! It is what the Creator would have wanted!"

"Yes! We will continue the precedent set by our parents, who died in the war!"

"Now, now." The Barberry patriarch calmed everyone with a wave of his hand. He put a palm to his chest as he lowered his gaze and continued in a sorrowful tone. "My own father was killed by one of these rogue alchemists—in our own ancestral castle, no less. An orphan he so graciously spared because he thought she deserved a chance. Yet she came back for him to drag him to the Discord's Underworld. That is why we need to eradicate them."

"War!"

"Kill them all!"

Unnatural. Anne sat there and felt faint.

She thought of the girl with red hair, whose smile lit up the room. She thought of the boy who was as hard to warm up to as a glacier, but whose nature was as clear as water in the purest spring.

They were right about this all being unnatural.

They were just wrong about who the unnatural ones were.

"My necromancy," Chely murmurs; she sounds hollow. "You were the first subject of my necromancy. I just didn't realise it at the time. I wanted you back. But that's why you're here—isn't it? The reason why you and Anne are both here is because of the attempts I made at using necromancy-adjacent alchemy on you. But I was only half-done with you, Cole. That's why you are only here as your spirit—the crow."

"You shouldn't bring back what has died, Cai-Li." Cole's voice is pained. "You should have let me fade into your memories. My spirit should have dissipated back into the world, like my mum's. I am half-dead, Cai-Li. Even more so than Anne. Her body was also revived by you, so she's technically In-Between, while I am not even the Cole of the Yamalan you remember. Half of me is gone; the other half is filled in with whatever matter death is made of. The reason why I am a crow most of the time, it's…it's because I no longer even have the level of cultivation necessary to remain at the level of clarity of a human."

Chely's world has always been one of constant change. A mirage of things, bright and colourful, like a supernova. It is the daily view when you are an alchemist. Everything in this world moves in alchemical friction against one another. In the land of Aixauh— where every inanimate object has its own rhythm and energy, where trees can gain sentience and mammals can take the form of humans with enough cultivation—everything has a colour.

The alchemist's job is most akin to a painter's.

Fireworks are mixed together using different metals by non-alchemists, but they are equally beautiful because of the different metals that are mixed in. Barium gives off a grassland, strontium is the colour of poppy flowers, copper is the ocean on a sunny day, and sodium results in sunflower fields.

Alchemists simply replace the metals with concepts. They use the energy to make symbolic things into supplements for the metals required for chemical reactions. But the theory behind it remains the same.

Chely can cut any ordinary herb and use it as barium in her cauldron. The same logic applies to the others. Chely had a lot of bluebells planted next to The Cottage, as copper was one of the most common things people asked of an alchemist—for they wished for her to fake forged copper coins for them.

Strontium—that is one Chely doesn't want to think about much, as it turns out nothing is colour—the exact shade as blood itself—required to be the alchemical equivalent of the metal.

The Creator that the magicians of Inabri so proudly claim is responsible for everything? In the land of Aixauh, He is only seen as a magnificent alchemist who could see all the weaves and colours of energy—Qi, as they call it—and do whatever He liked with it.

It didn't make Him the master of everything simply because He gave something an outline. Like a parent, a country couldn't claim the victory and failure of a child. The Creator did not have the right to demand respect from His fellow alchemists.

Chely looks at Cole, whose youthful face twists with anger. His voice sounds so different, even though he physically remains the same. She thinks about how she held Cole's hand as they watched his mother decompose by death, part by part, as if nature were an alchemist disassembling a creation it no longer needed.

She thought that by preventing Cole from disappearing into nothing like Auntie, she was sparing him.

Instead, she trapped him as a creature that went hand in hand with death.

Cole of the Yamalan was made of clear fresh water, glaciers, and snow.

Cole the familiar is a black, solid creature cloaked in feathers, who can fly, but never high and far enough to leave the In-Between, a land of ghosts.

"None of them stood up for me. Only you did."

Except Chely didn't stand up for Cole. She thought she was protecting him, yet all she did was deny him the right to move on.

And Annie, who has been silent this whole time, she does not look angry. Instead, the oracle in black looks like she's going to break from guilt. She turns away to avoid looking Chely in the eye.

No, not because Anne blames Chely, but because Anne sees herself as a monster for trapping all these people.

Anne thinks Chely doesn't know she prophesied Cole's death. She barricaded herself from the outside world in solitude because she was too ashamed to tell Chely the truth.

Cole and Anne both went through the same war as Chely.

The boy who was Chely's brother made peace with the fact that he was a casualty of war and was ready to be returned to his roots.

The woman who was Chely's wife found herself in the war against the path set for her by her family, seeing the future clearly with her own eyes, but still able to feel love for her sister afterward.

Chely starts laughing as she finally sees the truth in the mirrors that are the ones she claimed she was doing all this for.

Anne and Cole might have died because of the war, but the one who was truly lost to it was her.

Ying Cai-Li, the descendant of the Flaming Hawk who once was the immortal sun, is unable to let go of the sun's heat and anger.

Until it burns the ground to cinder, until the archer has to shoot it down to allow new life to grow.

Anne Barberry only ever wore black. It is the colour of mourning in this land.

The colour one would wear for an eternity, if one was widowed.

She was mourning me, Chely thinks. *For what I have become.*

The Blood Hawk.

A monster.

"You are the descendant of a sun god who was also a bird."

"Hey, quit laughing." Chely gave Anne a nudge on the shoulder. "You're going to choke on that pie, Oracle. Have you prophesied that?"

"Oh, I might." Anne shrugged; she was such a lightweight.

She was comfortable. After a full year of dating, The Oracle had finally peeled away that layer of skin and showed the true Anne Barberry that Chely had known was there all along.

"You see, Chely. Being The Oracle isn't, like… linear. The future is more like the night sky. The stars are events of each person's past that knit into constellations. An oracle's job is to decipher those constellations—to study the past of the collective of humankind—in order to predict the bigger picture the future might take."

"I'm sorry." Chely sighed. "Can you explain that again in a human language, please?"

"All right, all right." Anne rolled her eyes. She indulged Chely, for no matter how mad she pretended to be, the oracle was all mush on the inside.

"Basically, for an oracle to predict the future, they must also study the past. People always think they're original, but they are really not. Everything moves like a wheel. People keep making the same mistakes they did in the past—and will likely continue to make again in the future. That pattern is what prophecies and divinations are all about, Chely.

"The Visions I have, they are just a jumble of mistakes that we as humanity have made in the past, now being repeated."

Chely thought about that.

"It's still gibberish," the alchemist concluded.

"You're a lost cause," the oracle replied.

"So, which star am I?"

"That's your whole takeaway from this very deep, philosophical conversation?"

"Well…yeah."

"Fine." Anne threw her hands up in surrender. "You're not a star, Ying Cai-Li. You are the big dumb sun whose brain is meatloaf baked in an oven."

21

The Witch and the Sun

AFTER MUCH SCOLDING and throwing things against the wall, Cole of the Yamalan retreats back to his room in the west wing of the Castle.

"Er," Anne tries to break the silence, thick like stone walls, while also tentatively trying to swipe away the debris that stings in the wake of Cole's departure. "So, Cole had half of the castle to himself this whole time. I always thought it was just extra space. This explains…a lot."

Her words echo in the room as if it were empty.

Chely's eyes linger where Cole left, the door he slammed shut still vibrating. The alchemist's raven-black eyes are hollow and unseeing, as if she were hypnotised into an endless void.

"Don't take Cole's words to heart." Anne sighs. She fumbles with her words like an ugly duckling fumbles as it treads across water with its little webbed feet. "You know how I reacted when I didn't have my memories and you showed up at the castle doorstep? He just needs time—then he'll come around."

Chely chuckles. It's a guttural and foreign sound, like the grinding of carriages against rocks.

"Time is not the issue here," The Blood Hawk replies. "Besides, we both know that's not true."

Anne didn't expect that response. "What is not true?" she asks, slightly alarmed at the tension that dissipates from Chely's shoulders as if the alchemist has shrugged it off like snow.

The unnerving yet persistent smile pressed on Chely's lips looks like a slit throat.

"You *coming around?*" the alchemist says with no accusation in her tone, only a merciless sincerity. "Annie, you don't need to tend to my feelings. Despite our growing acquaintance and familiarity again during the time you've hosted me in this castle and the In-Between, that does not mean there is some kind of rekindled spark of fondness."

Anne lowers her head and says nothing.

"See," Chely's eyes close as she smiles in gentle sadness. "I'm right. You have not forgiven me for what I have done, nor will you forgive me for what I am about to do next. Our love story reached its end long before this tale started."

"How do you know I cannot forgive you?" Frustration builds in Anne's stomach. She can't help but let the veneer of calmness slip as she raises her voice at The Blood Hawk, who is as horrifyingly calm as an executioner holding a bloodied axe. "I have done awful things too! You think Cole is solely pissed off at you? I *trapped* all the people in the town under the hill and *wiped their memories* to keep them imprisoned *on purpose!* If anything, you are the one who shouldn't forgive me. I am a massive hypocrite for shunning you all the while I remained idly unaware of my own crimes!"

"Yes, I am not denying what you did was troubling," Chely agrees. "But I wouldn't call you a hypocrite, Anne Barberry. You did not choose to have your own memories wiped. You didn't have a choice in being brutally murdered. You didn't have a choice when I dragged you from your peaceful rest. This place—the In-Between— you didn't create it out of malice. It was a natural occurrence from being caught up in waves upon waves of devastating circumstances outside of your control. Your amnesia—that's a natural response from the trauma."

"Right," Anne says, her hands fisted at her sides. "Tell that to the people in the neighbourhood. That innkeeper—I guess you recognised him?—he was the tailor who did our wedding. He had a wife waiting for him in the Beyond. I barred him from leaving for *years*. The same goes for all of them—they are almost all people who lost someone to the war, either the one that happened a decade ago, or the one before that."

"I know," Chely says. "But I have been here each year in the past decade on the Day of Zhong Yuan (中元节), when the veil between life and death is the thinnest. I could never cross over physically like Maev, who could travel here in corporeal form. But I have seen the faces of the residents of the town under the hill. These souls you claim you've trapped here, as if that indicates your own wickedness, none of them are the innocent victims you're making them out to be.

"Plus, Annie, you always asked them to drink from the Chalice of Truth. When a soul enters the In-Between, they are sent directly to your oracle room. They would think they were asking for your divination of their future, when in truth they are sent to you so you can judge their past. *That* is the source of the so-called disappearances, especially of those whom the locals called 'tourists.' They did disappear after an oracle session with you—but not because you did something horrendous to them. Instead, it's because you deemed they had earned their right to leave. It's more than what some *monsters* deserve."

Anne shakes her head, a little unnerved by the intensity with which Chely utters that last line.

"If you could see the motivation behind my mistakes," The Oracle says to The Blood Hawk. "Why can't you see they are not all *monsters*, Chely? We are all children of war. We are *all* bathed in the blood of those who died in the wars before us, raised by societies who sang stories of war crimes as lullabies to their children. We are all casualties, but we are also the instigators. You see the contradictions, don't you? The Aixauhan soldier you killed in revenge for Cole's death; he was as innocent as Cole. We don't know if he enlisted of his own free will, but he sure must have been scared and tired when he killed Cole. We were all scared and tired. Do you truly think he deserved to die? Any more than me or Ark Li or even Cole?"

Chely sighs, her eyes foggy and dark like a swamp that swallows creatures whole.

"I made a mistake killing the Aixauhan soldier," The Blood Hawk admits. True regret flushes across Chely's face for the first time, a rare sight. "I killed because I was furious. You're right, he didn't deserve to die. He was the same age as us. A scared kid, really. Probably just wanted to go home to his family. He would likely have felt guilt for the rest of his life—for the blood on his hands when he was a soldier. Even the blood of a Yamalan boy, one of his fellow Aixauhan kin, who are seen as almost celestial in our culture."

A spark of hope enters Anne's chest. The edges of Chely's face soften, like a sizzling stove fire that was given too much oil that's finally cooled down. A steady fire flickering and dimming like a lady dancing in a red dress.

She's getting through to Chely, just as the necromancer Blood Hawk had once softened back into the girl in the tavern.

That red-haired girl, who had casually struck up a conversation with Anne, even when knowing full well Anne was The Barberry Oracle. The girl with a bright smile and twinkling black eyes that looked as if they had stars in them, who brushed away Anne's invisible walls as if they were made of cotton.

Anne's hand twitches. Instinct overtakes her as she steps forward.

Before words can be uttered, Anne clutches Chely's face and brings her own mouth down on the alchemist's lips.

Chely's pupils dilate for a second, surprised by Anne's sudden advance. However, the alchemist does not pull back. She does not let go.

The fire that has tickled at their hearts since Chely showed up outside of Anne's castle ignites into an avalanche.

Their tongues intertwine, as do their limbs. Anne's black, laced sleeves brush against Chely's crimson hair. The alchemist's hands first scratch at the laces stringing the oracle's old-fashioned gown until it fall off with more threads torn loose by Chely's nails.

Anne does not mind.

All the oracle feels as the layers of clothes are peeled off her is the bliss of having Chely Hawk's skin against hers. Like throwing oneself into a hot spring after being starved in a blizzard for eternity.

Chely's skin is a furnace. The only living soul Anne Barberry has seen in a decade-long isolation, among ghosts who are lost and cold. Alone in this realm of In-Between, where the oracle is both queen and slave. Without any memories of how she got there, or who she was.

For a decade, she was The Eyeless Oracle. For how could an oracle not be blind in a world filled with ghosts who have no future to be told?

As Anne brings Chely into herself, she feels the currents of air circling around them, as if a giant bird has flapped its wings.

Anne opens her eyes and gasps.

She is indeed entangled with a giant, flaming creature with wings that has fused with the light pouring into the room.

This is when The Oracle remembers the prophecy from long ago.

A prophecy she scribbled down as a child, not knowing what it meant.

The witch has finally caught the sun after a lifetime of chasing it.

The prophecy that defined The Oracle for her entire life but was forgotten as soon as it was spoken. It has come back, like an old friend, watching smugly as if winning a bet.

Anne Baberry moans as her sun melts her with its light.

That is until The Blood Hawk's cursed words overtake the gentle warmth of Chely Hawk.

"You're right, Annie. Not all of them are monsters who deserve the horrible things I did to them," the alchemist says with a mirthless smile on her face, as if the words that come out do not taste like acid, but citrus. "Except for your sister, who I made sure screamed her throat out before I tore the ingredient I needed for your revival out of her eye socket."

Cole hears the ruckus all the way from the other side of the castle.

He's not sure if Cai-Li and Anne are having the most passionate magic lesbian sex ever after seven years of separation and several months of pent-up tension, or if they are killing each other in a magical duel to the death that could bring down the entire In-Between.

Depending on which truth and plans of Cai-Li's are revealed prematurely, there is an equal chance for both.

Maybe at the same time, even.

Even the fire god Chi'You has nothing on Ying Cai-Li when the alchemist is hell-bent on burning down her own life and any chance she could have at happiness.

Cole knows that better than anyone.

Even if he is angry, he can't *truly* be mad at her.

Unlike Annie, Cole's field of vision does not end at the borders of the In-Between.

The Oracle still has no idea what Chely's plans truly are.

Idiots, Cole thinks.

"We can't let this go on any longer," says the dark-skinned girl who emerges from the wall, not bound by the laws of the In-Between.

Maev is bestowed with the talent of walking across all the realms of life and afterlife, so of course she can move through the fabrication of Anne's little kingdom as if it is nothing but a hologram or an illusion—which, in a sense, is exactly this place's nature.

"I know," Cole replies. "Have you located the captain?"

"Yes. She was hard to find. The realms of the afterlife are plentiful, and the ocean that links them is vast and unending. I choked on salty seawater for about a week just trying to teleport onto her ship! I really hope you know what you are doing."

"I'm so happy to see you again, all grown up." Cole shakes his head. "I'm sorry to drag you into this, Maev. "

"Nonsense," Maev replies. "You three saved me when I was just a kid. You were barely adults yourselves. No one was watching you, yet you carried us with you anyway. No matter what you have done, no matter what happens next, you, Anne, and Chely will always be heroes to me."

Cole lets out a laugh. He moulds his own form like one would mould fresh dough bread until he is a crow again, only ten times the size of before.

"Then let's hope Captain Ark takes a trip by flight as well as she does sail. Because I do not want to puke all over my amazing feathers, which are also my shirt."

"As I have recently come to learn"—Chely dragged one finger across the bookshelf that hosted crystal balls and books of scribbled prophecies, coming away with dust under her nails—"you will not be the only Barberry who was murdered by an Aixauhan alchemist under your own roof. Maybe you can find comfort in that, dear sister-in-law. Since you want to be an oracle like your grandfather so badly. It is almost an honour to die the same way as him, isn't it?"

Patricia Barberry, the golden-haired doll that scrambled backward, was all tears and panic. Her voice was blocked out by a noise-concealing elixir, which she had drunk unknowingly after getting it from a servant at the party who she hadn't even taken a good look at.

It'd been so easy that it bordered on comical. No danger detection spells. No wards against concealing magic or glamour.

The Blood Hawk hadn't even disguised herself very well. Her head had not been the clearest when she decided to infiltrate the party at Barberry Castle. Nauseated and enraged at the thought that these people, who were responsible for so much pain and suffering, were allowed to roam free when everyone she had cared about had been reduced to nothing but tearful memories.

Annie, who was found crumbled outside this very castle. Her left leg bent in the wrong direction, her nails broken and the nubs underneath them caked with dirt and blood. Her white bones protruded from pale skin, like a fish being flayed alive. Her blonde hair, near the colour of silver…the blood that ran from her corpse was the only shade of warmth at the crime scene.

When they had shown the alchemist her wife's body in the morgue for identification, Anne was little more than a bloody lump.

However, even that image didn't fill The Blood Hawk's mind with as much disgust as she felt now, watching the squirming blonde girl, who was a spitting image of Anne, about to die by Chely's hands.

This girl was the same age now as Anne and Chely had been when they'd first fallen in love.

The Blood Hawk did not flinch at all as she plunged the dagger into the heart of the younger Barberry.

"She could change, you know?" Anne's voice resonated in her ears, like a daydream slipping through her fingers. Too good to be allowed to last in this nightmarish world.

"She just needs someone to show her there is a bigger world than Barberry Castle. You were the one who did it for me when I was her age. You gave me the gift of acquainting me with those the Barberrys teach their children to hate. You, Cole, Maev, and the other kids. You gave me a family. A real one. I could give it to her. Give her a chance."

The Blood Hawk methodically plucked a pair of tweezers from her back pocket, then used those tweezers to carefully maneuver and dislodge the eyeball out of the dead girl's head.

You gave her the choice, Annie. It appears she has declined and proven you wrong.

Ark didn't take chances with Brutus Barberry. Neither do I.

The alchemist took the eyeball and placed it in a small jar. She pulled back her red cloak, revealing a hidden arsenal-like inventory tucked away in the pockets of the fabric. The only ingredients left to acquire were mercury and another eyeball.

The Elixir of Immortality that the Founding Emperor of Qin, Ying Zheng and his clan of alchemists had searched for centuries.

They had been so close to solving the puzzle, but they had lacked one piece to figure out the last clue.

One cannot concoct the Elixir of Immortality for themselves, for the alchemist making the elixir must ingest mercury as part of the process. Subsequently, all who had attempted this had died from mercury poisoning, even though when their bodies were tested afterward by fellow alchemists, it was determined that they had been successful in brewing the elixir.

They'd succeeded in their goal but had not survived long enough to reap the rewards.

For those who wanted to claim immortality, it had never occurred to them they could ingest mercury but then pass the successfully brewed Elixir of Immortality to someone else instead of drinking it themselves. Seeking to live forever meant one needed to not care about anyone besides oneself. That selfishness—that had been their fatal flaw.

The dilemma that had perplexed Aixauhan alchemists for millennia was, in fact, not a dilemma at all.

The Blood Hawk left the corpse of the last Barberry who would ever live in this castle on the ground. When Anne returned to this world, the alchemist doubted she would ever want to see Barberry Castle again, let alone live in it.

Before The Blood Hawk left, she spotted a scrap of paper on the bookshelf.

It was clearly the work of a child. Even with surprisingly elegant handwriting, the paper was covered in crayon drawings. A sun that was in fact a gigantic bird with feathers of gold and red. A brown block, probably meant to be a cottage with a windmill on top, surrounded by every shade of colour of the rainbow—a sea of flowers in blue, purple, pink on green grass. And a tiny stick figure with a black rectangle dress, who raised their tiny stick arms into the sky, as though they wanted to take everything into their embrace.

With trembling fingers, she took the scrap of paper down from the bookshelf.

She read the scribbled words beside the child's doodles.

The Blood Hawk was shot down from the sky. Her flames dimmed as Chely Ying came back to life.

"Once upon a time,
a witch fell in love with the sun.
Ever since then,
she has been chasing her light."
by Anne Barberry, 6 years old

22

The Chalice of Truth

"WHY?"

The temperature drops as if a bucket of ice water had been thrown directly onto a kindling fire. The dying flames sizzle, screaming in agony at being smothered and suffocated like babies in their cradles.

Anne's mind goes blank. Her lips are still stained with warm blood, with Chely Ying's teeth marks from when she bit into her with that scorching kiss. Now, it feels more like the throbbing pain of being slashed open by a blade—a blade poisoned with the venom of a creature that was all fluffy feathers and warm colours.

For a moment, Anne thinks the eternal winter has thawed. She sees colours for the first time. The crimson hue of the sun at dawn, Chely's fiery red entangled with Anne's moonlight hair. Their powers dance together as if a shattered jewel is finally being assembled into one whole masterpiece. Their magics weave around each other in alchemical sigils, hungry and desperate, devoid of the tentativeness and caution that has resided there for a decade.

If someone were to run into them at that moment, they might believe they were viewing an illusion of some kind.

The strands of Anne's power summon the shadows, pale and silver like a river under the moon, reflecting the blazing glory that is the scarlet flicker of flames bursting like tiny firecrackers with Chely's alchemical prowess.

Chely is the day, and Anne is the night. For a single moment, they are seen together in the sky at the very same time. The blazing dawn that Anne envisioned them having on the edge of tomorrow.

That moment is broken, because the sun bursts this precious world apart like a raw egg with its deadly heat.

"Why?" The Blood Hawk is still smiling. "It's ironic; that's the same question you asked Ark." She's never looked more like a descendant of a celestial being than right now—detached and amused at the devastation of a mortal's follies.

"You're so sweet, Anne Barberry," Ying Cai-Li says; her voice is damning. "So sweet yet filled with guilt that does not belong to you. Instead of hating the captain for ending your childhood, you asked why she didn't take your life as well."

Darkness closes in from the edges of Anne's Vision. She's losing herself again, so soon after gaining herself back.

The Eyeless Oracle snickers in her head. *Weak girl, foolish girl, this is why you needed me to handle the hard truth. You are so fragile, like a porcelain doll, naïve to the point of having such blind faith in the future and thinking you could change things this time. Thinking you could change the end of this story. The story of the two girls whose love conquered against the trials of war and lived happily ever after.*

"Why did you kill my sister?" Anne screeches. Her voice sounds like metal scraping against metal. She tries to drown out The Eyeless Oracle. She refuses to go back into the darkness, not before she pierces herself through the heart with the truth of Ying Cai-Li. "My sister was a teenager! She was Maev's age at the time of the war! How could you?"

"Patricia Barberry was the sole heir to and head of the Barberry's noble lineage," Chely replies, sweeping away the argument as if dusting dirt from her clothes. "Sure, she hadn't reached the age of adulthood by the end of the war. But she had done plenty of awful things as the head of the Barberry family. She had a seat on the Inner Circle of the Magician Alliance. Do you need me to remind you what that means? It means she was part of all the military strategic decisions made in the war that led to the deaths of millions—Maev's parents, Cole, Captain Ark. *You.* "

"So, you think you should hold her and her alone responsible for all the war crimes of Inabri?" Annie bites back, spitting blood onto the floor. Her lips are stained a deep scarlet; it tastes bitter and metallic. No longer the warmth and passion of a lover, but the venom of a monster.

The Blood Hawk stares back at her. The prickle of pain that twitches at the corner of the alchemist's eyes almost makes Anne recognise her as Chely Ying.

"No." The alchemist's next words wipe away the last lingering spark of hope residing in The Oracle's heart. "Her life didn't matter to me, Annie. I don't care if you loved her despite everything. She needed to die for what I'm about to do."

The Blood Hawk's eyes are not the black pearls of an Aixauhan alchemist, instead the colour of days-old dried blood left to rot on the road.

"I killed your sister for you, Annie." The Blood Hawk smiles, her hair dampened by the shadows into a wine colour. "You're so eager for your life to end. No, I'm going to let that happen. This is only the beginning of your story, dear Oracle."

"What—what are you talking about?" Anne asks, her head swirling like a sail blown off the chart.

The image of The Blood Hawk and Chely Ying cascades into two in her mind, just like the two sides of The Oracle and Anne Barberry.

"Do you know what I found on the bookshelf in Barberry Castle, after I took out Patricia Barberry?"

Anne shakes her head. Numbness replaces the throbbing wound of betrayal. She stares blank-eyed at the monster wearing the mask of her wife, not knowing how else to respond.

"I found plans, documents, reports." The Blood Hawk closes her hand into a fist, white half-moons forming on her palm as her nails dig into flesh and skin. "All in preparation for *another* war. And *another*. And *another*. All the way mapped out from decades ago until the end of the next century. All with the end goal of annihilating Aixauh."

"Impossible," Anne murmurs instinctively. She sees Chely again, like a reflection of light on the surface of a lake. Only for a second, brief and then gone like a ghost.

"Oh, I'm afraid it's more than possible, Annie." The Aixauhan alchemist smiles a tired grin. Her eyes are filled with blood vessels, all the way until the redness seems to leak out of the corners like tears. "That's not the worst part, you know. From what Captain Ark helped me to gather before she died—the plan was *working*. They might have lost the war, but they were *winning*."

"How could they be winning?" Anne asks, her voice bordering on hysterical. "The ones who started the war were tried and executed. Aixauhan alchemists were offered compensation for both wars by the International Magical Alliance that was newly formed to keep peace. All the war criminals were gone!"

Unless…

Anne's eyes grow wide. The Eyeless Oracle chuckles at the blind-sided idiocy of the girl who is its host.

"They passed on their plans and their wills to their children," Anne mutters. "'*The magical lineages who pass down the Creator's Magic by blood will also pass down the Creator's Will.*'"

"I guess so," Chely replies. "Those were the last words of your sister. I hate to cause you pain, Anne. But what the Inabrian magicians need is not another oracle that promises them a greater than life future—what they need is a historian, someone who can teach their children of the past. The past that was paved in blood led Inabri to where it is now. To do so, they need a magician, one of their own, but someone who will not leave out the ugly parts. Someone who will ensure the past wars will not be repeated in the future ever again."

The same ideas that came from Anne's parents, drenched in the nostalgia of childhood honey. Once upon a time, Anne was a bystander too. She watched the Inabrian kids at the summer camp trashing the hearts of the two people she'd later come to love the most in the world. Even after Brutus's murder, it still took years for Anne to slowly crawl up that line of indoctrination. Upstream and clumsily, she thought she'd gained enough perspective to understand what the war meant for Chely, for Cole, for Ark Li.

Except, here is Anne's Aixauhan wife, standing true to show the cycle of the Barberrys' sins has not ended. Even after seeing visions of mountains of corpses from the coming war as a child in her nightmares. Even after fleeing in the war as refugees with starvation churning her stomach until they ate bark carved out from the scorched trees.

Even after a war in which she lost the closest thing she had to a brother, Anne Barberry still walked back into that castle, because the Inabrian oracle, she held out the foolish hope of reconciling with her fellow Inabrians.

At the very end, she was murdered for the very same reason. Anne Barberry remained blind to the extent of suffering Inabri would cast on those they thought outside of the Creator's Will.

She truly is the biggest fool that has ever lived. No wonder her Oracle persona in the In-Between has no eyes. Anne Barberry does not deserve them, for she chose to remain sightless, even in death. She chose to be blind to the malice and trepidation her country held to those she considered family and still forgave those who only by blood were called her kin.

Yet, she still had the audacity to call Chely's actions those of someone lost to dark magic. Wasn't that the exact same rhetoric as the sugary words of her parents?

"The magical lineages who pass down the Creator's Magic by blood will also pass down the Creator's Will."

Anne might have recognised Brutus Barberry as a monster for what he did to the Aixauhan alchemists, but she'd never viewed the power of The Oracle itself as anything less than natural. Even though the Barberry family used The Oracle's power for great evil, setting up a war that would claim millions of lives. Far more than the grotesque necromancy that Chely has been practising and the handful of lives that belonged to the perpetrator that The Blood Hawk could take in a lifetime.

Who is the Creator? Anne does not know. She only knows there must be one, since that is what The Oracle is. The Oracle uses the Chalice of Truth to trace the past like stars into a shape that leads to constellations of the future.

But what kind of Creator would let His instruments misuse the power of The Oracle for their own benefit, all the while claiming other forms of magic and powers as evil in nature?

Anne Barberry had the choice to hide away in the In-Between. She had the choice to be blind to the world of the living, erecting walls around herself in the name of punishing those who did bad deeds in war because of her grief.

All the while, Chely Hawk was still fighting a war in the real world. The love of Anne's life, her wife, lost everything to the war, but still hadn't given up on searching.

"Cole was right about me when I first met him," Anne said, her voice monotone. "You never should've got involved with me, Cai-Li."

Chely's eyes grow wide; this was clearly not the response she had been anticipating.

The alchemist opens her mouth to say something. "Annie, what are you talking about?"

"I'm talking about my death, Chely," Anne seethes. "Patricia killed me not because she thought I was a traitor. At least not only for that. *The magical lineages who pass down the Creator's Magic by blood will also pass down the Creator's Will.* Do you know what that means?"

"I have my guesses," Chely says. "None of them are good."

"Well, you're right to assume." Anne nods. "My sister killed me as part of their plan for the next war. She interpreted that saying as meaning the power of The Oracle would pass down by blood, and rightfully so—in her eyes—to one who is serving *'the Creator's Will.'* She thought that by killing me in a ritualistic sacrifice, the oracle power would be passed down to her by blood. The Visions of war were how Brutus Barberry prepared the first Aixauhan alchemists' massacre. And…my Visions also gave him the reassurance that there would be another war with a Barberry Oracle in its midst even as he died."

Anne can't look the flame-haired alchemist in the eye. Chely's face is a contortion of a thousand emotions. She surely did not expect how the tables have turned during the course of this one conversation.

"So, you can go now," The Barberry Oracle says, her voice dry.

"Wait, why would I do that?" Chely's head shoots up. "I thought we got past the stage of kicking me out of the house because we are talking about difficult topics—"

"No, Chely. It's not *you*," Anne replies. "It's *me*. I'm the one who doesn't deserve you wasting any of your precious time on me anymore. You are seeing something in me that's not there. Something beyond selfishness. I thought I could be the person you think I am, but I never was that person. I am no saviour of Inabri's next generation."

"No, Annie." Chely shakes her head. "You are exactly who I know you as. Cole saw that as well, and that's how we became a family. Even Captain Ark saw you as hope. Because you are the one who picked Maev up and carried her when her leg was broken. For days on end. You refused to put her down even as she drifted between the land of the living and the dead."

"She was the same age as Perks—Patricia." Anne swallows. "It wasn't something noble, Chely. I am no saint. I wouldn't have cared if Aixauh had lost the war. I still blamed Ark Li to some degree for killing my grandfather. I still wanted my sister back.

"I didn't tell you that I foresaw Cole dying in the war. I chose not to listen to you when you warned me against going back to Barberry Castle to visit my sister."

"Again, the guilt," Chely says, her voice growing deep and painful. "They make you the human that the future needs. Not someone who believes themselves flawless or a tool of vengeance, not a monster. But a flawed human being who isn't afraid to reckon with the bigger picture."

Anne stares the alchemist—the necromancer—straight in the eye. "But I made you a monster." Before Chely can protest, the oracle continues, "Don't even try to deny it. Isn't that the reason you are really here? Your words just now made your intentions clear. I saw it as The Eyeless Oracle, the night you left the castle and slept on the hills. I saw it before too. During the war. You fly into the sky, ascending into the sun. I saw it as hope, but it wasn't! It's death, isn't it? You're going to die because of me."

Instructions for reviving/granting immortality to Oracle Angelica Barberry Written by Cai-Li of the Ying Clan (嬴彩黎), The Blood Hawk (赤鹰)

List of Ingredients:

1) Mercury (水银), 3 inches, liquid form. Must be pure and condensed into liquid form that is transparent and clear (enough to be confused with water droplets). (Note: must be drank by the alchemist brewing the Elixir of Immortality)

2) One eyeball taken from an individual that belongs to the subject's bloodline (the alchemical symbol of birth) to make The Eyeless Oracle see Life. (Note: Patricia Barberry)

3) One eyeball taken from the individual who first made the subject fear death to instill the desire for revival within the subject to escape from death. (Note: Captain Ark Li)

4) The life force (Qi) of an individual who learned to cultivate it for at least two decades, preferably someone who is either an alchemist and/or a spirit of nature. (Note: Chely Hawk)

5) Following 4, it should be noted that due to the nature of life force (Qi) circulation, when resurrecting an individual (such as the subject, The Oracle) who has aspects of a supernatural nature that are alternative/equivalent to alchemy, it must be an individual whose life force (Qi) who is also magical in nature who could transfer enough Yang (阳) energy to balance out the Yin (阴) energy of the subject.

6) Following 5, said individual would also be me, Ying Cai-Li.

7) The Elixir of Immortality will be brewed in the Chalice of Truth after the Ritual is complete. The subject will drink the elixir and return to the land of the living with eternal life and youth.

P.S. The ritual will result in the death of the alchemist who drinks mercury (as it is essential to the brewing of the Elixir of Immortality but is lethal to ingest) and also the magical individual who will give up their Yang (阳) life force in order to restore the subject to life. The eyeballs could be acquired without killing the individuals supplying the ingredients (Captain Ark has agreed to provide me with her eye upon her natural death, but Patricia didn't agree, so I had to take drastic measures).

The memories that return to Anne Barberry are not just of her death, of the fact that Cole is the crow trapped with her, or that her sister killed her in cold blood—but also the memories she locked away as if slamming the door of a warm, lit-up cottage amidst a snowstorm raging in winter.

If all Anne had cut out of herself when she died were the bad things, then it wouldn't explain why she had forgotten the first prophecy she'd ever made as an oracle. It was not Cole's chest being torn apart by a spell with blood blooming into a barberry bush, all just to save Anne.

No, the first prophecy that Anne Barberry was as an oracle was a cottage, a field of summer flowers, and the sun.

She was a child, yet somehow, she had full faith in herself, and in this world being exactly the way it was in that Vision of hers.

That child believed this was her future.

A beautiful, peaceful existence, bathed in eternal sunlight. Where she made flower crowns for her friends and would always be happy and secure.

Over a decade later, Anne Barberry saw The Cottage as Cole took her and Chely there when the war first started. There were no flower fields, only dead grass covered in a thin layer of frost. As it was during the tail of autumn, they finally dragged their tired bodies to The Cottage, escaping the urban areas.

The Cottage was there, but it was not the hot chocolate wood and fresh scent of morning dew from Anne's Vision.

Mice squeaked as Cole opened the door. Spiderwebs hung like lingerie from the walls. Tentacles of mould crawled from the corners to the ceilings. The dust-covered wooden floor creaked under their feet, so brittle that the boards groaned like an old man whose spine would crack in two with each step.

"This place…" Anne couldn't help but pause. The words simply fell out of her cracked lips; they bled due to dehydration. Her limbs were leaden. "It's nothing like what I imagined."

Chely perked up. Even after barely consuming anything for the past week as their food and water supply ran dry, Ying Cai-Li was still as sharp as a hawk. She picked up Anne's incoherent murmurs, even though Cole had already collapsed onto a cot like a bag of old bones, halfway unconscious.

"Nothing like you imagined?" Chely repeated, her eyes glistening like stars in the pitch-black night. "Have you been to this place before, Annie? Did you see it in a Vision of yours as an oracle?"

Cole snorted. "The noble Barberry Oracle probably just meant she was expecting a royal tavern."

"Be nice, Shui-Yin." Chely sighed. She scolded Cole, but without much heat. "We're all tired. Let's just all enjoy a night where we can sleep under a roof."

Chely only ever used Cole's Aixauhan name when she was acting like Cole's mother. There was a special dynamic to them, a bond that had been forged by age, like a sturdy tree trunk that grew rings over a millennium. It was a powerful thing to share a foundational history with one another.

Chely lit a small fire at the stove of the cabin, muttering Chi'You's name. The small, flickering flame painted the grey walls orange and yellow. Cole let out a happy noise, yelping in triumph as he smacked Chely on the shoulder.

Anne watched as the fire in the stove danced. She watched her two companions quickly engage in a conversation that made both of them laugh. It was as if they themselves were fire, even as the world outside was encased in an ice age. Still, they made their own warmth. They created their own tiny sun in that cottage, with no frost in their hearts that separated them from the rest of the world.

"I'm going to take the first shift," Anne said. She took a few pieces of dried meat and went out the door. "Going to look around and make sure there are no wild animals who can maul us to death at night. Also going to see if there's a pond somewhere so I can get some water stored."

"There's a well nearby," Cole replied. "But it's not been used in ages. The water's probably like, filled with a metal residue that can kill us or something. If you drink from it, you might die, Barberry."

"Don't pretend you're worried about my well-being, Cole of the Yamalan," Anne replied, equally cold. She loosened the strap she always tied around her belt and took out a small, rusted cup. "I have this."

"What will a stupid cup do?" Cole furrowed his brow.

Chely, on the other hand, who surprised Anne with her depth of knowledge, made an almost comically excited noise.

"Is that legendary…Chalice of Truth?" Chely asked, her face warmed up by the fire and now pinkish-red instead of ashen as it had looked for the past few weeks. "The one that can purify any poisonous liquid? Once you drink from it, you can only see and say what is true?"

"I'm confused." Cole scratched his head. "I heard the Barberry Chalice can eradicate an alchemist's soul. You probably should stay away from it, Cai-Li. "

Chely's eyes glimmered and the alchemist opened her mouth, excited like a child who was going to explain their favourite toy to their best friend. "No, Cole. You see, I actually saw what's inside. Also, Anne's been using it for tea, I think."

"You what?" Cole scrunched up his nose. "Yikes, Barberry."

"You don't believe me?" Chely raised an eyebrow. She turned to Anne with a flirtatious smile. "Brew some tea for Cole; let's see if he likes it."

"Ew, what the hell, Ying Cai-Li! 你他妈的是不是有病 (Are you fucking insane?)" Cole cursed in Aixauhan.

Anne grimaced at Cai-Li. She loved her flame-haired alchemist, but her feet had way too many scrapes and calluses accumulated through hiking the mountain range, narrowly escaping patrolling soldiers on both sides, only to listen to Chely scare Cole with horror stories about the chalice.

The truth was that Anne didn't wish to know more about the chalice. She'd had it since she learned how to walk. It was the thing she hugged to sleep. She would one day untangle its bloody history, like figuring out what being a Barberry meant to Anne from here on out, but not when they were all exhausted and famished from the hike.

"All you need to know is that this cup," Anne emphasised by putting weight on the word, "is a magic cup. No matter how muddied or polluted, any water brewed in the Chalice of Truth will be the safest and tastiest water known to mankind."

"Just like no matter how cunning and conniving a person is," Chely added with a smile. "No matter how good at self-deception. Whoever drinks from the Chalice, the truth will be pulled out like a half-formed moth from its impenetrable cocoon."

Anne's eyelids dropped so her eyes formed half-moons as she turned to stare at her girlfriend.

"What?" Chely asked, completely oblivious.

Cole made a splattering noise. "How do you know so much about the Barberry Chalice, Cai-Li?" he asked.

Anne wondered the same thing.

"That's a story for another time," Cai-Li said. "How about you tell Anne here how we are going to get the dirty well water filtered for drinking, Cole?"

"I'm not going along with it," Anne says. "There's no way I'm letting you carry this plan through. Did you think I would be happy to let you die for me? That somehow this cursed existence…this cruel ritual of granting me the curse of immortality without my consent would *please* me? Please stop. I am telling you to stop."

"If I had a penny for every time in the past seven years someone told me to 'stop'"—Chely smiles, as if this were an amusing inside joke they were sharing—"then I'd be the richest woman in the world, Annie. Alas, I am still going through with it. Like I said before, I am a selfish creature, one made of rage. While you, my wife, are a creature of guilt and sweetness.

"Once you are back in the living world, I know your good heart will lead you to the happiness you deserve. I know you'll finally come to see with those clear eyes of yours that you can be the *hope* that guides the world into a more peaceful and introspective era, where people are more focused on the bigger picture instead of being sucked into this cycle of never-ending violence. I cannot do that. I am made of rage. I can see nothing beyond the red—you, my love, you have been the light that guided me since the war, grounding me to my last shreds of humanity."

Anne stares at the crimson-haired alchemist, utterly dumbfounded by the nonchalance she's displaying at the chilling revelation.

"This isn't our usual schtick where you say something horrifying with a smiling face or suggest some bloody solution to minor inconveniences and then I scoff and that's that. This is your *life* we're talking about!"

The sun sets on the horizon of this place that was neither of the living nor the dead. It's been a long day in the In-Between, from breakfast when The Oracle Queen regained her memory till the revelation that Cole the familiar crow was the actual dead boy he was named after.

Exhaustion hits Anne Barberry like a hurricane. Her head lulls and pounds like it's being repeatedly bashed like a watermelon, yet somehow still not swallowed up by oblivion.

Chely Hawk—no, Ying Cai-Li. The Blood Hawk. The Aixauhan alchemist of the Ying Clan.

She stands next to the window frame, the last glow of white yarrow-coloured light framing her skin the colour of honey and gold. Her black eyes are exposed to the light, and her pupils are a deep crimson that resembles blood freshly spilled from veins.

In the twilight that she was named after, Cai-Li shines like a statue made of gold, and her hair is threaded with the flickering of a flame. Behind her, the evening sky explodes in soft and gentle pastel hues. They spread along the blue shores of the waning sun like watercolour soaking into white sheets.

The blinding light dims into a gentle beckoning, the sun waving goodbye with an invisible hand as it drops to its death off the cliff from the western sky.

Chely smiles, the muscles around her lips relax; the curve is thin but unshaken. Her eyes, which usually spark mischief like twin flames, are now heavy-lidded and half-closed as if the alchemist were falling asleep. Rays of sunlight pass by the window. The alchemist's eyes darken to the colour of ebony. Like spilled blood has dried on the wall, finally forgetting its heat and colour, fading away with only the remnants knowing it was a stain.

The Blood Hawk, the descendant of sunbirds that caused famine and devastation, is gone. Replaced by a simple mortal woman, who smiles as if admiring her wife's beauty before her partner has fully risen from their bed.

"From the moment I stepped into your castle, Anne," says Chely, "it's been like waking up from a nightmare of my own making. All those people I killed, the blood I shed and tried so hard to justify—when I was again in your presence, my love, all those excuses I made up to soothe my own conscience collapsed in an instant. I am filled with shame; the sins I committed hit me all at once. Horrific. Unjustifiable. *Evil.*"

Anne's heart stops. Those words repeat in her head, like the smell of fresh blossoms in spring, like the first sea breeze when taking a walk on white-sand beach, feeling the gentle waves of the ocean washing footprints clean. Step by step.

Could this be true? The oracle's heart quakes like a deer that just found a nice patch of leaves to munch on. *Could it be true that we are finally getting through to each other for the first time since the war ended?*

"I have no moral high ground, Chely." Anne doesn't realise she's opened her mouth; her presence feels detached from her body and her cold and hard words. "I don't care if you murdered those people; they deserved it. I don't even care now, I think, about what you did to Cole or what you plan to do with me. Because I understand. Your grief, your sorrow, your despair. I never wished to leave you behind on your own. I can forgive everything you've done because I love you, Ying Cai-Li. I *know* you. Everything you have done, the good and the bad, you did it out of love. Desperate and blind, hopeless love."

"So, you understand," Cai-Li says slowly, "why there is no world in which you can convince me to stop my plan?"

"I know you." Anne shakes her head in denial. "Once you set your mind on something, you never quit. Come heaven or high water. I tried to freeze you out several times over the first months when we first started dating. I left you because I was still pretty brainwashed. But you—you were always there, waiting. Then, there was the war. You were the one who dragged me and Cole through the mountains to reach The Cottage, even when we both said we wanted to simply lie down and nap. You said that it was a death sentence—that even if we were just taking a nap, we would not be able to get back up and would die right there. Once you start something, you see it through to the end. "

"It sounds like you're complimenting me," Chely says. Her voice is morose. "But I haven't been that person in a very long time. Trying to bring up the good deeds that person has done is like reminding a ghost of the taste of food. I can conceptualise it, but I do not feel it. Trying to appeal to my better nature is not going to save me."

Anne pauses, but then a resolve fills her like never before. She's tip-toed around the truth for a full decade, unwilling to say her fears out loud. As if she could build a wall that can withstand the storm outside, when the true enemy is the mould and fungus that hollowed out her memories and her sense of self.

"I never thought you were descending into darkness, Ying Cai-Li," Anne says, turning her head to watch the setting sun which sets the horizon aflame into a crimson red. Like a forest fire engulfing the world. "I *saw* you in a Vision, do you hear me? You are going to leave a mark on this world *in the form of the sun.* Not a shadow that casts toward the future but light. It's the prediction of a Barberry Oracle; the only people whose future we can divine are those who will play a part in changing the world. Your light. Your fire. Your will. These are the things that will make the future brighter. You say I'm your light? Well, you are mine too.

"I held onto you because you are the light that made me realise the shape of myself. I followed you to meet Cole. I followed you into the war. I followed you onto Ark's ship. I followed you into marriage. I followed you like a shadow chasing the sun. Without you, I am nothing and no one."

Chely's eyes grow wide. The shadows rose. Her cheekbones were giving a darker edge, Anne could tell.

"Maybe, for a while, you were the witch who chases the sun that you prophesised as a child, Annie," Chely says. Her hair is cast in shadows, no longer the shining metal copper, but a thick and finely aged wine. "Not anymore though. Not after the decade we spent apart. Not after you were killed by your own sister. From the ashes, you rose as The Eyeless Oracle. A shadow, but chasing the sun no more. You suspected I was lying from the moment I got here—that was why you offered me tea. Isn't it? Not because you wanted my company, despite knowing the despicable monster I have become. But because no one can lie after drinking from the Chalice of Truth."

Anne does not respond. She doesn't need to. Chely is right.

There has always been love between them. But that love was once a summer flower that sparked like a flame, a summer blossom that defiantly grew its petals for all to see. It was their rejection of the adult world which tried to confine them to old grudges and animosities between people who were old or long dead.

How foolish and naïve they were. The love between Anne and Chely was one that had no concept of The Barberry Oracle or The Blood Hawk. The granddaughter of a war criminal or the descendant of people who thought immortality gave them rights above mortals. They were just two girls at a tavern, exploring each other like flowers tasting the morning dew.

But summer flowers only last for a season.

Autumn came, and so did the war.

Prophecies made by oracles have so many interpretations, they might as well all be null.

Their love did not die. Instead, it transformed. It was brutally eaten by the last hungry creature and digested. Then dropped into the soil as feces and left there to rot and be trampled over by powers large and small.

It lay there dormant, dying and decaying. It provided a lot of self-reflection to the nature of its existence.

Can I truly love you no matter what happens next? Not just till death do us part. But beyond it, when death becomes mundane and grief takes place in your heart where once trust was, when hatred fills your drive where once it was filled with the will to save and protect?

Can I still love you when I no longer know who you are?

"Yes," Anne closes her eyes and answers. *Yes, to both those questions.* "I did use the Chalice of Truth to make sure you would not lie to me when you first came. You are also wrong. I did not offer you tea because I wanted to hear you confess to all the horrible things you have done. I offered you tea because I wanted to talk with you for just a little longer. Talk honestly, like we used to as kids in that tavern. When you didn't have to mince your words, and I didn't have to fake moral objection. I just want *you*, Chely Ying. I just wanted you to *stay with me*."

The red-haired alchemist clumsily facepalms to cover the fact that she's trying to hide her tears.

When Chely lowers her sleeves, she says in a quiet tone, "That was not what you said, Annie." Chely sounds so small and fragile, like a chastised child. "You told me to leave. You suspected I was responsible for the disappearances. You hated that I was doing black magic. You didn't trust me anymore. How could you want the company of someone who you cannot even believe to be a good person?"

"Because nothing you can do will ever stop me from loving you!" Anne shouts. Her silky voice and impeccable manners, drilled into her by Barberry education, fall away like the tide. She feels a hot burst of fire inside her—it is not the crimson flame of Chely's hair, but molten gold.

Chely's jaw drops. Her eyes grow as big as diamonds, like glistening stars that hold a whole constellation within them.

This person. Those eyes.

This is the future that baby Oracle had foretold for herself. Anne is not the witch who fell in love with the sun when she first glared up at the sky.

Chely is.

And since the sun was snuffed out of her world, The Blood Hawk has done all she could to feel the light of her sun again.

23

Difference in Perspectives

"SO, COLE, YOU called?"

Captain Ark Li is nothing like Cole remembers. No longer the tough and cutthroat woman with cropped dark hair and a silly tricorn pirate hat she eccentrically wore as the captain of the refugee ship that stowed away Cole and his friends during the war.

That woman had a face of steel. Captain Li was in her forties when the trio and their little band of orphans stepped into the belly of her cargo hold. She had a darker shade of skin, both due to the constant exposure to the sun out at sea but also because she is a native from the southern province of Aixauh, close to the port cities that Inabrians used to do commerce with before the Inabrians grew greedy and wished to take everything instead.

That was where Ark Li had learned her seafaring skills. The Li Clan and the alchemists from Captain Ark's region had been the first massive casualties of the First War. The first true carnage that made alchemists and spiritual beings in Aixauh realise the Inabrian magicians didn't just ideologically oppose them but were actively campaigning for their extinction.

Her parents had been executed in a manner that would ensure the destruction of their spiritual core, their soul that existed beyond death. It had not been plain murder; it had been a higher form of eradication. Alongside the captain's little sister, who had been taken from Ark Li and reemerged as a pile of bone, whose condition had indicated a violent and brutal fate too bleak to speak of.

All this was information, Cole only learned by re-establishing contact with Captain Li after she died.

Truthfully, Cole thinks he doesn't grasp the meaning of war. Not like Captain Ark, nor like Anne or Cai-Li. He was born after the First War ended and died a relatively clean death without having witnessed the aftermath of the Second War that ground his two best friends into the shells of their former selves that Cole no longer recognised.

Surprisingly, it was the cold and staunch captain who reached out to Cole through a letter sent by a…seagull, of all things.

It read: *Dear Cole. How is Anne Barberry?*

Cole sighed.

Throughout their voyage with Captain Ark Li, during the toughest and deadliest years of the war, Cole had no doubt Anne realised and recognised that Captain Ark was the murderer who'd gutted her grandfather right in front of her.

But it was so like Anne Barberry to leave out important details of her own past trauma and suffering, as if they were embarrassing secrets that she herself had somehow deserved and should feel guilty for.

Looking back, Cole can't help but notice how much his initial hostility and mistrust toward Anne could have contributed to the unwarranted guilt she carried around her wrists and ankles like shackles—which she had been born into through no choice of her own and which she had tried to break out of in the short time she was alive by trying to mend the wounds her family had wrecked upon this world.

After Anne and Cole spent some time in the In-Between—with The Oracle having amnesia about the fact that the crow she thought was her familiar was actually her deceased best friend—she told Cole-the-crow about her nightmares, about Brutus Barberry, about how she found the bones of Captain Ark's sister scattered around Barberry Castle, along with so many other unclaimed remains of hungry ghosts.

"Caw—"

Cole couldn't speak to Annie directly, but he hoped the sentiment could transcend words.

It's not your fault.

"*Caw—*"

For some reason, even though Cole's cawing as a bird was indecipherable to anyone else in the In-Between, there were still some remnants of Anne Barberry that made her understand him.

Even when Anne did not remember the black bird of death that was her only companion in this cold place between Life and Death was the brother whose demise she blamed herself for.

"Cole, I was angry and terrified about Ark Li for the longest time," Anne said, her locks framing her face like the moonbeams against the dark silk of her dress, a beautiful silver-haired ghost who was born from darkness and filth and shadows. "She was the bogeyman of my childhood. I knew how death looked on people—the first person I ever saw killed in my Visions was your namesake."

Cole plucked a little at his own black feathers, knowing full well she meant *him*.

"And for the longest time, I thought it was my fault all these bad things in my Visions were going to happen to those people I saw dying," Anne explained, absent-mindedly stroking Cole's feathers, as if noticing his distress. "But that monster who murdered my grandfather? She was tangible, blood and bone, all gnawing teeth and howling words. She was a solid predator, a true monster I saw doing something terrible to someone I loved. And for the first time, I stopped blaming myself for all the dead people in my Visions as The Oracle. I blamed them all on her. Ark Li, an Aixauhan alchemist."

"*Caw—*"

Cole had never heard Anne speak in such a venomous tone. The Oracle's beautiful pale face twisted like spiderwebs, the blood vessels in her eyes popped, and he could taste the poison of hate—the same thing that had destroyed so many lives and led to all this death and war, leaking out of Anne Barberry like a powder keg that had been dampened but was still ever at risk of exploding.

It surprised and scared him a little. The Anne Barberry in Cole's memories had always been a wall of ice, a marble statue dressed in an overly complicated black funeral gown. She had been the definition of stone-cold beauty.

When he still had not known what lay in her heart, Cole had thought the coldness radiating off of Anne Barberry was an apathetic arrogance, a nose turned up toward the high heavens and an aristocratic arrogance that made her indifferent to people's sufferings. He'd thought her emotionless and devoid of empathy, like someone who was born to privilege and thought they were entitled to the world.

Then came the war. Along came the nights where screams tore through their campsite or The Cottage that woke Cole from a dead sleep, thinking some sort of animal was being torn apart, flesh and skin flowing amber river as they died in the surrounding woods.

But then he'd turn around and see the screaming prey, whose inhuman cry did not belong to an animal from outside The Cottage or tent, but instead to the blonde oracle, sobbing into Chely's shoulder like a broken doll.

The first time this happened, Cole was dumbfounded. He never realised that Anne Barberry, The Oracle who held the entire future within her Visions, who could predict the rise and fall of empires and map out the deaths of millions in wars and disasters, actually was very petite.

Especially when she cried like that, it was like witnessing a silk-worm's hard cocoon being violently torn apart as the butterfly was dragged out—limping and half-formed—drooping in misery and on the brink of death.

That was when Cole had realised: the mask of cold indifference, the extravagant black mourning clothes, the forever expressionless face and monotone voice... they were all the cocoon of a silkworm. They existed because the true creature inside was confused and vul-nerable yet trying its best to reflect and grow.

Had they been living in peaceful days, Anne Barberry would have soon emerged from that cocoon as a magnificent butterfly, who knew how to laugh, who loved people with kindness.

A butterfly who kissed Chely on their wedding day while smil-ing like an idiot, who scolded Cole for being reckless during the war because she knew he would die and only went into war to prevent that from happening.

That was who Anne Barberry was.

"Caw—"

You idiot, Cole replied. *You think you can fool me, Annie? I know you like the palm of my hand. You are my sister without sharing my blood, just like Chely. You have no anger in you, not toward Ark Li, not toward anyone.*

The only thing within you is a sadness as deep as the sea. It is endless and contains compassion for all those who suffered in your Visions, those who come and go from this place. You have a heart of gold that is as shiny as the colour of your hair.

Of course, Cole couldn't exactly say any of this to Anne. Not as a bird. Not when his sister did not yet wish to relieve the pain. Not when she did not want to remember what she had left behind.

So, he cawed.

I'll make sure you get your happy ending, sister dear.

I'll make sure of it.

You will have the love that you tried to secure for me and Chely. You will have the peace that you allowed even Ark Li, who never afforded the same grace to you.

You might be The Oracle, Annie. But my vision will come true.

Ark Li knows from the bulging eyes of Shui-Yin, the half-Yamalan, half-Inabrian boy, that he is neither delighted to see her nor did he expect to see her in this form.

Death is an interesting thing. It grants some people peace, others suffering.

Captain Ark Li, however, received neither of those things.

Instead, her afterlife is like many of her days on Earth.

The sun that hangs overhead and the stars that direct ways for the ships that travel the high seas and that connect different realms of the afterlife are almost the same planets as those in the living world.

There are still storms that can flip a ship right over as if it were made out of paper. Only instead of the sailors choking to their deaths and the ship becoming bone wreckage at the bottom of the sea, a new habitat for the local sea life, the sailors always miraculously find themselves floating above water as if they weigh no more than a wooden plank, and the ship reassembles itself after the storm passes, like it has a mind of its own.

Ark's parents don't go sailing with her. They stay in the Underworld realm under the fair Yan Luo King, Judge Bao Zheng, the fairest judge to ever exist in Aixauh's long history.

They blame their departure on seasickness and on wishing for a quiet life to devote to their alchemy after the traumatic end they suffered, alongside all Aixauhan alchemists and the millennia worth of research that went up in flames, burned by the magicians and the noble lineages of Inabri.

"We don't want to be a bother to you," they told their one-eyed daughter, their eyes glazed over as if they were searching for a different black-haired girl somewhere behind Ark who would pop out and denounce this woman in front of them as an imposter. "You are not an Aixauhan alchemist, Si-Ya. You are a pirate."

"Agreed," Ark said.

She had not heard her Aixauhan name since she was a teenager; it was a stranger she hadn't met in half a century.

Si-Ya, 思雅, a girl's name that means thoughtfulness and elegance. Ark Li is neither of those things, and if her parents wish for that daughter back, then the pirate has nothing to offer them.

Ark dropped them at the port on the mountaintop of Kun Lun, where alchemists and cultivators resided after noble deaths. The waves of excitement brought on by the reunion after death diminished, like a low tide preceding the natural occurrence of a high tide.

She knew they had eternity here for her parents to reconnect with this pirate whose hands are stained the blood of the people who were innocent or not-so-innocent, with the little girl they left behind who cried herself dry at witnessing the whole Li Clan's execution.

Maybe Ark's gentle, healer parents could come around one day. But it is not in the nature of a pirate to wait around for others' forgiveness.

So, Ark left her parents and went on to explore the afterlife on her own.

She is a pirate captain of her own ship and crew. She selected each and every single one of the crewmen herself, like picking up dying crabs who wandered too far off on the burning sand trying to find their way back to the ocean.

"The Inabrians have a saying. They believe their Creator made an ark that sailed through a tsunami that wiped the world. You're our ark, Captain! You're the one who fared us through this blasted war and created this sail that's a haven."

Thus, the legend of Captain Ark Li in the afterlife is born.

However, the story of the pirate captain is one of the past wars. It involved another girl, another empire, another pair of girls who waded through the worst together and fell in love in the process but parted ways in unfortunate circumstances, never to be reunited again.

Maybe one day Ark will tell her little sister about this story. Her sister, who remained the age she died, was the quartermaster of their ship in the afterlife. She is tiny as a rat and ten times as fast. She can climb the bowsprit like a spider with eight legs.

Ark's sister seems to possess no memories of Barberry Castle and the horrors she endured there. Maybe it is a mercy granted by the afterlife, to wipe those soul-shattering barbs clean from the minds of children who die young.

When Maev came along, the girl who was blessed with the gift of being able to safely walk between life and afterlife, appearing out of nowhere and crashing right on top of a very unhappy seagull, Ark was finally persuaded by the little miscreant that was her little sister to let her try rum for the first time since, "I technically have been dead for over four decades, making me perfectly legal in terms of drinking age."

"Hey, Maev." Ark waved at the dark-skinned young woman with dreadlocks. She still remembered Maev as a dehydrated, malnourished orphan stowaway hiding in the barrel of Ark's ship. That bold little girl, who had been shrunken to near bone and had a dying look, was now taller than Ark—Ark now looked the age of a teenager while Maev was in her prime. "I haven't seen you since I popped off the mortal plane. How are you doing?"

Maev didn't respond, which confirmed it wasn't a social call. Ark shrugged, not caring much.

She could already half-guess why Maev had shown up on Ark's ship deck.

The girl had never liked the captain. No one could blame her. Maev, Kong-Ming, along with all the scrappy orphans that the bothersome bird trio brought onto the ships, were more mouths to feed and an easy target for being taken hostage during a time of war.

The idea of saving orphans had never occurred to Ark Li. She was a navy-trained soldier before having mutinied and turning to piracy. Somewhere along the way, saving civilian children had become low on her priorities. The whole myth of Captain Ark Li saving orphans was just that: a myth. It was the bird trio that insisted they continue their heroic venture of turning Ark's ship into a charity, used to escort the orphans to safety, away from the war zones.

It was not a bad trade, Ark thought. Hope was supposed to be annoyingly righteous and impractical for someone like her, who valued human lives no longer by the merit that they deserved to live, but for it to be something people must earn the right to.

Might made right. Survival of the fittest. A form of thinking that Ark did not wish to contaminate the future with.

Cai-Li and Shui-Yin wanted saving the orphans, like Maev, to be their top priority, or they wouldn't follow her command to work as part of the crew. And Ark had fought in a war; Shui-Yin's Ya-malan ability made him perfect for espionage.

Cai-Li? Well, Cai-Li had a full arsenal. A bird of prey sweeping across to the enemy ship alone, and minutes later, with the colourful yet corrosive stink of alchemical compounds, leaving behind sludge and blood and brain matter scattered with no survivors.

After the war and after Patricia Barberry's gruesome murder, people would say that Cai-Li was a radical terrorist, a murderer and a monster who'd gone outside the peace treaty and international law because The Blood Hawk liked to taste the Inabrians' blood as revenge.

However, on Ark's ship and Cai-Li's homeland, the sentiment was reversed.

Unbeknownst to Maev, or the current Barberry Oracle, or even Shui-Yin of the Yamalan, The Blood Hawk is not a derogatory term given by the Inabrians to describe Cai-Li's descent into blood-related alchemy and necromancy.

Instead, it was a mistranslation of the honorifics of the legend that was beginning to build surrounding the red-haired alchemist and assassin in the land of Aixauh. 赤鹰, directly translated as the 'Crimson Hawk,' was a species of birds found on the island in the very south of Aixauh, in the island dock region of the Aixauh coast where Ark Li came from.

Yes, it was Ark Li who pushed Cai-Li's deeds as tales that slowly spread like wildfire after the war.

They reached the shores of Inabri as the name of a necromancer and a monster, but in the land of Aixauh, without even Ying Cai-Li's own knowledge, she had become a folklore hero, a name that the Aixauhan alchemists muttered with reverence and pride as they rallied behind her, as she was the sunbird she descended from. A goddess who did not forgive and forget the wrongs that were done to her people just because the pale ghosts had decided the war was done.

赤鹰, 金乌之后, 蚩尤之徒. The Crimson Hawk. Descendant of the sunbird. Disciple of the fire god Chi'You.

Cai-Li was too busy pulling people's eyeballs out and sulking in The Cottage of Shui-Yin's over the dead Barberry Oracle. She did not know that, across the ocean, her people were erecting statues of her in temples with her name.

They drew her in murals, with hair haloed by crimson flame. She wore an elaborate alchemist garment in the Aixauhan style, red flame-like sunbeam threads woven around the tunic of her neck. A pair of red wings erupted from her back, starting with ebony black and growing into wooden brown, and slowly the feathers cascaded into wine red, the spider lilies crimson, then lustrous orange, until they faded into the wingtip that was gilded with gold.

Ying Cai-Li did not know there were gilded murals of her in temples, paintings of her that hung on the front doors of alchemist families and clans.

She had become a protector goddess in the short decade after the war, for she did not fear bloodshed and sought vengeance.

Before her death, Ark told Chely all of this.

It earned only an amused laugh from the red-haired godspawn who had become a legend. "I don't want to be a goddess, Captain," The Crimson Hawk said. "I want the person I love to be alive and happy. I want to grow old with her until our hair is grey instead of the colours of the sun and the moon. What use is immortality when I cannot even spend my last breaths with her?"

Ark sighed. Her vision was surely becoming blurry due to the infection that was claiming her. For a moment, she saw a younger version of herself in Cai-Li. The two faces mingled and overlapped perfectly.

As if staring into a mirror of her past, Ark remembered how similar she and Ying Cai-Li were.

There had once been a girl, too, named Si-Ya who had loved the dock city. Before the Inabri ever set foot on the land that did not belong to them. Before Captain Ark had been born, there had once been a girl she thought she'd be with until death did them part.

"The Barberry Oracle will never understand what you are doing," Ark said softly. She was no longer the hard-boiled captain, commander of a ship that rescued refugees of war. She was the closest thing Ying Cai-Li had to a mother.

Cai-Li's face grew stern. "Annie proved herself, even to you, Captain." She pulled her hand away from the aged captain lying on her deathbed. "She is kind. She isn't like them."

"That's exactly why she wouldn't understand, little hawk." Ark smiled; she closed her eyes and laid out the observation and perspective only age and experience could grant at Cai-Li's feet. "杀人偿命, 天经地义. 君子报仇, 十年不晚."

"The person who killed someone should pay with their life; it is as natural as Heaven's morals and Earth's law. An honourable one will always take revenge; a decade is not too late."

Cai-Li translated those Aixauhan idioms, but then she suddenly laughed.

"Hell, Captain," Cai-Li mused. "We Aixauhans sure do have a lot of sayings about revenge. Are we really so good at holding grudges?"

"It's not about grudges. It's about setting the world's balance by settling a blood score," Ark said, serious and shaking her head. "You know I'm the one who killed your wife's grandfather, right?"

"…Yes," Cai-Li admitted, her face rarely so unsure.

"Why do you think I killed Brutus but spared your little love?"

"Well, because you are an honourable person," Cai-Li responded naturally. "Brutus Barberry deserved his fate, but Anne was innocent. A life for a life. You wouldn't have killed a girl for revenge, as it would make your revenge no longer honourable."

Ark nodded. "*Exactly.*"

"What are you trying to teach me, Captain?" Cai-Li asked, slightly confused.

"Your wife, she loves you, but she is still an Inabrian. Her last name is still Barberry, and she still grew up with this society's morals and values. To us, taking revenge by killing the one who killed someone we love is not just natural, but required, for if a loved one goes unavenged, it is a sign we let the deceased down.

"However, the Inabrians Creator preaches forgiveness. Revenge killings, in their eyes, are inherently an act that people who have fallen to Discord would take. They were taught to turn the other cheek when struck. I can see Anne Barberry clearly now. She is a girl of virtue and goodness. But her morals and values aren't aligned with yours, sunbird."

Cai-Li fell silent. She understood what Ark meant.

"That's why Anne went back to that castle for her sister in the first place," the red-haired girl said. "She said forgiveness was the road forward. I thought it was ridiculous, but she was The Oracle, so I thought maybe she knew something I didn't. But instead—"

"Anne Barberry simply thinks that forgiveness is the way to right a moral wrong," Ark said. "While you and I, we Aixauhans, we know that a blood debt can only be paid by blood. That is the natural law of Heaven and Earth. I killed Brutus Barberry so he could no longer harm another. You killed Patricia Barberry so she couldn't do so either in the future. Sometimes pretty words are not enough to stop a force that wants us dead; we can only strike back until they are no longer a threat."

"Maybe you are right, Captain," Cai-Li replied, her voice quiet. "But we are still different. I grew up in Inabri. Cole, my sworn brother, is half-Inabrian. I fell in love with Annie, the oracle heir of one of its noble magician lineages. I do not find their morals fully nonsensical. I didn't kill Patricia Barberry for some greater good, or cosmic balance. I killed her because she took the one person I loved from me. And I would do it again. And again. Because no matter how many times Patricia Barberry perishes, it will not bring Anne back. So, I will find another way."

"The way of necromancy," Ark understood perfectly. "The pursuit of the Elixir of Immortality is the natural quest for an Aixauhan alchemist. It was from the days of the Founding Emperor."

"So, will you help me?"

"An eye's just an eye." Ark waved a hand at Cai-Li. "Maybe our idiom was never solely about vengeance; maybe it can also be applied to your love for The Oracle."

Chely chuckled, but this time, she only sounded sad.

"Captain," The Crimson Hawk of legend said, "we aren't the only ones who have idioms. 'An eye for an eye will make the whole world blind.' Anne believes that. So, what do you think she'll do when she finds out I am about to exchange a life for a life? If an eye is enough for the world to become blind, what evil would make someone unwilling to be revived as an immortal bring into the world?"

Ark Li shook her head, not because she did not know the answer, but because she found the question pointless.

"Nothing will happen, Cai-Li," Ark Li said. "No alchemy is inherently evil. You know that. Your ancestors, the Flaming sunbirds, did not know they were scorching the Earth into famine and drought. That was just the way it was. The immortal you revive and cast upon the world will just be Anne Barberry. Do you think she's evil?"

"No," Cai-Li answered as if it were the truth of the universe. "She is the best of us."

Ark arched an eyebrow. There surely was some history between Cai-Li and Anne Barberry that the captain did not know of. Neither did she care to know.

"Then you have nothing to worry about," she said. "Go ahead and do what needs to be done to bring your lover back."

"No?" Cole seethes angrily. He is trying his absolute best not to punch the former captain in the face, even though he knows she'd duck and return his clumsy attempt at combat tenfold. "What do you mean, *NO?*"

"It's as simple as it sounds, Shui-Yin," Ark replies. She pats the eyepatch and says, "If I had any moral objections, I wouldn't have given an eye as an ingredient for the ritual in the first place. Cai-

Li is doing what she wants. You care about that Barberry girl too. Didn't you tell me how sad you were to see her here so soon? Don't you want The Oracle to be alive again?"

"Yes," Cole sputters. "But *not like this*—"

He wants Anne to be alive more than anything. Hell, only minutes ago, he made world-shattering declarations of giving Anne the happy ending he knew was long due to his friend.

But what he meant was peace, saying goodbye. He wants Anne and Chely back together again. He wants them both to be at peace. He wants them both alive, but that's not how death is supposed to work.

One could grieve. One could rage. But one shouldn't let those things replace the space in one's heart for hope and the future.

"Anne doesn't want this ritual to happen," Cole says. "She'd never agree to Chely giving up her life so Anne could live. You can help us convince Chely to back off from this plan and let them say goodbye and have closure. Chely always looked up to you. If you can convince her simply to let go, then Anne can be at peace. *I* can be at peace."

"I'm sorry, Shui-Yin of the Yamalan." Ark dips her head, as if for the first time truly feeling a slight amount of sadness. "I'm sorry for what you had to go through. To be ripped back from a peaceful death gives serious whiplash, or so I heard from some of my crew members. But instead of me, you should be talking to Cai-Li, before you run out of time."

Maev's face drops. This is bad. For some godforsaken reason, Cole thought that because Captain Ark saw Chely almost like a daughter, a reflection of herself—the captain's protégé—that would mean Ark Li wouldn't want Chely to die.

"Sorry I wasted your time, Maev, Shui-Yin." Ark Li stands up. "Excuse me though. My little sister is my quartermaster, but I still don't particularly trust her not to boss my crew around. She's smart, but she is probably also very drunk on rum by now. I have a ship to run, so don't waste any more of my time."

"Stop!" Cole yells. Desperation leaks into him, the patchwork he plastered across this whole miserable affair crumbling. "Please, Captain. I can't—I can't lose them both again."

"You won't lose them both," Ark replies matter-of-factly. "You'll lose Anne Barberry, since, well, she will be forever alive, and you are dead. So, that's an eternal farewell. But Cai-Li will be dead too, so you two can hang out. It's been the pair of you against the world since you were kids, right?"

"You are a monster," Maev murmurs. "How can you be so cruel? Human lives, they aren't subtraction."

"I don't deny I am a monster, Soul-Gazer," Ark says. "But we all die in the end. If you look at this from the bright side, it is actually an enormous win. Since Anne Barberry will be alive forever, Cai-Li won't be stuck in the war that never ended in her head. Cole, you are finally not a bird that can only caws all the time. Why aren't either of you happy? You have made great progress, yet all I see are whiny children bickering about trying to reverse something that has already started."

Cole's head snaps up at that.

"What do you mean?" His voice is suddenly as grim as the blackbird of his familiar form. "What do you mean by '*already started?*'"

24

The Farewell

CHELY YING IS many things. A paradox, for one. The embodiment of saying horrifying things in a cheerful tone. An accomplished and famous alchemist, albeit not for the most savoury kind of magic. A necromancer. A survivor. Someone who never returned from the war.

Despite the decade between them, the fact that Chely ripped out Patricia Barberry's eyeball, went on a murderous rampage against war criminals, and used human body parts of alchemists as if they were herbs, means that Anne—for all her skill in seeing the future—can never predict what Chely will do next.

The blonde Barberry gives a soft laugh. She isn't enraged or flabbergasted at this point. Not after Anne just admitted when backed into the corner that she would love Ying Cai-Li, no matter what The Blood Hawk did in the past or would do in the future.

Before those words were squeezed out from the depths of her soul, Anne didn't even know they were the truth.

It was like plucking a pearl that started off as a speck of sand in an oyster. The sand would grind against the clam's soft and vulnerable flesh, breaking every gentle thing and leaving the clam's insides a grisly and gory clout. It wasn't the speck of sand's intention to hurt the clam. It simply drifted through the thin opening of the clam's walls coincidentally. But the result was that its nature was cut, clambered, and trussed until the clam was bleeding from the inside.

However, in the end, the pearl was born by absorbing all the pain of the clam, blossoming into the most precious thing in the world. Pure, beautiful.

And the clam was proud and delighted by the loveliness of the pearl, despite everything that ground both parties into shambles before they were reformed.

That speck of white sand was how Anne and Chely started off as kids, hiding from the world to talk together in that tavern. Their blushing faces and grazing fingers.

They were the clam, and the speck of white sand—a tiny but common thing that was so puny that it was nothing but one in a trillion that formed the beautiful beachside—it snowballed through the decades; first, it was the war, then it was death, there were Chely's murders and necromancy, and there was Anne's isolation and imprisonment of all the souls within the In-Between.

After all of that, the clam should be dead.

Instead, what Anne finds within is a pearl. The indestructible heart that is the compressed essence of everything they've been through, the combination of Anne and Chely together.

It is love. Love without condition. Love while knowing each other's every bump and flaw. Every awful thing they have done and everything rotten within their nature. All their vulnerabilities and their broken pieces and jagged edges that will definitely hurt the other party.

None of it matters in the end.

It's still Chely and Anne.

"You know I'll never agree to that," Anne tells Chely softly. "I will never let you kill yourself so that I can live."

"I know." Chely smiles. She reaches out a hand and brushes away a single strand of Anne's golden hair. "I share that sentiment. But, Annie, I cannot live in a world where you do not exist."

The alchemist tucks the hair behind the oracle's ear, but Anne catches Chely's thin wrist with an iron grip.

"I think you have forgotten who is in control here," Anne says, trying to crush the tears welling up in her eyes and sound menacing. She ends up sounding like a slippery squid. "I am the queen of the In-Between. I control everything here. The kitchen, this castle, even all the townsfolk down the hill and their memories. You may be the most talented alchemist in history, Ying Cai-Li, but you have no power here. I will not allow you to die for me. You cannot make me."

Chely smiles. She lifts her free hand in surrender.

"I know, Annie." The alchemist is calm, as if she hasn't just been told the thing she sold her soul was for nothing. "We may both have changed a lot. But I knew from the moment I set my eyes on you, you would let no one suffer except yourself."

Anne snorts. "Quit joking." She laughs. "You saw a loser getting drunk in the corner of the tavern reading a book and decided she must be a saint? Quit buttering me up with your silver tongue, my love."

A light enters Chely's eyes. It is like a meteor shower has suddenly entered the alchemist's dark, night eyes. Cai-Li Hawk's eyes are lit up by emotions that Anne does not understand.

"We shared two-thirds of our lives entangling together, Annie," Chely Hawk says gently, as if she is seeing across time to a place of nostalgia in her childhood. A place that Anne has no access to. "Yet you still don't know that I fell in love with you back at that summer camp."

Cai-Li snuck out of the tent after Cole's tears dried. The boy had finally fallen asleep. His transparency kicked in, so all Cai-Li had to go off of was the snoring. It had taken her a few hours to calm him down by promising they would never return to this summer camp. They'd tell Cole's mum what happened, and the kind-hearted but clear-eyed Yamalan woman would definitely not let her son be subject to such cruelty again.

Then for another few hours, Cai-Li and Cole had played silly games so the Yamalan could cheer up until at least half of him was transparent and glacier-like again.

The Yamalans were free spirits born of the wild. They were shapeshifters, but they were made of metals and elements of the celestial energy due to their home being the Yamalan Mountains, which were so high that they absorbed the celestial properties of the sky. The less solid they became, the freer their form, the happier they were. The more solid and human-looking they got, the more distressed they were.

Cole, who was half-human, was born to be trapped in a sense of predetermined melancholy. The pure Yamalans experience only joy, pixies and animal spirits. They have no sense of human sorrow or the problems that come with being mortal.

That was why it was extra unforgivable, what those magician kids did.

In the dark, surrounded by emerald grass and silver moonlight, little fireflies sparkled quietly in the silent woods like tiny lanterns. The breeze on her face was warm as it was summer. The humidity of the woods should have soaked the little Aixauh girl in sweat.

However, all Ying Cai-Li felt was a bone-chilling coldness.

It was like a tiny fledgling first bursting out of its shell only to watch its parents being ripped into pieces by the talons of a stronger predator.

Cai-Li knew kids were mean. Unlike Cole's gentle mother, Cai-Li's mum had laughed when Cai-Li begged to go to this summer camp so she could make some new friends.

"Friends? Silly, there is no friendship that can be formed between them and us. They have their Creator, while we have our gods. We are from two different worlds. There is no mixing."

"Cole's parents mixed!" Cai-Li protested, proud that she had cracked her mother's seemingly impeccable logic.

"No, they didn't." Lady Ying smiled the same ineffable smile that one day Cai-Li would learn to inherit as well. "In a couple of years—maybe a decade—you'll see, my little sun birdie. There is no bond that could survive between an Inabrian and an Aixauhan."

"But—"

"Believe me, Cai-Li. I've lived longer than most people. Not a single friendship or relationship between them and us has lasted. Don't waste your time before you lose your already short life."

Cai-Li had thought her mum was exaggerating until she had slowly come to the age to realise the bitterness that underlined Lady Ying's worldview.

Now, standing in the middle of the forest, surrounded by those bullies, Cai-Li thought her mum might have been right all along.

Those Inabrian children. The way they'd looked at Cole as if they were watching an insect they'd caught in a jar. They'd had a look of hunger and delight on their faces, shimmering under the summer sun in perfect innocence. They had laughed and chuckled cruelly as they'd each taken turns poking at their trapped insect, entertained by its jerky movements.

When Cai-Li had stepped in, they had stopped. But they had not seen her as an equal. If Cole was an insect they'd toyed with, then Cai-Li was the venomous snake hidden in the grass.

A camp full of kids who had stood by and watched as their peers treated Cole like a piece of meat. All white-faced with skin so pale that they would sunburn simply by taking a stroll outside. Their cheeks had been flushed, but they'd had skin the colour of corpses floating in rivers, pearl-white as ghosts who haunted the living.

Today, it had simply been bullying. What if tomorrow it became a murder? Would they bat an eye if someone blasted a spell at Cole or pushed him off a cliff?

They'd all stood there and *watched*, the people of this land.

They had eyes as light as the shade of a rainbow. Eyes like gemstones, as if their Creator had merged the most precious metal to form the window to their souls. Hazel that glistened amber with jade around the edges. Blue, some light as aquamarine and some the colour of sapphire. Gold, the colour of wheat during harvest season.

They had eyes so colourful, contrasting with the Aixauhans' eyes that were all dark as night. Cai-Li had once wondered if they saw the world through an enchanted lens.

Now she knew why they had eyes that were so light.

Because they had no soul behind those mirror-like gemstones.

They'd watched as Cole fell apart. Not one single person had muttered so much as a protest.

The Inabrian magician children might have had no concept of war, but no infant born of Aixauhan parents had forgotten what happened.

It haunted them through the absence in their family trees in the form of aunties and uncles, in the mass graves that were covered in joss paper in an attempt to appease the spirits. It haunted them in the names whispered of family members they had never met and through the silence that befell the older generation as they clutched tight tokens of loved ones whose bodies were never found.

The Inabrian noble lineages passed down their Creator's blessings.

The Aixauhan alchemists passed down scars of the dead.

"I went to that one girl's tent," Chely remembers. "I wanted to beat her up bloody so I could get an excuse for me and Cole to get kicked out of the summer camp. I didn't want her to win, and we were not going to run away. We were going to leave as the monstrous gremlins, children of Discord, just as they saw us."

"Fair enough," Anne replies. "Who could blame you? None of us did anything to warrant their cruelty. I guess you always had that fighting streak in you; I just kind of…idealised you too much. I doubt Cole would have been thrilled though. He isn't too happy about your whole killing people and necromancy thing."

"Let me finish, Annie." Chely can sense Anne's sanity is hanging on by a thread, but she's still slow in her delivery of this ancient memory. "It might not sound so relevant. But I promise you, it was the key that opened a particular door that led us to this future."

Out of professional habit, Anne objects by instinct.

"The future has no keys to doors, Chely," Anne says, hating herself for the need to correct the misconception of what an oracle can do even at this critical moment. "You're describing everything as if it's all predetermined. As if that one decision bore some kind of cosmic significance to every event to come. I heard it a thousand times as The Eyeless Oracle, those people who came to me over the years seeking the future—wishing me to give a definitive answer that would save them from making their own decisions in life so they could either rely on or blame the prophecy."

Chely pauses, then she says, "The future is the forming of constellations. There are no key decisions, no doors to a set path. An oracle gazing up at the stars, as they reach Earth from a distance, saw that what we saw was in fact the past, so instead of predicting the future... oracles are much more like historians. You read the patterns among the stars of the past and try to map out what constellation they will form in the future."

Anne opens her mouth, both in surprise and in awe.

Only for a moment though. It should be obvious, if anyone was capable of getting the gist of what an oracle is, it would be an oracle's wife.

"If you know my stance on fate and predestination," Anne asks softly, at the same time a lover's gentle caress and a desperate plea, "why bring it up now? Are you trying to use what happened back then to justify why you are giving up your life now?"

"No, Annie." Chely shakes her head. "That would go against everything I just said, against everything you, as The Oracle, told me. I am not telling you this memory to convince you to let me trade my life for yours. This story is about me finally telling you that long before you knew I existed, I had already fallen in love with a girl at the summer camp when I found the wrong tent."

Chely did not remember the names of the girls who had taunted Cole earlier that day.

They all blended together, like a kaleidoscope. A bunch of confusing and enigmatic but bright colours that had vaguely the same shape but were blurred and distant like dabs of acrylic paint instead of actual girls one would know.

The important thing was they were many, and Cole only had Chely.

Cai-Li knew she couldn't get back at the girls and start a fight amidst the summer camp, as the supervisors there were all Inabrian magicians. Cole's mum had sent them there for that exact reason: so they'd be outnumbered by the people of this country and have them soak up Inabri and their magician culture like baby cats being drowned in a river.

It was a bad day. Cai-Li's thoughts swirled like the currents about to form a city-destroying tornado that wished to swallow those girls and that camp whole for trying to make Cole feel small about himself.

She didn't have authority on her side, so she'd make her own method of making those girls pay. By sneaking into their tents in the middle of the night and pranking them with something that was humiliating but couldn't be traced back to Cai-Li.

During the days they'd already spent in the camp, which was about a week and a half by that point, Cai-Li had observed quietly as Cole talked at her during dinner which direction the girls who always liked to stir up trouble retreated toward at the camp.

The summer camp had about fifty tents. Almost all of them were shared, two and two. No one wanted to share a tent with Cai-Li because she was an Aixauhan alchemist. It was a blessing in disguise, since that meant Cole could sneak into Cai-Li's tent without worries. They kept each other company so Cole didn't have to deal with his tent-mate's friends' endless, seemingly innocent questions. "Is it true your alchemists have corroded blood that is pure liquid metal instead of blood?" "Is it true that Yamalans are cannibals?" "Is it true..."

The girls who had come after Cole that day were all the ones who had slept in the same area, in the northwest corner of the campsite. The numbered thirty to forty tents. Cai-Li and Cole had been assigned tents when they'd arrived, but apparently those girls had handpicked their own all in one area. That kind of privilege wasn't afforded to the others.

"So, are they, like, a big deal around here?" Cai-Li asked, seemingly innocuous and clueless, to one of the Inabrian magician kids who weren't outright hostile or avoidant.

"Oh, yeah." That kid lowered their voice, as if announcing some kind of secret that could unlock the recipe for the Elixir of Immortality to Cai-Li. "You don't know, Chai, but they're the lineage kids."

Cai-Li furrowed her brow, feeling like she really should pick an Inabrian-sounding name for herself just so these idiots would stop butchering her beautiful name that was dedicated to her immortal sunbird lineage by spitting their saliva out every time they tried—and failed—to pronounce it correctly.

So, what does that mean? Do they have a family disease that got passed down or something?

That was what she wanted to say, but instead Cai-Li thought that would paint her in a threatening light that would block her chance of learning more about the targets of her little revenge plot. Plus, it would put Cai-Li on the radar of the kids at camp so they'd see her hostility toward these so called "lineage kids" and suspect her as the culprit of whatever Cai-Li was going to do to them.

So, instead, she scrunched up her nose in innocent confusion and schooled her face into a blank look.

The Inabrian kid sighed, as if Cai-Li were a toddler asking why the sky was blue.

"The lineage kids are the magician nobility's heirs. Unlike the rest of us, they are the first-born children of lineages who were blessed with one specific magical talent each by the Creator during the Great Times of Depravity. There are the Ollies, who control the tides on the ocean. The Logans, who could tell what you're thinking from ten feet away. And the Henrys, they could control the weather—as in lightning to strike down their great enemies during the War!"

The kid babbled with such speed and fervour that they clearly didn't notice Cai-Li's fists clenching. Here sat a child, the same age as Cole and her, who talked about the war as if it was from some kind of storybook. Participants hadn't slaughtered people and piled their bodies into holes; they themselves had been forced to dig their own graves and had been massacred within them.

They talked about the war and the magician lineages as if they were mythical legends of their era, instead of murderers and monsters.

It made Cai-Li nauseated.

"You all right? You look like you need to breathe."

"It's just the sun." Cai-Li waved away the concern from the boy and gave him a bright, encouraging smile. "Don't stop! This sounds so exciting. The Henrys—that's Lisa's last name, right? So, she's one of the lineage magicians who can manipulate electricity?"

"I said she can summon lightning—"

"Sure, but the underlying principle that allows that level of manipulation requires the baseline ability of manipulating electricity. Also, the thunder gods of Lei Gong and Dian Mu (雷公和电母)," Cai-Li smiled and said.

The kid sighed again. "Aixauhan alchemists," he mumbled before pulling away and joining his friends.

"Before you go," Cai-Li gave the sweetest grin she could muster, like the brightest poisonous red mushroom with white spots on it. "Who would you say is the one lineage kid that all of them would listen to?"

Finding the leader of the pack was important. Lisa Henry had surely done most of the taunting that day, but if Cai-Li wanted to create enough chaos amidst a group, striking the head usually created more discord as they would all blame each other for the one person they all wanted to impress.

The kid, to his credit, gave an honest and straight answer.

"Anne Barberry," he said. "The heir of the Barberry Lineage, which is the blessed family of oracles. She apparently developed her oracle powers when she was only six. Imagine that! She's set to take over for Brutus Barberry as his protégé. She speaks only to the other lineage kids, not the rest of us at all. And when she says something, the other lineage kids always take it seriously."

Anne Barberry. Cai-Li chewed on that name like a piece of garbage stuck between her teeth. That was one hell of a name. Rolled off the tongue. But she also sounded like a real asshole.

If even Lisa Henry, who had been nothing but horrible even to her own people, listened to this Barberry Oracle, then she must have been the worst of the bunch.

She checked the spreadsheet and spotted Anne Barberry's tent number. The girl conveniently shared a tent with Lisa Henry.

Cai-Li hadn't seen Anne Barberry when Lisa and the other kids had picked on Cole. Where had she been? Sitting nearby and not willing to get her hands dirty? Watching her lapdogs do her dirty work? Whatever it had been, she'd have it coming when Cai-Li got to her.

The night was dark and damp. It was technically summer, but Inabri was an island country that had temperatures jumping from a single-linen day under the sun to a three-quilt-and-still-shivering day under the moon real fast.

All the tents were warded against the cold so the children wouldn't catch a cold and have their parents come complaining. Cole had laughed at this and told Cai-Li that if his mother knew the camp was using a warming spell to guard her Yamalan son against bad weather, she might have reconsidered sending them there.

"Why?" Very rarely did Cai-Li find Auntie's ideas strange. "I don't want to get a cold. This place already hates us, why risk bad weather making life even worse?"

"Well, maybe not for *you*," Cole had said with a grin. "But we are one with the world, Cai-Li. The Yamalan embraces whatever nature gives us. We do not shield ourselves or try to alter what was intended."

"That's rich." Cai-Li had rolled her eyes and punched her best friend in his invisible stomach. "When you have a conveniently well-built aptitude for enduring cold weather because your people are literally children of the snow mountains!"

Cai-Li could feel the rain-drenched grass clutching her crouched legs like frostbite. She waited patiently, trying to convince herself the numb terror and sudden craving of a warm bed, snuggled up in blankets, were only the persuasion of a coward's mind.

She thought of Cole, of the way he literally disappeared as the kids laughed at him.

They were killing her brother, Cai-Li thought. If she kept allowing it, then there wouldn't be much of Cole of the Yamalan left by the time they reached adulthood.

She needed to give the Inabrian magicians a taste of their own medicine. Cai-Li didn't intend to hurt them—even though the idea was tempting—but she'd make sure there was a sad accident that would leave them preoccupied with Anne Barberry's rage and forget about picking on Cole for the rest of the summer.

"Are you coming, Annie?"

Cai-Li threw her whole body onto the ground, where the shadows hid her while Lisa Henry called from outside of the tent.

Ew. The wet soil stuck to her cheek and lips, and her white shirt and pants were drenched in mud. She was miserable, and she was determined to pass that misery onto the person she saw as responsible for this.

"Don't call me that," another voice came from within the tent, a monotonous and level voice that didn't sound like it belonged to a child who'd been asked by her friends to join along.

"Ah, but Mr. Barberry asked us to take care of you." Lisa laughed, as did her friends that were gathering around the tent. "I'm pretty sure that's what he called you when he kissed you goodbye."

An odd and confused feeling rose from Cai-Li's chest. It felt damp and dark, as if something was deeply wrong. Why did it sound like Lisa and her friends were *taunting* Anne Barberry?

The looks on their faces… They were like vultures circling prey that was about to die, waiting to dive once the target's self-esteem dropped to the point of being nonexistent.

Just like they had with Cole.

Anne Barberry was not one of them; that was Cai-Li's first realisation.

Then, Cai-Li saw the girl hidden by the tent walk out into the light and to face Lisa Henry. Her white-blonde hair was silver under the dimness of night, like moonbeams on water. She had skin pale as a lily, but ashened by the night and the coldness of her disposition. She wore a black puff-sleeved dress, like a figure who'd stepped out of an oil painting of old.

Cai-Li thought she looked ridiculous dressing up like that for camp.

Cai-Li thought she looked marvelous, and her cheeks flushed the same shade as her red hair.

The second thing Cai-Li realised was that Anne was the most beautiful girl of her age she had ever seen.

Anne Barberry carried herself like a queen, with her chin tilted up as she watched Lisa Henry and the rest of the lineage kids in utter deafening silence, a swan among a bunch of squawking ducks.

"Lisa Henry," Anne spoke in a tone as soft and gentle as a lullaby. Her words, however, were as damning and ominous as a curse. "You know I'm The Oracle, yet you interrupt me during one of my divination sessions, believing that it will somehow yield good results?"

Lisa scoffed, slightly annoyed as her group of sidekicks shushed one another at this. Despite Lisa Henry's grip on them, it seemed the boy had been right that the lineage kids listened to Anne Barberry.

However, he had clearly gotten the reason wrong.

The third thing that Ying Cai-Li realised about Anne Barberry was that people feared her through no fault of her own.

"You…you don't scare me! I know your power, Anne. Our families worked alongside each other for centuries! You cannot divine individuals who aren't part of the larger picture."

"Yet, I actually just caught a glimpse of you in my Visions just now," Anne replied, her face expressionless, which made her words even more eerie. "Before you rudely interrupted me, of course."

Lisa started shaking, as if Anne had just sentenced her to death.

"What do you mean?" Lisa muttered. "If I'm in your nightmares, does that mean I'm the catalyst for the war to come? You must be lying! My lineage isn't one made for battle."

Nightmares? War to come?

Every single word was like a drum against Cai-Li's already ringing ears. What the hell were they talking about?

Anne Barberry's voice was the only clear thing that still caught her attention.

"You know better than anyone else, Lisa," Anne replied calmly, "as we share the same tent. I have been having a hard time sleeping at night recently. An oracle does not lie about the future. And I have been seeing someone die, again and again, in my dreams. That is why I was screaming in the night until it drove you to ask for a transfer that was denied."

Lisa's knees buckled. The lineage kids surrounding her caught her elbows and ushered her away from the tent. As she left, Lisa Henry looked like a ghost herself. As if the words from the girl who had moonlight for hair and the posture of a black swan had determined her future.

They really do listen to her.

Mesmerised, Ying Cai-Li stayed in the grass, with the soot and mud clinging to her clothes. She forgot all about the cold as a new feeling seized her that lit her up from the inside.

Curiosity, confusion, and a dash of vindictive delight.

"How… What?" Anne mutters, discombobulated. What Chely is saying makes absolutely no sense. "I don't remember." The oracle gulps, a fear suddenly gripping her throat. "Am I still missing memories? Is this why I can't—"

"No, Annie." Chely rests her hand on Anne's shoulder, only for Anne to flinch away.

There is a flash of hesitation and hurt that crosses Chely's eyes. It makes Anne's heart ache, despite the fact that the alchemist lied to her again. Anne is entitled to feel angry, but all she feels is empty. Empty, tired, and in need of a good sleep to wake from so these earth-shattering revelations will end.

Then maybe Anne could wake up in The Cottage that she reached in death. She might be accompanied by Cole, but she might be alone. Either way, she would be happy. She'd sit and watch the sunrise, and the sun would be a bird, a flaming sunbird.

That would be her heaven.

That would be death.

"Why are you even telling me this now, Chely?" Anne lifts her head up and looks Chely straight in the eye. "Why now? You want to trade your life for mine. I tell you to stop, and you go on this tangent about this thing that happened when we were children that doesn't matter—"

"It matters," Chely cuts Anne off. There's a quiet determination behind the alchemist's gentle but firm voice. It is the strength behind her constant smile despite the bleak situation before them.

"It matters to *YOU!*" Anne yells back, trying to push that sense of something tingling in her mind again away. The same feeling she had when she first recounted the truth of her death and the In-Between. No. She refuses to go through this.

Chely flinches, second time in less than a minute. Her face grows pale, despite usually holding a healthy bronze colour.

Anne must be seeing things. Her mind jumps to empathising and trying to humanise the woman she loves. Chely leans against the wall, her body trembling as if she were standing in the winter cold with no warm clothes nor a temperature regulation spell.

But no, there is no way Anne is letting Chely get away with this again. This vulnerability. Chely is *fine.* For all they know, this might just be the In-Between finally repelling Chely's soul—a living and healthy soul—out of the place where only the dead or near-dead should be able to enter.

"Look, Chely. I see that what you're trying to tell me… it matters to you." Anne clears her throat. She tries to regain her patience, even as she feels her ability to take anything else—absolutely anything—crumble away.

"And I told you; I love you. No matter what you have done in the past, whether I know of it or not. You are not a monster, not to me. I know why you did the things you did—and I understand. I do not begrudge you any of it. Hell, I probably couldn't have done better myself. *Haven't* really done better myself."

Anne gestures at the In-Between and gives a crooked smile. Before Chely can interject, The Oracle shushes her.

"Let me finish. This story so far, this dance between you and me, you were the one who had the upper hand all along. You knew I died; you knew I was the one trapping people in the In-Between. Now, you are trying to bring me back to live through necromancy. It's *enough.* I know why you did it all, but the fact remains, you are doing all this against *my will* and *my choice*. It's time you heard what *I* have to say in this whole matter."

At last, Chely seems to be listening. She gives Anne a final signature Chely Hawk smile and then nods.

"You're right, Annie," Chely says quietly, hoarsely. "I'm sorry I forced this onto you, my love. All this time… I was simply working off the belief that once you were alive, then you could make actual choices. You could choose to hate me; you could choose to do what you want with your life. You could choose to go live in The Cottage or travel the world. You could be The Oracle, or never again tell anyone you have the gift of prophecy. You could be anyone. You could finally be free."

"I have always been free, Chely." Anne sighs. "I might not have been free because my sister killed me on the last day of my life. But before that, I had a lifetime of choices. I made each and every one without regret. I chose not to be like my family. I chose to join the war. I chose you and Cole and every child we managed to save. I even chose not to tell you once I realised who Ark Li was, because it didn't matter to me anymore that she had killed my grandpa. He had it coming, and she was protecting us on her ship amidst a war. I chose to let it go.

"Most important of all—I chose *you*, Chely. I chose to go back to that tavern for a second date. I chose to be with you during wartime even if it meant I might lose you. I chose to marry you. In my singular, limited lifetime. Every choice I ever had was between something else and you, Chely Hawk, Ying Cai-Li. I always chose you."

There is a short silence from where Cai-Li stands. The alchemist seems to have frozen on the spot. The smile is still plastered across her face, but Anne can tell the words have sunk in by the trickling tears now forming and spilling from Chely's red-rimmed eyes.

"You're right, Annie," Chely says finally. "You're right. That story—forget about it. We had a lifetime together. We were in love.

We were married. How it ended…that didn't change a single part of what we had together. "

"Yes." Anne smiles. She can feel the sting of tears in her eyes too. She tastes salt on her tongue as she swallows tears and an ugly laugh. "You're stubborn as fuck, Blood Hawk."

Chely lets out a little laugh. "You say that name as if it's some kind of endearment," she laments. "Never thought I would see the day coming—Anne Barberry condoning murder."

"Don't push it." Anne rolls her eyes. "You know what I mean."

"I do," Chely replies, her skin turning a pinkish shade—is it because of the colour of the sunset coming through the window? It's been a long day. "So, tell me, Anne Barberry, what do you have to say to me? What will happen now?"

Anne closes her eyes. Birds sing amidst the trees. She envisions The Barberry Castle crumbling due to time and neglect with all the barberry bushes dying out and withering away. Until all its sins rot with the people who lived within are forgotten, leaving nothing but a smudge upon the green soil and earth.

Anne listens. She can hear Maev, Kong-Ming, and all the other children laughing. She can hear the branches of Cole's tree grow as the boy's soul cascades into a thousand leaves and flowers and seeds. They spread and envelope the mountain on which The Cottage lay.

She sees Chely growing old, tending to Cole's tree as blossoms of every colour bloom on the field. She sees Chely muttering Anne's name in a whisper for the breeze to carry away, to wherever True Death is, until they can be reunited again.

Anne Barberry, The Oracle, sees the passage of time laid before her with two fully opened eyes. The constellation forms as if it was always meant to be, with the stars winking at her, commemorating her for a job well done.

Finally, the future whispers to its beholder. *You have accepted your gift.*

Yes, Anne replies, soft and gentle, with no hard edges or sarcasm. *I'm sorry I denied you for so long, Future. You have always been a gift; I was just too jaded to appreciate you when I had all the time to lose.*

All's forgiven, my child, Future whispers back to The Oracle like a mother to a child. *You have all the time in the world now to figure it out. The constellation has finally set in its form. You will have all the time in the world now that the future which had been on a balance scale is finally set into motion.*

What?

Anne snaps back. Whiplash seizes her as her Vision retreats into the back of her head, and all that peaceful passage of time—the future that Anne thought was determined—disintegrates in front of her like ash.

The scenes she saw. The constellation was in her mind. The one where Anne had uttered her choice back to Chely. The path where her wife would go back home to live a long and happy life, alone yet never unloved.

That is not going to come to pass. That is not what the future holds.

Anne's eyes snapped back to Ying Cai-Li.

The Red Hawk collapsed onto the floor while Anne spoke to the Future. The Oracle gasps and runs toward the alchemist's sprawled form, which trembles as if some ancient creature is trying to claw its way out of her.

"I know what you'd choose, Annie," Chely replies. Her weak voice is nothing but heavy breathing. Still, her eyes are the solid ebony of the Aixauhan people. So solid and full, like rich soil. So solid, like Cole's eyes as he took his final breath.

"You will say you choose death," the alchemist continues, her smile still lingering like a flicker of flame—defiant until the very end. "You say this—all this was nothing but a prolonged goodbye. You'd say it's a gift, for us to get the closure we never did when you went off and got killed. You would then try to lecture me on how we are privileged, as we got the time to say goodbye, unlike the tailor and his wife, unlike Cole, unlike so many people who loved each other but were torn apart by war. *We* alone got to make peace with each other and untangle all the misunderstanding so *I* could live on in a peaceful future."

Anne's grip on Chely's shoulders tightens. She's certain she'd be squeezing the alchemist to death if Chely weren't already at Death's door.

"So, this is why you were so smug and certain all this time." Anne scowls. She sees the cruel smirk on Chely's face, even as the alchemist's eyes shut like twin-blinds. "You didn't travel to the In-Between to seek me out. You didn't come here willingly at all. Death brought you here, as naturally as it would anyone. You landed in the In-Between because you made the choice for me from the *very start*. You already *started* the necromantic ritual. You have been dying of mercury poisoning this entire time."

The alchemist's skin is not just pale, but a rose-coloured pink. Her skin isn't a healthy shade, and it is peeling back like dried orange slices.

All signs of mercury poisoning, which Chely repeated and again since coming to Anne's castle. Chely has talked way too much about that one ancestor, the emperor from eons ago, the one who shared her last name. The Founding Emperor of Qin, who sought the Elixir of Immortality but died of mercury poisoning.

"You idiot!" Enlightenment storms Anne's mind as she cries out loud. The Oracle did not see what The Blood Hawk was planning, not until the very end.

Ying Cai-Li's last expression is triumphant yet apologetic. She tips her chin back to kiss Anne on the head and leaves one last lingering metallic breath before fading into the sunset she was named after.

"I cannot let you speak, Annie. Because your answer will always be *no.* I need you to be alive, so you can see yourself the way I see you. And since you are always so goddamn slow, I'll give you an eternity so you can do so."

Cai-Li stayed in the grass until all the camp lights were out. The world plunged into darkness, and she was pretty sure she was becoming some kind of stinky swamp monster by now.

Lisa Henry and the other girls did not return to the tent. Probably still reeling from the aftermath of what the oracle had said.

Cai-Li's plan of revenge was fulfilled, but not by her. So, with her initial plan being thrown out the window, what the hell was she still doing there?

The answer was the oracle girl who stood with the elegance of a swan.

The night covered the campsite until no one was looking.

Even the voices of the animals in the wilderness had died down. Night capped the world in an eternal sleep. It was so deathly quiet that the only sound Cai-Li could hear was her own breathing.

Suddenly, a loud and clear voice broke through the peaceful campgrounds.

"A war will come," it said. "Many will die. Bullets. Bloodshed. A cottage on the hill. Old scores will be settled in old homes. A war only begets another war. He will die. He will die. He will die. Cole of the Yamalan will die. His death will mark the start of the birth of The Blood Hawk. The Blood Hawk will rise and become the Sun. She will change the history of Aixauh and Inabri for centuries to come."

The last words were like acid that made Cai-Li almost choke.

She sprinted up, forgetting about stealth or caution. The campsite was beginning to stir. Some candles were lit by magicians who had control over fire or light or anything close to illumination. The words were a thunderous roar. The voice was all-encompassing. In Cai-Li's shocked state of mind, she failed to recognise it as the same one she had heard mere hours ago.

The Deity making the proclamation was speaking from the Heavenly Court. It was how Cai-Li imagined her ancestor sounded, the sunbird who illuminated the sky.

Except this voice promised nothing but shadow. It was a creature of darkness, cloaked in the night. It was the fate that lurked for everyone at the end, with its emissary sounding a trumpet, heralding the doom of the one person Cai-Li cared about.

Against all rhyme and reason, the red-haired girl sprinted toward where fate had made a claim on Cole's demise. It was the same direction Cai-Li had watched for hours, the tent a girl occupied all by her lonesome, who had scared all the bullies away with only one sentence.

It wasn't a sentence though. Cai-Li only then grasped why Lisa Henry's response had been so dramatic—as if the moment Anne Barberry had opened her mouth, the bully was already a goner.

It was a *sentencing*. The Oracle could see into the future, to who lived and died.

"YOU'RE NOT GOING TO TAKE MY BROTHER—"

Cai-Li shoved her hand into the tent and ripped the protective layers apart. Burn marks were left singed where the protection wards were placed. They were effective magic, but only against Inabrian magicians.

Cai-Li was an Aixauhan alchemist, a descendant of the Sun. This damn oracle and her evil curse and this godforsaken fucking country wanted to tear Cole to shreds. Cai-Li would not let them.

She would burn the source of that darkness away from this world. She would smother the seed before it could grow. She would end the war that this voice promised and all the children at camp who laughed at Cole's humiliation and would do so again at his death.

Cai-Li's eyes burned with the crimson of fire and scarlet of fresh blood. In the night, it was hard to tell the difference. She was a bird of prey, hunting down the threat that cast its long shadow over her nest.

However, she did not find the creature of darkness chanting deadly curses within the confines of the faint yellow tent.

There was still chanting, yes, but it was not from some evil entity that presided over Cole's fate.

A girl whose long hair dripped down to the ground, covered in the moonlight now streaming in from the torn part of the tent that Cai-Li had burned through.

She was curled up in a ball, her tiny hands holding her bent knees against her cheeks. A cup that looked common enough slipped from Anne Barberry's fingers and clattered to the ground. Its landing sounded like the resonance of bell towers, or the hourly dong Cai-Li used to hear back home in Aixauh. That cup was heavier than it looked, and liquid spilled from it. The liquid was as clear as the moonlight cast over this whole eerie scene.

Cai-Li hesitated. The crossroads of the future lay ahead, but she did not know it yet.

The choice she made next was like a spindle that intertwined Cai-Li's fate with that of the crying girl on the ground, who was wide-eyed and seeing into a time that had not yet come to pass.

Cai-Li picked up the spilled Chalice of Truth and took a peek into the depths of the content inside.

It was as if she was suddenly pulled by a hand that peeled back her skin and age from the moment Cai-Li was born. She was an infant, then she was a teenager, then a fully grown woman. Time lost its meaning, as the Chalice of Truth held the possibility of every path offered to its beholder, everything they could be.

Ying Cai-Li was not just Ying Cai-Li. She was also Chely, a strange Inabrian name she had not yet taken on. She was The Blood Hawk, hands coated in blood and filled with rage. She was a necromancer dying from mercury poisoning.

"Because nothing you can do will ever stop me from loving you!"

Those words broke through the musty clouds in the sky that threw a long shadow over the future of Ying Cai-Li—a life that would be filled with blood and loss, victims and perpetrators, a war that she would never escape from.

That sentence, it caressed Cai-Li's face gently, like the warmth from a stove fire.

The voice was golden strings of gilded locks. Under the dark clouds that were Cai-Li's future, which was an eternal night, the voice was the moon—the only source of light in dark times.

"Why?" Cai-Li, no, Chely replied. She knew who she was now, and she was terrified of who she would become. A monster. "How can you say something like that?"

"Is that you?" the girl asked, fully visible now. It was Anne Barberry, a six-year-old child, with big pigeon-grey eyes that were wide in surprise at seeing her first Vision.

Her voice was high, and her words tripped over one another. It was not the girl who saw Chely at that moment who spoke those words, but the future version of who this six-year-old child would eventually become.

In Anne Barberry's childlike eyes, Chely could see her red hair was like a ball of fire.

"Are you the sun that I dreamed about?"

No, Cai-Li wanted to open her mouth and say to the little girl who did not know her yet. *You are mine, Annie. I will be chasing after you, even long after I am gone.*

Then, the future that had pulled apart its curtains for her closed in like a pomegranate peel closed in its seeds. A thousand futures entombed inside the fruit that was now planted to blossom.

In every single one of them, Cole of the Yamalan would die.

In every single one of them, Chely Ying and Anne Barberry would meet each other, and then leave each other.

The witch would forever be chasing her sun. Which one of them would be chasing the other would change with the season, but nonetheless, their roles would switch and then settle and then switch again. Forever entangled together by fate of meeting, doomed to a future of separation.

The Chalice of Truth told all of this to Ying Cai-Li, long before she understood what any of it meant.

In the morning, they found Chely with an unconscious Anne Barberry, who was exhausted from her oracle powers, and a screaming Lisa Henry who had finally come back to her tent at summer camp.

Lisa Henry zapped Chely with her powers. Two weeks later, Chely was woken up when a crying Cole almost tackled her to death with a bear hug. She would only remember what she saw after drinking from the chalice, like one remembered a distant dream.

Except for the odd urge to give herself an Inabrian name, Chely Ying remembered nothing about Anne Barberry.

Not until the very end, as she drank down the pure liquid form of mercury.

The cup fell from the alchemist's hands as she recalled the story of their lives and all their variations, clarity granted only to The Oracle and the ones who were about to die.

Ying Cai-Li, The Blood Hawk, smiled for the first time since Anne had gone.

"Being an oracle truly is as disorientating as you make it sound, Annie," The Blood Hawk said to herself, wishing The Oracle's Eye would someday show her love her final farewell. "For you, it must have been a lifetime of nightmares. For me, one time was enough. So, I'll take The Oracle with me and let it trouble you no more, my love.

"You will have all the past stars with you. Draw your own constellations, Annie. I am truly the end of The Barberry Oracles. I will be with you forever, watching over you from the Great Beyond."

25

A Life for a Life

THEY'RE TOO LATE.

As soon as Cole of the Yamalan flies in from the window and lets his black feathers fade into glacier skin, he knows that Ying Cai-Li is gone.

"You idiot!" he curses out loud.

It startles Maev, who blows in from the nearby door, puffing and huffing after climbing through this labyrinth of a castle. Without the aid of wings, she came just in time to catch sight of Cole shouting at the Chely's corpse.

And Anne, who holds Chely in her lap like a mother would hold a child who had simply drifted into an afternoon slumber. There is a stillness that she retains despite Cole's sudden intrusion and bellowing sound.

The oracle does not flinch or drop her wife's body. Anne Barberry's eyes are the colour of steel. Her lips thin, showing she acknowledges they have company. This is no longer a private mourning.

It does not shake Anne Barberry at all. Instead, she holds Chely's corpse like it has always been there. Like it is second nature for her to hold her lover.

It's almost as if she's making up for lost time. A grim and distant part of Cole's mind resonates with that feeling.

Despite not exchanging a glance or a word, the bond that has developed between him and Anne Barberry over their shared seven years in the In-Between recognises the grief in each other. When Anne finally looks up at Cole standing there, their faces are a reflection of each other's, both strung tight with emotions threatening to spill out. Lips downturned, anger churns while tears gather.

"She'd already started the necromantic ritual," Anne answers the question that dances on the tip of Cole's tongue. Her voice is monotone and explanatory, as if she were as large as the sea and Chely's death was a mere drop of salt water. "She was able to enter the In-Between so many times because she was experimenting with failed attempts of the Elixir of Immortality through the last decade, trying to reach a point where the alchemical balance ratio would kill her while also granting me the same amount of life energy."

"Fucking bastard." Cole's reply is simple and succinct. A strange and foreign sensation floods his chest. It is grief, he recognises, but not the same shape Cole has grown used to.

When his mum went, all Cole felt was the mountain cold of the Yamalans' home that he was never welcomed to return to. When the kids they tried to save had died in the war, grief was a burning forest fire of rage at the unfairness and futility of it all. And when Anne died, it was like standing on white sand under the hot sun. A familiar agony, especially when one needed to feign a smile while a layer of one's feet burned off on hot coals. Cole still embraces Anne with a sense of familiarity and joy.

The peace and longing and wonder of reuniting with a loved one after death.

There is nothing more miraculous.

Yet, Ying Cai-Li didn't even allow him that.

She's left him with a black hole where his heart is supposed to be. They parted on angry words, with actions undertaken by this now-dead woman who Cole still cannot forgive nor understand.

But there she is, lying on the ground, as limp as a snake shedding its skin. Except Ying Cai-Li was not a snake, she was a sunbird. Unlike the phoenix of Inabrian lore, the red flaming birds of Aix-auh's myth do not rise from its ashes. No, they were shot down due to their own hubris. Just like Cai-Li did to herself, to Cole, and to Anne as well.

"She got what was coming to her." Cole feels his jaw move its muscle as those words tumble out. "She got what she deserved."

Maev sucks in a gasp at Cole's remark—again, this was why he didn't want her there, despite what the orphan girl meant for all of them, she was not part of this inner circle of mourning who knew Chely for the full asshole she was.

Anne says nothing as she tips her head in Cole's direction. The oracle is always quiet, but Cole's used to reading Anne Barberry through body language, just as Anne learned to understand the meaning of different pitches of the cawing of a crow. Cole can't tell if Anne is angry at his remark or angry at him. Either way, it doesn't matter much as Cole brushes it off.

Ying Cai-Li is dead. Cole's sister and protector is dead. The firebird who once told Cole what mortals knew about love to ever throw away longevity for it. Cole's last courage and tether to the living is gone.

How does one give a name or feeling to such a calamity?

The answer is: you don't.

"Anne, let go of her," Cole says, averting his gaze. "You don't want to see her body fade into dust like all the ghosts who eventually move on to the Beyond. She was an asshole for going out like this—letting you see her. We don't owe it to her to stay here and watch the last great selfish act of The Blood Hawk."

"This isn't the end," Anne utters calmly, as if she is bargaining with Death itself. "She isn't fully deceased. If she were, she would already be gone—"

"Then let her be!" Cole raises his pitch. "She was gone—*long* before she arrived here! You said it yourself, Anne. She was here over the years because she was experimenting on human beings, as well as herself, like the fucking creep she turned into. This is not Chely. Chely would never have hurt you like this."

She would never have hurt me like this.

Anne falls silent again, as if not hearing his words. She simply pats Chely Hawk's hair like she is a wounded bird who fell from its nest and not the flaming bird that brought calamity upon everyone in his room.

"I'm fucking over this," Cole says. "You can find me downstairs with Ark Li once you're done cuddling the dead, Annie."

"Cole!" Maev finally lowers her hand from her face, pulling herself out of her shock and bellowing in shocked disgust. "What has gotten into you? Chely is *dead*! Everything we did—"

"It's all right, Maev," Anne interrupts, despite only seeing Maev for the first time in the In-Between. The oracle does not appear surprised. "Is Captain Ark here too? Did Cole bring her here from the Beyond?"

Maev lets out a sob. "I'm sorry, Annie," she cries with an energy that only the living can afford. "We didn't mean to upset you. But Ark was there with Chely while she was trying to revive you, far longer than I was in the living world. She was the closest person to Chely; we just thought maybe she could help."

Cole lets out a sound that earns a terrified glance from Maev.

Anne finally snaps out her mother's hand long enough to lift a surprised and annoyed eyebrow at Cole. "You *agreed* to this?"

"Yeah, sorry about that, Anne." He knows his apology rings hollow like an empty seashell. "I didn't mean to trigger your history with trauma. I was trying to get the captain to prevent Chely doing something stupid. *Something exactly like this.*"

"You don't need to apologise, Cole." Anne furrows her brows. "I'm actually more surprised…she was willing to come."

"I'm not as cold-hearted as you think I am, Barberry."

The captain strolls into the room with a confidence that has always been jarring, like a thorn thrashed into the backside of soft skin.

Ark Li wears one eyepatch, a long cape, and a tricorn pirate hat. She has a devil-may-care air about her that is like pouring boiling water into the room—the entire atmosphere suddenly sizzles like a hot kettle with white steam coming out. Threatening to explode at any second.

Anne freezes the moment their old captain's voice buzzes in like a lazy bee, completely unaware or just not caring that she just entered what was the eye of a hurricane.

Cole can feel the tension that grips the oracle's shoulders; Anne's hand squeezes Chely's as she tries to shield The Blood Hawk's corpse from the captain's gaze.

It is a futile gesture. But Cole knows Anne has probably realised, somehow, with The Oracle's ability and hold over the In-Between, that Captain Ark Li had a willing hand in contributing to Chely jumping off the ledge once both Cole and Anne were gone.

"Why are you here?" Anne asked; her tone was laced with ice. It is some semblance of emotion that brings some life back to the oracle's voice; suppressed anger is better than the empty shell she was mere seconds ago.

"Same as you." Ark shrugs, as if her presence isn't a nightmarish childhood monster to the girl she's talking to. "To say goodbye to Chely. Sad though. Seems I'm a bit too late. She appears to be a goner."

Anne remains frozen, her face as frozen as a dove's from lack of shelter during a harsh winter. The glimmer that had returned to Anne's pigeon-grey eyes to make them moonlight silver is completely gone.

Cole has had it.

"Fuck off, Ark." He lets his anger shoot out of him like an arsenal, like the cannons Cole used to admire that fired at the captain's command. He can't discern the threads of anger from the depths of grief reserved for his dead sister, but Cole is sure that he is willing to strangle Ark Li. "You have no right to speak to Anne like that. You said Anne and Cai-Li were the hope for Inabrians and Aixauhans, but then you poisoned Cai-Li's mind until all she could think about was reviving Anne instead of moving on!"

The captain doesn't deny Cole's words or respond to his animosity with anything other than an amused smirk, like a seagull finding a baby crow's cawing endearing.

"I'm not going to deny that I didn't exactly stop the sunbird here from indulging in necromancy," Ark Li replies. She lifts her eyepatch, exposing the flesh that has knitted into a twirling scar. "Even gave her a precious part of myself. All to bring back the granddaughter of the man who slaughtered my family and give her immortality. Yes, I'm totally the villain here, Shui-Yin."

The words spilling out of her mouth are smooth like honey, but Cole only sees acid. He feels like a powder keg, and Ark Li is the final spark teasing him to explode.

"You're insane!" Cole screams, swinging his right fist at Ark Li. "She trusted you. I trusted you. *We ALL TRUSTED YOU!* Because we were dumb children flying blind in a war, terrified to our cores. And you saw that, and like a vulture, you dove in and ate us whole. You made us into soldiers, sailors on *your ship*. Chely *hero-worshipped* you. Yet you used her; you used her when she had no one else left. You were the last person around she listened to. But instead of telling her to fucking stop and take a holiday, you stirred her to poison herself and now she's *a corpse on the ground*."

Maev lets out a yelp but cannot intervene fast enough. Cole's fist almost lands a square hit to Ark Li's jaw…because she does not dodge. She merely stands there, unflinching, as the fist closes in against her face like lightning striking a tree rooted on the spot.

"ENOUGH!"

The queen of the In-Between's voice is an earthquake that makes the ground below their feet scramble and shiver in fear. Jars and containers slam into one another. The door groans as if it's being torn off its hinges. The window's glass cracks like the frozen surface of a lake in winter, and everyone in the room feels the temperature dip and their clothing growing crisp in an icy dread.

Cole buckles under the sudden suffocation, slamming into the table beside him.

He would have hit the floor head-first if a chair didn't suddenly grow the ability to move its four legs and catch him like an oddly shaped wooden horse.

This is the work of The Eyeless Oracle, the one who holds complete control of the castle and the town below.

In his blinded fury and sorrow, there is a small part of the familiar in Cole that is almost in awe.

Anne must be overwhelmed with the revelation, then crushed by Chely's nastily wrapped surprise gift of immortality. The Anne that Cole has grown to know—who hid in a castle to ward off the storm outside, the one who wore all black but refused to even see Cole as the lost brother she had—that girl would be falling apart.

Maybe, in the long years seeing Anne meander with self-loathing and dosing everyone with amnesia in the In-Between, even Cole, who is the closest thing Anne has had to a companion in a decade, was disappointed into forgetting who she truly was before death took her.

The Barberry Oracle who did not yield to the wishes of her family and who dedicated her life to her Aixauhan friends without a moment of doubt and fear for the so-called consequences or the life she left behind.

"Li Si-Ya," Anne stands up. She finally lets go of Chely Hawk, leaving her to lie on the floor. Her eyes are now steel and storm clouds. Her voice is both calm like the moon and as vastly unknown as the sea. "You know more about what Chely was doing than anyone in this room."

The captain's eyes widen, caught off-guard that Anne knows her by her true name. It tickles Cole a little inside, and he cheers for Anne for putting a dent into the unshakable glamour of the pirate captain.

"Huh," Captain Ark Li—no—Li Si-Ya shakes her head, almost in disbelief. Still, her next move is to let out an exasperated laugh. "Of course you know my name, granddaughter of Brutus. You did some digging after watching your grandpa die, didn't you?"

"Yes," Anne replies, her face firm and diplomatic. She recounts her words like a historian. "The Aixauhans kept a list of every single casualty of the war—both of the wars. The alchemists massacred, and the alchemists lost. That was how you found out Brutus was responsible for your family's demise. Your people are ones that wouldn't forget your grief so easily. You hold them close to your heart, never letting go of the past, of those who took them away, so that you won't lose them again. Not a second time.

"You and all of Aixauh remembered, even as we in Inabri thought that unimportant. But that is why Inabri *lost* the war to Aixauh. Because your people *remembered*."

Li Si-Ya's eyes lock with those of Anne Barberry. An unspoken jolt of electricity sparks between that lone exchange.

Two wars. Decades of hostility. Millions dead and gone. Generations of ghosts still not put to rest. Cole feels them all. Like Chely Hawk's necromancy was never intended for Annie alone. Instead, he feels every single person who has ever lived and died around them.

His father, who murmurs in Cole's ear how he truly loved his mother but had to leave lest his family kill his son and wife.

His mother, who returns with the salty taste of the ocean and a fresh perspective of travelling the sea currents. She talks of how well Cole has grown; she laments Chely's quiet yet calm-looking corpse and sheds a tear as if she were her own daughter. A girl who shares the same facial features as Ark Li, and a husband-and-wife pair. They all wear the gear of sailors at sea, and they chant Si-Ya's name.

The Aixauhan soldier who killed Cole apologises clumsily before vanishing, "*I'm sorry, I just wanted to go home.*"

All the dead they knew are there with them. How it is possible, Cole does not know. The room is too small to host all the ghosts one gathers after living through a war.

What he does notice is that none of them belong to Anne Barberry. There is no Patricia Barberry nor is there Brutus nor Anne's parents.

Then, the moment passes. All the dead fade back into the stars, and the only ones remaining are those who are supposed to be in that room.

Cole, Maev, the oracle who brought the ghosts together as a show of good faith, and the recipient who the show was for.

Ark Li is back. The woman aged back to the seasoned captain who commanded a rogue warship on the seas. She removes her hat and stares at Anne, as if seeing her for the first time.

"You truly are the future of this world," Captain Ark Li says, her dark hair flattened down from the hat's restraint. She looks a lot more human this way, a lot less intimidating. "Anne Barberry."

Anne nods solemnly. "I remembered who you were when we were on your ship," the lady of the castle says. "It is kind of hard to forget the voice of all your childhood nightmares. But it was war, and you kept us alive. Maev and the other kids. They needed someone to protect them. You made soldiers out of Cole and Chely, but they had to be to make it to the finish line."

"So, you kept quiet about me murdering your grandpa," Ark Li replies. "For their morale?"

"No," Anne's voice is that of the hardest metal. "Because I understood. Your family was killed by Brutus in front of you. A life for a life is the law of Heaven…"

"A life for a life, as it's Heaven's Law and Earth's Moral," Ark completes the idiom.

Maev looks slightly unnerved by this entire conversation, but Cole knows what they're talking about.

杀人偿命, 天经地义.

An old Aixauhan saying. But it underlines the difference between Inabrians and Aixauhans. It was the fundamental fracture that separated Chely from Anne and Cole.

Despite everything, Cole is still half-Inabrian, whose mother encouraged him to learn from his father's land and use an Inabrian name. While Anne Barberry, no matter how much she tried to peel herself out of being one of a magician lineage, was still born from the soil and blood of the same vein of thoughts.

For Chely, it was different. For Ark, it was different.

They were not even Chely and Ark.

At their core, they were Ying Cai-Li and Li Si-Ya.

Aixauhan alchemists who worked on a distinct line of morality but never strayed from their own code at all.

"I was angry with Chely for the longest time," Anne says softly. Her eyes dart to the still figure on the ground. "I thought what she did was monstrous, even before I died. I didn't understand why she would want to preserve Cole's corpse. I didn't understand why she would go after my sister and that Aixauhan soldier. It was all so meaningless in my eyes. To waste one's life chasing after revenge and ghosts. It wasn't going to bring the dead back."

"Except it literally does," Ark Li finishes Anne's sentence. "In the rule of Aixauhan alchemy. A life for a life is the most natural of laws. You cannot invent the energy required for alchemy from nothing, Yin and Yang demand balance. Revenge is not something cruel or self-destructive for us. It is the righteous path. A life for a life, both applied to the taking of a life, and the gifting of one as well. Cai-Li thought you would never understand it. That's why she took the mercury without telling you—because Chely thought you'd never understand the ways of Huaxia Aixauhan alchemists."

"She thought I saw her as a monster," Anne replies dully. A wail spills out from her small body draped in black. "I didn't even get to tell her until the very end that I understood."

Li Si-Ya's face softens. She steps forward, putting a hand on Anne's head.

It is like witnessing a predator develop a vegetarian diet. Under any other circumstances, Cole would have enjoyed the bizarreness of this whole situation.

But this is not it. Chely still lies on the ground. She is still dead, no matter how heartwarming this reconciliation between people who held blood grudges is.

Cole's brain spots something roaming in the sea of his mind. Something that has been teasing him like it was playing hide-and-seek. The true reason he was so mad when he saw Chely's body on the ground.

It was so unnatural. It doesn't make sense. The symptoms Ying Cai-Li's body is displaying, it doesn't make sense that she is dying.

That is when Cole of the Yamalan finally blurts out what has been bothering him this whole time: "Wait… Did you say she is dead because of mercury poisoning?"

26

The Cottage of the Flowering Fields

CHELY REMEMBERED THE first time she went to Cole's cottage to visit him and his mother.

The humid summer air made her sweat to the point she almost felt like she was an alchemist's cauldron melting from the inside out. If she hadn't brewed a dozen orbs of condensed ice water supply that could be tucked into her alchemist ingredients belt, Chely was pretty sure she could never have made it through the hike.

"Why do you and Auntie live so far away from civilisation," Chely complained. "How do you ever do your groceries?"

"Well, Mum and I are Yamalan," Cole, who looked tired but not nearly close to a sponge soaked in sweat like Chely was, said. "We are shapeshifters and one with nature. This isn't far from civilization, mate. Nature is its own civilization."

"That's wise," Cai-Li said. "And I fully believe that's the case for Auntie. But you are a city boy. I am the one who has to sit through your countless temper-tantrums because your favourite food stand at the night market doesn't operate on workdays."

"Shut up, Cai-Li," Cole replied. "We Yamalans are one with nature; we're wise beyond your human comprehension—"

Chely was way past the point of being polite after seven hours of muddy mountain tracks through the woodlands that kept going upwards. "Yes, you're very majestic. The same way you tripped over that rock and hit your head."

"Sod off. I get your point, all right? Mum can just melt into the water and drift down the stream until she reaches a town," Cole rolled his eyes and said. "She says it's as easy as a dream. What's inside her veins is closer to what river streams are made out of—minerals, yada yada—than blood. So, she basically can take, like…a ride on anything similar to her anatomical structure? I don't get half of it, but it sounds cool."

"Oh," Chely's awe and professional curiosity of being an alchemist overshadowed the exhaustion she felt. "That is so interesting. I wonder how Auntie is calculating the anatomical balance as she's doing such things. It's like…natural alchemy with one's soul. Even the sunbirds, the Ying Clan, don't have that level of control over themselves like that."

Cole warned drily, "Don't sound too excited, Cai-Li. It sounds like you want to dissect my mum."

"Not Auntie, never." Chely waved her hand dismissively, but then she turned her gaze to Cole with the most morbid grin ever. "You can dissect me to see if the sunbird has any actual alchemical manifestation in me in exchange."

Cole physically stopped moving, looking firmly creeped out by Chely's sudden change of tone.

"Keep your insides to yourself," Cole yelled back. He dashed along the woodland trail about a hundred feet ahead of Chely, his voice reverberating through the trees and branches and scaring a few squirrels. "Ew! Who the hell asks that? Was that meant to be flirtatious or just horrifying? Serious invasion of boundaries, Cai-Li!"

"Aw, don't flatter yourself, Cole," Chely sing-songed like the long black-haired hungry ghost who was haunting people who ate their tributary food. "You know I'm as lesbian as they come. If I wanted to flirt with someone, it would be Auntie. Not you."

Cole's response was to throw a stone at Chely while blending into the background, only for it to be incinerated into black smithereens by the fiery ring Chely placed around herself for protection.

"Okay, you don't want me as a stepmom," Chely relented. Still, her smirk did not fade at all. "Got it. I'll stop."

"No, you won't." Cole didn't sound any less alarmed. "You're horrible, Cai-Li. Don't make me puke all over you."

"Speaking of puke," Cai-Li mused. "Did you know when I was a baby, I actually could puke fireballs? Courtesy of being the sunbird's descendant."

"Wait, really?" Cole asked. "My puke just looks like…water."

Chely shrugged and said ominously. "Maybe it *looks* like water," the red-haired alchemist smiled to her half-Yamalan best friend. "But maybe it's something more than that, Shui-Yin (水银)."

Cole grimaced. "I hate this sometimes," he muttered. "The way we just…are imbued with these non-human characteristics? It's why the Inabrian magicians think we're not fully human."

"Oh, shut up." It was Chely's turn to scoff. "Don't you go on this road to internalise the bullshit they spill, all right? We're fully human. You think the Inabrian magicians don't all have a few screws loose? That's the nature of magic. We touch the core that common folks don't tap into, which means we get a few side effects that come along with it. Inabrian magicians or Yamalan or Aixauhan alchemists…either we're all humans, or none of us are."

Anne's head snaps toward Cole. Her best friend and familiar's face is changing colours in all the shades of a rainbow.

Those words "*Is that why she is dead?*" are another knife twist in the insides of Anne's chest, where she previously thought she had no senses left. There is a great emptiness, a blurred white space after Chely collapsed and stopped moving.

Her heart stopped beating after that. Although Anne supposes no one in this room has a pulse except Maev. But her heart may as well be gone, replaced by an eternally dark sky. No stars. No constellations. the oracle is blind again, for what use is her sight when the sun is gone?

But now, something about the way Cole blurts out those words churns Anne's heart into beating again. Heat rises within her cheeks. Her head pounds suddenly, as the implications swirl before her mind can catch up.

A spark of pure, irrational exhilaration fills her. The oracle does not know why, but she senses something like a caterpillar senses it's the season to start crawling out of its cocoon to become a butterfly.

A possibility.

"I thought you knew." Ark Li, who seconds ago was all Anne could focus on, is now nothing but background noise to the possibility that is hatching. "It's basic alchemy, Shui-Yin. How come you didn't know?"

"Because I'm half-Inabrian and half-Yamalan, Li," Cole bites back. His bitterness and rage toward their former captain clearly has not loosened as the room is suddenly filled with a renewed air. "Our relationship with the elements works differently from most of the Aixauhan alchemists. The Li Clan and most alchemists cultivate them. The Ying Clan and the Yamalan? We *are* the elements."

We are *the elements*. Those four words break the dam in Anne Barberry's mind like a flood.

"That's it, Cole." Anne rushes to her brother's side and grabs Cole's shoulders. She doesn't even feel the movement or the fact that she's screaming her lungs out. "That's why she used mercury to preserve your body! *That's* why you didn't fully die but instead became the tree itself! *That's* why you're here! Damn the Creator, Chely was batshit crazy, but she was also a fucking *genius!*"

Cole's face blurs as he's shaken back and forth. He clearly does not realise the significance of the words he's just said. He looks like he wants both to vomit and to deck Anne in the head.

"Has she…" Maev's murmuring voice came from the edge of the room. "Completely lost it to grief?"

"No," Ark Li responds, the older alchemist's voice conveying an assurance as if she's known all along this would be the result. "I think Barberry has finally arrived at the natural conclusion you all somehow missed."

"What?" Cole and Maev ask in equal confusion. Cole, especially, sounds like he's walking through clouds.

"Mercury!" Anne can't hold it in any longer. She turns to Cole. "*You're* made of mercury, Cole! You didn't die at all! In fact, you were the first successful necromancy Chely performed. Well, maybe saying that isn't accurate, since you're a tree growing near The Cottage and stuff. But that explains why you're in the In-Between but outside of my control. We were both revived by Chely's necromancy when we were supposed to die. So, unlike the ghosts without a physical body tethering them to life in reality, you and I are both half-alive and half-dead thanks to Ying Cai-Li. The queen and king of the In-Between."

Cole only gapes at Anne. His face shows more conflicting emotions, as if he wants to come forward and give Anne a hug or maybe push her headfirst into a well filled with cold water.

"Annie, you're not making any sense," Cole replies, his voice grave.

Why? Anne is almost pissed off by the lackluster response from the only other person in this room who should be jumping up and down at this revelation.

"I know my body composition has a strong resemblance to mercury. My mum told me that. She resembled water the most, specifically mineral water of the mountains. It's why she was half-invisible all the time. So, the same for me—kind of fading in and out since liquid mercury appears like solidified clear drops of water. It's what alchemists put into temperature testers for patients who have a fever, because mercury can detect temperature."

"And you still can't *see?*" Anne bellows at Cole, who flinches back, clearly mistaking her mind being blown as grief-driven hysteria. "Chely's not dead, Cole. She's still in the In-Between. Which means her body in the real world hasn't completely died, nor am I fully resurrected, and *that* means the ritual or necromancy or the Elixir of Immortality, whatever the fuck Chely had going on, it *is not finished.*"

That finally sends a glimmer of understanding up Cole's face. His eyes fade away into pure white without colours, before returning to solid black but with specks of glistening tears.

"We can stop her, Annie." Cole understands. He grips back Anne's arms that clutch his shoulders with equal strength. A blossom of hope travels from Anne's face onto Cole's as well. "We can still save Cai-Li."

"Yes," Anne says. She utters that again and again and again. *We can save her. Save Chely. Save her.*

"Not to burst this hopeful bubble of yours," Ark Li's voice suddenly cuts in, like a flaming sword plunged into cold water. "But what you're thinking, grandchild of Brutus. Even if it worked, it's still too late."

Anne's state of delirium takes that as a gnawing annoyance. She flips back toward the captain, who appears honestly grim for some reason.

"Why can't it work?" Anne asks. "You haven't even heard what my idea is—"

"Oh, you think *I* have no idea that Shui-Yin of the Yamalan here is the physical manifestation of a mercury container?" Ark Li scoffs. The short period of understanding Anne thought they reached less than half an hour ago dissipates like morning dew. Now she's back to being the adversary of Anne's nightmares, sneering and condescending, filled with the malice of wanting to tear Anne apart. "Cole's name is Mercury (水银, Shui-Yin) in Aixauhan. The Yamalans were never known to be subtle in naming their children."

"What?" Cole jumps back as if someone just took a swing at his face. "I always thought my Aixauhan name meant like…water silver or something like that. You know, because I look translucent like water and appear silver under the sunlight at times?"

Ark Li facepalms, as if wishing a rock could fall onto her and end her misery.

Maev catches on. The girl who walks between the living and the dead gasps. "It's why the Aixauhan word for *mercury* is translated character by character as 'water' and 'silver.' Chely always said that Aixauhan characters are descriptive, and they name things according to appearance and metaphors."

Shui-Yin (水银), silver water. Liquidated mercury was as clear as water but appeared more solid and metallic under the light. Just like Cole.

Anne never met Cole's late mother, who passed away before Anne started dating Chely, and well before Cole and Anne were friendly enough for the boy to disclose his sad past to her. Anne had never known a Yamalan up close, so she assumed Cole represented all of them.

Stupid, tunnelled-vision Inabrian magician thinking. The truth is, if Aixauhan alchemists can be different enough to be an umbrella term for the Li Clan, who were mortal healers that dabbled in alchemy, and the Ying Clan, who were straight-up descendants of the

Aixauhan gods, of course the Yamalans are not all the same. Maybe not even between mother and son.

She's only seen Auntie through photos. She appeared half-invisible in most of them, just like Cole did. So, Anne assumed that it was all Yamalans. They were half-invisible, resembling the mountain glaciers, the permanently snow-covered mountains they get their namesake from.

Anne almost wants to laugh in self-mockery. Her ignorance has blindsided her.

"Of course," she mutters. "Cole, remember what Chely always said? What do you always say to me? In Aixauh, everything has a spirit, and when something is cultivated for long enough, it gains sentience and a human form. But it doesn't change what they actually are. Yamalans, your people are born from nature and return to it—you are metal, and water, and air. Cole, you are mercury. Same with Cai-Li, she's fire itself. What is born of fire will return to fire. For her ritual to complete, she has to become the sun, and *you* have to be present at the scene of Cai-Li's death, as you are the final component to the ritual. Mercury, the element that's crucial to the brewing of the Elixir of Immortality."

Ark Li lets out a gasp that sounds half like she's amused, and half like she's finally being let off the hook from something extremely painful.

"That would make sense, wouldn't it?" the captain says, infuriating as ever. "The Yamalans don't all look like Cole and his mother. I had crewmen on my ship over the years who were from the Yamal region. One of them was made of pure gold, he cut off his fingernails to sell at every port. I always wondered why he ended up wanting to be a pirate. He certainly didn't need the money."

"*You knew?*" Cole's grasp on Anne's arms slackened. The Yamalan boy solidifies into a dark cloud that rounds on Ark Li. "You knew this information all along yet you treated us like fools—"

"There's all the time in the world to rip Ark's head off her shoulders, Cole." Anne pulls on Cole's arm and forces him to focus. She's burning like a furnace. *Is this what Chely felt like all the time? Burning from the inside out with forbidden knowledge and ideas so crazy it set the world aflame?*

"She's right, Cole," Maev joins in, her voice shaking, but the orphan girl manages to ground Cole's attention back to them. "You called Ark here because you wanted her to talk Chely down, right? Now, Anne seems to actually have a plan to wake Chely up…and the captain is probably still more qualified than any of us to bring that plan to fruition. She's the only one of us who is an Aixauhan alchemist and who knew what Chely was up to!"

Cole still seethes. He breathes like a boar about to trample someone to death.

Anne grips his shoulders harder. *Please*, she calls out wordlessly to Cole, the companion and only friend she's had for seven years. *We have to save Ying Cai-Li.*

Cole meets Anne's gaze, his eyes flashing white and then black—how could Anne never have noticed the metallic quality of it all? Chely surely had. His tension-filled shoulders loosen, and he embraces Anne.

"I'm up for whatever your plan is, Annie," Cole says while holding her, both clattering like twin pine trees shaking off snow in a new spring. "I'll knock some sense into that thick skull of your wife until she comes home to you."

"Thank you," Anne says. "Don't refrain from punching her in the face if you have to."

"Sure thing," Cole replies.

The queen and king of the In-Between smile at each other with silent understanding. They are ready to bring their wayward sun-bird home.

They made it all the way up until trees no longer obscured their view of the wider landscape around them. Chely gasped as Cole lent her a hand to climb and sit on top of a particularly high rock.

They were overlooking a cliff-side. As far as the human eye could see, hills rolled like stagnant ocean waves. Wildflowers bloomed on every foot of land that wasn't covered by greenery. Patches of yellow dandelions were like wheat fields at harvest season. Bluebells were fairy ladies with their gowns twirling in unison. White flowers that Chely cannot name were freshly washed sheets, or diamonds being scattered across a green grassy field. Apple trees with their soft pink blossoms danced happily in the wind. Wisteria trees hung their heads lazily, their purple eyelids drooping shut in the breeze.

She must have made a series of embarrassing sounds, for Cole laughed behind her, as only annoying younger siblings showing off something cool would do.

"Worth your legs turning into jelly, right?" Cole shouldered her, which almost made her lose balance and fall off the rock. "Oops, sorry. Almost pushed you to your death there."

"You could do worse." Chely laughed and shouldered Cole back. Her heart fluttered like the birds people always compare her to. "I'll die for you a thousand times, Shui-Yin of the Yamalan. Dying with my last vision of this breathtaking scene? There are definitely worse fates out there."

"Hey, quit being morbid," Cole shushed Chely. "I'm here to show you our humble abode. Can you spot The Cottage? We're nearly there!"

There is nothing "humble" in the excitement Cole showered his home with as pride glistened in his eyes. Chely gasped aloud again once she spotted The Cottage.

A windmill lazily rolled as the season's wind turned it along with birds flying across the sky. It was the sunset, a soft pastel pink hue overtaking the clouds like cotton candy. The sky was still blue, an azure-blue, gentle and kind. The two shades danced together to form the most beautiful colour Chely had ever seen.

The Cottage was a paintbrush, watercolour, drenched by the flower fields beneath it and the sky above it. It stood at the center, patient in its solitude. Stern in its age, but quiet.

"It's beautiful." Chely let the words and laughter spill out. All the weariness and exhaustion had been sucked out of her. She was as light as a feather and as fresh as a newborn.

"I know," Cole replied. He sounded old, which was odd. He was always a child in Chely's mind. Maybe it was an unfair assumption, since they were the same age. But ever since they were small, Chely had always been the one who shielded Cole behind her as they marched forward in the world.

"Thanks for bringing me here." Cai-Li enjoyed the breeze and let out a breath. "Thank you for showing me your home."

Cole didn't answer her, but she didn't not mind. They would get to The Cottage in time, even as dusk was about to swallow the world up into an endless night.

"It is going to be your home too," Cole replied, sounding agitated. "Is that what you want, Ying Cai-Li?"

Chely finally turned her head from the mesmerising scene back to Cole. Her best friend looks unfamiliar just then, as if a doppelgänger has taken his place.

He is still the same age. The same age where stubble pops from his chin that has never fully grown into a beard, despite his best effort. Even as the war dragged on, Cole of the Yamalan remained young, despite everyone around him aging.

Shui-Yin, *mercury*. An adaptable element for alchemists. Aixau-han healers used it in traditional thermometers, as the alchemists and their obsession led the element to be studied so thoroughly, they'd discovered even a small change in temperature caused the mercury to rise and fall.

Sensitive. Translucent. Clarity when one is burning up with a fever.

Poisonous. Deadly, especially in alchemy, as alchemists and emperors ingested it again and again, seeking glorified immortality.

Until even the metal itself had become synonymous with death.

Cole, Shui-Yin, mercury. The crow, a harbinger of death.

The first of them to perish. The one who died in his prime. He who became the black bird that was Death itself. The reason Chely started her journey into necromancy. The loss now grinds heavily upon both the alchemist's and the oracle's hearts until they have forgotten what it was like to have him there.

"Why did you follow me here, Cole?" Chely asks. "You shouldn't have been able to. This is Final Death. Aren't you supposed to be at the castle? Why aren't you staying at Annie's side?"

Cole is no longer pretending to be someone he isn't. His rage flutters into the air that smells metallic and nauseating, his translucent stature reflecting the light becomes piercing like knives.

"Because you never asked what I wanted, Cai-Li!" Cole's voice reverberates across the flower fields like the roar of thunder. The Cottage's windmill spins faster, like it's going to fall off.

"You never asked what Annie wanted, either. You just decided for us. Turned me first into a zombie, then a goddamned tree, then a freaking black bird who couldn't speak. Turned Anne into a zombie, and then the queen of the In-Between. Now you want to give her immortality? Are you some kind of noble martyr of lore, wishing for future Aixauhans writing poems about your sacrifice for millennia to come?"

"That's not…" Chely breathes out. She knew Cole would be angry, but she didn't expect him to follow her to the path toward the Beyond. "That's not a very good reason to drag yourself into the ritual, Cole. We don't know what effect another individual adding more mercury to the equation will do to the elixir. You might be wiped from the world. You could risk Anne's revival."

Cole's laugh cuts her off.

"Stop talking like you give a shit about any of us! You did all of it for yourself, Ying Cai-Li." He spits on the ground. "How do you think Anne will feel after you give her life back, huh? You always talked about how we shouldn't believe the bullshit Inabrians feed us, so in turn, you decided to feed yourself and the world with lies of your own?"

Cai-Li does not answer. Her expression remains blank. Cole knows her well enough to understand it immediately.

"People always assume just because you are made of fire, that somehow means you are rushed and impulsive," Cole murmurs. "But I know you, Ying Cai-Li, you are the cleverest and the most big-picture type person I've ever come across. You just didn't care, not even about the feelings of people you claim to love."

"I'm not going to lie to you." Chely watches Cole pityingly. "I know it doesn't work like it does with Annie. I needed her to have a dramatic last goodbye to me to fully snap her out of her state of solitary comfort and embrace immortality. You kind of ruined that, as now you've provided her with a hope of catching my soul and stuffing it back to the In-Between."

"You are truly an asshole, Cai-Li," Cole says.

"I know, little brother." Cai-Li gives a smile filled with determination and assurance. "You should go. The ritual is going to consume this place soon enough. It will then eat away the In-Between too. They are all part of Anne's death, and they will be no more once the oracle becomes eternal. I have drunk the mercury and will disappear into the sun. Even if you managed to use your own anatomy of being mercury to imbalance the ritual, you still can't stop me. You'd be adding more mercury into the alchemical equation. Then I'd have to add more fire. If you are set on the course to disrupt my plan, then prepare for me to burn into nothing—like what rumours believe the Chalice of Truth would do, my soul will dissolve without even the chance to enter the Cycle of Reincarnation."

"Is that a threat?" Cole scowls. "You are threatening me with your own destruction so that I'll let you die?"

"Yep," Chely replies cheerfully. "Sounds contradictory yet it's effective. Best things in life are oxymorons, brother. You should tell Maev and Ark to leave the In-Between too. They are not a part of this."

Cole's face scrunches up, and he appears to want to scream Chely's ear out some more.

Before he has the chance, the sunset that spread across The Cottage of the flowering fields explodes in a crescendo. The pink and fluffy clouds blaze into flaming orange and red, as the last of the sun strikes the horizon like a cannon hitting its target.

Chely Hawk feels an excruciating bite on her fingertips, like a thousand tiny hounds are tearing up her flesh with sharp teeth. The first jolt makes her want to scream; instead, she laughs, as she knows this is success.

The horror in Cole's eyes shows the reflection of a human-shaped torch spontaneously combusting into black char in yellow and red flames.

Her lower arm catches on fire, followed by her left leg. Her consciousness lasts for only a second before she is lost in the sea of scorching and blinding pain that devours her identity.

There is a screeching, worse than anything humans can make. "CAI-LI!"

The boy calls out a name that no longer has an owner. He is blocked by the wall of pain and flames that is turning her into shreds and flickers of ember. She must be screaming. It only makes sense. She watches as her fingers blacken, and then turn a lighter shade, a greyish ash.

At her center, she is blue. They were wrong when they called the Hawk a creature of blood. Fire is not the colour of Cai-Li's red hair, or Anne's luminous golden locks.

The purest fire is the same deep cerulean blue as the night sky engulfing The Cottage of the flowering fields.

There will be no flowering fields. They have all caught on fire. All the purple wisteria, the lavender, the bluebells and the dandelions. They are all now on fire, the blue flames scorching the field.

She knows, as her soul ascends into the sky, that the boy watches her from below, tears still not fully dried from his eyes.

It makes the girl-who-was smile for a single second.

Despite being angry with me, you are still sad at my departure.

Such gentleness is why you deserve to live, my brother. You and Annie both.

Then, she ceases to exist.

The sun sets in the western sky. It vanishes with a laugh of triumph. The Flaming Hawk, who brought famine, who was once shot down by a legendary archer, has risen again and taken her final bow.

Cole watches as his home burns to smithereens.

The Cottage he grew up in. The one where her mother cuddled him to sleep at night during his first days in this strange country. The flower fields where he and Chely made flower crowns for each other and played hide-and-seek.

The place where he welcomed and reunited with Anne in death.

His home. Nothing more than smoke and bones. White smoke and scorched land.

How could you do this? he wants to ask the sister who has destroyed it.

"I can do this, because you chased after me," the merciless goddess of the sun says gently as she flies across the horizon. "The ritual was meant for Annie alone. But your stubbornness in following me here brought me a new idea, Cole. Maybe when I preserved your body and you became a tree—that was not the end, only the beginning."

Is that why you have taken away my home? Shui-Yin, the boy of mercury and Death, asks. A single tear rolls down his cheek.

"Yes," the sunbird replies without mirth nor mercy. "You were right, I did this all for myself. But do you know what I truly want more than anything, baby brother?"

Cole stares in stunned horror. He has no response to the creature who swallowed death.

"I want the war to end," it says. "You and Anne. You both have grown compliant with death. That was why you stayed in the In-Between for a decade, when both of you could have willingly moved on. Neither of you did, because you wanted peace, yet you don't want to admit the nasty truth: that the war will never end. It lives inside you like a parasite, it takes root and births illusions. It even makes the most beautiful lie out of the most painful truth."

He shook his head. *No, Chely. No.*

"I am not Chely," the entity says, still patient, as it stands atop pitch-black nothingness. "I am The Blood Hawk. Your sister is gone, mercury child. Just like a cottage of flowering fields is not death. It is time for you and the oracle to recognise that I am always what I choose. Instead of trying to get in my way, you can appreciate the gift I grant you both."

"This isn't what Anne or I wanted!" Cole shouts at the entity of death, finding his voice only feeds the fire eating away at the edge of the world. "We will hate you for taking away our choice in the matter, Ying Cai-Li. *We will never forgive you.*"

"Sounds like a fair trade."

A final flicker of red flame, like the tail end of a girl's red hair. The last words of Chely Ying as a human are said with amusement.

"Hate me till the ends of the earth, Cole. Hate me every day when you wake up to the first rays of sun, for it is the dawn of a new day. Hate me until you and Anne both forget about The Cottage and the flowering fields and find a new place to call home. You guys have nothing but time."

27

The Voyage to Tomorrow

ARK LI HAS never tried to convince others she is a good and merciful person. Other than her sad past as a child caught in the middle of the war between Inabri and Aixauh, Captain Ark Li is the first to admit she has no other redeeming qualities. She was a pirate, and any self-respecting pirate would tell you they are villains in the story.

She has done a great many horrible things. She plundered her own people. She executed her own crewmates. She could have stopped after killing Brutus Barberry and settled down with her lover, but Captain Ark Li was in love with the life of being a free outlaw, so she lost her lover and a potential peaceful life.

It made sense that Ark's parents, who were healers, would not want anything to do with her, not that Ark cared much in the end. The Li parents made the mistake of choosing their stupid morals instead of the exit offered to them.

Still, sometimes, Ark dreams of her childhood home. The days when she went up into the mountain to pick barberries from bushes filled with thorns, as well as the days she'd go down to the port city where she'd rinse herself with salty ocean water. Smell the stink of fish guts, but be welcomed by the refreshing ocean breeze.

The place that marked the first Inabrians who set foot on the land of Aixauh centuries ago, sea merchants and traders who started off as singular oddities, but increased in number as their business grew, as the country of Inabri discovered tea leaves and porcelain.

And, even though they would never admit it, alchemy as well.

Inabri was originally an island, with its history not tracing back even a millennium. Yet, they were as wild and unpredictable as the sea. The tides rose high to cause tsunamis that ate away the entire population in the blink of an eye.

"That was what runs in Inabrians' blood," Ark's mother once told her when she was a little girl. She was a scholar, a historian. Still an alchemist, but one who focused on theory and self-cultivation rather than a practitioner like Ark's father. "They have seawater running through their veins. That's why they are salty, as salt makes you thirst for more. Greedy, never enough. Merciless, powerful yet viewing everything it swallows with an apathy. Wayward, like a sail without a tether. We Aixauhans, on the other hand, are people of earth and soil. Our history is defined by our connection to the history of our land."

Ark didn't get to be a child for that long in her life. She grew up in a time when there were pamphlets and newspapers scattered all around the port city, calling for the liberation of the Aixauhan people from the tyrant who ruled them, all written in Inabrian letters that crawled on the paper like caterpillars. Ark could not read a single word of it, but she did read the elegant willow shapes of the Aixauhan translation.

"Free the Aixauhan public from the tyrant that calls himself the emperor! Liberty! Free commerce! And the freedom of each person choosing their faith and belief in the Creator!"

Those words rang in Ark's impressionable young mind, like beautiful butterflies and flowers of spring. Filled with a beautiful vagueness that promises a sense of change.

Her mother was wrong. Maybe Aixauhans were people of earth and soil, but earth and soil was forever unchanging, dull, stuck in their old ways. It did not rise and fall, its charcoal brown did not glisten under the sun, it did not spit out white foam. It did not smell of possibility, as well as salt and soft breeze.

Ark Li was an Aixauhan girl, but she had the soul of the sea.

And those pale-skinned merchants and sailors and preachers all came from huge ships made of timber and had sails ten times the size of those of the common fishing boats that belonged to Aixauhan fishermen. They were marvels, like dragons with divine knowledge that rose from the unknown ocean. That, according to tales the Inabrians told to the only alchemist in Ark's clan who spoke their language, traveled through storms and the monsoon seasons and fought sea monsters to get here, and would return to their island the same way.

Ark's father had scoffed and that these "ghosts" (鬼佬) were better off being swallowed by the sea, the whole lot of them. "It would do everyone else a favour. Before they send armies to storm our land and raze everything to the ground like they have done to so many of our neighbours already. Aixauh always stood strong, and they are still wary of alchemists and the craft we passed down for millennia. However, I tell you, it will be only a matter of time before their greed and ego swallow us as well."

Ark cast the thought aside, for her father had always warned her about all kinds of things with the same grim look. *Do not play on the shore on your own, Si-Ya. Do not leave the alchemy furnace on when you need to go to the toilet. Yes, even if that means you will lose all the progress and have to start from scratch.*

She learned to treat her father's and mother's words like sand that stuck between one's toes. To simply wait for them to be forgotten.

Ark longed for the ocean. She was mesmerised by the pale-faced man who talked about a world with a singular divine Creator instead of a million local gods who were once human per town and region. She dreamed of this distant land and its people, where sailing to a faraway place was the norm instead being stuck in a dingy ocean-side dock town her whole life, learning and passing down alchemical knowledge until her body returned to the earth and soil that all Aixauhans believed they were made of by the half-snake goddess Nu Wa. Ark longed for the ocean, an adventure, and a glimpse of the island country whose people had somehow conquered the wild oceans and treated deadly trips around the world like an adventure.

It is obvious in retrospect that it was never the Inabrians who captured Ark Li's childish imagination—it was the concept of hope, of renewal.

Except, instead of believing in the change that they could bring themselves, Ark Li fell into the traps of someone else's false hope. A promise made by the same people who believed the world was an oyster granted to them by their own Creator, with no respect for the land and lives of those they conquered.

Blood ran through the streets of the port cities. Alchemists' remains were fed to the waves, human sacrifices for the will of the Creator preached by the sea ghosts. How could a Creator let some of His creations trample over others? It made no sense. When all the Li Clan was gone, Ark was in no mood to engage in a theological debate with those who wanted her dead.

However, in another life, where Ark Li was allowed a childhood free of deaths and revenge, she would have become a scholar instead of a pirate. In that life, she'd have come to believe in an all-encompassing Creator, whom she believed to love the Aixauhans and Inabrians equally.

Too bad Ark was trapped in this life. In this life, the Inabrians proclaimed that alchemy and Ark's people were not part of the Creator's plan, so there would be no place in her heart that wished to know the Creator, as He must be as cruel as the Inabrians who spoke for Him.

In this life, the caterpillar words scrawled down on newspapers and pamphlets were nothing but lies and illusions the Inabrians fed themselves. They were reflections of the image that the Inabrians had conjured up for themselves, so they could believe that the slaughter of Ark's people was somehow just and right. A right given to them by their Creator, against the "evil" that threatened their voyage to a tomorrow they believed they were owed.

In this life, the Inabrians lost the war eventually, but not before their beautiful lies left Aixauh in blood and ruin. Not before they left Ark an orphan, not just of her family, but of the entire alchemist clan of Li. The sole successor of a legacy that she had never cherished, Li Si-Ya died, and the pirate queen Ark Li was born. All in this one life.

Sometimes, however, Ark would dream of a different one. A voyage to a better future, somewhere Inabrians and Aixauhans could meet as equals on the wide ocean. Somewhere Ark could afford to entertain the idea of a singular Creator and come to her own conclusions.

In this life, Ark knew there would be another war on the horizon, for the ocean was greedy and the Inabrians had seawater running through their veins. So, she banished the thought of a Creator who might not agree with the actions of those who waged war in His name. The thirst for power of the Inabrians grew; Ark had to be prepared.

The greed of the Inabrians was that of an ocean swallowing so many sailors who dared to traverse into its vast belly. It never contemplated a world that was large enough for more than itself.

The Second War was coming, and Ark was no longer under the thrall of their words. She would make the Inabrians into the ghosts they resembled all along. If the Inabrians saw monsters in the alchemists, then Ark would give them what they believed to be true.

She would become the monster on the sea responsible for Inabrians never returning to their homes again.

For the rest of her life, Captain Ark Li would never again go by her Aixauhan name. The line of the Li Clan had died with her, buried with her parents, and later—as Ark found out when she finally reached the island that housed her childhood fantasies—buried with her sister as well.

Under the castle surrounded by barberry bushes, rotting into white bones on foreign soil.

Aixauhans were people of the earth. Nu Wa moulded them from the yellow clay along the shore of the Sunlit River. So, to the earth they would return, to their ancestors. Ark's sister, however, rotted away in the backyard of an Inabrian magician and was eaten by maggots.

In another life, Ark would have mourned her parents and her sister's death. She'd have uttered the Creator's words on their deathbeds, wishing them a precious eternity in His company.

In this life, Ark's sister was a pile of bones she buried with her last remaining shred of faith in something larger.

There were thousands upon thousands of bones just like her sister's… Bones that were tiny and skulls that had not yet closed off at their crest.

Tens of thousands of Aixauhan children.

Each was an unfulfilled promise. Each an empty voyage that could have sailed to a better tomorrow.

Ark would later prove to be a tremendous help to Ying Cai-Li, the gifted necromancer who, despite growing up in Inabri, was so well-versed in alchemy that it made Ark feel shame boiling in her chest.

"You are so well-versed at the Inabrians' belief in the Afterlife." Cai-Li, the alchemist who would concoct the Elixir of Immortality, the first in millennia of Aixauhan history to have done so. She said to Ark with a smile on her face, with a sense of piercing clarity that went well-beyond her young age, "It's almost as if you are a believer in their Creator yourself."

"Don't flatter me, child," Ark replied with a laugh filled with salt. Her mouth was dry as her illness ate away at her. She would soon join the rest of the Li Clan and all the alchemists, after assisting the greatest alchemist to ever live in a final quest to defeat death.

"There can be no Aixauhan alchemist in my generation who believes in the Creator without betraying the blood of our families. Not in this day and age."

"Captain Li." Cai-Li was not fooled. "You have the makings of a saint in the Inabrian beliefs—a childhood home destroyed by evil men, the last descendant of a precious lineage. Even the part about taking vengeance by your own hand. It's all rather in the style of the Creator's ordination, at least according to their Record."

Ark laughed for real. Her sore throat coughed out blood that tasted like metal and salt. A trail of blood dripped from the corner of her lips, and Ark licked it off.

Metal and salt. The same taste as ocean water, the same smell as the sea breeze.

Her mother had once told her the Inabrians had the sea running in their veins, making them forget their humanity, making them cruel and greedy.

"Hypothetically speaking," Captain Ark Li told Ying Cai-Li, "if everything goes according to plan, your wife is the one who most likely will become a saint. She's martyred at a young age, killed by those she trusted, and soon she will become immortal by your hand."

Cai-Li watched Ark curiously. "Do you ever regret not being able to be born into the new age to come?"

"The Inabrians believe in a voyage that ships humanity to a better tomorrow," the captain said. In another life, she'd have been a scholar or perhaps a priestess. "When man-made evil tears the world apart, there will be a great flood that cleanses everything, until there is nothing but a new dawn."

"Would you have preferred that?" Cai-Li asked.

"Who knows," Ark replied. "There is no maybe, like I said. We only have one life each."

"Not necessarily," said Cai-Li. "There is the Reincarnation Cycle."

"Yes, I suppose." Ark shook her head. She didn't like the idea of a reincarnation cycle, which was a thought she could not give voice to. It was too cold. How could anyone prefer that to be a solace? To know everything one was in this life was washed away into nothing of consequence? To become strangers to everyone that she loved in this life, no matter how painful, seemed wrong. "Let's get back on track. Talk of the afterlife makes me queasy."

"Okay," Cai-Li concurred. Neither of them spoke of another life again.

The Inabrian side of alchemy and necromancy yielded little to no results to their experiment anyway. Ying Cai-Li perfected the Elixir of Immortality on her own, because this was the life they lived in.

"Destroy the cycle, sunbird," Ark told Cai-Li. "Let there be no more bones for future alchemists to collect, and let there be no more monsters like me to be born."

"I promise I will," Cai-Li said as she watched the concoction of the Elixir of Immortality. "Anne is the key to a better tomorrow. Or, like how you would put it: the Ark of the Inabrian Creator. A voyage to the future. A future without death and war. I am sure of it."

"I really hope you're right," Ark answered drily, skeptical till the end. She was too old and tired to start having faith. "You better not fuck this up just because you're horny and love-struck, Cai-Li."

"I won't," Cai-Li promised, her eyes the shade of the most fertile and rich of Aixauhan soil. "Anne isn't going to accept any of this quietly, but I will make her do so."

"The future in which she is a saint," Ark said solemnly. "While you will only be remembered as the monster who used dark magic and boiled blood for the selfish pursuit of immortality. You are not going to tell the oracle girl the future you saw from her Chalice, are you?"

"She must never know." Cai-Li shook her head. "That is the key. Promise me, Captain. After I partake in the mercury and became part of the concoction, I can no longer ensure Anne's safe passage from the land of the dead to the land of the living. I have one last favour to ask of you: guide her back to life once I am gone. Protect her at all costs. Make sure she never knows the truth of my plan. She needs to realise it herself in the centuries to come for there to be no more war between Inabri and Aixauh."

"You will become a monster to all," Ark mused. "But to Anne Barberry, you will be the saviour and martyr of one. She will think you died out of the love you have for her alone."

"And that love is going to ensure peace between Inabri and Aixauh for the millennia to come." Cai-Li's eyes sparkled with light as if a fire were lit inside them. A furnace befitting the nature of a true alchemist. "No one will die like your sister did, like Cole did, like Anne did. No one will live to lose everything like you or me. That will be worth it, even if it means I have to manipulate the one I love."

"To tell the greatest lie to achieve the ultimate good." Ark sighed. She felt outmatched, for as long as she lived and all the terrible things she had done—none of it matched the scope of what Ying Cai-Li was about to enact.

Maybe it was good that in this life Ark Li believed in nothing at all, if she had known the existence of a Creator, then no one would be there to help Ying Cai-Li in becoming a god herself.

"You are truly the most contradictory individual I have ever come across, Ying Cai-Li. You are surely the blood and legacy of the Founding Emperor, with your selfish ambition. Yet you are still truly paving the foundation that will ensure Aixauh thrives for hundreds of generations from now on, just like your ancestor Ying Zheng."

"Thank you."

"It's not a compliment," Ark said. "But I promise you. I will make sure the lie you tell Anne Barberry becomes the truth. We never had this talk. Your secret will die with me. I will protect her, but I will make sure she remembers you as the selfish lover ravaged and changed by the grief of war if that's what is needed to save both Aixauh and Inabri from the cycle of violence."

"Thank you." Ying Cai-Li smiled like the dusk of a new world. A world that Ark had been born into, but hopefully, no one else would.

28

Grief

THEY ALL SIT in silence, this merry band of people Anne would never have pictured gathering together—especially not inside Barberry Castle.

Ark Li, the captain of the ship that saved Anne and her friends, but also the murderer of Anne's grandfather (albeit for understandable reasons). She looked younger than Anne did, like she was in her late teens, despite wearing the same outfit and having the same ridiculous straw hat on. It made this figure who terrorised Anne's worst nightmares look like a kid dressing up for a masquerade party.

Maev, the only living member who was a child when Anne last saw her, now apparently in her twenties. The girl who always had her head shaved bare during their time running away from the war now sported an afro. Her eyes were bright, like stars twinkling in the dead of night. They were devoid of the terror that Anne was used to seeing, as they were reflecting the endless gunsmoke and dead bodies. Maev survived the war, and she left it behind, more so than Anne and Chely ever had.

And then there is Ying Cai-Li, who lay on the floor with half a smile on her face. Her lips are drained of colour as her skin turns cold. Anne cradles the alchemist in her lap, shivering in a feverish cold.

Strands of red hair obscure Chely's pale face. Anne swipes them away. With her eyes closed, she looks as if she were simply visiting a sweet dream.

Anne Barberry has the sudden urge to laugh out loud.

If only all those people who once shuddered in terror at Chely's name could see her now. The fearsome reputation this sleeping beauty garnered throughout the years since the war.

Anne remembers now.

So many passersby walked through the In-Between. More who were trapped there. They came with tales of the necromancer who hunted them down, whose eyes were depthless voids, with hair that shifted between wine and the rising sun.

They spoke of how The Blood Hawk had always smiled as she ended their lives. How utterly calm she was at each and every murder scene. There was no emotion. She was a goddess of death.

Chely has that same look on her face now.

Anne is numb as the gears in her head continue turning.

Even before the black bird shot through the window and startled everyone.

Even before Cole transformed back from his disheveled state, pale and unstable.

Even before the anger exploded from the Yamalan boy.

Even before Maev gasped at the words tumbling out of Cole's mouth, stitching together a picture of how Ying Cai-Li destroyed The Cottage on the fields of flowers at dusk.

That cottage that housed them through the war. The Cottage that Anne first stumbled upon when she died. The Cottage where

Cole welcomed her home. That little home represented safety and sanctuary but was also the final destination.

Chely had destroyed it. The final place of rest and peace for Anne and Cole.

It was their home. A symbol.

It was where they learned to trust each other. Cole's jabs at Anne in the early days of war, Anne's failed attempt at finding a clean water source and burning any food sources they could find. The tree where they buried Cole. The place where Anne and Chely lived in the short time they spent together after they were married.

It was like throwing your favourite stuffed animal into the garbage. Smashing a family heirloom into smithereens.

Anne's hands tremble as she finally stands, letting go of the body of the one who caused this concave into the abyss in Anne's heart.

Silence falls on everyone again as Cole finishes recounting his tale.

Finally, the storyteller lets out a huff.

"That's it," Cole of the Yamalan says. He looks more solid than Anne can ever remember him being, even counting the times when he was alive. "She killed herself. The ritual is complete. She destroyed death. And she said that Anne is alive, and so am I? I don't exactly know what she meant. But it can't be. It just can't be."

Maev shakes her head in disbelief. "It's not possible. I don't know what Chely did, but no one can bring back someone who was fully dead from Beyond. Even if Chely somehow smashed the place that symbolises death? That doesn't change the fact that you and Anne are… I mean, you are both still *here?*"

"So, she died for nothing," Cole replies, his voice cold as the snow of the mountaintops. Anne's heart skips a beat. The emotionless way Cole speaks of Chely…it's like watching the death of both of them again, at the same time. "What a shame. But I guess it should be expected. None of us really knew her in the end. She is a stranger. I guess that's what it takes to kill yourself while believing you are doing the world a favour—she truly lived up to her moniker as The Blood Hawk.

Maev sucks in a breath. "Don't say that," she shushes Cole while her eyes flicker in Anne's direction. "Maybe she turned into someone we don't know. But she is—she was—our friend and family. We should mourn her, like we do all the others."

The others, as in the sailors who died on Captain Li's ship, as the kids they took in but couldn't keep alive amidst quadrants of magicians and soldiers. It almost makes Anne smile, as this is the girl she remembers they saved from a burning building that was torched by the soldiers. A timid little thing.

Cole lets out a bitter laugh. "You're right, Maev." He turns to Anne, anger still coming off him in waves, yet his gaze softens as it meets Anne's—as if he's suddenly stumbled onto thin ice. "Anne… I'm sorry. But I think we should bury her."

Anne finds herself mute. She's stuck in a realm of her own.

A scream tears through her, yet no voice comes out.

An angry cry of despair, yet she does not necessarily feel surprised.

A violent urge to shake the body growing cold until it reanimates back into the red-haired alchemist with the smug apologetic smile, yet Anne Barberry knows the truth. There are no oracle powers needed. There was no other way this could have gone.

From the moment Chely stepped into the In-Between, Anne knew this day would come.

For Anne knew the nature of the sun. It was a fiery ball of heat and warmth; that was why she huddled toward Chely, disregarding everything her family had taught her. The witch who chases the sun, for Chely was the warmth in the eternal dead night that is Anne Barberry's life. The first rays of dawn. The first flicker of flame. It lit a beacon in her world, yet it kept burning until the morning came.

Anne tried everything to quench the fire of her sun. She knew if Chely kept burning, the fire that brightened the night would turn inward and consume the sun itself. For what use is a lantern when the night has passed? Who needs more heat when summer has come and the world has warmed back up?

The sun that keeps burning will devour all that is beautiful and natural. It turns into a forest fire, a furnace fueled by Discord. It devours the natural order of things before dying out.

That is the nature of fire: to smoulder and fade when denied the fuel to keep it going.

When Anne finally feels her limbs again, she finds her body trembling as if an earthquake has ravaged through her. Her stomach heaves as a deafening patch of fireworks explodes from her throat. Cole kneels next to her, and then so does Maev. They put their arms around Anne, holding her as she sobs and pukes.

Her eyes burn like open wounds on her face. Anne swears they must be running crimson blood, but as Anne's vision blurs, she realises the liquid dripping onto the floor is only transparent tears.

Grief engulfs her so entirely, she no longer feels human.

An animalistic growl sounds and echoes throughout Barberry Castle, down its ancient halls and past its portraits that trace back centuries of lineages. All the ghosts of children and monsters who linger here, some innocent while others deserved to suffer forever… all of them are quiet, shocked into silence at the oracle's grief.

She is really gone.

29

One Last Funeral

THEY HOLD A funeral for Ying Cai-Li in a field of barberry bushes.

Clouds roll in the sky like puffs of sheep's wool. The sky is a deep, dark night with no stars to be seen. The town is quiet, with no resident moving an inch. The permanently lit and lively inn finally closes its bar.

The queen of the In-Between, the mistress of the castle, everything in this realm moves according to her chosen obliviousness. the oracle's state of mind of wishing to trap those who deserved such pain in this place like an insect in amber, because Anne believed these people didn't deserve to truly cross over and meet the kin waiting for them on the other side.

It will be the last night of it. Now, Anne Barberry has no more resentment or hatred in her heart for the people of this town. Not when she herself loved someone who was also as guilty and stubborn and unrepentant as those souls that are stuck in the permafrost of the In-Between.

After this night, this one last funeral, the In-Between will be forged anew in someone else's image. Someone who is far kinder, far more clear-headed, who sees through the war and death, who dealt with all the bullshit yet still has a pair of clear eyes unmarred by personal vendetta and pain.

"I will stay behind," Cole says to Anne before the funeral, when she is finally lucid enough to listen after shutting herself in her black curtained room, drinking, for the weeks that rolled by. "I don't care what Cai-Li did and said. But I lived, and I died. That's the natural order."

Anne doesn't flinch beneath the lingering sparks of anger coating Cole's voice. However, that anger does not burn hot, it does not scorch or eat away at the world until there is nothing left. Like the mountains Cole's people came from, his anger is something steady and logical.

In the end, Cole truly is the best of them.

"You'll make the In-Between a better place, Che… *She* wasn't lying to us," Anne replies truthfully. Yet her lips tremble and her words twist when they touch that name. "I can feel my life running back into me like a river that flows upstream. I'll go back to The Cottage, and I'll keep the tree that contained your life force there evergreen. That way, you will technically be alive to run the In-Between for centuries to come. Let's be honest, you *were* the one who really ran this place for the last seven years, since I was playing house with myself half of the time."

"You weren't playing anything," Cole replies. "You were grieving, Annie. For me, for yourself, for your little sister, and for Cai-Li. Maybe she was alive, but you mourned her. Cai-Li wasn't the only one who lost everyone they loved, you know? Even though that bastard made it all about herself."

Anne stays silent at that. She and Cole walk through the hills around Barberry Castle. The ground they tread on is the same place where she met Chely again, where Anne shouted at the alchemist, accusing her in rage and anger.

All those feelings are gone. Fizzled away like foam in the sea. Or like the fate of the little siren in the Inabrian fairytale that Brutus Barberry used to tell Anne when she was a child. The protagonist of that story was a daughter of the sea, who fell in love with a non-magician boy who walked on land. She saved him, but he did not recognise her when they met again. In the end, the little siren refused to kill the boy to gain back her ability to go home and evaporated into sea foam as the dawn came upon them.

Anne never understood that story. It had been buried with all the other memories—the gentle and quiet ones of Brutus being a grandfather with wrinkled eyes when he smiled that filled her with a sense of safety as he tucked her into bed—after Ark Li murdered him, after she found out who he truly was, after the war ended.

Anne thought it was an either-or question. She was either the Aixauhan alchemist's family and friend who was a traitor to Inabri, or she was part of the bloody Barberry legacy who carried on committing unspeakable crimes. Cole was either the boy who died young and pure, someone they lost at war, or the crow who stayed with her for a decade that was a symbol of death. Ark Li was either the murderer of her grandfather, or the innocent woman seeking rightful justice by taking out human scum.

And Chely Hawk, or Ying Cai-Li, she was either the girl with flaming hair as warm as a summer day who Anne chased after like the only light in her life, or she was the broken glass of a crushed chandelier. A goddess corrupted by something unspeakable, a necromancer with no morals and a taste for blood, a daydream that turned into a nightmare. It was that black-and-white thinking, this selective obliviousness, which had caged Anne and every single soul that came into her realm.

Barberry Castle loomed large as its mistress, cloaked in the shadows, built walls around herself, as if her entire world would crumble into dust if she didn't. Ying Cai-Li's last act was bringing those walls down. Putting aside all the lies and deception, all the murder and necromancy. Those last few weeks they spent together is the image of Chely that Anne chooses to remember.

Chely could have simply done the ritual of resurrection instantly without those excruciating weeks as mercury seeped into her every muscle and bone. The poison that drained away her life and made her every move like walking on knives—so much like the price of the little siren's deal with the sea monster—all to spend a little more time with the girl she loved till ruination.

Ying Cai-Li was truly gone, yet Anne Barberry had gotten her back. One piece at a time, with the bickering banter and jabs. They fell in love with each other again, seven years after death did them part.

However, just like Anne decided her stance on how she felt toward Chely Hawk, with no more secret-hiding behind that ever-present smirk on the dubious alchemist's face that kept one guessing—Cole has an even longer history with Chely; he has every right to not forgive who Chely became.

Anne puts her head on Cole's shoulder as they watch the sun rise on the horizon of a new day.

"I think you'll make a brilliant king of the In-Between, Cole."

Forever truthful, and in good fashion of always butting heads with her, Cole of the Yamalan replies as he hugs her tight, "Thanks, Annie. I wish I could return the compliment, but I can't. You really sucked at running this place."

"I really did fuck up pretty bad." Anne giggles, the first sound of laughter coming out of her dry throat. She sounds like the mournful bells of a funeral, or the cough of a dying old crone. Not someone who has been given a second chance at life, the first human to drink the Elixir of Immortality and live an infinite lifetime.

"It's okay," Cole says while patting Anne on the head. "I'm still pissed at Cai-Li. But the last thing she said to me was, 'You have nothing but time.' And if anyone will spend the rest of eternity well, it is you, Annie. You, who was born from the Barberry Lineage but made a family with those your family deemed as subhuman."

"Oh." Anne puts the back of her palm against her forehead and feigns fainting in shock. "Are you saying we are family, Cole of the Yamalan? Gosh, have you finally recognised me as your sister-in-law? Let me make us a meal to celebrate this monumental moment!"

"Fuck off." Cole rolls his eyes and pushes her away. "No way in the world I'm touching any food you make with a ten-foot pole. For the sake of humanity, don't ever cook anything for anyone once you're back in the land of the living. Or I'll probably have souls turning up in the In-Between crying about how they've been poisoned to death."

They laugh at his silly joke. The sun would be up in the sky soon enough, after the funeral and after Anne departs this place once and for all. The town will buzz again, even with half of the residents moving on.

There will always be souls that linger after death, who cannot move on from what happened to them during their lifetime. But with Cole as the guardian of this place, it will no longer be a prison, and he will be no warden. Instead, he will be a welcome host, the crow accompanying every soul from one side to another with quietness and understanding. Just as he had been at Anne's side for all this time.

"Burn Barberry Castle and all its black curtains to the ground after I'm gone, will you?" Anne asks Cole softly. "I know Chely destroyed The Cottage that marked all three of our ends. But maybe you can build a new one. Maybe you can weed out all the barberry bushes and let all the wildflowers grow."

Cole shakes his head. "No, Annie. I think I will keep our castle just the way it is now," he says with the surety of a monarch. "Cai-Li burned down The Cottage and all the flowers at our end as she died. I do not agree with her, but I think I am beginning to understand. That cottage was my childhood home; it was our first shelter during the war. But none of us can truly return to that cottage. It is time to stop looking back at one beautiful scene in the past and remembering what we could have had; it's time to move on."

"I get what you're saying." Anne nods, still her brows knotted as she turns back to observe Barberry Castle and thinks of all the white bones buried underneath. "But this place—this place is the image of all the Barberrys who came before me, Cole. They were the ones who killed so many of your people; their war killed *you*."

"Well, I never knew any of *those* Barberrys." Cole turns around, his eyes gazing upon the castle not as a tomb or a prison, but as a misunderstood friend. "The only Barberry I know is you, Annie. And despite you not being yourself half the time, while I had feathers instead of skin, this was still our home for a while. I think I like it just the way it is."

Maev comes to tell them the funeral pyre is ready. Anne and Cole exchange a glance, a gesture that communicates everything they need to know. It is time to say goodbye to the one who brought them together, and the one whose funeral will mark the beginning of their parting.

However, before they can follow Maev, Anne spots a figure standing at the other side of Barberry Castle. Overtaken by the castle's towering shadow, Anne cannot tell where the darkness the castle ends and where Ark Li's shadow begins. They melt together, like the castle has somehow eaten away the soul of the sea captain.

The sun is out, but it does not reach where Ark Li stands.

"You go ahead." Anne waves Maev and Cole onward. "I'll catch up in a minute."

Anne finds Ark Li at the tallest tower, overlooking the cliffs.

"That is a steep fall," Anne says. She tries not to tremble in the face of the pirate captain. The tower is high. The wind howls.

"None of us can die," Ark replies, not turning around to see Anne. The captain stands at the edge of the tower. Her black hair takes to the wind like the flag of the ship she once commanded. "This is a good view."

"It really is," Anne admits. She closes her eyes and imagines herself taking flight. The heat of the sun is diluted by the wind.

Anne Barberry never liked the height of Barberry Castle. She was afraid of falling. The height made her dizzy if she stared down a window for too long. She never came to this edge of her own house.

Ark stands there, however, determined and casual as if she owns the place. The whole scenario is ridiculous, Anne thinks. The sea captain, who broke into this very castle to murder Anne's grandfather, is more comfortable in Barberry Castle than the mistress of the castle itself.

It's something Anne will never understand. This very castle that overlooks the barberry fields in which the captain's sister is buried, the bones that form the foundation of this place, should be enough for anyone to want to fling themselves off this tower.

Anne still feels the urge to hurl in her chest. She can't die. Not after Chely Ying. The curse that Chely gave to Anne out of love, the gift that was the same as poison.

Immortality.

"You are not going to die even if you choose to jump," Ark Li recognises the glint in Anne's eyes. The captain comments casually, her young face as blank as the clouds of an open sky. The best way to set sail without worrying about storms or lightning.

Anne's lips curl up. It's a more painful jab than if Ark had stabbed her through the heart. This pain is a dull ache, much how ingesting mercury must feel. A slow and dull ache that comes in waves like an endless ocean made of acid, slowly spreading through one's bloodstream like tentacles.

"Why did you help her?" Anne asks. A thousand ghosts stand between Ark Li and the last Barberry. Everyone who deserved to die and those who did not. The innocent and the guilty. "Your letter said you saw hope in me, but that can't be true. You loved Chely. She was like a daughter to you. You helped train her to become a weapon. You were proud of her. You were…like her. Why kill someone you love to grant immortality to the bloodline that slaughtered yours?"

Ark Li turns her head back. Her youthful face is unblemished by scars or age. She is about the age of sixteen, a decade younger and more daring than Anne. Yet, the smile on Captain Li's face is one of a seagull watching its young.

A smile plays on Ark's face. "After everything, that's the only thing you want to ask me?" The captain's voice is so unburdened. Anne has the feeling Ark Li could really grow a pair of wings if she wanted.

No, Anne wants to scream. She wants to tear that smile off the captain's face.

Anne has every conviction to push Ark Li off the tower, for Chely, for herself. Will Ark Li fall apart? The captain who seems undefeatable in battle. The girl who lost her whole family. The captain who plotted to murder Anne when she was on her ship. The girl who came to Barberry Castle to slay a monster.

The monster in Anne's nightmares. The captain who took them under her wings. Safe harbour. Dangerous predator.

The one who poisoned Chely's heart. The one whose heart was poisoned by Anne's family.

Ark Li is an enigma.

"Yes," Anne replies.

"Do you not hate me?" Ark lifts an eyebrow and spreads her arms. The captain hugs the sky with her small frame. "I wanted you dead, Anne Barberry. I definitely killed your grandfather. I sort of had a hand in the death of your wife. Yet all you have to say to me was 'that's a steep fall?'"

Anne thinks about it. She truly contemplates the question.

"I always imagined death as something horrible," Anne says. "It's like falling into the abyss when one is believed to be soaring toward eternity. I saw death the first time you came to this castle. Death was simple back then. It was to be feared. I think I know death up close. Death is an enigma. *You* are an enigma. Chely was an enigma. I guess I am an enigma too. You died, I died, Chely is now truly dead. I don't see how I could hate you without hating Chely as well."

Ark Li blinks. A smile blossoms across her face. It is sincere, a peachy colour that is the same as the twilight that could be seen over the board of the ship. It is brutal, but it hides no treachery and bears no ill-will.

"I guess it is above you now," Ark says. "To hate someone who is deceased, Anne. I cannot believe I am saying this to a Barberry. Still, I bid you good health."

"And I will tell the world who you are," Anne replies. "I will tell them the truth about you, Captain Ark Li. I will tell them the truth about Chely. Everyone will see you. There will be no one who enters the In-Between again who will forgive the sins done to you, nor will they forget the sins you committed."

Ark Li walks toward Anne. She is much shorter as a teenager than Anne, who is now going to look thirty forever. It is weird to get a pat on the head by a girl.

"I am counting on it," Ark Li replies. "An oracle who is determined to become a historian… Tell them about the war. Tell them never to start one ever again."

Anne does not hate the feeling of Ark's hand against her head. It is odd how Ying Cai-Li's death went along with the anger and vipers that curled up in Anne's stomach.

Everyone is a stranger after Ying Cai-Li. Everyone is a friend after Ying Cai-Li.

In one way or another, the blood alchemist blurred the line between friend and foe. When blood mixed with blood, there was only red left. The same colour as Chely's hair. The same shade as the sun at dawn.

Anne blinks and then she sees Captain Ark Li no more. There is no shadow blocking the light showering the In-Between in its golden rays. There is only a girl, returning to her family after a long journey at sea.

"I saw you in a Vision," Anne shouts toward the back of the captain who flattered her. "It's one where you were a priestess of the Creator, Captain Li."

The captain nods before leaving the tower. She does not jump off the edge. Instead, Ark Li takes the steps down.

"I can see that," echoes the pirate captain. "In a different life where the Inabrians didn't slaughter my clan, I could see myself making the Creator's acquaintance. Too bad we're stuck in space and time, where His speakers are murderers and conquerors."

When Anne goes to find Cole and Maev waiting to send her off, Ark Li is nowhere to be found.

She melts away with the sun. Chely Hawk's corpse burns away as easily as paper.

Smoke rises into the sky in white clouds. It is nothing but a carcass left behind. Anne tilts her head toward the fireball that brims with golden and red threads. The blood alchemist watches her funeral with the same perplexing smile as she had as a human being.

There are so many things left unsaid, yet it is the end.

Time to say goodbye.

Cole and Anne stand next to Ying Cai-Li's remains as the sunbird's taunting rays cover the hilltop. They wait quietly and defiantly until the being of pure flames has left her steadfast watch atop their heads.

Neither Anne nor Cole say a word. She wonders if he was secretly wishing for the sun to stay put. Anne was waiting for it to linger, as that was what Cai-Li did; she latched onto things like a barnacle when she should let go.

Yet, as the cotton candy pink and lilac hues grow like a field of wildflowers across the blue sea of the sky, the sun retreats west without slowing down. Sweat forms on her forehead. She tastes ash in her mouth.

She wishes for Ying Cai-Li to stand up from the fire. It is what Cai-Li is, a corpse that has dragged itself through the world due to flames that ate away at the alchemist until she was cinders in the shape of a human being.

Anne waits as the crimson tongue licks the cheeks of the alchemist. She remembers the taste of Cai-Li's cheeks—the first time they kissed, the alchemist's cheek tasted bitter, like the ale she had just drank. They fumbled and Anne's teeth clattered with Cai-Li's. Flesh was torn apart in their clumsy youth that turned the kiss into iron and saltwater. They giggled together, unaware that was the taste of blood.

Anne would give anything for it to have remained that way.

She closes her eyes and utters a final goodbye.

The sun rises to the peak of the sky.

Cole pulls Anne into an embrace. "Good luck, Annie."

She knows he means it; for the king of the In-Between and the immortal oracle, this will be a more final goodbye than death itself.

"It's time to go," Maev quietly interjects.

Anne nods. She turns her back on the sun as she takes Maev's hand.

Maev begins to sing. It is a melody as soft and gentle as the spring wind. The world becomes distorted.

The castle that trapped the oracle in life and death fades away. The barberry bushes melt into a crimson hue. It is the colour of the sea being stained by the blood of sailors under Captain Li's ship. It is the colour of the battlefield where Cole had fallen.

It is the colour of Ying Cai-Li's hair. Her soft lips and gentle stare.

"May we meet again in a kinder world."

It might be nothing but a hallucination, but Anne Barberry wakes up an immortal with those words echoing in her mind with heat like that of the sun.

Epilogue

Five Centuries Later

I AM A historian whose life is about to go out in a blaze of glory.

I am going to present my pitch for a project that is sure to be rejected.

The historical institute where I am a scholar is called The Castle, even though it's nothing of the sort. It was designated a historical heritage site, according to both the Inabrian and Aixauhan Historical Institutions. Both countries no longer go by those names, with one falling into civil war about two hundred years ago and the other fracturing into city-states that each govern their own terrain.

The history of the two wars that led to the decimation of almost 80% of the alchemist and magician population of the world are remembered by everyone. Decades passed, historical accounts were written, both Inabrian versions where they denied the existence of the genocide of alchemists during the First War and the Aixauhan versions where it was seen as a humiliation that would motivate their hostile and closed-off diplomatic approach for the next three centuries.

Amongst the documentation of the Wars, a few names pop out. There is Saint Ark Li, the pirate general whose family members were documented victims of the First War, who became a benevolent roguish figure that dedicated her life to saving alchemist and magician orphans regardless of their origins in the Second War. For her selfless endeavour in saving orphans, the Central Church of the Creator actually canonised her as a saint about fifty years ago, which had nothing to do with the historical figure herself but was more an act to rally their crumbling power in the city-states.

Ark Li is, in fact, the subject of the thesis I wrote which gained me entry into my position at The Castle. Like I said before, it truly is nothing like it sounds. It is a library and a university dedicated to the study and preservation of history.

It is nothing like a university of anyone's imagination. No floating metallic walls with sparkling scientific research labs mixed with the world's leading alchemists and magicians. No machinery or AI that helps the students customise and design their everyday life and studies. The Castle Institute is as old as its founder, whose bones are no doubt buried nearby. A witness of history itself, The Oracle Anne Barberry. A place befitting the person—both endured like a fossil fuel from an ancient time.

Warm brown wooden logs are bound together as walls with a stove that constantly burns at the center. Each student is assigned a cabin-like dormitory where they cook their own food harvested from the wild fields and woods with their own hands.

The library that houses ancient documents tracing back through the millennia is indeed a castle with spires where green vines cloak them like a gown, with ancient corridors with windows that are forever open to sunlight in.

It was the head professor's personal preference, some say. Others say the professor was driven mad by obsession with her subject of study. No one knows the true story of Anne Barberry, who is undeniably eccentric in her taking on the same name as the famous oracle. I used to think she must either have a massive ego or that she must just be a plain kooky fangirl of the historical figure she studies. Professor Barberry's questionable sanity aside, she is well-renowned in the field of historical academia. She penned the universally recognised *A Record on the Age of Magical Desolation* around thirty years ago.

Some students believe she is *the* same Anne Barberry of the Second War itself, the martyr oracle whose pursuit of peace after the Second War led to her own demise, and also the rise of a monster.

It's nonsense, of course. I mean, there's the fact that Professor Barberry doesn't look a day beyond thirty. The history professor has blonde hair, cut short. She styles it into a tousled bob, which is the same hairstyle that women of my mother's age love to wear. On Professor Barberry, it does not appear old. If anything, it is the oldest thing about her.

Professor Barberry wear contact lenses that adjust her eyesight to perfection. She always wears a headpiece that allows her to simultaneously communicate with different groups of researchers of The Castle at once. She wears a pristine white lab coat, a dazzling shard of modernity in contrast to both her occupation as a historian and writer renowned globally for her works on New and Old History and Archaeology.

The castle is the perfect blend of contradictions, just like Professor Barberry herself.

My lifelong work on Ark Li was filled with pursuits of the seaside town interviews that recounts folklore of the legendary pirate captain synonymous with a sea goddess and spending most of my adult life living within the carcass of Li's old ship—a hologram, as the reconstruction of the original vessel proved to be a failing project. The original ship was a protected relic for about a century after the second Inabrian-Aixauhan war. It was turned into a museum until the general public got bored of hearing about the sea goddess two centuries later. Now, it is nothing but my old tomb, me, an unaccomplished and washed-up historian who has no idea what I am doing.

The day I brought my project to The Castle Institute, I was as exhausted as I am today. There was a mountain trail between where the midair car park was located to the point where The Castle Institute resides.

"Why?" I asked incredulously. "Who designed the climb to the Castle Institute to be such a difficult task?" It was almost like the university didn't wish to be found in the first place. I didn't voice the second part of my thought.

The taxi operator AI beeped at me, which I angrily gave a middle finger in return.

Many months later, as I passed my apprenticeship and became a formal scholar of The Castle, Professor Barberry presented the answer to my question.

"Oh," the blonde woman said emotionlessly. "It's so those who don't think history is worth the hike give up on the way here. I don't have time for people who lack devotion to their studies."

I nodded, albeit with a slightly pained smile. This was typical of our Professor Barberry; she is dismissively arrogant in the same way my grandma is. It is absurd, as she can't be that much older than me. She might have just been a genius kid who wrote the Record when she was eighteen or something, and anti-aging technology has truly advanced in the past decade. But the fact that Anne Barberry acts as if she is somehow above the time we live in truly grates on my nerves.

There was no way that what some whispers say about her is true.

That somehow, she was the final product of the infamous Necromancer Ying Cai-Li, the murderer and corrupt alchemist who almost plunged Aixauh and Inabri into a third war by killing Anne Barberry's sister. There were so many versions of The Blood Hawk's story, each sinister and grotesque. Some say she dabbled in necromancy that led to her turning her closest friend, Cole of the Yamalan, a fallen war hero, into a tree as part of her pursuit of immortality.

It has nothing to do with my own unspoken feelings toward Professor Barberry. Sometimes, I do think she's a lot like an ice-cold statue frozen in time instead of a flesh and blood human being.

Yet somehow, I cannot stop admiring Professor Barberry purely from an intellectual perspective. She is the embodiment of my adoration for the subjects of history and archaeology. She is unflappable in the face of any flattery or error, always calm and objective, like a polished silver blade or the steady mountain terrain.

On my first day, when I nervously presented my findings on Ark Li to Ms. Barberry, I knew I was doomed. The angle of my argument on Ark Li, an ancient figure who was revered for her heroism, was next to blasphemy in historical academia. It was what drove me to The Castle Institute to begin with, for there was nowhere else I turned to willing to publish my account of The Saint Captain.

"What is wrong with you?" they had told me. "You are trying to argue that Ark Li was some selfish figure who was consumed by revenge? That kind of revisionist take might be popular with the youth in their virtual reality games. We are proper academics, Miss Ying. Not storytellers."

Professor Barberry, however—she welcomed me into her office at The Castle after hearing about my accounts on Ark Li becoming a laughingstock among our profession.

At first, I thought it was a joke. A cruel humiliation. I did not know what kind of person Anne Barberry was back then. I knew only that history was a solid and fixed thing. Ark Li was seen as the hero who suffered a great loss; there was no room for her as a human being.

That was my idea fixed in stone until I watched Anne Barberry read through my files right then and there with the concentration of the sun illuminating the earth. Hours ticked by; the sun drowned in the east and rose in the west. I slept in Professor Barberry's dorm and awoke to go back and find that she was reading the conclusion paragraph I had on Ark Li.

"Miraculous," the head historian said. Her voice was flat and her face expressionless. She could proclaim she murdered someone with the same tone, and it wouldn't make a difference. "Did you say you were turned away by a dozen historical institutions before this, Miss…Ying?"

"Y-yes," I nervously clutched my skirt.

My skittish nature seemed to surprise Professor Barberry. There was a tremor across her lips that almost bordered on being a smile. An amused one, for some personal reason that I could not decipher.

"Then those historical institutions should be run out of the field of study. Ridiculous," Anne Barberry commented. "Your work is exquisite. Why are you so nervous about it?"

"I…"

"Why are you stammering?" Professor Barberry asked. "This is good work. But if you don't even believe your own research, who's going to take you seriously? You sure are nothing like your surname suggests."

My face flushed red. Panic seized me as much as embarrassment. I thought I was about to faint.

"Please," I said as tears welled in my eyes. "Don't turn me away."

Because I knew, despite the sophisticated and polite excuses given to me by every historian I've ever worked with, the true reason no one wished to hear my controversial direction on Ark Li was because of my last name. The cursed infamy that followed my family for five hundred years following the two wars.

The name of the necromancer. The Blood Hawk. Ying Cai-Li.

Professor Barberry frowned. I was not used to the naivety and out-of-touch scholarly innocence that the head of The Castle Institute possessed.

"Why would I turn you away?" Anne Barberry asked. "You backed up your argument well. There was plenty of evidence that the orphans were not saved by Ark Li, but instead they were present only when Chely, Cole, and Anne had boarded the ship. You also brought up the fact that Ark Li's assassination of Brutus Barberry was not an act of ending the First War, but happened after it, with no apparent motivation found that could result in long-term peace. I agree with you; if anyone found out Ark Li, an Aixauhan alchemist, had been behind the assassination of Brutus Barberry, the Second War might have happened a lot sooner."

That was the moment I lifted my head to see the golden hair illuminating Professor Barberry's grey eyes. She was a sword that was cleared of all the spindly unspoken rules of our profession. If the sun had a personification, it would be in the shape and frame of Anne Barberry.

Okay, so maybe my coworkers' teasing was not entirely unfounded. It only later struck me as odd how Ms. Barberry referred to these long-dead figures by their first names, as if they weren't ink on paper but her personal friends. Maybe that was the epitome of a true historian.

I grumble about Professor Anne Barberry being a snob but can't help thinking that she is what I should aspire to be. She dedicated so much of her life to her studies that I also had the crazy urge to change my name to some historical figure, just to emulate Professor Barberry's dedication to her studies.

Some of our coworkers think it is a form of madness or blasphemy to fashion one's looks and name after a dead historical martyr of old. I secretly agree, but defend Professor Barberry publicly, for who hasn't had a friend or an uncle named after Cole or Ark due to their parents being infatuated with the legends and heroics of The Desolation Wars?

Professor Barberry might have her flaws, but she is sincere and serious about the subject of history in a way that goes directly against the common attitude of our era—which is that the historians are a useless bunch of nerds who should be abolished.

It's time to look forward to the future with the combination of technology the ancient magicians and alchemists crafted, they say. Humanities subjects like history and literature are relics of a bygone time. They should be put aside for progress forward.

I think that's *true* madness. Dump humanities subjects in the garbage? History as a field of study is the essential work of the human soul. The history of the world is often a circle; a well-versed historian is often like the oracles of old, who could predict the patterns of social and global issues today by looking into the past.

Not to mention, I was immersed in the legends by blood, not choice. I was a child who grew up with my family name squandered. The same way I imagined they spoke of the Barberrys before Anne— the historical figure, not my fellow historian—with personal ire and in fear of evoking an evil spirit that could come to haunt the living with malice because of the crimes they committed in life.

There wasn't any bullying or shunning of my family, for the name of Ying Cai-Li is a complicated one back home. In some rare places of the remaining Aixauh, she is the symbol of nationalism, an ascended goddess who fulfilled the ambition of her ancestor, Aixauh's first Emperor Qin, and achieved immortality despite foreigners trying to eliminate her bloodline.

If one can peel myth out of the socio-political context of the day and age we live in, this isn't particularly a bad thought. I like it, secretly and unspoken, for I do not agree with the nationalists who see Ying Cai-Li as a return to the ancient god-like power of Aixauh, neither do I see her as the villainous blood necromancer who pursued immortality as a form of escaping the war.

When the topic finally came up one afternoon, Professor Barberry and I were finalising the translation of a piece of engraved document:

"Once upon a time,

a witch fell in love with the sun.

Ever since then,

she has been chasing her light."

"Professor Barberry," I asked timidly, "who do you think Anne Barberry, er, The Oracle, was referring to with this prophecy?"

"You can call me Anne," the professor responded, her voice cordial despite its distance.

Our coworkers like to tease that I'm the head professor consort, despite there being no hierarchical structure at The Castle. I dismiss these claims, thinking them stupid. I'm sure my silly crush is not reciprocated by Professor Barberry, who is kind but always interacts with the world as if she is not part of it.

"Professor Barberry," I continued. This earned a snicker from her, as the head of The Castle Institute saw the thorny defiance that poked out of my timid veneer occasionally but never resented me for it. "Who do you think The Oracle was referring to when she made this prophecy?"

This was the oldest prophecy made by The Oracle Anne Barberry that historians had on record. It was written in the scribbles of a child using crayons (an old tool for writing without laser beams) before the First War occurred. She was probably a preteen, if not younger.

"Are you asking me that as a fellow historian, or as Ying Qian-Yang?"

I didn't answer. Professor Barberry's pronunciation of my full name was perfect, unlike most descendants of the former Inabrian city states in this part of the world. She must understand the meaning of those words.

千阳, Qian-Yang, meaning the ray of a thousand suns.

It had the same connotations as Ying Cai-Li, 彩黎, "the radiant dawn." My parents were still chasing after the tales of the ascended Blood Hawk. My path to becoming a historian was partly to escape them and their fanaticism.

"Well, if you're not going to choose, then I'll give a response to both."

Professor Barberry was chattier than usual. I had an odd stray thought wondering if she was drunk. The scribbled prophecy in front of us seemed to rejuvenate her in a way I could not understand. It was as if water that kept dripping down on a stone had finally managed to penetrate its solidity; there was something old sparkling to life that I did not understand.

It was at that moment, entranced and bewitched, that an image hit me like a lightning bolt, like déjà vu.

Annie in her black gown, the sun lit up her eyes like silver.

The moment washed past me like the sunlight that blinds one's eyes when staring into it. Once I tilted my head back, Professor Barberry appeared as she always did: stoney but gentle.

"As The Castle's head historian, I represent the conclusion we reach as a team. I will tell you this is most likely referring to Cole of the Yamalan. After all, so much of her motivation in recorded history stemmed from her love and loss of him. Just like your ancestor, Miss Ying. Chely shared the same love of Cole. It was the one thing those two seemed to have common ground on."

"But…that's the common consensus among scholars," I pointed out. My stomach lurched as if I had a personal stake in her answer. "I don't think you truly believe what you are saying."

In return, a flicker of emotion peeked out from Professor Barberry's eyes. It was the tear of a stone maiden.

"If you're asking me as Ying Qian-Yang," Anne Barberry replied, "I will tell you that The Oracle was not the witch in question. Whoever this witch was, she was chasing a future that was bright as the sun. There is nothing more hopeful than an oracle."

"Are you saying the witch is Ying Cai-Li?" I pressed on, my professional curiosity piqued. "Do you believe she and The Oracle Anne Barberry were in love? That she loved her because she thought of Anne as having a better future?"

"I think Chely believed Anne to be an oracle that would have a better impact on the world than she herself," the head historian replied. "What an idiot. She never realised that by carrying all the blame, she indeed gave the world a more hopeful future than some Barberry Oracle ever could."

The goddess of Past and Future, Chely thought. *I am sorry I have to leave you. I wish more than anything to come back to you one day.*

Except I will change my ways. I will be humble, and I will be kind.

Wait for me, my love. Ten years. Twenty. A century.

I will come back to you through the Reincarnation Cycle.

As a different person, at a different time.

Afterword

When I was a little kid, I used to dream of Cai-Li and Anne as best friends. There was a short story, that cannot be found but in the minds of those who read it online, about them getting to know each other. In that version, Anne was solemn, kind, but very haunted. Anne hasn't changed much since then, not in looks or temperament. She is the same character you read in this story.

Cai-Li, however, started off way different. She was what Anne imagined her to be, I think. Gentle, kind, unflappable. She'd face anything and any odds, any adversity, with a smile on her face and zero fear or anger.

As you can tell, that's not the version of the character that became in this story. Growing up is a lot about building oneself up, but equally it is about the erosion of ideals. Ideals that one starts to realize are imposed on you by other people.

There is a version of Cai-Li featured in a future story that is that person. Gentle, kind, unflappable. But that character goes by a different name, wears a different face, and exists in another genre.

When I first engaged with fantasy as a genre, I believed in the magic of it all. However, like Cai-Li, there was a war in front of her that she didn't survive unscathed.

I have always joked about how Chinese dramas and legends "bury everyone equally," and that is very much true. Chinese culture seems to thrive on tragedy. But I think it fundamentally is a different perspective on the world. The fantasy of the west is about heroes or villains, while in the Chinese cultural landscape, it is about how the era makes a tragedy out of everyone.

This is very much a tragedy, I think. It is also about new beginnings. There was a time when I wrote this final version that the story was purely a cozy fantasy, with Anne and Cai-Li reconciling after a war they survived together. Tending The Cottage, Cole was alive in those tales too. They were all together like they were meant to be.

But that's not the world we live in. In this world, I watched COVID-19 happen. Initially no one in the UK at my university talked about it as the death toll piled up high in China. Then later, stuck in a room, I watched as the west raged about how Chinese people were responsible for the virus. The uselessness and pointlessness of the existence of my people's lives, only in relation to whiteness, was more blatant then. Having bottles thrown at me by people shouting slurs, people joking about whether I'd eat their pets, all the people talking about how much they loved Chinese food and claimed it was part of the British culture turning around to make fun of me with my home cooked meal.

There was a point when I knew I had died like Cai-Li, that gentle, kind, and unflappable version of her. The hero whose virtue and humanity are valued by me and Anne. But then there was no Anne in my life, the people I loved kept turning out to be…not Anne.

That's the thing, Anne is an ideal. She exists unchanged because the idea I had of her didn't change, but Cai-Li as a reflection morphed. Became scared and angry, hurt but slowly unshaken by the desires of others. A sun that scorched itself dry of tears and rose into the sky. Not necessarily to anything better but enraged to burn the world down. Because whatever comes next, it must be better than what it used to be.

But I don't think this is a tragedy. Because in every Chinese story, the idea of reincarnation is always assumed to be present. That's the ultimate comfort anyone gets, the idea that somewhere down the line, there will be a happy future. That after we fight and tell our truths and reveal our scars and accomplish our plans, we'll be able to find peace.

The reason Anne gets to be immortal isn't because immortality is a gift. It is because it is Anne's responsibility. It isn't Cai-Li's responsibility to mend the hearts of those who lived. Cai-Li died, very much like most characters in this story, because of war and trauma and colonization and bigotry. So, Anne changed as well; she is still the same person, but she needs to face the fact that in the world they live in, Cai-Li was never going to survive what they put her through.

I watched them meet, fall in love, and get married or torn apart by death in a thousand universes over the years. I think if you read this story with any honesty or sincerity, you understand what I mean by this.

There is no tragedy of the era. There are people. People who can choose to do something before it is too late. People who need to change and teach the truth of the past. But I am not going to do that—this is only a story.

Dawn Chen is a sapphic fantasy and horror author who grew up in Beijing, China. When she was thirteen, she moved to Germany to live with her family. Since then, she has both lived in Canada and UK. She writes in both Chinese and English, wishing nothing more than to keep writing, and has a perfectly healthy obsession with ghosts.

She's the author of the Chinese queer diaspora horror short story collection *Dawn's Cozy Horror Corner*, the Chinese-inspired anti-British colonial sapphic fantasy *The Witch Who Chases the Sun* and the sapphic vampire epistolary horror novel *A Vampire in Beijing*.